Praise for the author's previous book

The new book by Dr. Sharifullah Dorani... is ı
Afghanistan's troubled past, but rather is a rem
country's modern history with details, facts and figures that presents in its
entirety the reasons that made Afghanistan, in spite of its ancient and rich
civilization, renowned globally for all the wrong reasons. — *U.S. Studies
Online*

His is the art of synthesis: of letting the known, verifiable facts speak for
themselves ... *America in Afghanistan* documents forensically how the
incapacity or unwillingness of the powerful to imagine the conditions of
the conquered can prove devastating to the imbalances of geopolitical
power... The book is most powerful precisely when the anthropological
distance is set aside and Dorani allows everyday Afghans to speak... Their
voice gives the book a human scale. — *Charged Affairs*

The fact that Dorani spoke to Afghans from 'all walks of life' in
researching the book is a strength that yields many of his most cutting
insights... Dorani's Afghan perspective is truly invaluable. Americans and
Westerners should pay attention. — *Carter Malkasian, The Strategy Bridge*

A valuable contribution to understanding the complex motivations, causes
and consequences of US policy towards Afghanistan and the internal
disagreements between the actors. — *LSE US Centre*

The book is extremely valuable in terms of understanding decision making
towards Afghanistan... Academics and practitioners can…gain an accurate
and deep understanding of America's longest war. — *Professor Rahman
Dag, CESRAN International*

Gives a fascinating overview on events in Afghanistan and the 'thinking'
behind the decisions made by successive US administrations. — *Bedfordshire
Refugee & Asylum Seeker Support*

Dorani's work... provides an interesting overview of U.S. political history
throughout the course of the Afghanistan war. — *The Palestine Chronicle*

Eminently readable... a must-read for Afghans and others alike. — *Peggy
Mason, Rideau Institute, Canada*

THE LONE LEOPARD

A novel by

SHARIFULLAH DORANI

S&M Publishing House

Bedford, England, The UK

ISBN 978-1-7396069-0-9

(Paperback)

ISBN 978-1-7396069-1-6

(Electronic)

ISBN 978-1-7396069-2-3

(Hard Cover)

To my parents, wife, noor *of my eyes, Elham (Hamid), Husna and Raihan (Amaan), and, most notably, the women of Afghanistan, who have received nothing from the four-decade-long war but an extraordinary amount of suffering, and who continue to face discrimination on an unprecedented scale.*

CONTENTS

They unashamedly call it 'Little Moscow'…

PART ONE

Early March 1992

Chapter One

Why did the female teachers march at the back? And who was the 'fat man' with a head as large as 'the nomad's dog'? Two questions Baktash whispered and, I bet, every student asked himself. The overweight man with a long moustache broke from the crowd and crawled up the volleyball seating stand.

'Quiet,' he roared, his eyes popping out like a mad cow.

All the chatting, walking on the spot and blowing on hands died down in the assembly, except the sound of drizzle hitting against umbrellas.

'I'm Mullah Rahmat, your new *mudir*, and your new instructions are: follow Sharia law and stay away from *lundabazi*.'

My hair stood on end. How come he pronounced before the teachers the repulsive word starting with L, meaning 'boyfriend-girlfriend relationships'? And instead of *Good morning* us and welcoming us back to school – or, like the old mudir, Raziq Khan, cracking a joke about how many marbles had we won or kites had we cut over the winter holidays – the new 'school principal' jumped into ordering us to follow our 'religious commitments'.

'It's a school, not a nightclub. Anyone caught doing lundabazi, it'll be my feet and their stomach.'

This was the first time I ever remembered someone speaking openly in school about using religion to punish immoral behaviour; the first time a *mullah*, an imam, heading our school instead of a pro-Communist; and the first time a mudir wearing shalwar kameez in school.

'Why have I chosen this school?' Mullah Rahmat asked, his eyes travelling from one corner of the assembly in the schoolyard to the other.

Silence. Everyone stood with blank faces, especially those who did nothing else but chat up *jelais* or young women, including female teachers. Raziq Khan, in a dark blue suit and a red tie under a black coat, cast his eyes down. He was in love with our geography teacher, Huma *jan*, and so wasn't immune from Mullah Rahmat's threat.

'If Kabul has turned into the capital of corrupt behaviour, Makroryan has evolved into the capital of the capital, and this school has been reduced to the capital of the capital of the capital.'

Silence. Drops of drizzle like ice cut into my face, making the first day of school even more depressing.

'The red Russians left, but Makroryanis still follow their corrupt behaviour. They unashamedly call Makroryan "Little Moscow".'

Silence. I wiped my face with my jacket and blew against my hands.

'But I won't allow this in my school.' He wiped his forehead with his hand. Any jelai who complained of a *halek*, a young man, he warned, and he'd get his bodyguards to hang the halek from the school gate. 'Is that understood?'

Heads nodded and mouths uttered yes. Teachers stood indignant, however. Mullah Rahmat held them liable for having transformed the neighbourhood into Kabul's Little Moscow.

Raziq Khan was the main culprit in the school. He was a *Parchami* comrade of Agha, my father; like Agha, he was affiliated with the pro-Soviet People's Democratic Party of Afghanistan. Like thousands of Afghans during the past decades, the old mudir had studied in the Soviet Union and publicly promoted the Communist Union and its way of life. Raziq Khan once said if a parachutist got blown away and landed amidst the grey apartment blocks, he'd mistake it for Moscow. 'Because Makroryan is a minor photocopy of Moscow,' he added with a smile.

The Soviet Union had built the Makroryan apartment complex, located in the north-east suburb of Kabul, less than three miles away from Kabul International Airport. In the popular musical duo Naghma and Mangal's song, *My Beloved Air Force Pilot*, on television, Makroryan from the sky looked like rows of rectangular matchboxes situated neatly behind each other in a gigantic garden full of trees and flowers. As spring set in Makroryan, as purple foxgloves, blue morning glory and pink roses in the gardens put forth new flowers and produced heavenly scents, as butterflies flew from one morning glory to another, and as the morning birds twittered and chirped in cherry blossoms, acacias and willows encircling the lawns, Makroryan was transformed into a *janat*: Heaven on earth.

A gardener tended the flowers and the grass in every block. The municipal officials risked losing their jobs if they left the district dry or untidy. Every other district of Kabul received electricity every other night, some even twice a week, and many electricians had their faces smashed in when the blackout happened on Thursday evenings for the weekly Indian movie; no one dared to cut off Makroryan's electricity even for an hour. Relatives and friends from other parts of Kabul overcrowded your flat if the television showed a new Indian movie, especially if it starred the Indian legend and my favourite Indian actor, Amitabh Bachchan.

As you strolled around Makroryan on a hot summer evening, you witnessed families sitting together on lit-up garden lawns, drinking tea and listening to Ahmad Zahir or Sarban while little children played around them.

The water supply dried up in Kabul during the dry season of autumn; in Makroryan the government supplied water 24 hours a day. Kabul's biting winters covered the city with up to 20 inches of snow, and nearly two million Kabulis struggled to afford wood and coal to heat their homes. The central heating kept our apartments as warm as a sauna. *The Mirror Show* on television broadcast Kabulis queuing up with their coupons and complaining that their Soviet-subsidised cooperatives had run out of this or that. Supplies were never exhausted in Makroryan; every Friday, Mour, my mother, and I saw bags of flour, cans of vegetable oil and cartons of soup lying in our cooperative. Those characteristics turned the Soviet-style apartments into a dream home for Afghan parents.

If you loitered in the area, the chances were that a secret agent from the most feared state intelligence, Afghanistan's equivalent to the Soviet KGB, known by its acronym KHAD, stopped and searched you. If you failed to satisfy them as to the purpose of your visit to Kabul's highly classified district, you ended up in the notorious KHAD prisons. I didn't remember hearing an apartment being broken into or a person getting burgled in Makroryan.

The security forces had to be alert, as nearly all high-profile government officials and their families, not to mention President Mohammad Najibullah himself, and his wife and daughters, as well as most Russian advisors and their families, resided in Makroryan. Police officers guarded 24 hours a day those blocks in which Russian advisors or Afghan ministers or deputy ministers lived. Owing to Agha and the presence of a few other high-profile government members in our block, two policemen guarded it day and night.

Makroryan was also famous for its liberal way of life, and Mullah Rahmat, I reckoned, particularly alluded to this aspect. Nowhere in Kabul did there exist a swimming pool for women, but the Old Makroryan Swimming Pool opened once a week to women swimmers, and on another day of the week to Soviet citizens. Nowhere in Kabul was there a nightclub, but the Makroryan Cinema doubled up as one on Thursday evenings for Russians and Makroryanis. Every cinema in Kabul showed Indian films, but the Makroryan Cinema screened Russian movies. Nowhere in Kabul did Afghan husbands with their Russian wives amble hand in hand along the road, but you saw such couples in dozens if you took an early evening stroll to the Makroryan Market.

This so-called liberal lifestyle of Makroryan turned the district into a janat on earth for the pro-Communist haleks and jelais. Makroryan likewise constituted an earthly janat for me and countless other traditional young haleks and jelais – albeit I disapproved of its liberal nature, and agreed with Mour that something needed to be done about it. The starting point was, as Mour often said – and now Mullah Rahmat was also going on about it – good parenting. Parents needed to instil moral values in their children. Especially mothers... Someone poked my right shoulder, a signal from a friend to pay attention.

'Can you name me a father who doesn't drink?' Mullah Rahmat said, glowering at us. His eyes shifted to the humming old-aged school keeper, who plodded into the concrete school building holding a shovel. 'Quiet,' the mudir roared when a few brave souls tittered.

Mullah Rahmat had a point. I didn't know about the rest, but at least one-third of pro-Communist comrades I knew drank alcohol,

Agha included. As Wazir once put it, a comrade was 'less patriotic' if he abstained from alcohol. You bought a bottle of vodka or brandy in stores in the Makroryan Market. According to Wazir, a factory in the Pul-e-Charkhi District of Kabul produced our particular brandy.

'How many parents pray or fast?'

Again he had a point. I never saw Agha or any of his comrades stepping into a mosque or fasting. Wazir often said that a real comrade risked being seen as a traitor if they fasted. The entire district didn't have a mosque; last year, President Mohammad Najibullah ordered one to be built by the Makroryan Market, which Wazir and I attended.

'None,' he said, tightening his grip on the metal stand.

Someone from the assembly coughed. Followed by another. I blew against my hands.

'Stroll past any given block and I guarantee you will catch jelais and haleks snogging left, right and centre.'

He now told lies. Some jelais and haleks exchange love letters, but I never caught them snogging.

'Today an Indian film is shown on television; tomorrow you shamelessly follow its fashion trends.'

I fastened the top button on my jacket to hide the Russian-style red- and white-striped T-shirt.

'It's our responsibility as adults, as parents, teachers and school administrators to tell our kids to follow the way of Allah.' Drizzle drops flowed from his thick hair down past his square-shaped forehead. 'Alas, teachers themselves copy their outfits from the unbelievers,' he went on. His eyes rolled to Huma jan and Mahbuba jan in black coats, under which both wore the semi-official school uniform: beige leggings with a dark green outfit – a knee-length dress buttoned from top to bottom. Like them, most female teachers and deputies shielded themselves under the black, blue and purple umbrellas. Their male colleagues stood like fear-stricken chicken flock deprived of grain. Raindrops flew down their red and blue cheeks and noses.

'The Communist regime has deviated Kabulis from Islam. Kabul must be abolished and rebuilt with an Islamic foundation.'

Raziq Khan's eyes widened, his grey hair drenched.

Mullah Rahmat's negative propaganda about Kabul and Kabulis equally astounded me. The new mudir dared to publicly criticise the very way of life the pro-Communist Party had fought for decades to establish. Was he too powerful for the KHAD to arrest him? Or did Mullah Rahmat ascertain that the government's days were numbered? As each day passed the pro-Communist *Khalqis* and the *Parchamis* kept losing their grip on Afghanistan, causing Mour and me to worry more and more for Agha's life.

Mullah Rahmat wasn't entirely right about Kabul, though. Even in the liberal Makroryan (forget about the rest of Kabul) in Ramadan, Wazir and I scrambled for a place in the mosque to perform the *tarawih* prayer and recite the Quran. By the time we broke our fast after sunset, and Mour insisted Wazir ate some rice palaw and *yakhni* lamb, worshippers had filled the mosque. We ended up praying outside.

Someone tapped on my right shoulder.

'Stop it.'

'Not me,' Wazir said.

'Bad timing for a joke,' I said to Baktash.

'What joke?' Baktash said.

'Shall I tell the buffalo-headed mudir you're one of the naughty haleks?'

I peeped behind and, with a sinking heart, saw a chubby jelai smiling.

'Stop telling lies. I don't even know you.'

'Or shall I inform my uncle and aunt?'

'Who?' Jelais involved their fathers or brothers to fight harassers, never uncles and aunts.

'Your parents, cousin.'

'I'm not your cousin. Liar.'

'You'll find out.'

Goose bumps pricked my skin. I turned my face. Her unashamed smile demonstrated that she enjoyed seeing me frightened. If only the mudir would let us go to our classes.

'Nice to meet you, Ahmad jan.'

I turned my face around. 'How do you know my name?' I asked, praying in my heart to *Khudai*, Allah, that Mullah Rahmat missed me doing the very thing he warned against. My friends overheard every nonsense she uttered. I feared they might assume I was up to something. My heartbeat increased. *Please, save me from her*, I prayed to Khudai, hating the jelai and her outrageous manner.

'Friends?' Her eyebrows were raised, her right hand stretched between Wazir and me, and her teeth chattered.

She was crazy. Instead of the white headscarf and black outfit school uniform, she wore a fluffy coat, a loose-fitting kameez and shalwar with no decorations, and a long, green headscarf. You saw no jelai wearing a traditional dress with hair fully covered in Makroryan, let alone in the school, or heard a jelai asking a halek to become her friend.

'*Friends?*' Rain dropped from her headscarf and flowed down her red cheek.

Baktash pinched me in the thigh, whispering that Mullah Rahmat might catch me talking.

'Don't want a jelai to be my friend.' I turned my face.

After some more advice, linked with threats, Mullah Rahmat ended his speech by saying that he looked forward to punishing the 'unlucky womanisers'.

Chapter Two

Curiosity took Baktash and me to an empty school a week ago. The mujahideen daily fired rockets at Kabul from the capital city's outskirts, indiscriminately killing and injuring Kabulis. Fortunately, last week's stinger missile hurt no one, but it created an enormous hole in the schoolyard's garden and smashed almost all the glass, which the school had yet to install. Schools in Kabul lacked a heating system and they thankfully closed in winter. In mid-March the first few weeks of the academic year felt like you sat in a fridge. This year's winter, coupled with the rocket's effects, was worse. Cold air blew in through the missing window panes. My feet felt numb on the concrete floor, and even my T-shirt under my jacket stayed moist, thanks to Mullah Rahmat's lengthy speech under the drizzle.

'Still giggling,' Baktash said.

'I swear on Mour's head I don't know her.' As a child I visited Mour and Agha's birthplace in Surobi, an outlying district of Kabul. Husbands and wives met at night when the men returned from their headquarters, the *saracha,* to the bedrooms. Haleks and jelais went to separate schools, and jelais dropped out in year six. I preferred that tradition, but the stupid schools in Kabul put us all together, and today some foolish jelais from the right row peeked and sniggered. The shameless jelai threatened my reputation. I shifted my legs to the left to ensure my back was to the jelais.

'The new mudir will bring real Islam and punish her kind,' Wazir said, putting his notebook on the wooden desk with metal legs.

Shirullah got the second-highest grades in the class and was meant to sit at the front desk next to me, but who'd dare to remove Wazir?

'*Inshallah*,' I said, 'God willing'.

'How can a jelai become a halek's friend? She's a lunatic,' Wazir said, tapping his feet on the floor like many in the class.

'I don't see a problem with it,' Baktash said.

'We're open with each other. Talk about men's matters. Wrestle. Can she?' I asked Baktash.

'It's forbidden for the Sunnis. The Hazaras don't care because they've deviated,' Wazir said.

'The Hazaras are proper Muslims. I'm not sure about the Panjabis,' Baktash said, searching in his schoolbag.

'The Panjabis are brothers; Mongols aren't.'

'Please, stop the name-calling. We're all Afghan brothers.' I echoed our mosque's mullah.

'Consider what I told you,' Wazir said to me, pointing with his eyes to Baktash behind me.

'It's a matter of motives. If your heart–'

'It's as sinful to mingle with a non-*mahram* woman as it is to gamble or drink. Period,' Wazir said about women who weren't related to men in blood, cutting Baktash short.

'A boyfriend-girlfriend relationship is one of the five vices Mour warned me against,' I said.

'Find yourself new friends.'

Baktash stopped searching. 'I'm Ahmad's friend.'

'Ahmad doesn't want a Shia friend. Tell him, Ahmad.'

'Please, Wazir. I have a serious worry on my mind,' I said.

Wazir's insistence on throwing Baktash out of our circle troubled me. I'd known both of them since I knew myself. We opened our eyes to the world in the same block, learned our alphabets in the same class, and mastered kite-flying rules on the same site. Every year Baktash and I saved up for winters, bought strings and kites and flew them in the kite festival in the Makroryan playground. Wazir couldn't afford to contribute, but he flew the kites as he was 'good at cutting' the opponents' lines. Baktash or I held the spool. Baktash loved to fly, but Wazir refused to give him a chance. They often argued and exchanged names, and I thought that factored in Wazir hating Baktash. I was wrong. Wazir's loathing for Baktash ran deeper.

Wazir's uncle sent him books from Pakistan over the past two winters. Obsessed with them, Wazir shared with me their radical messages about the *jihad*, the holy war against the Red Empire, but never with Baktash. Wazir believed the 'gullible' and 'untrustworthy' Baktash might give Wazir away to the KHAD. Worse, Wazir's Salafist books described Shias as those who caused 'more serious damage' to Islam than the *kafirs*, the unbelievers. The books turned a 15-year-old friendship into an enmity. Wazir suspected Baktash was a Shia due to his round face, flat but long nose and narrow eyes, and because Baktash refused to join us in the mosque; he waited outside until Wazir and I finished our prayers. Baktash, in turn, called Wazir 'Panjabi' due to his dark skin and thick, black hair, and because Wazir defended Pakistan – and taunted me with *Shorawi*, Russian, owing to my light brown hair and fair skin, when I provoked Baktash.

A month ago, after the Friday Prayer, I asked our mullah with a chest-length beard if Wazir's books told the truth.

'These books have destroyed Afghanistan. Throw them away. We're all Muslim brothers and have lived in this country for centuries. We all believe in Khudai and the beloved Prophet, peace be upon him. We all are meant to encourage a feeling of mutual love and respect, not hatred. Understood?'

Woh, yes, mullah *saheb*, sir, I remembered replying.

'Khudai has created this world for living; live in it and let others live. Understood?'

'Woh, mullah saheb.'

'Go and give love to your friend,' he said, stroking his beard.

11

I already adored the clean-hearted Baktash like a brother, but Wazir said the mullah was 'aligned' with the government, and he considered changing mosque. Baktash wasn't Shia. Even if he was, we all were 'Muslim brothers'. I reckoned his leniency towards religious commitments didn't stem from un-religiousness or 'reading' his father's collection of books by Vladimir Lenin, Karl Marx and Friedrich Engels. I often reasoned with Wazir that I hadn't seen Baktash opening those books or talking about Communist ideas. Baktash wasn't a hypocrite. The lack of commitment derived from laziness. His Taekwondo instructor complained of Baktash's lack of gym attendance. Our teachers scolded him for missing schooldays. His mother told him off for copying my assignments. They all knew Baktash loved to 'chill out', especially with me. He loved movies. We borrowed videocassette tapes from shops in the Makroryan Market and watched them. His ambition was to become an action hero like Bruce Lee. He even played a part in a film as a child artist, and his father promised to make him a star once he finished Honar-haayi-Ziba, Afghanistan's Drama School, at Kabul University. He'd rather practise his dancing skills and Hindi in case he got an offer like another Afghan actor, Hashmat Khan, from Bollywood, than do his homework or learn a religious *dua*, prayer. Wazir hated the idea of Baktash becoming an actor – another reason Wazir would invoke to finish with Baktash. I likewise disapproved of him becoming an actor; he could choose a career from hundreds of respectable professions. We loved movies but hated the profession; this was hypocrisy, he'd respond, adding with a smile that I'd be over the moon when he got me to meet Amitabh Bachchan in person once he made it in Indian cinema.

'Stand up,' I said as there was a knock at the wooden door. Every student stood up in respect. Raziq Khan, the Dari-language *ustad*, teacher, Mahbuba jan, and to my horror, the crazy jelai walked in. Had she reported me to Raziq Khan? *Please save my honour, Khudai.*

Raziq Khan gestured us to sit down, and we did.

Mahbuba jan put her bag on the desk with a chair before the blackboard and stood by the front window. She praised the left row for having shifted closer to the middle one, ours, to avoid the rain that came through the glassless windows, adding that at least their row got a better scent of the acacias in the school gardens once they blossomed.

First things first, Raziq Khan said: he planned to go nowhere and the school would be administered the same way as before. Mullah Rahmat had imposed himself as a mudir without 'the Minister of Education's order' and he was 'gone'. Raziq Khan wanted no more discussion about the 'imposter'.

Everyone cheered, except Wazir and me. Most students liked the cool Raziq Khan because he acted like he was one of us. In fact, if the middle-aged Khan dyed his grey hair black like his moustache, and wore jeans with a T-shirt, the thin man would easily pass himself off as one of the stylish students.

'Of equal importance is' – Raziq Khan added and nodded at the crazy jelai – 'that you're a brave jelai. You can do it.' He walked to Mahbuba jan and gently pushed her away from the rain-splashed window recess. Both stood with their heads turned to the crazy jelai.

The crazy jelai stood before the desk with a red nose and cheeks. Her eyes roved and she waved at me when her gaze caught mine. I quickly averted my eyes to the world map poster hanging on the right side of the blackboard. Titters from the jelais' side. She had no shame. My heart pounded against my chest.

'*Salaam alaikum*,' she greeted us with the two Arabic words meaning 'peace be upon you'. 'My name's Frishta and I'm thrilled to be your new classmate.'

The words 'new classmate' raised my heartbeat. The smiley face ruined the first day of year nine and, I feared, would turn the entire academic year into hell.

13

'This's a school, not a wedding hall,' Sadaf said, sitting parallel to Wazir and me on the right row.

A burst of laughter and cackle subdued the sounds of blowing on hands and tapping feet.

'These are our traditional clothes. Malalai Anna wore them to the Maiwand War,' the crazy jelai said, her face blushing.

'We're not at war,' Sadaf said.

'Wake up,' the crazy jelai said.

'We don't want a villager in our class.'

Laughter, chuckles and cackles. Even Roya's mouth stretched. The jelai school gangster, Sadaf, would turn the school into prison for the crazy jelai and hopefully compel her to leave our class.

'Shut your ugly face,' Sadaf said to Roya.

Roya's face turned as pale as the three pieces of chalk on the blackboard's nook behind the crazy jelai.

'Quiet, everyone. Is this how you treat your new classmate?' Raziq eyed everyone, Sadaf a little more, but couldn't name her because she was Rashid's girlfriend.

'Carry on, Frishta.'

'Just returned from Moscow, where I took a one-year course in the Russian language.'

'Ooh?'

Titters.

'Sadaf?... Please,' Raziq Khan said over the sound of muffled clapping from the adjacent classroom.

'Before that, I studied in a school in Kunduz... Now I'm back in my dear Afghanistan...' She looked at Raziq Khan, who nodded. He averted his eyes to the mini-Kabul River getting built by his feet and said something in Russian.

The crazy jelai spoke back in Russian.

Raziq Khan's jaw dropped. 'Would you?'

The crazy jelai touched pieces of soaked mud scattered on the floor and held up her palm. 'I won't change this mud for the entire Soviet Union, let alone Moscow.'

Mahbuba jan flinched. Raziq Khan wondered and uttered a sentence in Russian.

The crazy jelai went on and on speaking equally in Russian, and we shivered in the cold.

'Very proud to have you in my school,' Raziq Khan said. He poked his face out of the wooden window frame, to let the rain wash his skin, inhaled and exhaled the scent of bloomless acacia trees, and wiped his face with a handkerchief. Did he dry tears or drops of rain? Mahbuba jan, like many students, had a blank expression. Raziq Khan turned to us and motioned with his hands. We clapped.

'I'll make an exception in your case and let you sit in year nine. But you must pass year eight where you left your studies for Moscow.'

'*Thank* you.' Her face brightened.

'Remember, in effect, you'll be studying two years simultaneously before you pass the year eight exams.'

'I've been revising over the winter holidays. Inshallah, I'll be OK.'

'Ask your ustads if you need help,' Raziq Khan said, eyeing Mahbuba jan for confirmation, who was in her own little world but quickly checked in to say an enthusiastic 'Of course.'

'Do you know any student who has year eight notes?' Mahbuba jan asked.

She pointed to me. 'Ahmad's my cousin.'

Eyes turned towards me, including those of Wazir. My lips remained sealed; her accusation exhausted all my energy.

'Excellent. You're related to a student who is at the top of his class,' Raziq Khan said.

'Of all year eight classes,' Mahbuba jan chipped in.

'I know, he's a bright young man like his father,' Raziq Khan said, hands in his moist coat pockets.

I had got the top grades throughout all year eight classes, but I'd never help the liar.

'I don't know her.' I found the courage.

'Ahmad, I don't want to hear a complaint from Frishta,' Raziq Khan said.

***

FOR THE FIRST TIME I ever remembered, I didn't go on the 15-minute break. Roya must feel every day like a prisoner in the lonely class, I wondered. Roya's loneliness was her comfort zone, and the crazy jelai earlier on tried to remove her from it. No wonder Roya mumbled a *no*, perhaps wondering whether the crazy jelai, like the rest of the students, Sadaf in particular, mocked her. Maybe it was nine-year-long students' intimidation, or perhaps her stepmother's alleged cruelty, which had turned her into a Roya who hardly spoke. Never went to the blackboard to figure out a formula. No teaching went into her head, no matter how many times an ustad repeated it. In the end, I supposed, the school let her stay on just to get away, even for a short time, from the oppression of her stepmother. But the school cared less about students' bullying.

My heart fell as the crazy jelai dashed in. 'Roya, you're coming with me to the canteen. No more excuses.'

Talking to Roya even embarrassed other jelais, but the crazy jelai seemingly picked her as a friend. The crazy jelai leaned over the wooden desk and withdrew a notebook, her hair fully covered in a wet headscarf. She wore the hijab but broke the Islamic rule of abstaining from lies. How dare the notorious liar make me her cousin? My classmates might think she was my girlfriend.

'Why did you lie?' I heard myself say, my heart beating faster.

She jotted down something in her notebook.

'I'm talking to you.'

She put her pen into a pencil case, placed the pencil case and the notebook into a leather bag, pushed the desk with a *qeghgh* sound, and walked in my direction. 'Friends?' she extended her right hand, towering over me. A mixture of roses and jasmine entered my nostrils.

My heart kept pounding. What if someone caught me talking to her? It'd only prove her accusation correct.

'I've asked you a question.'

'When are you lending me the notes?'

'Never.'

'You are. Tonight. At your house.' She gave me a broad smile, her black and white coat reflecting the dim light from the window.

The words 'your house' made me numb.

Sadaf entered with her loyal friends, all three as tall as their boss's shoulders. She threw a closed umbrella towards her table, but missed and it hit the damp floor, splashing water around. 'Pick it up,' Sadaf said to Roya.

'Roya, let's go. We've got five minutes left,' the crazy jelai said.

Roya's face lost colour, her body frozen.

The crazy jelai lifted the purple umbrella with water dripping and placed it on Sadaf's desk.

'She's crazy, and so's her choice of friendship,' Sadaf said. Her friends cackled.

'Come on, Roya,' the crazy jelai said.

'Sit down, stupid.'

'Her name is Roya.'

'And yours is fatty potato.'

Sadaf's friends snickered. A student, pretending to be a motorbike, rode in and out, making a *vroom-pt-ptta* sound.

'Why are you hurting your sisters?'

'You told me to wake up: we're at war.'

'You're not my enemy.'

'Scared?'

'Not of my sister.'

'Say sorry.'

The crazy jelai took a step closer to Roya. 'Let's go.'

Roya shivered. 'I don't want to go. She'll hurt me.'

Two jelais poked their heads in and said, 'Hi cutie.' They sprinted off, yelling and giggling in the corridor. I'd warned them of a complaint to ustads and even their parents, but the stupid jelais wouldn't stop.

'She won't. She's our sister.'

'Stop fucking calling me sister,' Sadaf said to the crazy jelai.

'She's going to hurt me,' Roya broke into tears, covering her ears with her hands.

'Show me,' the crazy jelai said and checked Roya's cauliflower ears like the famed wrestler, Khalifa Nizam.

'Has Sadaf done this?'

Roya wept, her body shivering.

'Speak to me?'

'Yes, I have. Will do it again if she disobeys.'

'Is it better to remain quiet and wait to be stomped upon, or stand up for yourself and get stomped upon?' the crazy jelai asked Roya.

'Shut the fuck up,' Sadaf yelled and rushed towards her victims.

Roya screamed.

The crazy jelai blocked her leg and slipped her body in between. Sadaf went into the air and landed on her back with a banging sound. The crazy jelai let her hands off Sadaf's armpit and shoulder. Sadaf's legs gave way as she rose, and her body moved to one side before her friends steadied it and then sat her on the chair.

An *aah* sound. 'What have you done to her?' a friend asked, pointing to a goose egg on Sadaf's forehead.

'It's called a side throw,' the crazy jelai said. She took Roya's hand, touched the black, red and green Afghan flag stuck to the left of the blackboard, and kissed the hand, and then both raced out. Roya's face was as pale as Sadaf's goose egg.

Baktash sauntered in and moaned about Wazir and Shirullah ignoring him, wanting me to go out. I didn't have the energy to stand on my feet, let alone venture out. Baktash shook his head and placed his umbrella in the bag.

'Ooh, what happened?'

'The crazy jelai.'

'Really? Punched her?'

'No, a side throw.'

'A side throw? It isn't Taekwondo.'

'What time is it?'

'10:13,' Baktash said.

Today's break felt like a year. Wazir and Shirullah's eyes widened as they entered, wanting to know what had happened to Sadaf. Baktash told them – I was glad Baktash made an effort to keep our group unity and held no grudges against Wazir.

'She's just threatened to tell lies to my parents.'

'You may have done something.'

'Baktash, how many times do I have to swear I don't know her?'

'She's blackmailing you,' Wazir said.

'Why?'

'Your brain,' Wazir added.

'I think she fancies you,' Baktash said.

'She's stayed in Moscow by herself – she's dirty,' Wazir said.

'Please, Khudai, save me from her. Mour will kill me.' My voice broke. The school bell clanged.

'Lend her nothing. We'll tell Mour she lies,' Wazir said.

'Rashid'll get her. She's beaten up her girlfriend,' Baktash said.

'I heard he's back,' Shirullah said.

'What if they put him in our class?' Baktash said.

We looked at one another.

The grey sky from the windows roared. Lightning. Rainstorm. Cold. Something was wrong about this year. My heart had sunk in my chest. Maybe Mullah Rahmat was right and Khudai was angry with us Kabulis for our disobedience. I prayed for His mercy.

Chapter Three

My routine went like this every academic year: perform the noon prayers after coming home from school, have lunch, take a siesta, drink tea with what Mour called 'brain food' – almonds, pistachios, walnuts and raisins – study until the five-minute cartoon film at 18:15 on television, chill with my friends until dinner around 19:30, do my homework and help my sisters with their studies, and go to bed at 21:30. I hated the last part of Mour's timetable – it prevented me from watching the Sunday evening movie, the only American film in a week, and it upset me more if it starred Schwarzenegger or Rambo.

The first day of the routine, coupled with the crazy jelai's threat, stopped me from napping this afternoon. How would Agha and Mour react to her lies? My heart had sunk to my stomach. I'd been expecting a knock at the door at any moment.

Mour required me to stay at home that day to help with new neighbours' hospitality. A brigadier, his wife and their son had moved into the opposite apartment last week. According to Mour, Brigadier and Agha met in the notorious Pul-e-Charkhi Prison in the late 70s when President Daoud Khan locked up the pro-Soviet Communist Party leaders to thwart a military coup. But their junior-level comrades, with KGB and GRU's secret assistance, succeeded in toppling Khan's Republic in the April Revolution. Ever since the Parchami Agha and the *Khalqi* Brigadier had remained friends – their parties in power and in a constant war with the mujahideen. Brigadier served in the north, and Agha throughout the capital. Agha now arranged the transfer of his 'trusted brother' to Kabul and obtained a

Special Order from the President for the ownership of the flat opposite that an Afghan singer and her family had vacated over the winter and 'run away', like most celebrities, to the West.

I overheard Agha listening in the lounge to the BBC World Service Pashto. Surprisingly, he was home earlier, maybe for the guests. Agha had two wives: Mour and his job. He had three children with Mour, and a child from his second marriage named Politics. Every day Agha left in the early morning and came back around 7:30 at night. He occupied most of his time with his other wife and my step-sibling when he was even at home, listening to the variety of news: the Voice of America in Pashto, Kabul News, Iranian Radio and his favourite and the 'most reliable', the BBC World Service in Farsi and Pashto. Lying on the sofa with a smouldering cigarette, he saw or heard nothing once the damn thing was broadcast. We all stayed mute. He gestured or, in extreme cases, whispered a word if he required our service. I yearned for the day Agha stepped into my room and asked how my day had been, if I liked something, or just talked about *anything*. Agha forgot that his other wife and three children also had a right to his love and attention.

Baktash's father took him everywhere: to the theatre, live shows on television during *Nowruzes*, New Years, and Eids, and to the Soviet artists' concerts in Kabul Nandari. Baktash told me stories of how the celebrities shook his hand and how the Tajik and Uzbek performers spoke in Dari. Some argued that he was spoiled because he was the only son; I likewise was the only halek in the family, but Agha never took my sisters or me out, not even to a shop. Even on Fridays, a family day, when many families drove to the Qargha Lake or Bagh-e Bala for a picnic, Agha was away with his other wife and son.

I once asked Agha if we all could go on a picnic on a Friday at the Paghman Gardens. My history ustad recommended a visit to our Arc de Triomphe at the entrance to the gardens, which King Amanullah had brought in foreign experts to create as part of his quest to Europeanise Afghanistan. Mour's leek *bolanis* with *doogh*, diluted yoghurt, coupled with the monument's visit, would've given us a great day out there. Agha deemed it unsafe. Safe to be a holiday retreat for the Baktashes and hundreds of other Kabuli families, I complained to Mour, but life-threatening for us. Mour shushed me, reasoning that Agha was busy providing for our livelihood. Mour never let me raise the issue with Agha again; she thought it wasn't Agha's responsibility.

The door knock startled me, but Mour and Agha greeting the guests in the hallway reassured me.

Tap, tap, tap at my door.

'Tell Mour I'll greet them later,' I said.

My annoying sister tapped again.

'Nazo, go away.'

Another one.

I pulled the door open. 'Go away–' The smiling face's presence numbed me.

'Don't faint. I'm your new neighbour.'

I tried to take a breath.

'Don't you invite me into your room?' She stepped in and filled the room with a jasmine aroma. 'Wow, my favourite colour. Brown bedlinen, brown pillows, brown curtains, even a brown desk cloth. And bookcase, wardrobe, desk... All brown, brown, brown. Impressive,' she said, raising her eyebrows. She let herself loose on my bed, her fat, round bangles hitting against one another with a clacking sound. One bangle matched her blue kameez and headscarf, and the other complemented her white shalwar.

'Except I don't like the layout.' She got back on her feet. 'I shall move the desk and chair into the corner opposite your bed... The front of the window is a bad place for the tape recorder. Move it... over the table before the bookcase next to the alarm clock... even though it isn't easily reachable... Now my cousin's room looks better.'

'I'm not your cousin,' I said, feeling tightness in my chest.

'Who do you listen to?' She pressed the button of the tape recorder. 'This is my favourite Ahmad Zahir song.' She stood opposite me and offered her right hand. 'Friends?'

Her eyes beamed with pleasure, the cheeks glowing with redness, and the wide lips stretching to her ears. She reminded me of a mammal: a snow leopard with olive skin, a perfectly round face, large black eyes and long eyelashes. A wrestling mammal who refused to give up on its prey. Actually, she inherited a wrestler's characteristics: plump but flexible, chubby but fit. A wrestler who dared to wrestle with a reality that was impossible to beat.

I never had a female friend. A woman never asked me for friendship. And never was a jelai alone in my room. Her presence in my room embarrassed me. How come her father allowed the daughter with a non-mahram halek? Well, if he let her stay alone in Moscow for a year, a few minutes in my room mattered little. I, on the other hand, didn't wish to ruin my reputation. A young jelai and a halek alone in a room approximated a ticking bomb that could explode at anytime.

'You know my answer,' I said over her favourite Ahmad Zahir song: *Life eventually ends, never submit to aggression, if the submission is a must, then it is better to die.*

'I shall tell Uncle and Aunty you're harassing me.' Her smile broadened under the yellowish glow of the chandelier.

'Are you blackmailing me?' My chest tightness got worse.

'Absolutely not.'

'Why do you invent lies, then?'

'I don't. Your father and mother *are* my *aka* and *tror*.' In keeping with tradition, you called your elders from the father's side aka, uncle; aka's wife became *akanai,* not tror, aunt. But I didn't correct the crazy jelai about the common mistake and instead took a deep breath.

Noisy chatter and waves of laughter came from the lounge. I feared Mour would open the door and see a jelai in my room. What an embarrassment. I switched off the tape recorder and rushed out of my room, into the lounge.

'*Wah-wah*, my nephew has grown into a handsome man,' a tall man with curly hair like a jungle said after I said *salaam*, hello, embracing my shaking body against his gigantic trunk. I felt my heartbeat against his stomach. He let go of me.

'So handsome, *mashallah*.' An obese woman with a brown face and a well-defined nose echoed her husband, using the Arabic word for 'Khudai's protection of me'. Did her face look familiar? 'And I'm told he's a well-mannered gentleman,' the woman added, kissing me on the right and left cheeks, her strong powder foundation smell entering my nostrils.

She embarrassed me; women kissed each other's cheeks, not men. I said salaam to their son playing marbles with Zarghuna on Mour's precious leather sofa. The halek's chocolate-stained hands full of marbles must've infuriated Mour.

The crazy jelai followed and sat next to her father, opposite Agha and me, on the three-seater sofa. My heart pounded against my chest. Brigadier half unzipped his grey tracksuit, closed his eyes and inhaled deeply. 'I feel like I'm in Jalalabad.'

Ironically, Wazir also called our reception room Jalalabad, the capital of Nangarhar, known as 'The Always Spring'. As in Jalalabad, Mour's six flowerpots on the window recess smelled fresh throughout the year.

Brigadier's wife, whom Mour called Mahjan, told me she was 'pleased' the crazy jelai and I were in the same class, we should be 'friends' and 'look out' for each other. Parents even abstained from small things like calling out their women's names in public, yet the unashamed family befriended their daughter to a halek? What happened to their courage, their *ezat*, honour? Mahjan took her leather jacket out and asked Mour to turn off the heater. Sweat had erupted on her forehead. Now I made her out. She appeared with the celebrated actor, Haji Kamran, in comedy plays on television during Eids and Nowruzes.

Her profession and the dress style – short-sleeved green dress with leggings, and open hair without a headscarf – explained that the family was too progressive to bother about shame. Why did the crazy jelai wear traditional Afghan clothes and a large headscarf, though?

'Except for you, *zoya*, Frishta knows no one in school.' Mahjan called me 'son'.

I looked at trays of green raisins, almonds, pistachios, dried peas, cakes and *kulchas*, cookies, on the black glass coffee tables before Brigadier and the crazy jelai.

'You're a bright student, Mashallah. Frishta needs your help,' she added.

I counted six cow chocolates over the glass tray full of sugar-coated almonds. I neither knew the crazy jelai, nor wanted to associate with her.

'Go and bring the notes Frishta jan needs,' Agha said.

I stayed put, and wished Agha understood me.

'There's no hurry, aka jan. I can have it tomorrow,' the crazy jelai said.

'Raziq Khan phoned me today. We all want you to help Frishta jan. Make sure she passes her exams. Am I clear?' Agha said.

'Woh.' Why did he torture me? He offered no help with my studies. On top of this, he pressurised me to share my time with a crazy jelai. I concentrated on my studies, not just for school, but also for a medical degree in three years' time. Every year thousands of students undertook the entry assessment for a medical degree at Kabul University; only a couple of hundred got in, those who did exceptionally well at school.

'I'm not sure if he's got the time,' Mour chipped in and picked up the nickel silver teapot.

'He must make the time,' Agha raised his voice.

Mour's face turned red as she poured the steaming tea into Mahjan's cup. Mour wouldn't rescue me even if it meant I'd fall behind with my studies.

***

AFTER SEVERAL CUPS of tea, *after* all the news ended, after Brigadier complimentarily compared Mour's house with 'Munar Jada' – a place in the heart of Kabul where hundreds of Uzbek businesses sold Afghan hand-knotted rugs; and like Munar Jada, Mour laid rugs in each of the four bedrooms, the hallway, kitchen and the balcony – Brigadier, whose cheeks were as rosy as Mour's rugs, told us how he loved his only daughter and how he'd make her an example to the other Afghan women. 'I give my princess the same freedoms as my Safi,' he went on, pointing towards his son, who played marbles with Zarghuna in the corner near the bulky Russian TV set.

'Thank you, *padar* jan, for not clipping my wings,' the crazy jelai said to her 'father', holding Nazo's hand.

'One day you'll make history, princess. I'm sure of this.' Brigadier planted a kiss on his daughter's head and told her how proud a father he was. His eyes, lips and whole spirit smiled at once.

The crazy jelai kissed her father on the left cheek. Did I feel jealous? I placed two sugar-coated almonds in my mouth and let them melt.

'Once the piece of my heart becomes the Prime Minister and Zahir Shah the King, she'll punish all Afghanistan's enemies.' Brigadier sipped from his teacup. 'She's written to the king. He'll come to Kabul soon after the "mujahideen's takeover".'

The BBC reported tonight that the mujahideen captured strategic outposts beyond Khost and reportedly executed high-profile pro-Communist officials. The news predicted the fall of Kabul as 'more likely than ever'. Recently I'd been praying to Khudai every day to keep Agha from the mujahideen's harm.

'I'll have to start with those who've sold our *watan* to the Red Shorawis.'

Brigadier burst into laughter, his belly like the Bimaro Hill moving up and down.

Talking in front of the elders, and speaking in such an open manner to her father, accusing him of selling his 'homeland', alarmed me. Didn't she know Agha was a high-profile member of the pro-Communist Party?

A *taqq* sound. Mour told Safi and Zarghuna to play marbles by the door, the only vacant space in the room, away from her treasured TV cupboard.

'Princess, we haven't sold our watan. The mujahideen have.' Brigadier's eyes and mouth remained stretched. He asked his wife to extend her hand and turn the volume up on the television. Ustad Gul Zaman sang *Oh My Homeland*. I put a cow chocolate in my mouth and chewed on it.

'Padar jan, the mujahideen defend our watan. Our religion. They look after the refugees and the poor.'

Agha's lips pulled back. 'Frishta jan*, we* defend our watan. Our reforms tackled illiteracy, gave women equal rights, offered the poor more land. We strove to protect the interests of workers, peasants and toilers. The mujahideen kill them. Burn schools and bridges. They've pledged to cripple Afghanistan and then gift it to Pakistan and Iran.'

Zarghuna peeked at Mour, grabbed two chocolates and offered one to Safi.

'Aka Azizullah, the Communists invited the Shorawis to invade our watan. Afghans will never forgive them.'

'We so-called Communists also asked them to leave, and they did. America and her puppets persist in their support to the mujahideen in Peshawar.'

'As the Shorawis support Najibullah's Communist regime.'

'The Soviet Union no longer exists. It's disintegrated,' Agha said.

Agha shared with Mour a few months ago how everyone in the Kabul government was in anguish about its future because the new administration in Russia under someone called Boris Yeltsin had vowed to disconnect its supportive pipeline to the Najibullah regime. Like most Afghans, Agha looked to the United Nations Special Envoy, Benon Sevan, to broker a peace settlement to the 14-year civil war between the mujahideen and the pro-Communist government in Kabul. The Cold War was long over between America and the Soviet Union, but their proxies continued to fight in Afghanistan, Agha said.

'I understand the April Revolution wanted to topple the President Daoud Republic, but I don't comprehend why your comrades martyred his 17 family members, all children and women,' the crazy jelai asked.

'A mistake made in the heat of the moment,' Agha said over one of his favourite songs, Ustad Awalmir's *This's Our Beautiful Homeland*.

'Martyred: millions. Forced to abandon their watan: six million. Lost limbs: hundreds of thousands. Widows: tens of thousands. Political and social system: shattered to pieces. Construction: entire villages turned into dust. Has all this been done in the heat of the moment?'

'We publicly acknowledged our mistakes and have attempted to fix them.'

'The destruction you've left is irreplaceable. The Communists have crippled our watan.'

'Afghans will one day find out who really has crippled Afghanistan, Pakistan or the Soviet Union,' Agha said. 'Having said that, I'm impressed by your knowledge.'

'She reads a book every day,' Brigadier said, making it sound like the daughter travelled daily to the moon.

I dipped a kulcha in my cup and took a bite on it.

'Well done, zoya.'

Agha never referred to me as zoya, even though I was his real son.

'Politics has nothing to do with religion and everything to do with interest. Powerful countries have no permanent friends or enemies, and certainly no concern for one's religion. They're prepared to use any means, even religion, to further their interests.'

The crazy jelai's eyes fixed on Agha. Her father unwrapped a chocolate and threw it in his mouth.

'America or Pakistan isn't here for the mujahideen to help them promote Islam. We're *already* Muslim. America aids the mujahideen to turn Afghanistan into the Soviet Union's Vietnam. Pakistan assists the mujahideen to establish a puppet government in Kabul against India. The Pakistanis crave for a slave Afghanistan that'd have no ability to claim its rightful territory on the other side of the current border where our 20 million Pashtun brothers and sisters live.'

Brigadier put his left hand around the daughter's shoulder, telling his 'princess' to listen to the words of 'a wise man', my Agha, and to read about the so-called Durand Line Agreement.

'I know, padar jan. The British Empire imposed a border in 1893, which separated one Pashtun from the other.'

'*Afarin*, hence no Afghan government has accepted it as its official border'. I heard the first 'bravo' from Agha, not to my sisters or me, but an ill-mannered jelai. Agha sipped his tea. I dipped the other half of the kulcha and put it in my mouth. Took a tissue and removed moist bits from my fingers.

Mour asked me to fill up the cups. Mour and Mahjan, sitting on the two-seater sofas opposite each other, listened to the debate between Agha and the crazy jelai as Afghan women always did.

'Do you have a book on the Durand Line Agreement, aka Azizullah?'

Agha said he'd find her one.

The crazy jelai thanked Agha. '*Manana*, Ahmad jan.' She put her hand over the cup and 'thanked' me.

I filled Brigadier's cup. Counted four chocolate wrappers in the waste bowl in front of him.

'I hope I haven't been rude, aka Azizullah.'

'No, zoya, you haven't. Sadly, you were right on most things. Try to stay calm, though, when you debate your point. Hmmm...' Agha cleared his throat. 'The trick is to see yourself as a nursery teacher.'

Brigadier stroked the crazy daughter and advised her with a mouth full of green raisins and almonds to note another important point.

***

MINUTES LATER THE CRAZY JELAI had a quiet conversation with Nazo. 'Medicine, mashallah,' the crazy jelai said excitedly, her hand curling over my sister's. Mour asked Nazo to go to bed; the crazy jelai wanted 'some more chat' with Nazo about school.

'Now. It's nearly nine,' Mour said. Mour intended to keep Nazo away from the crazy jelai, or else our bedtime was 21:30.

Nazo peeked at Agha and put her cake-encrusted hands over her eyes. I knew she was faking it.

'Let her stay a little longer,' Agha said.

'She wants to go to university and become a doctor,' the crazy jelai said to Brigadier, her face beaming as if my sister had done *her* a favour by going to university.

'Afarin,' Brigadier said. He took a mouthful of the home-made cake and sipped his tea.

Nazo removed the crazy jelai's hand and peeped at a glaring Mour. The crazy jelai had already rubbed off on my sister. Mour would put Nazo in place once the insane family departed.

'We don't send our daughters to universities,' Mour said.

'What about Ahmad?' the crazy jelai said.

'He wants to study Medicine.'

'Ahmad can be a doctor; Nazo can't be a doctor.'

'Ahmad's a halek.'

'Everyone has an equal right to learning.'

For Mour, words such as 'Communism', 'capitalism' or 'human rights' formed empty concepts which had no place in Afghan society.

'Education helps them discover themselves. Their talents. Their identity. Helps them become an asset to their family, children and watan,' the crazy jelai went on.

'That's why they go to school.'

'Not university, though, where her future lies.'

'Her future is in her husband's house.'

'I object.'

Zarghuna rolled a handful of marbles across the carpet and yelled.

'Besides, an Afghan woman must read the Quran and learn about her traditional duties. Righteousness is more important than education,' Mour said.

'The first word of the Quran says, "read", which calls on both men and women. *Khuda* jan wants us to learn about our Islamic and human rights.'

First Agha irritated me, and now Mour's debate with a spoiled child. I'd rather watch *An Hour With You* on the muted television than have a worthless conversation with a rude jelai.

'She's inexperienced, but you're the mother. Teach her. She's putting her future in jeopardy,' Mour said to Mahjan.

'Why's everyone scared of a woman's voice?' the crazy jelai said.

'You must teach her the importance of respect. Life will become much easier in her real home.'

'Tror jan, you're insulting *madar* jan.'

Mahjan, the crazy jelai's 'mother', frowned. 'Frishta, your tror jan isn't wrong.'

No Afghan disagreed that respect constituted an important concept in Afghans' lives. The crazy jelai violated it regarding both my parents, yet she accused Mour of insulting Mahjan. Safi yelled *ooh* and threw a marble, hitting Mour's crystal chandelier. Mahjan chastised him, warning she'd take him home if he misbehaved again.

'OK, you teach me what madar jan's neglected.'

'Frishta, behave.' Mahjan raised her voice, frowning.

I loathed her. Didn't she know elders talked and juniors listened?

'I tell Nazo and Zarghuna that life's demanding with the in-laws. They want you to be skilled. Cook, clean, look after the young and the elderly. If not, the in-laws would curse us, the mothers, for having given them unskilled daughters. They'll force you to learn the hard way. So, get well prepared now if you want to have a comfortable life with the in-laws. Rudeness gets you nowhere in there, I tell them, apart from subjecting you to beating. Respect is the only means to save you.'

'Who said we'll knock the in-laws out?' the crazy jelai said.

'By respect, I mean to *shut up* and abstain from complaints. Endure hardship with closed lips and do nothing that dishonours the in-laws. Like a dutiful Pashtun bride, carry your responsibilities quietly, and I promise you, I tell them, things would turn out good.'

'I hope Azizullah hasn't subjected you to hardship for making us the tea,' Brigadier said to Mour and burst into laughter. His sweaty face reddened. Except for Mour and me, everyone else joined him.

'Ahmad jan's father is a diamond. But you know, brother, we live in a conservative society and have to raise our children accordingly.'

Mahjan nodded.

'The discussion has heated the room,' Brigadier whispered to Agha and wiped his face with a tissue. He steadied Mour's pot with one hand and with the other opened the window. Fresh air touched my cheeks and eyes. Agha took two cigarettes out, handed one to Brigadier, lit his and passed the lighter to his trusted friend.

'Like water, we must adapt to any object we're poured into,' Mahjan said to Mour after a pause, sounding like a politician agreeing with an electorate before an election.

'I'd rather live for one day and be free than live for a hundred years and be a slave,' the crazy jelai said.

Mour shook her head, her eyes travelling to Brigadier.

'I'm staying out of this,' Brigadier said and laughed, holding a burning cigarette.

'A wise choice,' Agha said and inhaled cigarette smoke.

'Mour prepares Nazo and Zarghuna to be housewives, like herself, raising children and washing cutlery.'

'Frishta?' Mahjan glared at the daughter.

'Daughters: imprisoned; sons: free. Is that fair?'

'Not your business,' Mahjan said.

'Only women have to become slaves? Ask tror jan if she ever taught Ahmad how to behave towards his wife?' Did her voice break? 'On the contrary, sons are advised to beat the shit out of their wives.'

Mour and Mahjan hadn't touched their tea. Perhaps the heated debate and the aroma of cigarette smoke spoiled their appetite.

'Frishta jan, I'd want my daughters to be in place of President Najibullah, but I have to be realistic. Daughters need husbands for financial support. Agha and I won't be around all the time. The best future for them is to have their *own* homes. It isn't slavery to cook for their children or wash their clothes.'

'They don't have to get married. They'll have their own salaries.'

'Jelais don't find employment even after university. Say they miraculously get employed and endure their bosses' harassment, their salaries won't even be enough to cover the rent.'

'They can live with Ahmad.'

'I'd rather have them be slaves to their children than Ahmad's wife.'

'Let them finish university and then marry them off.'

'University will take away that opportunity from them.'

'Thousands of jelais study at Kabul University?'

'Our Pashtun families don't marry a jelai who's been to school, let alone university.'

'Is my father not a Pashtun?' the crazy jelai asked.

'Your views aren't for everyone. How many times do I have to tell you?' Mahjan said to the daughter.

The orange and silver light was turned off and on. Mahjan scolded Safi to let go of the switch. He deserved a smack.

'We need change. Lasting change.'

'I don't want to sacrifice my daughters' lives for change. So please don't brainwash them.'

'Education is a right, not a crime.'

Mour's brow wrinkled as her face turned to Mahjan. 'I have to tell you the truth. With such a tongue, no suitor will ever step on your doorstep.'

'Telling the truth is a message of Islam. A message of Afghanness. If a suitor is scared of hearing the truth, shame on them.' The crazy jelai's voice broke. She dashed out.

Mahjan apologised to Mour.

'I hope this doesn't cost us future teas,' Brigadier said, bursting into laughter. He shook Agha's hand and rose to his feet.

***

ONCE THEY HAD DEPARTED, Mour told Agha that the crazy family was too Westernised for us; it wasn't wise to socialise with such a family.

'Liberty doesn't mean corruption,' Agha said and puffed his cigarette smoke.

Mour put a cup on the tray. 'Mahjan is an actor.'

'*Was* an actor: a respected profession worldwide.'

'Not appropriate in *Pashtunwali*, though, especially for a woman,' Mour said. My mother lived by 'the way of the Pashtuns'.

'Wazir says it's un-Islamic,' I said and picked pistachio shells from the sofa where Brigadier had sat.

'That halek has lost his mind. Don't listen to everything he says.'

'Wazir's a good halek. Misses none of his prayers,' Mour said and walked out with a tray full of ceramic cups and saucers.

'Baktash's father isn't happy. Stop harassing Baktash. It isn't your business if he's Shia or Sunni. Don't let Saudi Arabia and Iran's proxy conflict ruin your friendship. Am I clear?'

'Woh.' I picked more shells and oily pieces of cake and kulchas from the rug and placed them on the tray.

'I've already got enough worries on my mind.'

Mour and his children's needs were always secondary concerns.

Mour entered and voiced her disapproval of the decision to let a 16-year-old daughter live by herself in Russia. 'A young woman without her parents becomes corrupt like that,' Mour added, snapping her fingers.

Agha smiled. He agreed or disagreed with Mour, I didn't know; probably his thoughts were elsewhere, with his other marriage and its worries.

'The daughter of Brigadier will bring shame on her family. Remember my words,' Mour said.

Agha smiled again, observing only Khudai knew His subject's future. Agha talked with the crazy jelai like she mattered; with us, he sounded as though every word that came out of his mouth cost him an Afghani.

'May Khudai show no one a daughter like Frishta,' Mour said.

'*Ameen*. And a son like Safi,' I said and wiped away chocolate stains from the TV screen.

'Have to keep Nazo and Zarghuna away from her. She's a bad influence.'

'Let the jelais socialise. Overprotection is harmful.' Agha pressed the cigarette butt in the ashtray and then pushed it along the glass table with a scraping sound.

'With a rude jelai like her?'

'I believe you, too, overstepped your *melmastia*,' Agha said. He had a point. Not once did Mour remind them to eat the food on the tables, an essential tenet of 'hospitality', and one Mour never forgot regarding other guests. Showing profound respect to all guests irrespective of their backgrounds, and doing so without any hope of remuneration, constituted a critical component of national honour.

'I had to be candid. It's my daughter's future.'

'I don't know why you've declared war on diplomacy,' Agha said.

'She wants to be a prime minister,' I said.

'And change the world. Futile teenage dreams. Wait until she meets the harsh world,' Mour said.

'Frishta is different. There's something about her,' Agha said.

'What?' I sat on the sofa. Didn't remember Agha complimenting anyone. His comment intrigued me.

Agha wondered. 'Integrity, I suppose.'

'What's integrity?'

'Shamelessness,' Mour said. 'The family is not for us.'

'I've known the family for years. They're honourable people.'

After Khudai, Mour obeyed her husband. If it weren't for Mr Right, the crazy family wouldn't set foot on our doorstep. A dutiful wife respected her husband and cared for him: grandparents had instilled this in Mour. Disobedience meant disrespect, which had no place in Pashtunwali. For Mour, care and respect needed to be shown in action, and Agha had passed the test.

Believing in marrying someone from one's own tribe, the Ahmadzai, Grandma married off a 16-year-old Mour to her distant cousin, Agha, shortly after the demise of my grandfather, an imam. Agha attended school during the daytime and made mudbricks nightly to support his family, including Grandma. Mour remained grateful to Agha for letting Grandma live with them and providing Grandma's treatment in 'her dying days'. Grandma never saw her daughter getting pregnant, and died with worries. Agha's parents pressurised him, as many Afghan parents would, to get a second wife; Agha wouldn't change 'a piece of Mour's hair with the entire women of the world' even if it meant they remained childless forever. Three years after Grandma's passing, Mour's womb showed generosity and prevented another woman from coming into the marriage. Mour developed more respect for Agha – though traditions required that Mour herself would've got a second wife for Agha if Mour hadn't conceived me for a few more years, Mour once told me.

After my conception, a government job arrived that was accompanied with accommodation. 'Who'd give us an apartment in Makroryan if it wasn't for Agha?' Mour often said.

I wished Mour one day had complained to Agha about his lack of interest in family life. Fathers and husbands interacting with children and wives weren't a man thing, Mour reasoned. To compensate, Mour acted as both our mother and our father. She helped me with my school studies up to year five, the level she could teach. Taught my sisters and me the Quran. Reminded us not to lose our traditional values in the otherwise liberal Makroryan. Bought our favourite clothes in the overcrowded Mandawi Bazar: mine were baggy T-shirts, light jeans and high trainers. Packed the fridge-freezer with fresh fruit juice in summer, and filled our pockets with dried berries and walnuts in winter. Cooked meat every other day. It was 'all for Agha' that we could afford meat; Mour tasted it 'from one Eid to another' when she was our age.

Mour spent every single moment of her life for the sake of her children and husband. If after Khudai Mour worshipped anything, it was her family – and the apartment. I never saw Mour doing anything but preparing the three meals, washing the cutlery and cleaning the apartment. I begged for the day Mour did something for herself. The word 'relax' was not in her dictionary. She'd preoccupy herself with tidying up rooms – if there was nothing else to do. She kept the apartment as clean as the mosque. That night, Mour stayed awake until midnight, tidying the lounge and the kitchen.

Chapter Four

A short man in a washed-out suit was gesturing. He leaned against a Russian jeep parked on the pedestrian way in front of the Russian-subsidised cooperative. My heart fell as the short man showed his red-coloured card: a KHAD agent.

'*Asnad?*' The KHAD agent checked our 'documents', *tazkiras* or birth certificates, and handed them back to Baktash and me. 'This is fraudulent,' he said to Wazir, holding his birth certificate. 'You're not 15.' He pointed to Baktash and me. '15-year-olds look like them.'

I pleaded with Wazir last winter to shave his uneven beard with bald patches in between and his thin moustache, but he said the beard was part of the natural order, and the Prophet, peace be upon him, cursed those men who assumed the manners of women, and those women who assumed the manners of men. I warned him one day that his six-foot height, large muscles, and, above all, his facial hair would come to bring him harm.

If the security forces found you hadn't done the two compulsory periods of military service and were between 18 and 40, they conscripted you. We still had four more years to finish school before they lawfully enlisted us. But if you looked bigger and stronger for your age, they picked you up from the street regardless of your student status or age, and soon you found yourself in the first line of the battlefield, fighting the mujahideen – an almost guaranteed death. Every day we saw or heard of Afghan security forces' coffins getting transported to Kabul.

In 1933, a student shot dead King Nadir Shah, who'd gone to a school to award medals to students. His tomb sat atop the Teppe Maranjan, which became home to hundreds of kite flyers during kite festivals. However, its outskirts served another purpose: a graveyard to which the security forces' coffins made their final journey. The Kabul government called it the Teppe-e-Martyrs, and it almost ran out of space. To compensate for the loss, the KHAD, the Ministry of Defence and the Interior Ministry scattered their people in the streets of Kabul to check documents. Haleks acted blind or mute, and even wore women's clothes to save themselves from *askari*, conscription.

'How come you're 15 when you're taller than Amitabh Bachchan and more muscular than Rambo?'

'None of your business,' Wazir said.

'Don't give me that look.'

'I swear on Khudai he is. We were born in the same year and grew up in the same block,' I said, praying Wazir didn't do something stupid, like punching the agent and running away. The two men in *khaki* military uniforms sitting in the jeep and holding their Kalashnikovs would shoot him dead.

Like any other morning, business as usual pushed on for everyone else around. Drivers from white and yellow taxis shouted, 'To town, to town,' while loud Indian and Afghan music played on their cassette players. Civil servants – in suits and ties, skirts and leggings, jackets and coats – waited for their work transport on both sides of the road, with a handful of men puffing on cigarettes. Overhead on the balconies, above the acacias and willows, Makroryanis, mostly women, in warm pyjamas and jackets, carried on with their daily routines of hanging their washing, talking to neighbours, or observing the hectic road with steaming cups of tea in their hands. No one cared why the KHAD agent conscripted a 15-year-old student – not even the students and ustads walking to school.

'We've been in school since year one. You're mistaken,' Baktash said.

'Hazara and you, handsome, you're getting late – go to your class,' the agent said, pointing with his head to the school walls located two hundred metres away.

'I'm Uzbek, not Hazara.'

'Is there a difference? They all have a flat nose.' His eyes travelled to the sudden movement of people towards the opposite side, the Makroryan Market. A white and blue Tata pulled over at the stop, and scores of men and women pushed and squeezed past with yelping and swearing to get into the already filled bus.

'He's big because he goes to the gym,' I said.

'Good, we need people like him in the frontline,' he said, still gaping at the bus pulling out with passengers hanging out from its doors. His moustache covered his upper lip; his lower lip and face had turned purple.

'But he's not 18 yet. You can't take him away,' I said.

'We'll let him go if his tazkira wasn't fraudulent.'

'Will you?' Baktash said. The chilly weather had caused a fluttering of redness across his nose and chubby cheeks.

'No, he won't. He'll do what they did to Mustapha from Block 15. We won't go without Wazir,' I said.

Last autumn, security forces picked up the 17-year-old Mustapha from outside his school. A month later the family had lamentation over his coffin. Mustapha entered in the flesh. The mother fainted; the sisters and other female relatives rushed out of the room, shrieking. Men in the adjacent room abandoned reading the Quran and dashed in, wrestling Mustapha down. Mustapha cried out that he wasn't a ghost and that the Ministry of Defence had got it wrong, as, unlike his colleague in the coffin, he made it out alive. The family broke the wooden coffin in disobedience of the military, only to discover stones with pieces of human flesh drenched in rose water perfume. But three months later the family wasn't lucky: this time, Mustapha's corpse lay in the coffin sprayed with rose water fragrance.

To my horror, he placed Wazir's birth certificate in his jacket's side pocket and made Wazir sit between the two military men in the jeep. The rear left side door remained open, perhaps for more conscripts.

Agha had already left for work; so had Baktash's father. Clueless about a solution but desperate to do something, I looked around in despair, supplicating to Khudai to help me spot a neighbour or one of Agha's friends, or even a male ustad to help release Wazir from the death penalty, when my eyes caught the crazy jelai in the school outfit across the road. Not at this time, I thought, and turned around, my heart beating faster. Because of her, Mour hit Nazo's palms with a stick this morning, warning my sister to stay away from the crazy jelai and telling me to be vigilant.

A taxi on the road put on Naghma and Mangal's *attan* song and drove off, its passengers grumbling about the 'incompetent government'.

'Why's Wazir in the jeep?'

I took a deep breath of fresh air and read *Ice Cream and Burgers for Sale* on the window of our favourite shop.

The agent signalled to a tall student. Changed his mind as the student got closer. You couldn't miss the relief on the student's face.

'I've *asked* you a question, mister,' the crazy jelai said.

Dark clouds rolled in the sky above the trees and the blocks of flats behind them.

'He doesn't believe Wazir is 15,' Baktash said, blowing on his hands.

'I confirm he is,' the crazy jelai said.

'How?' the agent asked.

'He's in my class.'

'Hold up your jeans.'

Wazir glared.

The agent told one of his men in the military uniform to execute the order.

Please don't do something stupid, Wazir, I said in my heart.

The man pulled up Wazir's black jeans and revealed his lower hairy legs.

'Look, he's got more hair on his legs than I do. Twice as tall as I am, yet *you* confirm he's 15.'

'That's how Khuda jan has created him,' the crazy jelai said.

'Because he eats too much.'

'Shut up, Baktash,' I said.

'It's true,' Baktash mumbled.

A coach bus pulled over. Its doors opened with a hissing sound before a queue of civil servants emerged.

I swore again that Wazir was what his birth certificate showed, my hands and feet becoming numb with the cold. He pushed me and asked one of his men to switch on the engine. The military man stepped to the front, behind the steering wheel.

'You will *not* move the jeep,' the crazy jelai said and waved away the black exhaust from the coach.

The agent snickered. 'What can you do?'

'You'll see.' Her eyes moved to a Makarov on the agent's right hip.

'Is he a classmate or *lunda?*'

The military man behind the steering wheel sniggered at the word 'boyfriend'. The sky roared.

'My brother.' The crazy jelai stepped before the jeep, dropped her schoolbag and stretched herself out on the concrete.

The coach bus doors closed with a hissing sound and pulled out, its passengers' eyes fixated on the crazy jelai.

Could she have not stood before the vehicle? It'd still prevent the jeep from moving. The shameful jelai treasured drama.

Now onlookers gathered around to watch a jelai in a black outfit and white headscarf, having lain down on the wet ground, passionately arguing with the most feared people in Kabul, warning them over her dead body they'd take Wazir for askari.

The crazy jelai lifted her head from the schoolbag, and her headscarf fell. 'Ahmad, go and get padar jan.' She sounded like she'd given birth to me. 'For your information,' she flicked her eyes to the agent, 'my father is a deputy in the KHAD, and my aka jan, Ahmad's father, is Azizullah Azizi.'

The agent eyed me up and down.

'That's right. It's him, Senior Political and Foreign Policy Advisor to the President,' the crazy jelai continued. She pulled her headscarf up and tightened it against the chin.

'The law applies equally to all.' You couldn't miss the sudden softness in his otherwise harsh tone.

She told Baktash to go to school and let the mudir know. Asking me by name and ordering me what to do embarrassed – even angered – me, but I had no chance except to obey the crazy jelai. Her father was the only remaining hope to save my best friend. I sprinted in between the blocks of flats and the dark green Russian Volgas and jeeps parked before them, breathing in and out the fresh air coupled with the scent of trees about to wake up for the spring. My heart sank when Mahjan said Brigadier had already left. I hurried back to Wazir, panting and gasping. They weren't there. Had the agent taken them? I felt lost. Besides, I dreaded Mour's reaction to me running late for school. I didn't remember a day entering the class after the ustad. Learning was built on previous learning; you could never make up for an absence, Mour believed.

I raced back to Mahjan's to see if she could inform Brigadier of her daughter and my best friends' disappearance. The day brightened as my eyes caught Wazir, his mother, Aday, the crazy jelai, and Brigadier by the garden of Wazir's corridor. Brigadier's two

43

bodyguards in military uniforms stood by the dark green Russian Volga a few metres away near the lawn where the gardener trimmed the bushes. I uttered a salaam, suppressing my breathlessness and the pain from my arm, which I must've scratched on a thorny bush.

Brigadier discussed the government's desperate need for more security forces and how we had to take caution. Luckily, earlier Brigadier spotted Wazir and the daughter driving past the road; otherwise Wazir would've had his head shaved and on his way to the frontline.

Wazir nodded. The Volga engine started.

Aday told Brigadier she had one child left, but the government wanted to have him dead, too.

The mujahideen killed Wazir's elder brother, a second lieutenant in the Army, in the Jalalabad Battle following the departure of the Soviet troops. A year later, the Parchami President Najibullah bombed the Royal Palace of Darul Aman to defeat General Shahnawaz Tanai and his Khalqi followers' coup. Aka Iqbal was 'unrecognisable' when they pulled his body out of the rubble, as were parts of the palace that European architects built in King Amanullah's era.

Wazir and Aday lived on Wazir's father and brother's inadequate death gratitude payments. His clothes no longer originated from the posh Jamhuriat Market but from *bazzar-e-lilami*, second-hand markets in Foroshgah. He had worn the same pair of black jeans and shirts for a year now. Aday could afford to cook one type of food: *piawa*, onion, oil and boiled water. Mour and khala Lailuma, Baktash's mother, often dispatched a plate of 'tasty' food to the family, especially Wazir's favourite *kichri quroot*, short-grained rice, quroot made from dried yoghurt, and meatballs. A dish only tasted delicious when Wazir received a plate.

Wazir told me that Aday never stopped mourning the losses. Every night she spoke to aka Iqbal's Army uniform with one star on the shoulders hung as he'd left it. Wazir hid emotions, but I discerned he was sad on the inside; he missed his father. Initially, he hated the

Parchamis for political autocracy in the power-sharing government and, after the unsuccessful coup, for killing his father. Later, he despised both the Khalqis and the Parchamis. The poverty and Aday's constant sorrows compelled Wazir to spend time away from home. Mour and khala Lailuma threatened us with a father's punishment if we disobeyed our timetables. There was no father to discipline Wazir. No schedule to follow. No future career to aim at, apart from pumping up his body and dreaming of the jihad. He was a loose cannon.

Aday expressed her gratitude to Brigadier, who told the dark brown woman with a shoulder-length black headscarf that she really should thank us. He placed his cold hand on my hair and gently shook my head. If only Agha were such a cool father. We must leave now or Mour would notice, I thought. I peeped up and, to my relief, our balcony was closed. Two corridors down above the exhaust steam of the Volga, khala Lailuma hung clothes on the patio, but the trees comfortingly obscured her view.

Aday stroked the crazy jelai's head and kissed her on the forehead, thanking her for giving another life to her son.

Wazir wasn't only a son to Aday, but also a brother to the crazy jelai, replied the crazy jelai. Aday said that from that day on she was her 'daughter'.

Brigadier planted a kiss on the daughter's head and said how proud a father he was.

***

THE METAL GATE made a screeching sound as the school keeper opened it.

'Frishta's the type who'd sacrifice her life for you,' Wazir said.

The sound of students reading the renowned Pashtun poet and philosopher Rahman Baba's poem out loud echoed in the corridor.

'You're the smartest, Ahmad. Help her with the exams.'

I suggested we needed to be more careful where we went. We were to stop taking evening strolls to the Makroryan Market, where we ate burgers and ice creams in restaurants and listened to loud Indian songs, to save ourselves from not just the askari, but also the random rockets. Wazir and Baktash to give up their gyms. I sounded like Mour, but I didn't want to lose my best friends. Wazir spent two to three hours daily in the body-lifting gym, where he worked on his own. Last year he persuaded me to join as he needed a training partner. Agha said to ask Mour, but Mour didn't permit it in case I sustained a spinal injury. I must advance my education instead of strengthening my muscles, she advised: 'A quality education lands you a good job like Agha has. Get bodyguards then.'

We asked for permission to enter the classroom; the Pashto ustad wrote on the blackboard with a scraping chalk sound: *Your beatings were sweeter than the love of others, Your harsh words were better than the prayers of others.* The ustad asked for the author's name and who they wrote the poem for.

Blank expressions in the classroom.

'Ghani Khan, son of Abdul Ghaffar Khan. The poem was for his mother, whom he adored,' I said with hesitation.

'Why? Not you, Ahmad.'

Jasmine aroma and panting came from behind.

'Why did he adore his mother...? Come on.'

Blank faces.

'Ahmad.'

'He was seriously ill, dying. His mother prayed and supplicated to Khudai to take her away instead of her six-year-old son. She died; Ghani Baba lived.'

She uttered an afarin and gestured to come in, saying no word about our lateness. She carried on scraping the chalk against the blackboard, writing the remaining poem.

'I've been so worried,' Baktash whispered from behind.

'You were meant to get the mudir?' I murmured.

'Baz Muhammad sat me in the class.'

'Did you tell him about Wazir?'

'He said, "The school will have one dumb student fewer".'

'He'll burn in the Hell, the Communist,' Wazir said.

'Can I be your friend?'

I looked at Wazir and wanted him to say yes. Wazir was in a world of his own.

Chapter Five

The wooden canteen – big enough to accommodate the salesman and a few jars of spicy *simyan* or a home-made snack, chickpeas, biscuits and lollipop – often took up half of our break owing to its location in the far corner of the schoolyard, and its lengthy queues. Today was no exception, but Baktash's stories of Mazar-e-Sharif absorbed us, or rather me; Wazir ignored him.

Like tens of thousands from all over the country travelling every Nowruz, Baktash took a trip with his father to Mazar-e-Sharif a few days ago to celebrate the Red Flower Festival. Baktash participated in Jahenda Bala, the banner-raising ceremony in the central park around the Blue Mosque in Rowze-e-Sharif, and even 'touched' the Jahenda itself.

He conversed about how red tulips covered Mazar-e-Sharif's hills and green plains when Frishta and Roya muttered a salaam and joined the line behind us. Baktash pointed with his eyes to the back and raised his eyebrows. I whispered to ignore them. The salesman gave a lollipop to a jelai, and we took a step closer.

'It's a good omen to touch the Jahenda, right?' I asked Baktash, walking on the spot.

'Woh, they say–'

'You're a sinner. Celebrating Nowruz is *haram*,' Wazir cut Baktash short, making Nowruz 'forbidden'. There's going to be another argument, I thought with a sinking heart.

'What's wrong with celebrating the arrival of spring?' Baktash asked, shrugging.

We celebrated Nowruz for thousands of years; it was news to me.

'Any celebration imitating the age of *Jahili* is haram,' Wazir said, hands in his black jacket pockets. In Wazir's Salafi books, Jahili referred to the time of 'darkness', the period before the Prophet, peace be upon him, lived, and no one practised Islam.

'It's a tradition. We celebrate it for fun,' Baktash said.

The salesman served a pack of three biscuits to a jelai, and we stepped forward on the wet concrete.

'Shias don't care about sins, anyway. They follow Iran.'

'At least we don't follow Wahhabism.'

'Please calm down,' I said. Agha had a point about Wazir. Did he mean celebrating birthdays, Mother's Day, or National Independence Day was also forbidden? I asked him.

'Eids are our main celebrations, the rest—'

'Excuse me, there's the back of the line.' Frishta's voice interrupted Wazir's sentence.

'Where I stand, the line starts from there.' I overheard an Indian movie quote and knew without looking who the voice belonged to. I turned around and stopped on-the-spot walking. Rashid towered over Frishta, hands in his pockets. He wore a headband on his forehead, his blue shirt under the khaki jacket knotted at the front, with a jackknife and a nunchaku tucked on the right hip: an exact copy of the gangster, Raja, from the Indian movie, *Mashaal*, shown last winter on television.

'Frishta?'

'Yes.' Frishta's eyes flicked from Rashid to his three friends behind him. Their eyes riveted on Frishta.

'You're so really hot.'

'You're so really ugly.'

Baktash tittered, drawing Rashid's penetrating eyes onto himself. Thanks, Khudai, his eyes travelled back to Frishta. Frishta had no knowledge of him so told the truth; Rashid's nose resembled a turnip.

49

But you couldn't miss the paleness on Roya's face, as white as the walls behind her.

'What was it?' Rashid asked his friends.

'A side throw,' they said in unison.

Baktash peeped at me. His nose and cheeks had gone red.

'You want to side throw me, beautiful jelai?'

'She's my sister, Rashid. Leave her alone,' Wazir said. I bet it was the first warning Rashid received from a student, and I dreaded the consequences.

He took a few steps, stood opposite us with an overwhelming smell of hashish, and looked everyone in the eye – into Wazir's a little longer. 'See you at *rukhsati*.' Rukhsati was the end of the schoolday. 'I'll see if these fags can save you,' Rashid said to Frishta, pointing to us. He and his entourage stalked off, but the sinking feeling in my chest wouldn't go away.

Wazir was famous for his 'two-kilo punch', the force of which had knocked a few students unconscious. You called him an unofficial school gangster, but he was nowhere near as infamous as Rashid. Any student who dared to fight the school gangster was left with a scar – not on their faces or stomachs, but on their buttocks. Rashid stabbed his opponents in the bum so they couldn't show their wounds to the doctor.

Not just students but also ustads feared Rashid. He doubled up as a secret KHAD agent. Rashid's tip-offs had landed several ustads in the brutal KHAD prisons. The KHAD arrested, tortured and executed without a trial thousands over the years; a few more ustads could easily add to the number. This year was his third year in year nine. Ustads strove to see the back of him. But he wouldn't attend exams. Everyone knew he missed them to stay in our co-ed school to prey on more jelais; for year ten, he had to join an all-male upper school.

Rashid disappeared into the frontline for months and then reappeared. I reckoned he came after Frishta to avenge Sadaf, who'd been missing since yesterday, but sounded like he fell for Frishta. Bad sign for any jelai if Rashid chose her as prey. Last year a jelai dropped out once she found the school was powerless to stop Rashid from harassing her. Mullah Rahmat was mad at people like him.

A halek elbowed me and sprinted, but the ball caught him and he was out in *toop danda*, Afghan cricket, causing the opposing players to scream. Scores of other haleks and jelais circled around the school building, chatting, giggling and even playing while snacking on simyan, chickpeas and biscuits. But we stood frozen like the Buddhas of Bamiyan. The queue in front of us had moved miles away.

'I'll knock him out,' Wazir said.

'Why did you get involved?' I said to Wazir.

'Don't chicken out.'

It wasn't cowardice to have a knife in your bottom – it was pure stupidity to fight the notorious gangster. Baktash and I dreaded year nine in case Rashid became our classmate. Today he challenged us to a duel, thanks to Frishta, who'd vanished like the Russian cinema in Makroryan.

According to Baktash's book on Chinese face reading, a person with an aquiline nose discarded an approach to ease a situation if faced with difficulty. Wazir unquestionably made things much more complicated for us today. Wazir acted on his impulses and considered no consequences. Threw his punch and cared less if it fractured a nose or knocked teeth out. Didn't give a damn about his face getting smashed up or legs broken, or if the victims came back the following day with a dozen friends. Above all, he didn't stress about parents' reaction.

I was in awe of his bravery. My heart beat fast and dropped into my stomach, my hands and legs trembled, and sweat covered my body the moment my brain sensed a threat of violence. Then something took over and immobilised me. I'd fail the Pashtunwali test without a doubt if it was founded on courage alone.

51

Wazir would pass with flying colours every single tenet of the code of honour. My best friend lived by Pashtunwali. He called Frishta a sister, his *naamus* or pride. His ezat obliged him to defend Frishta's sexual integrity and chastity at all costs. Failure put his loyalty in question. Cut a true Afghan's arm but don't call him disloyal, Wazir often said. The loyal Wazir would play on his life but not allow the shameful outcome of chickening out of a fight. I also knew I accepted a knife in my buttock but wouldn't be disloyal to him. To me, he was a brother I never had.

We missed out on our break's favourite snack, simyan and chickpeas. Our uncertain fate spoiled everyone's appetite.

Chapter Six

The rukhsati bell clanged. Every student cheered the occasion; I found it the scariest rukhsati of my life.

We crossed the black school gate in the chilling weather and, thanks Khudai, saw no Rashid. Hurried by the sideway along the school walls and onto the muddy playground with pools of surface water. My heartbeat increased as four henchmen rushed from different directions and stood before us, panting and puffing. They differed from the ones who accompanied Rashid at the break; the current ones wore long *perahan tunban*, shalwar kameez, with prayer beads on their necks. I followed their eyes and peeped back to see Rashid racing with two henchmen, one holding a Kalashnikov. Our bodies turned to him like coins to the pull of the magnet. A breathless Rashid stood like a hero, like Raja from the Indian movie. He, too, had a scarf around his neck. I spotted a Makarov pistol tucked into his right hip next to the knife; the nunchaku had disappeared. What if he shoots us? I wondered. As we did many times in the past, anxious-looking students gathered to witness Rashid's thrusts in our buttocks.

'I'm sorry,' Baktash said to Rashid.

Rashid placed his hand on Wazir's right shoulder, 'Wazir Gul Haqqani, the new school gangster in my absence.'

Wazir's gaze glued into Rashid's face. My best friend's eyes showed no fear. Unlike me, his body was still. Wazir's deep-socketed eyes like an eagle seemed eager to attack as soon as Rashid raised a hand.

'Why do students call you Arnold?'

'A real Pashtun defends the weak,' Wazir said.

'Bullies the weak,' a henchman said, his Kalashnikov pointing at Wazir.

'Ah, you side with the victims against the baddies like me?' Rashid said.

Wazir's eyes were fixated on the target.

'A fight between a villain Bruce Lee and a *hero* Arnold.' Rashid had a black belt in Taekwondo. 'Arnold will end up with ten holes in the buttock,' Rashid added.

His henchmen laughed.

Wazir didn't match his favourite actor in fame, but certainly in height and build. Like Schwarzenegger, Wazir would knock Rashid out provided the thug allowed a fair fight.

'By a *Tajik* Bruce Lee,' another henchman said, and they all laughed.

'We're all brothers,' I said.

'Shut up, stupid Pashtun,' the henchman said.

Wazir's gaze was still glued on Rashid.

'I've always feared those eyes,' Rashid said to his armed hooligan.

I expected any moment a dull ache in my buttock before the thickening crowd in the ground surrounded by blocks of flats. No one rescued us. The ustads barricaded themselves in the school until Rashid knifed his victims. A few brave souls peeked from the corner classroom, visible to us.

'Rashid, we've done you no harm. Baktash apologised. Please let us go. What's the point in fighting?' I said.

'You're as beautiful as Frishta, Shorawi.' Rashid stung me with Russian. 'You'd be very handy in the frontline. Cook for us daytime; keep our beds warm night-time. Isn't he as handsome as a *jelai*, soldiers?'

'He is yummy, Commander,' one of Rashid's thugs said.

They cackled, their *tunbans*, shalwars, stained with muddy water.

'With your beauty... this soft baby skin... light brown hair...' His cold hand touched my cheek and hair. 'I'd have a jelai every day, even gorgeous-looking ustads.'

'Ustads are like our mothers.' How could he talk about them in this way? To even mention the idea was an unforgiveable sin. My mouth dried and my heart rate increased when the pervert made the inappropriate comment and touched my cheek but, apart from the mouth, which was only able to plead for mercy, the rest of my body had reached the frozen-up phase, shamelessly rendering me incapable of taking *badal*, revenge, for his dishonouring act.

'Is your mother Afghan?'

'Woh.' If only I had black hair and a brown face, I wouldn't have to answer the same question time and time again.

'I thought she was Shorawi.'

Rashid's insult pained me like a knife attack in my buttock.

'I heard jelais fancy you in school?'

'I'm not that type of a halek.' I loathed this sort of talking.

'What type are you?'

'I'm Muslim.'

'We're all Muslims.'

The henchmen snickered.

'Womanising is haram in Islam.'

'Why's Frishta your jelai, then?'

'She is *not* my jelai. We live along the same corridor. Her father is my father's friend.' She'd thrown us to the wolves and herself might've lain in her warm room, crunching her midday snack.

'I've been told otherwise.'

'She's my neighbour. I swear to Khudai.'

'Have her. We don't care,' Baktash said.

'No. We do,' I blurted out, to my surprise.

'Shut up, *beghairat*,' Wazir said to Baktash, calling him a coward. 'We don't care about the Hazara,' Wazir said.

55

'He's our friend,' I said to Wazir.

'That's what the Pashtuns are good at.' Rashid glared at Wazir. 'Have you, fags, seen a doctor to treat your slain buttocks?'

'Let Ahmad go. Your business is with me,' Wazir said, perhaps having seen my frightened status.

'I won't go without you,' I said. My legs shook. My heart was in my stomach. I imagined the deep pain with insatiable throbbing. So let's get it over and done with.

'Who sniggered?' the henchman said, putting candy in his mouth and tossing its wrapper in the rainwater on the left.

'The Mongol with chubby cheeks and a double chin.' Rashid put the back of his two fingers on Baktash's right cheek and pinched it. Baktash made an *ah* sound. His cheek turned red, the eyes tearing up. Baktash wouldn't have been a victim of Rashid's if it wasn't for Wazir. Like me, Baktash hated conflicts.

'Though it's unfair to make the Hazara pay for centuries-long cruelty of the Pashtuns, right?' Rashid asked his hooligans.

'Right,' they replied.

'Go, Hazara,' Rashid said to Baktash.

Baktash flinched. Looked at me and hesitated.

'Now, Hazara, or never?'

Baktash sneaked off, getting a kick on his bottom from Rashid for 'the sneer'.

One of the henchmen took a cigarette, lit it, inhaled, and offered it to Rashid, who took a puff and blew the smoke in our direction, making me cough.

'Who wants who?' Rashid said, passing the cigarette to another henchman to the left.

The henchmen had no time for a reply. Frishta darted, to my surprise, her bag swaying from side to side.

'Why have you confronted my brothers? You wanted to settle with me,' an out of breath Frishta said, her face flushing.

Rashid flinched.

'Beautiful. Brave. Loyal. You aren't actually a girlfriend but wife material.'

'Making a *khastegari*, then?'

My Khudai, she talked about 'marriage proposal' like a halek.

'Definitely. Mum will be sitting at yours tomorrow, my beautiful pussy cat.'

'Except, I'm a leopard, and leopards don't marry a dog.'

'I'm a lion.'

'I object. You're given a gun to defend your watan. Instead, you use it to terrorise defenceless students and ustads. You've turned into a cancer in the school and must be cut out at its roots.'

I'd never imagined a smiley-faced jelai like Frishta, a female, was capable of confronting a bully.

'*You* going to cut me?' Rashid said. 'Listen, soldiers, a *jelai* is cutting Rashid, the bloodsucker.'

The henchmen laughed.

'If I give you birth, I can also eliminate you.' Her voice broke.

Did I hear a loud, screeching noise? I followed Rashid's alarming eyes and saw a Russian jeep braking a few metres from us, water and mud splashing. Another jeep. And another. Finally, a giant Russian truck full of armed guards pulled over. Armed men jumped off and surrounded us. Their guns pointed in our direction. The preparation sufficed to fight a battalion. A man like a giant gorilla emerged from one of the jeeps.

My Khudai, Agha would never come to school to save me from Rashid; he'd go through the roof for creating him 'extra problems'.

Brigadier ordered blocking off the area and instructed students to clear off. Brigadier squelched across the muddy water with a dozen armed guards, who disarmed Rashid and handcuffed the henchmen. Rashid and the armed hooligan showed no resistance when their pistol and Kalashnikov were removed. None of the other henchmen was armed.

'Have you called them?' Two guards held Rashid.

'I've used your language to communicate with you. Now, if you're the son of a real man, not a bastard, if you have sucked your mother's milk, then fight these men, the real men,' Frishta said. Her rage was as loud as the Kabul River in spring, tears coming down her face.

'No power can hold the bloodsucker for long. I'll be back for you, whore.' He headbutted one guard, punched the other, and snap-kicked Frishta in the face, then threw a sidekick, but Frishta lowered her head. Wazir's two-kilo punch landed on Rashid's jaw with a cracking noise, followed by Frishta's kick in Rashid's groin. Rashid folded with an *ahhkh*, his face as dark as the mud.

'Beat up the dog,' Brigadier roared. Punches, kicks and even Kalashnikovs' stocks and barrels bombarded Rashid. Brigadier grabbed Rashid, telling the son of a 'whore' he was a coward, not a bloodsucker, promising Rashid – whose left eye blackened, and a mixture of blood and saliva drooled from the corner of the mouth – that he'd never see Kabul again. Rashid spat saliva and blood on Brigadier's face. Brigadier pushed him against the ground and ordered his men to wash 'the dog' in the grey water. Hands pushed Rashid's face in the rainwater and kicks struck his thighs, legs and sides. Rashid spat water and gasped for breath as they pulled his dirt-soaked head out like a dying, laughing dove. Brigadier ordered his men to throw 'the dog' and his 'puppies' in the jeeps. 'Are you OK, padar jan's leopard?' Brigadier asked his daughter. She was fine. Brigadier asked if we were OK, too, wiping his face with a handkerchief. Better than OK, we were relieved. Thanks to Frishta, today's episode climaxed in Rashid's downfall.

Frishta jumped in the first jeep and faced the back seat, her hands and lips moving. The passenger door clicked open, and the person Frishta talked to got out. Ustads and Raziq Khan, along with some students, appeared, and after checking with us, Raziq Khan asked her what she did in the jeep and who these men were. Frishta had positioned Roya by the Makroryan Market to direct the vehicles on arrival, and the armed men were Special Guards from the KHAD, 'Frishta's padar jan's army'.

Raziq Khan, himself a victim of Rashid's public slapping, nodded, his head turning to the muddy water which had temporarily swallowed Rashid's head. Locked his widened eyes with an ustad, then another and another. Tears spilt out of the sides of the grey-haired mudir's eyes. 'Afarin,' he said, as if to himself. 'Afarin.' His head moved up and down. His eyes travelled to the direction Frishta had left in with her father's army. 'She's what I call the true jelai of Afghanistan, the Malalai of Maiwand.' Did Raziq Khan call Frishta the true 'daughter' of Afghanistan, the Grandmother of the nation?

Chapter Seven

Frishta held two thermos flasks of green tea and three plastic trays of sugar-coated almonds and chocolates, and placed one tray before Mour on the Afghan rug, and the other two on the oak table in front of Agha and me. Poured the steaming tea into cups and placed them next to the trays. I uttered manana – the rocket carrying Brigadier and Agha had landed on the BBC News planet. Frishta smiled and said a 'mention not'.

Frishta sat next to Brigadier on the worn-out sofa opposite me, and leaned her ears to the portable radio. I'd said nothing about today's incidents to my parents, and, to my relief, neither Brigadier nor Frishta mentioned Rashid or the Khalqi agent. Frishta had suffered a 'nasty fall' when Agha asked her earlier about the bruised eye. I yearned to discover Rashid's fate, but waited with a tightened chest for Frishta, who chipped in with a comment or a question about the news.

Mour whispered something to Mahjan, who sat opposite Mour on the mattress. Mahjan tiptoed by Brigadier, pulled the brown curtains and opened the window of the orange-lit lounge. The black sky revealed itself. The faeces smell nevertheless persisted.

I reckoned Frishta got bored once her questions and comments fell on deaf ears, and she sat next to Nazo on the mattress, handing my sister a cow chocolate. 'How are your studies?'

'OK,' Nazo mumbled and peeped at Mour. She touched Frishta's buckles. 'What's this?'

'Push-ups from the gym.'

'What gym?' Nazo ate the chocolate. I unwrapped one and put it in my mouth.

'Judo.'

'Really?' Nazo said.

My hair stood on end. I knew no jelai who attended a gym, let alone a fighting one. How come I'd missed those knuckles, hard like marbles?

'You let your daughter go to the gym?' Mour said to Mahjan, frowning.

'Brigadier says if a son can do it, why not a daughter?' Mahjan said and pushed back the antenna on the bulky television.

'Does he not think about her future?'

'What's wrong with going to the gym, tror jan?' Frishta asked.

I chewed the chocolate and sipped my tea, not knowing why Mour would again waste time arguing with a stubborn jelai.

'Wrestling, jumping, climbing trees, even screaming: all these acts can damage virginity,' Mour said.

'Scientifically it's untrue.'

Mour gave an exasperated look towards Mahjan. Someone outside on a flute played the *Let's Go to Mazar* tune.

'Haleks do them all,' Frishta added.

'Jelais are meant to take care of their virginity. They carry the ezat of the family.'

Why did other people's behaviour trouble Mour? It was up to Frishta how to live her life.

'Do haleks not have virginity?' Frishta said.

'Haleks are born differently.'

'So only we have to "carry the ezat of the family"?'

'We're also required to stay virtuous,' I said.

'A jelai loses the chance to marry if she loses her virginity,' Mour said, raising her eyebrows. 'She may be able to marry a widower or become a second wife *if* the loss isn't due to sinful behaviour.'

'Would a halek in a similar situation marry a widow?'

'Haleks don't have virginity.'

'Do you accept such unfair rules, tror jan?' The flute stopped.

'Breaking these Pashtunwali rules ruins reputations and destroys futures.'

'I won't sacrifice today for a better tomorrow.'

Mour's eyes rolled to Mahjan, who told Frishta to stop the 'nonsense' and asked Mour to drink her tea.

Zarghuna rushed in and informed us of Safi having pooped in his pants. She dashed out. Some of those pants may have lain behind the sofa Agha and I sat on.

Mour told Zarghuna in a raised voice to keep it quiet, asking Nazo to check on her sister. Nazo rushed out. Cold coming from the open windows: the nappies smell and the heated debate made the room as boring as the first day of school. If only we had left for our homes.

'Tror jan, bring your daughters up as strong as your son. Instilling in them that they bear the responsibility of the family's ezat makes them weak. Do you ever tell Ahmad jan to "take good care of yourself because you're the ezat of the family"?'

I chipped in and told Frishta that Mour advised me that if I committed the five sins of alcohol, drugs, gambling, womanising and mingling with bad friends, I'd burn down my life and the family name to a small pool of wax. To cool off the argument, I went on, Mour further advised me to plan for tomorrow, spend within my budget, think of providing *halal* for my family, respect my elders, *care* for my sisters and future wife, and be kind to my children.

Frishta shut up, and I handed her seven of my year eight notebooks. A dog howled, followed by another. Agha and Brigadier looked at each other; maybe the mujahideen popped up here, too. They recently crept at night-time into other parts of Kabul and assassinated government officials. Mr Barmak, the ground-floor neighbour, yelled a *shoo*. Visibly relieved, Agha and Brigadier carried on listening to the radio while Frishta kept skipping through my notebooks.

She thanked me and requested we worked in a separate room because she couldn't concentrate in the lounge when Agha and Brigadier talked about politics, and, though she didn't mention it, Mour threw troubling comments.

'My notes are self-explanatory.'

'Ahmad has his own studies,' Mour said to Frishta.

'It's just for an hour every day. Inshallah, it'll be over in a few weeks,' Frishta said.

'Frishta really needs your help, zoya,' Mahjan said.

I counted half a dozen colours in the room: Brigadier's sofa was black, mine and Agha's brown; Mour's mattress red, Mahjan's yellow; the walls purple; and the television walnut.

'It'll mean a lot to me, Ahmad jan,' Frishta said.

'I've got my own studies,' I said, detesting being pressurised into doing something improper. I wished I had the choice to get out of this prison.

Frishta's eyes welled up. Mahjan told her not to worry; she could seek someone else's assistance. Frishta cleared her eyes and mumbled an 'OK'.

What I feared all along happened. Agha turned down the radio and inquired into the matter.

Mahjan explained.

'Who's she supposed to seek help from, if not you?' Agha said. He told Frishta I'd assist her until she passed her exams. 'Let me know if he proves difficult.'

Did he care about my future? Why didn't he give a damn about tarnishing my *obro*, pride, and ezat?

'I don't know if Ahmad will be able to focus on two–'

'It's only an hour a day,' Agha snapped, cutting Mour short.

I had no choice but to carry out Agha's instruction; the sooner I finished with Frishta's studies, the better. Although Mour never opposed Agha, she might have on this occasion, had she known what was around the corner.

***

NEXT TO THE WINDOWS was her bed with brown bedlinen, brown pillows, a brown desk cloth and yellow curtains. Above it, on the wall, was affixed a postcard of two rabbits. Frishta's wardrobe, bookcase and a Russian television stood in the corner closer to the door; like those of mine, they were all walnut – not what Frishta described: brown. This was the ordinary part of her room. The extraordinary aspect constituted *owning* a videocassette recorder sitting on top of the television – and waste: chocolate wrappers, clothes, books and notebooks, a cassette player with cassettes dispersed around the Afghan rug with tears. I hoped she looked after my notebooks. Mahjan needed to ask her daughter to tidy her room. But waste nappies, dirty clothes and shoes scattered in the hallway signified that both mother and daughter lazed away their time and turned the house into what Mour later called 'a messy nursery'.

Frishta skipped through one of my notebooks.

If only I could bury my head and vanish. 'Frishta, my friends and I see you as a sister.' I spoke my mind in case she contemplated dirty thoughts about me.

She nodded.

'I'll help you if you tell no one about it.'

'Why?' She put the notebook next to her.

'I don't want to argue. This is my condition.'

She stared at me like a leopard, an injured one; her black, red and purple eye socket appeared more so in the bright light.

'And please don't quarrel with Mour. It causes her a lot of worries.' Earlier on, I saw Mour's muscles tensing over the argument about the gym.

'She's ruining your sisters' future.'

'She knows what's best for her daughters.'

'She believes what's right for her is right for everyone.'

'Are you not guilty of the same attitude?'

She grabbed the schoolbag from her bedspread, stretched her legs out along the bottom front leg of the bed, and leaned against the wall.

I asked her about Rashid, whose return I feared.

'The school won't see the coward again.' She unzipped her schoolbag. 'Women are patient but not feeble.' She took her green notebook out, unfolded it and put it on her lap. 'Roya told me the coward touched ustads' bottoms. Pulled down jelais' skirts. The bastard forgot he didn't drop from the sky but popped out of a woman's womb.' Her brown face turned darker when she spoke of him. 'I don't understand why you all turn a blind eye to him.'

'Who can match Rashid? Plus, he never bothered my friends or me. And, we're not the police.'

'I'd rather die ten times over than see my sisters being stamped upon.'

'And not everyone has a father in the KHAD.'

'They have Khuda jan, though.'

'Smell?' Even her jasmine scent wasn't strong enough to bury the faeces smell. No one took action when Zarghuna told them earlier on about Safi. 'It may be Safi's nappies.'

'Don't you like the natural odour?' She smiled and rose to her feet. Sprayed jasmine and opened the window. Someone played Indian music over a running car engine.

'Are we friends?'

'We can't be.'

'Why?' She pulled forward her white headscarf and sat in her usual place, the bangles hitting against each other with a clacking sound.

'Frishta, I hate arguments.'

'We're having a discussion. I genuinely want to know why you want to keep our private classes secret, and why we can't be friends.'

She was required to be enlightened about our culture and our religion; she'd been away from Afghanistan. According to our mosque's mullah, educating ignorant people was a spiritual virtue. I told her we abstained from behaving in a way that people disapproved of. We didn't want them to gossip, *Khudai knows what the halek and the jelai are up to in that room. Shame on both coward families. They have no obro and ezat.* Worse, *don't marry the daughters because it isn't a decent family – the brother has a girlfriend.* I wanted to be an honourable son and brother. It was enough of slander for the family that Agha drank and never went to the mosque.

She nodded. 'Do you live for yourself or "people"?'

'We do what custom allows,' I said. 'Friendship between a teenage halek and jelai is improper. Such an unnatural relationship would entrap us in scandals.' I chose to withhold stories of how hurtful improprieties had led to countless murders and suicides. 'On a personal level, it'll damage my image in school. Students would call me *zanchow.*' I didn't even want my close friends to perceive me as 'feminine'. Baktash wouldn't care, but Wazir would disown me as a friend.

Her massive eyes widened like she'd discovered a clue to a predicament.

'And for you, Frishta, if you hung around with me, you'd put your future marriage at stake.' Bringing in her marriage prospects embarrassed me, but I had to instil this in her or else the ignorance could cost her honour. 'It's your responsibility as a woman to avoid mingling with men, or else people are quick to think filthy thoughts.' I repeated in the hope she'd learn. 'Ask Mour about what shame brought on the next-door neighbours in Surobi.'

'Tell me?' The car and its music stopped running.

'The mother committed suicide and the father disappeared with the remaining children once the daughter eloped with a halek. A decade later the brothers slaughtered the sister, her husband and their two children to regain their stained obro and ezat.'

'I'm not asking you to elope with me.'

'You didn't get the point.'

'I get it. You're lecturing me that I must worry about what others think of me, rather than focus on what I want for myself.'

'I didn't say anything about giving up your wants.'

'You want me to suffer from anxiety?'

'You misinterpret what I've said.'

'I don't give a damn about social pressures.'

'Picking a war with the entire population is a sign of lunacy.'

'Not all Afghans are conservative. Look at padar jan.' Her padar jan and Agha listened in the lounge to Ustad Saifudin Khandan on the television singing *Masooma Jan*, accompanied by the sound of *dhol*, the double-headed drum, harmonium, *tambur* and *rubab*.

'You said you were *genuinely* interested, and I explained. I don't want to argue or "lecture".'

'We're not arguing; we're having a discussion. Tell me, did many jelais study in the same class with haleks 50 years back?' She folded her notebook.

I hesitated.

'It's a discussion. I promise.'

'No.'

'Were women allowed to go to school at all?'

'I don't think so.' I put a cassette in its case and gave it to Frishta. Stretched my legs and pushed my bottom forward on the hard rug; I needed a mattress.

'Why?' Frishta tossed it on the bed.

'Why don't you place it...' I inspected but found no cassette holder. 'By the videocassette recorder?'

She'd take care of it later, she said, and raised her eyebrows, adding another 'why?'; the bruising and swelling to the eye socket looked severe.

'Obviously society didn't approve of it.'

'Was King Amanullah's decision to send 12 jelais to Turkey for their studies received well in the country?'

'He's one of my heroes, but I disagree with some of his decisions, including the one you mentioned.'

'Because your conservative fellows interpreted the decision as un-Islamic and anti-Pashtunwali?'

'I'm not conservative.'

'Why are you against the decision, then?'

'We didn't have two tailors in Afghanistan, and he wanted all Afghans to wear Western dress.'

'Point noted. Do you think, though, the decision in question contravened Islam or Pashtunwali?'

'Pashtunwali doesn't like a woman working outside or mingling with men, let alone studying abroad.'

'Define Pashtunwali.'

I knew it by heart from Rahman Baba's book from year seven. Pashtunwali guided our conduct. Stood for independence, bravery, loyalty, justice, revenge, self-respect, righteousness, pride, honour, chastity, hospitality, love, forgiveness, tolerance, faith and respect of elders.

Her eyes widened. 'What's Islam?'

I didn't like this and the previous question. As an Afghan and a Muslim, she should've known both our sacred code of conduct and our dear religion. With such progressive parents, I quickly reminded myself, it'd be wrong to have high expectations from her. 'Islam's our religion based on the Quran and the deeds and sayings of our beloved Prophet, peace be upon him.'

'I am a Pashtun – a Durrani Pashtun, even though I don't fluently speak the language. But is it *just* to take away our independence? Does physically imprisoning us demonstrate courage? Where is faith if women aren't trusted to step off their doorsteps? Doesn't respect start at home? Don't we as mothers, sisters, wives and, above all, human beings deserve to be respected?' Her eyes welled up.

'You *are* respected.'

Brigadier erupted with a *hee-haw* in the lounge.

'We *aren't* or else you'd have no issue with those jelais being educated abroad.'

I shrugged.

'Society or "people" claim it's against Pashtunwali to have women outside the four walls of their homes because "we're a white cotton"' – she touched her white tunban – '"and easily get stained", right?'

I shrugged. Knew it was good behaviour for women not to venture outside but didn't know in detail why. Never asked Mour for details. Saw no need to question the way of life our ancestors had followed for centuries.

'If I lock you up and deprive you of an education, you'd equally become "stupid, frail, and a sex object".'

'Who said anything about locking up?'

'Educate us, and we'd be neither stupid nor a sex object. Or else there wouldn't have been a Margaret Thatcher or Indira Gandhi, or our own Malalai Anna. Did Malalai Anna not join her brothers in the Maiwand War? Was this against Pashtunwali?'

'Malalai Anna's case was different.'

'It wasn't. Anna aimed to have more Malalais struggle alongside their brothers. It's time to rediscover Pashtunwali's true essence.'

'Which is?'

'Equal treatment and respect for both men and women.'

Did she argue that women should publicly mingle with men? Wasn't she mad? I didn't tell her. Already explained the *status quo*. Up to her to accept or reject it. Wouldn't concern me whichever decision she made.

Nazo counted in the hallway, and Zarghuna told Safi to hurry up and hide.

'King Amanullah obtained independence from the British Empire, passed the first Constitution guaranteeing equal rights for all Afghans, promoted equal education for men and women, abolished slavery, and introduced liberal reforms. And what did we give him in return?' Frishta asked. 'Accused him of being a kafir and declared war against his Kingdom.'

I stood up, pushed the window with her permission, and shut out the women chatter and the muffled folk music from neighbours' apartments; the same music played at a low volume in the lounge.

'Because he refused to pay the conservatives' salaries,' she added, burying her legs in her loose orange and white kameez.

I sat back. 'That was only one factor. He made other unwise decisions.'

'It isn't un-Islamic either, but certain mullahs' interpretation of Islam made it so, just for their benefit. Was the Prophet's wife not a businesswoman? Did Prophet Muhammad, peace be upon him, not encourage *all* to study? Did women not struggle together with the Prophet?'

Her use of Islamic and patriotic references falsified my assumption about Frishta's ignorance. Her bookcase's five shelves bursting with books, some as fat as the pillow resting on the walnut headboard slate, weren't just a show-off.

'"People" abuse our human rights daily, and we're told to be mute or else society shuns us. Well, brave women like Malalai Anna don't fear "people"; they mould society to their definition.'

Zarghuna and Safi screamed, and Nazo giggled.

Malalai Anna had a purpose, I told Frishta. Malalai of Maiwand tended to the wounded and provided water to the mujahideen. The brave teenager clocked the flag-bearer's fall, and the mujahideen panicked. She grabbed the fallen flag and shouted the verse. 'Young love, if you do not fall in the Battle of Maiwand, by Khudai, someone is saving you as a symbol of shame.' The mujahideen shouted '*Allahu Akbar*', Khudai was Great, and launched an attack. The British soldiers noticed her effectiveness and martyred her – on the very day which was supposed to be her wedding day. But couldn't kill her cause: boosting her brothers' morale won the Second Anglo-Afghan War. She turned into the nation's 'Anna', Grandmother, and her grave was now a pilgrimage in Kandahar.

'I have a purpose. I want to prove a halek and a jelai can be friends without being in a romantic relationship. I want to demonstrate that a country would be better off if a woman could gain a degree and work with her brothers to build their watan. If this loses me a husband, so be it. If Malalai Anna lost her life for her people, I'm prepared to sacrifice a future husband.' She became defensive as if I'd personally insulted her.

I hated emotions, and sadly we suffered from it nationally. I was only describing what was and wasn't acceptable in our culture.

'In Moscow, men and women were best friends. Nobody accused them of anything.'

'They're kafir. We're Muslim. Khudai has forbidden the two sexes to be together unless they're blood-related or married.' I made another try, but her darker face convinced me she'd taken everything personally.

'They were Turkish students.'

'We're in Afghanistan. If I had the power, I'd get the police to imprison such minglings of the opposite sex.'

'Why are you here with me, then?'

'I have no desire; Agha told me to.' I got up from the rough rug. Hated being alone with her. Hated her presence. Hoped today was the first and last tea invitation in the cold and smelly home.

She stood up. 'I'm sorry. I got carried away. I need your help, Ahmad jan. I find science too difficult.'

Agha turned my life into hell. She spoke to me as if I was to blame for the parts of the culture she disapproved of – the parts I cherished. Unless over my dead body, my sisters would hang around with haleks. We'd marry them off as they finished school. They'd build their watan, as Mour put it, by supporting their husbands and children. I'd marry someone from Mour's village who never went to school – someone who, when Mour told her to shut up, shut up.

'A word of advice, Ahmad jan,' Frishta said. 'A) don't aim at being accepted. Do what you think is right. You'll feel as free as a bird. B) think about others. The great people you've filled your notebooks about made their marks on the world because they sacrificed their lives for you and me. They strove for change and were comfortable with being disliked. C) put yourself in our shoes and think how you would feel if someone cut off your tongue, arms and legs, and then dropped your trunk off in a well for the rest of your life.'

I had no desire to change the world, I replied. I wanted to finish school and get into a medical university. Second, I cared less about anyone when it came to the way I lived my life. I didn't follow the examples of successful people. My hero, Mour, had shown me the traditional way of doing things, the Islamic way of behaving. Third, women were born to be home ministers and men foreign ministers. We agreed to differ, and I pleaded with her to let the matter rest.

***

THAT EVENING FRISHTA told me she spent between '10 and 15 hours' a day with books. Her book collection revolved around Afghanistan history, Islam and Europe. Like me, one of her favourites was Ghobar's *Afghanistan in the Course of History*. She read books on the human rights of women, and the rights of women under Islam. Over the winter, she finished *Afghan Women under Centuries of Oppression*, a giant book, and it made her cry.

Since moving into the apartment she'd been 'all day' in her room revising for her year eight examinations. No wonder I hadn't set eyes on her. She'd seen me playing in front of the block and was overjoyed that we turned out to be in the same class. She called me a cousin because she saw me as one, she added with a smile.

Frishta had prepared for the exams as much as she could. From then on, she needed my support. I told her I'd help, provided she accepted two more conditions.

Her eyes widened like the two rabbits on the wall opposite me.

No more discussion on women's issues and get Mullah Nasruddin's book out and read me a story, I blurted out. Being alone with a jelai was the most awkward moment of my life, and like a fool, without thinking, I asked for a Mullah Nasruddin's joke.

Frishta's lips stretched.

She flashed out the thin book from the piles of red, green and pale yellow ones.

What is politics, Mullah? asks the wife, Frishta read *Mullah and Politics*, sitting in her usual place, her right side leaning towards the bed's footboard.

Do you remember how many promises I made to you before marriage? Mullah asks.

Yes.

Did I fulfil them after marriage?

Not really, says the wife.

That's politics.

We grinned. I felt like a fish out of water.

'I don't know why Afghans see him as a fool. He was a wise man,' Frishta said.

Frishta was right. Mullah Nasruddin was a populist philosopher, and I knew no Afghan who couldn't quote or allude to a few of his funny stories. His anecdotes, often with a pedagogic nature, fit almost any occasion.

Chapter Eight

The post-dinner evening teas became a nightly routine. To my surprise, Agha talked a lot to Brigadier. I soon discovered they'd fathered the same child: they sat on sofas in the top two corners of the room, opposite each other, with cups of tea and bowls of sugar-coated almonds and chocolates placed before them, and listened to the news or prattled on about politics.

Mour and Mahjan either gossiped about neighbours and relatives or talked about traditions. Mahjan had grown on Mour because she listened to, what Agha called, Mour's 'philosophical lectures', never contradicted her, and, despite being pregnant, stood on her feet as part of 'a younger sister's duty' whenever Mour entered the room. Mour and Frishta both made an effort to avoid arguments. Safi and my two sisters played with each other in a separate room or the hallway. Frishta stepped straight into my room, or I did into hers, depending on which family served tea.

I got to learn some striking personal information about her and the family. A Durrani Pashtun Brigadier saw a Kunduzi-Tajik Mahjan in a play in Kunduz. They got married, and Mahjan gave up acting. Frishta was born in Kunduz, but the family soon moved to Kabul, then to Kandahar. She attended school in different provinces over 16 years, owing to her father's military work. Visiting women in the remote parts of Afghanistan opened her eyes to the plight of her sisters.

Frishta toiled for her goal: join politics and help her 'dear watan' and 'sisters'. It didn't take long before she established herself as a hard-working student. She was one of the first students to go to the board to explain the lessons, and one of the few to achieve the top grades of fives with afarins in her non-scientific homework. Joined the voluntary work of cleaning the environment and tree planting. Stayed behind to help students with lessons. Unsurprisingly, won the Student Representative position two weeks into school, which earned her a desk in the *edara*, ustads and mudir's office. And thanks to Rashid, earned the nickname of 'the Leopard'.

Mour found it difficult to accept that Frishta secured a desk and I didn't. I dodged voluntary school activities and social events. Spent zero time addressing students' problems. Evaded the spotlight. Found it awkward to talk to ustads about anything apart from studies. Frishta's grades likewise disturbed Mour. She falsely assumed Frishta stole 'the five afarin knowledge' from me.

Mour's worries increased after Frishta and I shared the position of student head of the class; I for the haleks, and Frishta for the jelais. In ustads' absence, we took the registry, went through previous lessons with students, and jotted down the mischievous students' names. I held my hands with palms upwards and accepted the stinging blow from deputy mudir's stick, but refused to tell on a classmate. It was only fair because my friends and I were the first to converse about movies, arm-wrestle or play cat and mouse.

Mour's concerns were justified in a way. Frishta and I spent more time with each other than we did with our parents, or even our friends in the past four weeks. We hung around two or three hours in the evening, either in her room or mine. Talked about anything that intrigued us, in addition to our studies. I told her about the three Anglo-Afghan wars, about the bloody history of the Afghan kings where brothers blinded brothers, sons murdered fathers, and fathers assassinated sons just to gain the kingdom. She told me about the hardship the Prophet Muhammad, peace be upon him, had faced throughout his life but never gave up and rose above enmity and insult. Told me stories of her 'heroes', the mujahideen, and how they'd bring peace and security throughout the country. Read me Shirazi, Bedil and Rumi's poems. We analysed whether Salman Khan was a better actor or Aamir Khan, if Arnold would beat Rambo or vice versa. Discussed why the musical group of *the Rain Band* founded by my and Frishta's favourite singer, Farhad Darya, split up, and which countries its singers had emigrated to; why Afghans compared Ahmad Zahir with Elvis, and if Sarban followed Frank Sinatra or Sinatra followed Sarban; or whether Michael Jackson's automatic bed was bigger and better than President Najibullah's one. Gossiped about classmates and ustads. Listened to Ahmad Zahir, Farhad Darya, the Kumar Sanu and Alka Yagnik duet, Modern Talking, and Frishta's beloved album, *Grease*. And my favourite of all, watched movies at low volume on her videocassette recorder.

Politics and women's issues put aside, we had plenty in common, especially history. I'd deny she was my friend if you asked me about our relationship, but she was as close as Wazir and Baktash. Those times I experienced awkwardness in her room had vanished. Her presence put me so at ease I forgot if she was a halek or a jelai. All day, every day I looked forward to our one-to-one evening classes.

Apart from one time, we didn't argue either and guess what? – it centred on politics. When Mazar-e-Sharif fell to the mujahideen and General Abdul Rashid Dostum, a strong Uzbek commander from the north with thousands of armed militias, Frishta predicted the mujahideen could anytime capture Kabul. I shared my anxiety that the mujahideen would kill Agha, her father and all those with high-profile jobs in the Najibullah government. Frishta reasoned the mujahideen would invite King Zahir Shah from exile in Italy, forgive everyone, and again establish a genuine parliamentary democracy like the 1960s. She accused me of supporting the kafir Communists when I doubted her rationale.

The clear-headed King reigned from 1933 to 1973, during which time no bomb went off and no rockets hit the city of my birth.

Afghans went to different cities for picnics, and the streets of Kabul, the Bride of Asian cities, embraced thousands of Western tourists. I prayed Frishta turned out to be right, and the great man led us once more.

***

ON THE LAST EVENING of our fourth week, Mahjan placed a plate with four potato bolanis and a bowl of yoghurt on the rug before me, demanding I finish them off. At Frishta's request, she switched off the muted newsreader in a tie and suit on the television and exited, shutting the door behind her.

'Madar jan loves you,' Frishta said, her right side leaning to the bed footboard as usual.

'She's filled the place of a tror I've never had,' I said. Mahjan made no secret of her motherly love for me. Spoiled me with a variety of food. Once she discovered the hard rug caused me tailbone pain, she placed a mattress against the wall. 'Mour says she shouldn't move too much.'

'Scientifically, it's good for the mother and foetus to be active.'

'I can't eat all this,' I said, pushing the bolanis plate closer to her.

'In America, people eat all of them.'

We both giggled.

Frishta mimicked our English ustad, who always said in America people did this and that, and why didn't we follow suit? Anything we did that the Americans didn't do was wrong, and anything the Americans did and we didn't do was equally wrong. Frishta possessed a unique talent for collecting gossip about ustads, and she shared them with me.

'I need a knife and a fork.' I teased her.

'I'll say the same: Khuda jan has given you hands, use them.'

We both giggled.

'In America, people eat with spoons.'

77

Frishta's face brightened and the corners of her mouth turned up. 'I forgot to tell you what she said to me yesterday in the edara.'

'Go on.' I bit into the hot bolani and sipped yoghurt from the bowl.

'You're already laughing.' She put her pencil on the notebook.

'Say it in her voice.'

'No.'

'Frishta, you know I get what I want.' She hardly refused me something when I insisted. I took another sip of the sour yoghurt.

She smiled. Frishta bent herself, twisted her face and extended her head to me. 'In America you don't hold the air in your stomach, Frishta jan. You let it go and *enjoy* it. Nobody cares. Here, we keep it tight until we burst–'

I told ustads wouldn't converse about farts, and rolled around the floor.

She broke out into laughter, her face beaming like the bright chandelier hanging from the ceiling. 'You'd be surprised. Ustads talk about some weird stuff.'

'I don't think she's ever seen America.'

'She hasn't been anywhere beyond Kabul.'

'This time, ask her whether she lunched with Bush.'

'She'll say he invited her, but she turned down the invitation.'

We both burst into laughter.

I initially perceived Frishta as a cry-baby, but she turned out to be hilarious. She'd win an Oscar if she tried acting. Frishta also demonstrated her trustworthiness: she kept her word about our meetings – nobody knew about them.

The family likewise grew on me. Her parents loved her, but weren't overprotective. The danger of this or that didn't stop them from living a normal life. They lived as if Nowruzes and Eids were the same; as though rockets had no existence.

My parents no longer took us to Surobi owing to Mujahideen's fear. We no longer visited friends and relatives in Eids for fear of rockets. Most friends and relatives had vanished anyway. Abandoned Kabul for Russia, India and the West. Gone were the Nowruzes when Mour and her female relatives and friends stirred *samanak*, the wheatgerm, played *dayereh* and sang Nowruzi songs. All you felt was being left behind; left behind to be eaten by the soon-to-be-loose zombies.

Chapter Nine

Wazir waited in the bright morning under the acacia tree on the lawn in front of Baktash's corridor. Normally, Baktash joined me second, and Wazir last. Shirullah met us in the Market, and we dawdled to school. Why's Wazir first today? I wondered.

'It's the time,' Wazir said. Sunrays, coming through the trees, lightened his black hair.

I judged what he alluded to.

'Tell the Shia to fuck off.'

'He isn't Shia. He's Uzbek from Faryab.'

'I don't care. He is a hypocrite.'

'He isn't. He's just lazy.'

'He's all. Shia. Hypocritical. Bloody cowardly.'

'He had no choice; Rashid warned him to. Plus, he wanted to inform his father to save us.' I told Wazir Baktash's justifications a hundred times; deep down, I knew Baktash didn't have the heart to fight Rashid, especially for Wazir and Frishta.

'Could've chosen to stay, but didn't. He's fucking disloyal.'

'He's our friend.'

'He's not. We're Pashtuns and he's Hazara.'

'We're all brothers.'

'What sort of a Pashtun are you?'

Baktash emerged from his corridor, his schoolbag touching the tree branches, which showed no sign of blooming.

'We'll discuss it later,' I said, noticing khala Lailuma holding her little daughter's hand by the portable guard booth, sauntering to the nursery.

'Now.'

'Wazir–'

'Me or Baktash?'

'Did you watch Arnold's *Terminator* last night?' Baktash said to me.

'We are not friends anymore,' I said. Those words felt like chewing rocks.

Baktash stayed numb.

'I'll punch you in the face if you follow us,' Wazir said.

Baktash's eyes fixated on me. 'Really, Ahmad?'

'Let's go, Ahmad.'

'You, too, Ahmad,' Baktash said to me.

'Come on, Ahmad. Shirullah's waiting.' Wazir marched off, passing Brigadier and Frishta getting into the Volga with its engine running. I followed Wazir. Baktash dried his eyes as I peeked back.

The television showed games of *buzkashi*, Afghanistan's ancient traditional sport, on Nowruzes. Baktash attended one early this year when he travelled with his father to Mazar-e-Sharif for Mela-e-Gul-e-Surkh. Wrestlers rode horses, competing over a goat carcass, pulling it in opposite directions to place it in the hole, the goal. I felt like the headless goat between the two friends, more like the one getting pulled and pushed by Wazir in whichever direction he wished to throw me.

***

RAZIQ KHAN HIT a student on the foot with a wooden stick before the assembly. Shafih made no secret of loathing the school. According to his philosophy, we needed money, not education. The educated lived 'in the pockets' of the rich. He had another philosophy. What was the point in going to school? You became a doctor, an engineer or a pilot. What then? Ultimately, everybody died and turned into dust and thus 'nothing'. Shafih was already nothing, and all he wanted was to enjoy life.

The pleasure had gone too far; the first day of the fifth week in school and Shafih hadn't attended a single day. It was no surprise that the enjoyment subjected him to a public beating. Shafih confessed before the assembly – a confession he should've made last year, even the year before – that every day he buried his school rucksack in a carrier bag and went to the movies or played snooker. At home, he pretended how tired he felt because of 'too much study' at school. His mother spoiled him rotten. Everybody laughed at the last part of the confession. Raziq Khan warned it wasn't a laughable matter, adding that anyone who followed Shafih's footsteps would meet the same fate.

***

MINUTES LATER IN THE class, Shafih acted as if Raziq Khan had given him a medal for good behaviour. The halek had no shame. The ustad was late, and he, as always, flirted with jelais.

'You didn't return my *mina* letter last year,' Laila, Sadaf's best friend, said about her 'love' letter. They both sat on the desk, their legs swinging. Like Baktash, whose seat was empty thanks to his supposedly best friend's news this morning, Laila coveted to join the film industry – be the next Adela Adim of Afghan cinema.

'Busy with exams,' Shafih said, standing opposite them, his back to the blackboard.

'Shut up, you never open a book,' Sadaf said.

'My feelings for you haven't changed,' Laila said.

'Something's happening to me, too,' Sadaf said and giggled. Rashid was gone, so she looked for another halek. A few shameless jelais like her gave the entire neighbourhood a bad reputation.

'Sadaffff,' Laila said.

'I can't help it, he looks like a model.'

82

No idea why jelais found the ugly face 'like a model'.

'Who's this new jelai?' Shafih pointed with his eyes to the back of the jelais' row.

'She's not the type,' Laila said.

'No one can resist Shafih,' Sadaf said, giggling. 'Chief, can you resist Shafih?' Sadaf asked in a raised voice from Frishta, who leaned on the desk, like me filling in the registry, except I'd completed it minutes earlier.

Frishta and Sadaf had been friends after Rashid's departure. According to Frishta, Sadaf's father and stepmother starved Sadaf, her sisters and their mother if they disobeyed household orders. Sadaf's father had married another woman because Sadaf's mother couldn't give him a son. Frishta had warned the father to 'stop being unfair'. Otherwise, she'd involve Brigadier and his guards from the KHAD. Apparently, the warning had eased life for Sadaf and the sisters.

'Salaam, this's Frishta.' She stood before Shafih, her left hip parallel to my desk. Why did she move from her place for a bad halek?

'Shafih. You're beautiful.'

They shook hands.

'Frishta. You, too, are handsome.'

An *ohhh* sound from the jelais blocked the students' noise of talking to one another in the corridor.

'I don't agree with what happened this morning,' Frishta said.

'I'm glad they caught me, or else I wouldn't have met you.'

'Frishta, don't believe him. He's yet to return my mina letter from last year.'

'Do you believe in mina at first sight?' Shafih asked Frishta.

Frishta's lips stretched. The art ustad knocked on the door, followed by chairs and desks scraping the floor. Wazir returned with a sweaty face from an arm-wrestling match at the back.

Frishta shouldn't have smiled but put him in his place. I planned to fill her in with Shafih's colourful character in the evening, but I had no clue she'd drop the mother of all bombs.

***

FRISHTA CLASHED WITH MOUR over why my mother kept Nazo away from Frishta, as though Frishta suffered from tuberculosis. Mahjan scolded her daughter for showing disrespect to Mour. Tears rolled down Frishta's face when Mahjan opined how Brigadier's upbringing had cost Frishta manners. Frishta dashed out of the lounge. I followed her into my room filled with jasmine scent. She sat on the mattress, leaning against the wall, her left hand touching my bed. I abstained from criticising her for arguing with Mour, something she'd been doing her best to avoid. Frishta's accusation of Mour's treatment of her wasn't an exaggeration.

I passed her a pillow. She threw it away against the bookcase. Threw the bag when I asked her to crack on with the exam revision. The bag bashed against the table, and the alarm clock dropped onto the rug. She burst into tears.

'I think tror jan has gauged Mour's plan to stop our classes. She just wants you to be careful,' I said, sitting on the mattress by her feet. Last week Mour told Agha to end the evening teas as they 'affected' her children's studies and manners.

'I miss my mother.'

'Tror jan's talking in the lounge,' I said, overhearing Mahjan and Mour chatting over the Voice of America news.

'She's *not* my real mother.'

'Is this a new drama?'

Frishta pulled up her white tunban.

'For Khudai's sake, what're you doing?' My heartbeat rose. Ever since I'd known Frishta, a headscarf was wrapped around her head and neck. A loose kameez and a loose tunban covered her hands to the wrists and legs to the ankles. She dressed like a 'grandmother', as Nazo once said.

'Frostbite. The cowards abandoned me in the freezing cold.'

'Pull them down, please.' My hair stood as my eyes caught her lower legs. The skin had blackened with white patches in between as if burned.

She covered her legs.

'Who are the cowards?' I said and tried to recover.

'My biological father and his murderous mother.'

'Why did they do that?'

'The cowards strangled my mother to death and threw me on the snow.'

'Na. Why?'

'For giving birth to a third jelai.'

'Khudai. But that wasn't your mother's fault.'

'It was. She didn't defend herself.'

'Where are they now?'

'The coward was hanged, and the godless bitch rotted in prison from tuberculosis.'

'Sisters?'

'Grabbed into marriage by the cowards' cousins. Free meat.' She burst into fresh tears.

'I'm sorry, Frishta.' I felt dizzy, as if Frishta had bashed my head with the wardrobe standing opposite me.

'Are your sisters OK?'

'The Russians buried them under the rubble when they bombed the village.' She broke down.

'Khudai, na. I'm sorry, Frishta. I'm really sorry.' The concussion confounded me. I didn't know how to soothe her, apart from apologising.

'How do you know all this?'

'Padar jan arrested the cowards.' Tears came down her cheeks. 'Padar jan and madar jan told me that they loved me more than Safi, but they wanted me to learn the truth from them.'

'Safi is also...'

She shook her head. '12 years after my adoption, madar jan got pregnant with him.'

I wouldn't even have guessed if she hadn't told me, I said; Brigadier and Mahjan were caring parents.

'The minute I was born, I became a liability.'

'You're not a liability, Frishta. You're an asset. Everyone loves you.'

She tilted her head and gazed at the brown chandelier, its yellow glow pouring over her face, the eyes tearing up. 'How hurtful it must have been for her.'

'Don't think about it.'

'The murderers wouldn't have been able to strangle her if she dared to stand for herself.'

'She'll inshallah be in Janat.'

'I see in every woman my mother. That's why I lose it when I see us being treated like a piece of shit.'

I let her speak.

'I can't see them suffer.'

'I understand.'

'I don't want you sisters to be my mother.'

'Don't worry, Mour lives for her children.'

'We're seen as a burden. First, dependent on fathers. Then husbands. Finally, sons. We must end this dependency. I want your sisters to stand on their own two feet.'

'I understand.'

She wiped her eyes with her white headscarf.

'Do you think I'm rude?'

I didn't know what to say.

'Tell me the truth.'

'You are not unless people don't know you well.' I decided against telling her to keep her outbursts in check, though I had previously reminded her of Agha's trick to see herself as a nursery teacher when arguing her point.

She considered something and nodded.

Nazo, in the hallway, instructed Zarghuna and Safi to roll the marbles to the last square on the rug; whoever delivered the marble into the square won the game.

'Frishta, count me in as a father, mother, brother, sister. I won't say no if you ask for my flesh.'

'Best friend?'

I froze, feeling the heat in my jeans from the mattress.

She burst into laughter. I joined her. 'You're the trusted person in my life. That's why I told you all this.'

'I'll do my best to help you pass your examinations, inshallah.'

'I am sorry about burdening you with–'

'Good you shared it with me.'

'I don't want to talk about it again.'

'Sure.' Nazo cheered. Zarghuna told her to keep it quiet as Agha and Brigadier listened to the news.

'Don't feel sorry for me. Khuda jan has given me angels as parents instead.'

I asked her to stand by the window, close her eyes and let the fresh air blow against her face. I waited until she followed the steps and then took Mullah Nasruddin from my desk and read.

Mullah was busy hammering down, trying to break the lock of a bank.

A passer-by asked, What are you doing, sir?

Playing the tambur, Mullah replied.

Can't hear the noise.

You shall hear it tomorrow.

Frishta's closed eyes facing the starless sky widened, and her lips stretched.

That moonless evening, my heart ached for Frishta. I doubted if my sisters and I were Agha and Mour's children. I doubted if any parents were real.

Chapter Ten

The following day at school break, Shafih collapsed as we lay on the lawn to enjoy the warm sunshine and the smell of fresh grass. Students chilled out in twos and threes, eating simyan and chickpeas, sucking lollipops, or crunching on biscuits.

'When did Frishta join the school?' Shafih said.

Nobody acknowledged him. Wazir and Shirullah positioned their right arms over their eyes, empty simyan and chickpea wrappers in their hands.

'She's a beautiful bird.'

'She's a good jelai – stay away from her.' I grew assertive with Shafih since Frishta had banished his ex-boss. Rumour had it that Rashid had been killed in the recent battle in Maidan Wardag.

'Why are you jealous? Is she your jelai?'

'She's my neighbour.' I wanted to break his bones.

'So?' He chewed on a piece of grass.

'Frishta's my sister,' Wazir said, his eyes still buried in the arm.

Shafih knew he couldn't fight the most feared halek in school. I felt proud that Wazir was my best friend. Nobody dared to even stare at me.

'I know you've snitched on me,' Shafih said.

'The last thing I want to see is your ugly face,' I said.

'My best friend is waiting for me.' Shafih pointed with his eyes to the plastic sheeting that covered our class windows above, got onto his feet and dusted off blades of grass from his bottom. 'His name is

Baktash.' He jumped over the roseless bushes and vanished into cheering students.

I'd been trying to persuade Wazir to change his views about Baktash, but Baktash would make it more difficult by hanging around with Shafih. Baktash's emigration to the back seat was in a way a relief: it helped to avoid looking into his accusing eyes as if I'd cut his wings. The feeling of being a goat carcass had become worse. More and more, I felt like a dog whose collar was with Wazir.

***

TWO DAYS LATER in the warm sun of mid-morning, the sports ustad took us to the schoolyard. The sports classes instead fast-tracked the military training and prepared male students for the frontline.

'Knock, knock,' Shafih whispered. He lay on his chest next to me in the school trenches the size of some dozen graves. In fact, we nicknamed them 'our future graves'.

I pretended he wasn't there and instead listened to the bald-headed ustad, who lectured on the importance of keeping the skull safe in the trenches from the enemy.

'Frishta shows me green lights,' Shafih continued. His eyes travelled to Frishta, who tricked Sadaf and shot a basketball.

'You're a fucking liar.'

Frishta's thoughts centred on serious matters; she had no time, as she once put it when we worked on Hafiz's poem on mina, for 'trivial matters' like relationships. She saw lovers as 'weak' and believed in mina for one's watan and Khudai. Frishta smiled at his compliments because she had no knowledge of his filthy intentions.

He fished out a light green piece of paper and waved it at me. 'Mina letter. She'll be mine.'

I wished I had the courage to punch him in the face, as red (and ugly) as the monkey's bottom.

He smirked. 'Why did you lose colour?'

'Fuck you.'

'Rashid will be back soon. We'll teach you and your boss a lesson.'

'*Fuck* you, and *fuck* Rashid.' I raised my voice and called Wazir.

Shafih sneaked away and joined Baktash.

***

THAT EVENING, thanks Khudai, my parents went a little earlier to Frishta's. I dashed into Frishta's room before she said salaam to my parents and started exchanging political comments with Agha on the frightening rumours of elements from the Khalqis and the Parchamis having secretly invited opposing mujahideen groups, Gulbuddin Hekmatyar and Ahmad Shah Massoud in particular, to take over ministries in Kabul.

She suggested I help her with the Pashto assignment on Khushal Baba, adding that the essay constituted half of the course work. Frishta struggled with Pashto, too. She often complained that schools in Kabul taught only one subject in Pashto when at least half of the population were Pashtun.

'Have you noticed that Afghans punish their greatest when they're alive, and mourn them when they're dead?' Frishta said, sitting in her usual place, her right side leaning towards the bed's footboard.

'We appreciate them too late.'

'Baba's own people, in fact, his sons, deceived him for Mughal's *sim* and *zar.*'

'Money and gold' were our weakest point, I acknowledged, sitting by her feet.

'Baba was different, though. He preferred poor independence to a kingdom.'

'He died unable to unite Afghans or defeat the Mughals.' I unintentionally sounded annoyed.

'It's immaterial, Ahmad jan. His advice continues to influence us.'

Why did she chat and joke with Shafih if it did? I swallowed the words.

91

'It does so *because* he thought about his people. Accepted a hard life but refused to compromise on principles,' Frishta added.

'You're in a preaching mood again. Can we get to the essay?'

She smiled. 'I've chosen a quote from Baba's poem, which I think captures his message well.'

'Which one?'

Frishta read: *The very name Pashtun spells honour and glory; lacking that honour, what is the Afghan story? In the sword alone lies our deliverance.*

'Khushal Baba would see showing green lights to Shafih as dishonourable?' I'd have burst if I'd kept the words inside me any longer.

Her colour darkened like her wardrobe in the corner. She looked up into my eyes, searching for something. 'What do you mean?'

'Do you like Shafih?'

Her colour changed further. The door swung open. Mahjan stepped in with a tray and placed it on the rug before my mattress. Instructed us not to forget the tea and closed the door behind her.

Frishta leaned on her right arm and resumed writing with her left hand. *Khushal Khan Khattak Baba was an Afghan poet, warrior and scholar,* she wrote. *He's known as 'The father of Pashto literature'.* 'What makes you think I like Shafih?'

'Shafih told me. He's written a mina letter for you.'

Baba encouraged a revolt against the Mughal Empire in the 17th century and promoted Pashtun unity through poetry. She wrote another sentence and looked up. 'What do you think of our match?'

I disliked Frishta's question.

'Ahmad jan, every jelai needs to have a soul friend.'

Her reasoning dismayed me.

'Frishta, you know boyfriend-girlfriend relationships are haram.'

'Khuda jan is sympathetic to mina.'

'Are you in mina with Shafih?'

'He's handsome. Funny. Brave.'

Her last statements contradicted the Frishta I'd known not long ago, up to this evening, the true jelai of Afghanistan, the serious Frishta whose thoughts revolved around politics, duties for her watan, working towards a future in which the rights of her sisters were protected.

'You said you didn't believe in mina.'

'I do now.'

'And fallen for no one else but Shafih?'

'Shafih's the only person who dares to talk to me about his emotions after Rashid,' Frishta said and carried on jotting down notes about the quote, whose message her action opposed.

Nobody expressed their mina for her because everyone saw her as an honourable jelai, who refused to let the thought of a romantic relationship cross her mind. Plus, who could dare to become her halek even if she wanted one? She was too good for anyone in the school; she was the 'bird' who flew 'highest in the sky'.

I reminded myself that she asked me, the 'trusted person', for my opinion on Shafih, and I had better stay as one.

'Do you know Shafih was Rashid's friend?' I heard myself say.

'Shafih was hardly involved in Rashid's crimes.'

Things sounded more serious; she must have inquired about Shafih.

'You must also know he visits bad places.' Shafih often bragged about how he had sex with prostitutes.

Frishta considered the last revelation. Stood up and opened the window. Sounds of neighbours' chatter and fresh air pierced the room.

'He told everyone how he taught Laila lip-kissing because "cheek-kissing was old-fashioned".'

'What's the difference?' She leaned on her right arm and recommended writing.

'How would I know? Ask Shafih.'

She appallingly wrote down in the corner of the paper: *lip-kissing versus cheek-kissing – Shafih?*

'Ask him also if he fights dogs. Gambles on partridge-fighting. Flies pigeons.' His father and, now increasingly, he were renowned for *kaftar bazi*, the play of pigeons.

'Akbar Badshah was crazy about kaftar bazi.'

'He wasn't about partridge-fighting.'

'A halek proposes to a man's daughter. "Do you smoke?" the man asks. The halek says no. "Do you gamble?" The halek says no. "Do you fight dogs?" The halek says no. "What habits do you have?" The halek has none. "Sing me a song." The halek is not Ustad Sarahang. "Tell me a joke." The halek is not Mullah Nasruddin. "Fuck off," the man says. "A man who hasn't got a habit and can't tell a joke is like a flaccid penis that won't stand up when you need it."'

'The man must have been on hashish,' I said. What'd happened to her tonight to speak in such shameful language? Safi screamed in the lounge, followed by Mour's voice, telling Zarghuna to give him the doll.

'Shafih follows his passion. He's released himself from people's chains. You do it, and you'll fly as high as Shafih's pigeons.'

'You want me to abandon studies and stand on the rooftop, whistling, wielding and waving a long stick to flying flocks? Then come to school and endlessly talk about how my pigeons circled the sky of Makroryan, how they dipped and dived before settling down on the rooftop?'

'If this is your passion, why should we judge?'

'Shafih isn't true to his word. He's a pervert. A serial swearer. Talks a lot but thinks little. I'd prefer a smart enemy than a fool for a partner.'

Frishta stopped writing and sat up, casting a shadow on the wall behind her. 'Shafih listens to his heart. He's brave enough to mingle with me at breaks. You and I have been friends for weeks, yet you're even embarrassed to talk to me in public.'

'We aren't friends.' Did Frishta intend to befriend Shafih to prove her point because I didn't dare to be a friend?

'What are we?'

'Neighbours. I'm here to assist you.'

'Ahmad jan, what is it you really stand for?'

'To get into medical university. Get a job to support my parents and sisters.'

'Not your future plans.'

'What do you mean?'

'You once told me you weren't the police to fight bullies. You only interfered if it affected you or your friends. Right?'

I remembered telling her that in this very room, then untidy, but now, thanks to Frishta's efforts, the cassette players, the cases, clothes, chocolate wrappers, books and notebooks had ended up where they belonged.

'Wazir decides to kick out Baktash. You follow him like a sheep.'

'I'm not a sheep. I've been trying to make peace between them.'

'This is *not* the point.'

'Fighting isn't the answer either.'

'Standing up for what's right is, even if it doesn't affect you, even if it hurts your mother or best friend.'

'Frishta, I don't like you hanging around with Shafih. People think filthily.'

'You know by now I don't live for "people".'

'You know I won't publicly hang around with you and damage my reputation.'

'I didn't ask you to.'

If only Frishta wasn't stubborn and understood that immoral romantic relationships stained her honour and damaged the family's standing that saved her life.

'Shafih doesn't care about his reputation,' she said as if to herself.

'He's a gambler, drinks alcohol, bunks off school. He has no reputation to start with. But you have a good name and shouldn't go for a person like Shafih.'

'Who shall I go for?'

'No one. You aren't meant to. Just wait like every other Afghan jelai for your wedding.'

'You won't understand. You haven't been in mina.'

'No, I won't. We're meant to marry and then fall in mina. Mina before marriage corrupts you and disgraces your family.'

'I can't. I want a halek now.'

Her last remarks froze me. As the conversation developed, I became dismayed, then angrier. How on earth could Frishta grow so immoral? As far as I'd known her during these five weeks, she'd proved to be an honourable jelai. Never missed a prayer. In fact, we often prayed our Maghrib and Isha prayers together on the prayer rugs, which were neatly folded on Frishta's bed. How many stories she'd told of the Prophet Muhammad, peace be upon him. What happened to her religiosity? To her Afghanness? To Khushal Baba's philosophical advice?

'I suggest you don't give your heart away to a halek until you've done your *nikah*. Deep and lasting mina blossoms after the nikah.'

She tilted her head, facing the cauliflower-shaped chandelier, and sighed.

'Shafih and his friends wear burkas and "touch" women in Nowruz picnics.' I remembered another negative point about Shafih and told her.

On Nowruzes, women and jelais – including Mour, Nazo and Zarghuna – went to the Shah-Shahid Padshah Shrine. Mothers prayed for themselves and their families as well as kept an eye out for suitable jelais for their sons, and young jelais prayed for a good husband and fortunate life, Mour once told me. The occasion also enabled Shafih-type haleks to wear a burka and molest women and jelais.

Her gaze travelled to the untouched bowl of sugar-coated almonds and chocolates on the tray, then to the cups and the teapot, to my face, contemplating or listening to the loud BBC News from the lounge, and the neighbours.

'Shafih's using you. He'll enjoy himself and then dump you.' I went on telling her that once in a wedding in Kabul Hotel, Mour showed me a woman with a smiling face whose *qataghani* dance skills made everyone's jaws drop. The woman was in mina with a man as a teenager, but after 'using her', the man dumped her. He told her if she fell in mina for him before marriage, she'd do so for anyone after marriage. The man married another woman and had grown-up kids, but to date, no suitor put a foot over the smiley-faced woman's doorstep in Karte-e-Now District.

'I'll also enjoy myself.'

Her unashamed remark hit me like thunder.

What did I hear? To my astonishment, a burst of laughter. 'Don't explode. I was only joking,' she said, drying her watery eyes with her hands.

I had no idea what to make of her. Perhaps our geometry ustad had been right to claim that women were as complex as algebra formulas. Was she just laughing or crying? Did I believe her serious face, her logical reasoning, or her claim to a prank? Whatever it was, I didn't like the idea of Frishta letting Shafih compliment her and, on occasion at breaks, hang around with her.

'Frishta, I dislike you flirting with Shafih. You should stop it.'

'I'm a free person and can choose who I hang around with.' Frishta's face darkened. Her two rabbits – white and light brown – from the opposite wall peered at me with eyes wide open.

'In this case I won't help you from now on – ask Shafih.'

'Are you trying to control me because you're helping me out?' Her face turned darker, this time like the sky from the open window.

'Who am I to control you?'

97

'Precisely.'

'I can't help you anymore. I have my own studies.'

'It's up to you.'

'I won't come to your house anymore.'

She pointed straight to the front. 'There is the door.'

'Tell Agha you don't need my help anymore.'

'Of course.' She broke into tears.

I sneaked out, overwhelmed by a mixture of hatred, anger, disgust, and even loss towards her, society and, importantly, myself.

***

MINUTES LATER THERE was a knock at our apartment door. I opened it. She stood behind the door, holding notebooks. Her eyes had turned red.

'They belong to you.' She threw the notebooks in and dashed into her flat.

Chapter Eleven

The following day, to many students' horror, the buffalo-headed Mullah Rahmat showed up at the assembly. He'd dismissed Raziq Khan for failing to follow his 'clear instructions' and reiterated his 'feet-and-the-halek's-stomach' threat.

We marched into separate year nine classes: one all jelais; the other all haleks. We were in the nine *alef*, and Frishta and Roya in the nine *jeem*, the room opposite us. The segregation applied to lower classes, too, as appeared later. The partitioning turned out to be chaotic because the school lacked enough ustads for the newly formed classes. For the first subject of the day, history, Mahbuba jan had to join Frishta and our classes – an occurrence we soon got used to. The feminine Shafih and the new classmate, Jawad, clapped as jelais entered the classroom.

Mahbuba jan dropped the third bombshell of the day: the new mudir banned female students and ustads from wearing short skirts and leggings; they must dress in a long headscarf to cover all their hair. Although the school policy required the jelais – even female ustads – to wear a headscarf, many ignored it. Instead, the jelais wore a short headscarf or no headscarf, and female ustads put on short skirts and leggings. Raziq Khan turned a blind eye to both.

Students bombarded Mahbuba jan with questions. One didn't have a headscarf, another didn't like it, and yet another pleaded with the ustad not to impose it on them.

'This is an order from mudir saheb,' Mahbuba jan raised her voice, quietening everyone else. The new dress code also applied to the ustads, she reminded her angry students as she stood by the ustad desk in front of the blackboard.

'He's taking us back to the Middle Ages, ustad.' Frishta's voice came from the back of the jelai row.

We hadn't spoken a word since last night – Frishta had been avoiding me.

'Mudir saheb follows Islam.'

'He's using Islam. Islam is about respecting women, not oppressing them. Today he imposes hijab; tomorrow he'll order us to sit at home.'

'Frishta, stop crying. It's good for us all to dress by the Islamic rules.' Mahbuba jan walked through the aisle with a high-heeled click-clack sound and stroked her 'favourite' student's head. Frishta wouldn't be comforted – she still sobbed. Mahbuba jan buried her face in Frishta's bosom as though the ustad herself cried out for comfort. Jelais, one by one, joined them at the back of the class and put their arms around one another, weeping and sobbing as if the monster *div* had demanded a jelai each day for dinner.

I didn't understand why Frishta cried because Mullah Rahmat's new dress code didn't affect her. She dressed like her heroine Malalai Anna; her headscarf alone was long enough to make headscarves for all the jelais of the class.

***

AFTER THE break, the nine jeem joined us again for algebra. We stood up in respect once the ustad, Baz Muhammad, nicknamed Mr Stalin, knocked on the door panel with his famous wooden stick. His presence in the class ensured students sat with one hundred per cent discipline. Although he became our ustad only this year, he'd filled in several classes last year for his best friend, the geometry ustad. After Rashid, he and his stick constituted another reason we viewed year nine with trepidation. Countless students had gone to the edara to seek medical help for their tender hands, sometimes for their bleeding noses, all because of his stick. We cut our break short in the sunny schoolyard earlier when we heard he was back from an absence following his wife's 'serious accident'.

On the positive side, he loved his students like 'his own' children. 'That's probably why Khudai has failed to allow me to reproduce; the only purpose we human beings are put on earth to serve,' he often said. Passionate about mathematics, ustads classed him as one of the best in Kabul. Like any other member of the Hezb-e-Democratic, he touched no bribe despite living in poverty with his invalid wife, whom he took care of: perhaps this was the reason he always came across as sleepy. When you asked him a question, he stayed behind to ensure you learned, even if it required hours outside school time. And he never failed students.

We began to prepare an answer for the algebra formula Baz Muhammad put on the blackboard. I finished in a couple of minutes and glanced up. Mr Stalin's gaze fixed on Wazir, who was drawing Diego Maradona. I pushed my bottom forward on the hard, wooden chair and stamped on Wazir's right foot; too late – he asked Wazir to come to the board.

Wazir was terrible at algebra. He'd end up with red tenderness in the hands, so I dared to volunteer.

'I want him, not you,' Mr Stalin roared.

A hesitant Wazir stepped to the blackboard, picked a piece of chalk from its recess and stood with a blank expression.

Mr Stalin stared at my best friend with a face conveying that he expected zero knowledge from his student. Mr Stalin, whose dark brown suit had turned into a mixture of grey and white owing to several years of wear and tear, glanced at students and shook his head.

Everyone laughed. Wazir's face darkened. Wazir could have been intelligent if he made an effort. His heart wasn't in school studies; at times, I did his homework. His aka's extreme books had conquered his brain and drove his life.

'I know what you'll make. A donkeyman,' Mr Stalin said, provoking titters among students.

Everyone feared the same fate, I bet, but they sniggered because Mr Stalin was in a good mood and because some, like Shafih, loathed Wazir.

Wazir gazed at his worn-out shoes. My best friend wanted you to respect him, make him feel important. Mr Stalin was doing the opposite.

'Get your father to buy you a donkey. Sell tomatoes.' Mr Stalin cupped his mouth and raised his voice: 'Tomatoes *bakharin.*'

Bursts of laughter.

Men – what Mour called 'illiterate donkey riders' and she seldom warned me to excel in my studies, or I'd end up like them – rode donkeys that carried tomatoes and shouted out loud, 'Buy tomatoes.'

'He may already be a donkeyman.'

Mr Stalin had just crossed the red line. You stabbed Wazir in the heart if you disrespected his father.

The gentle aka Iqbal used to take us to Chaman-e-Hozori, where we played football with haleks from the other districts. He often talked about how in the 40s Afghanistan played in the Olympics, and beat Iran in 1941. Aka Iqbal wanted Wazir to become not a donkeyman, but a professional footballer like aka Iqbal had once been and play for his watan. Thanks, Khudai, he wasn't alive to witness what was about to befall his son.

'Look down.' Mr Stalin said to Wazir. He clenched his teeth – a sign he was turning into Mr Crazy Stalin, no longer a laughable matter.

Wazir continued his gaze.

'Look down, I said.' He raised the stick but froze…

'This's wrong,' a female voice cried out.

A few faces turned to Frishta; most, however, were cast down.

'Everyone's born differently, ustad. Some have a talent for solving equations. Others are skilful with their hands. Maybe Wazir isn't a natural mathematician.' Tears rolled down Frishta's cheeks, her left shoulder, visible from behind the jelais, trembling. She'd been in a foul mood since our last meeting. The new dress code and Mr Stalin's treatment of Wazir appeared to have upset her even further.

'It doesn't help to humiliate him publicly, and I don't know why some find the humiliation of a fellow student funny,' Frishta said, casting her eyes over some students, Shafih and Jawad in particular. She stomped out.

Mr Crazy Stalin's body trembled – another dangerous sign. I didn't remember anyone confronting him. He'd take the shit out of us.

'Is an ustad not allowed to discipline his students?' he asked, as if to himself.

His eyes travelled from the left row to the middle, and then to the right. Students cast their eyes down.

'Ustad, he'll learn it for next week,' I dared to say.

'*Chup.*' He 'shushed' me.

'You, chup. A Communist kafir,' Wazir said.

Unbelievable. Why did Wazir *not* shut up? Did he want his bones to be broken?

Mr Crazy Stalin pushed Wazir. Next, Wazir lay down on the concrete floor. The stick whacked Wazir's shoulder. Another the head. Wazir crossed his hands around his head, and the stick struck against his arm. Mr Crazy Stalin's right hand went up and down with the stick.

What followed next was too quick. Wazir's right hand flew to his shoe and flew back with a force of President Najibullah's Luna rockets and bashed against Mr Crazy Stalin's chest. The ustad screamed, 'Ahhkh...' His body folded, the stick dropped with a *taqq* sound, and his hands pressed against his chest. Wazir sprang up on his feet with a knife covered in blood in his right hand and hurried out, leaving the slain body of Baz Muhammad on the concrete floor.

Screams and cries filled the room. Sadaf and Laila, along with Shafih, shifted to the far corners; the jelais covered their eyes with their hands. It was a day of Qiyamat.

The deputy mudir, Amrudin Khan, together with Frishta, hurried in. Frishta was, alas, too late.

Amrudin Khan placed his hands on Baz Muhammad's shoulders and turned him around, revealing his eyes, white like the ceiling. Jelais screamed. The ustad's jacket was soaked with blood, giving it a reddish-grey colour.

'He's losing blood. Help me,' Amrudin Khan said.

The ustad's pupil-less eyes and the pool of blood on the floor convinced me he wouldn't make it. The knife had penetrated his heart.

Amrudin Khan, Frishta, Shafih, Jawad, Baktash and I carried the ustad's breathless body to the edara. Amrudin Khan, whose white shirt was stained with blood, allowed only Frishta to stay behind.

***

'Get prepared for Pul-e-Charkhi,' Shafih said to me as we marched back to the class. 'Pul-e-Charkhi, empty a cell,' he shouted, his voice echoing around the long corridor.

What's just happened is real or a horrible dream?

'I'll tell the police you gave your boss the knife.'

What's going to happen to Wazir?

'I'll be a witness,' Jawad said.

'Ahmad has got nothing to do with it,' Baktash said.

Has someone physically shaken my brain?

'Traitor,' Shafih slapped Baktash. Kicked me in the buttock. Jawad pulled my T-shirt, and a fist landed on my nose. A pair of hands pushed against my chest and moved up and down. 'More evidence,' Shafih said. My chest felt moist.

'Ustad,' Baktash raised his voice.

Shafih and Jawad sprang into the class.

'Your nose is bleeding,' Baktash said and passed me a tissue. 'The bastard smeared your shirt with blood,' Baktash added over the ambulance siren. 'They'll turn the school into hell for us.'

My heart had fallen into my stomach.

***

AFTER RUKHSATI, Baktash and I knocked on Wazir's apartment door; no one opened it. Aday had vanished together with Wazir. Baktash told me what he later said to the police when they questioned us about Wazir's whereabouts, that 'Wazir joined his Panjabis'. Baktash sounded relieved to see the back of him – he said no word about me siding with Wazir.

For the next few days, I knocked on Wazir's white wooden door every morning and evening, but it stayed shut and without any sound. Never heard from either again. Agha assumed they'd gone to areas under the mujahideen's control where the Kabul government had no jurisdiction.

I later thought Wazir was too popular for Baktash and me. His aims evolved around the gigantic idea of jihad. I sensed he felt stuck and would abandon us once he got the opportunity. Baz Muhammad gave him one.

Mour and Aday gave birth to us in the same hospital, Zayeshgah. We crawled on the floor of the same nursery. Rolled marbles in the same playground. In Barats and *Ashuras*, we distributed our mothers' dishes of halwa, sweet rice and chilli rice among neighbours. In Eids, we dashed to the fair, rode on carousels, swings and Ferris wheels, joined the egg-fighting game, and shot balloons with guns. In the last days of Ramadan, after breaking the fast, we, along other haleks of the block, went from one house to another in the neighbourhood and sang ramazani songs in return for sweets, dried fruits and kulchas. And six days a week, from March to November, we walked to school together. School without Wazir turned into a painless source of torture. Life without Wazir became a prison. In fact, Kabul had turned into a prison. Families left for the West by the day. Agha confided that President Najibullah had also shifted his wife and daughters to India. Agha believed 'something bad' was about to happen to Kabul as the mujahideen closed in on the capital.

Things changed in school, too. Raziq Khan had vanished. His substitute 'like the KHAD' tortured anyone, ustads or students, who challenged his 'instructions'. His bodyguards searched all haleks, and sometimes jelais, at the gate. In a way, you couldn't blame the buffalo-headed mudir. Students previously threatened ustads – in some rare cases, mostly when Rashid was around, beat them up – but never murdered one.

Chapter Twelve

The buffalo-headed Mullah Rahmat lumbered in, followed by the religious studies ustad, Rauf Khan. The mudir told his two bodyguards, armed with Kalashnikovs, to go back to the edara. Instructed us to get some chairs and the students from nine jim.

Baktash and I, together with a few others, executed the order with an eagerness to please the entourage. The relaxed atmosphere became tense as we broke the news, students bombarding Mahbuba jan with one question: why must they join the nine alef if they had religious studies the following day? A question Frishta, I and, most likely, Mahbuba jan knew the answer to.

The 'dangerous womaniser', as Frishta put it, aimed not at eliminating haleks chatting up jelais, but at 'hunting' as many attractive, single female ustads as he could. The mid-twenties Mahbuba jan with dark brown skin, medium height and curly hair passed beyond the 'pervert's criteria'.

Thanks to Frishta's research on Mullah Rahmat, Frishta and I learned a great deal about him: as an ex-Mujahid, he defected with his 400 militia to the government last year under President Najibullah's national reconciliation process.

A week ago, the day after Baz Muhammad's death, the school keeper didn't give Frishta permission to enter the edara because Mullah Rahmat conducted 'a private meeting'. Frishta intuited something 'fishy' and disobeyed the school keeper. The buffalo-headed Mullah Rahmat towered over our year eight ustad, Huma jan. Mullah Rahmat got mad at the school keeper and slapped the old man, telling him to 'fuck off' from the school. Frishta took the blame for disobedience because she'd left a notebook, and inquired why Huma jan cried. Mullah Rahmat threw Frishta's desk out and told her never to show her face again in the edara.

Huma jan was absent the following day. Frishta suspected Mullah Rahmat. I told her he was a good Muslim and wouldn't tell lies.

Two days later I opened my apartment door and saw a fuming Frishta standing there – a rare occurrence as after our argument we never set foot in each other's flats; we spoke in the class when we discussed school issues as the student heads of class. Twice bumped into each other in the block corridor, and on one of those times she told me about Mullah Rahmat and Huma jan. But that evening she delivered the breaking news: having been to Huma jan's apartment, Frishta discovered Mullah Rahmat in the 'private meeting' had given Huma jan two options: sex or career. Huma jan sacrificed her job. Thankfully, Huma jan was engaged to Raziq Khan and planned to join him in Moscow. The cunning Mullah Rahmat told other ustads he had caught Huma jan hand in hand with a young man in the Makroryan Market and fired her because such corrupt behaviour 'adversely impacted' the students.

Now the hunter found a new kill.

Every student carried a desk or a chair with them to our class. The lovable Mahbuba jan joined Rauf Khan in a suit and tie by the window.

Mullah Rahmat studied the registry, his large lips, as dark as cow's liver, kept moving. His golden Rado watch and a golden ring with an auburn, egg-shaped gemstone reflected the gloomy light coming from the plastic sheeting. Unlike Raziq Khan, his thick hair had no trace of grey. He dyed it like most middle-aged Afghans. He couldn't hide his massive belly behind his perahan, though. Nor could he have shortened his long ears. Frishta was spot on: he looked like a buffalo – an ugly-looking one.

'Yesterday, I shockingly discovered that year eight students didn't know *Dua-e-Qunoot,* a basic dua a 10-year child should know,' Mullah Rahmat said, blocking out from view half of the blackboard with his gigantic body. 'Sadly, you've been purposely kept away from religious studies by the system,' he added, glancing at Mahbuba jan, who, along with Rauf Khan, stood with blank expressions.

He called Naqib, the last name on the registry, right from the end of the window row, to my relief. Naqib's leg caught a chair with a scraping sound and almost fell on the way to the floorboard. He recited the first three words of the Islamic dua and stood with an expressionless face.

Mullah Rahmat towered over him. 'Run out of petrol?'

Naqib cast his eyes down, his body visibly shivering.

He buried Naqib's small head with his huge hands and kneed him in the stomach. Naqib dropped to the hard floor. Tears came down his pale face as he caught his breath.

'I equally blame his parents for neglecting their duty.' He glanced at Mahbuba jan, who stood with an offended face.

'What does your father do?'

'He's a—'

'Speak louder.'

'Performer in the Radio and Television Centre.'

'There you are, a prime example.'

His eyes travelled from Naqib to Mahbuba jan. 'Ask him to shake his body, he'd do it right, left and centre because, I bet, his father taught him. But he's failed to teach him the very basics of Islam.' The mudir ordered Naqib to stretch his hand upwards, stand on one leg without his back touching the globe map. Pushed a piece of paper in Naqib's mouth. 'You'll never forget the dua again.'

He called Shirullah next and himself plodded back to his previous position.

Baktash's hands rested on the desk, trembling. He now sat in Wazir's place. I peeked to the row on my left and couldn't miss the fear on haleks' faces.

Shirullah's recitation was faultless. In answer to Mullah Rahmat's questions, Shirullah kept the handful of hair on the chin because it was the habitual practice of the Prophet, peace be upon him, and Shirullah's father was an imam in the local mosque.

'Here's another example. An imam is aware of his religious duties.' Shirullah had two afarins: one for the beard and the other for the correct recitation.

'Children are like a wet plant stem; bend whatever way you want them to bend. Believe me, if your parents carried out their responsibilities properly, this place would've been nicknamed a Little Mecca, not a Little Moscow.'

Rauf Khan, himself a pro-Communist supporter, and many would doubt his religious commitments, nodded at every single statement his superior made. Mahbuba jan, in a dark green outfit and tunban, seemed like someone about to be tried for murder in a court of law. Maybe they appeared terrorised in case Mullah Rahmat asked them to recite the Dua-e-Qunoot. They needn't have feared, at least for a while, because Mullah Rahmat's stony eyes flicked to me.

I glanced at my jeans.

'What's your name?'

Silence. The sound of drizzle hitting the damaged plastic sheeting over the windows.

'I'm asking you.'

Quietness.

'The one with the denim jacket.'

Shirullah tapped my shoulder. Why didn't Mullah Rahmat go through the registry? My name was at the top, and by the time he got halfway through, the class would have been over.

'Ahmad, mudir saheb.'

'To the board.'

I executed the instruction.

'The dua?' He gazed down with his eyes half-closed, turning his ears in my direction.

'Mudir saheb, I know it, but I'm nervous,' I lied. First, we were never taught that particular dua in school. Second, the school took religious studies easy. Rauf Khan gave the grades without us doing the necessary work. It could've been the pro-Communist government's policy to keep its citizens from learning about their religion, or it might have been due to Rauf Khan's laziness. But we liked it – it meant less work. It also translated into more time to focus on scientific subjects, instrumental in getting me into the Kabul Medical Institute.

'What's your name?'

I told him a minute ago. 'Ahmad.'

'Father's name?'

'Azizullah.'

'Address?'

I told him. I reckoned he intended to complain to my parents. I was happy with this (happy even with making me stand on one leg), provided he spared me a beating.

'You're not nervous. You answered all the questions correctly because you *knew* the answers.'

He glared at me as if I'd burned his house down. I put my eyes on my hip hop trainers. My heart palpitated in fear as his legs moved like tree trunks in my direction. He towered over me. 'Why haven't you learned it?'

'I'm sorry.'

A blow on my face threw me to the ground. The religious book flew out of my hand. He picked up the book and screamed at me to get back on my feet. I stood back up with a ringing noise in my right ear.

'Look at the state in which you've kept the book. A Holy book needs to be wrapped in seven pieces of cloth.' He flipped the pages.

A folded piece of paper dropped from within the book. Picked the light blue piece up and unfolded it. His red eyes flicked from one line to another: each line caused his eyes to pop out more. Baktash was right, Mullah Rahmat wasn't entirely sane. He read it aloud.

A letter to the halek I am in mina with, whose name is Ahmad jan:

Every day I see you, I feel like Sandy found her Danny. When you tease your hair upwards and back, you're just my Danny from *Grease*. I love him because of you. Thinking of you fills my day with joy. You don't know how crazy I am for you. Your smiles at me turn my days into summer nights and make me believe you're in mina with me, too. You wouldn't imagine how much I'd cry if you said no to me.

Your Sandy desperately awaits her Danny's reply. You know who I am.

Your mina.

As the proverb claimed, when days of sorrows arrived, they came in multiple numbers. Someone intended to stain my honour in front of the whole class. The words would get to my parents. What would they say? The air became so solid I thought I'd die from suffocation.

'Who's written this?' He advanced towards me.

'I don't know, I *swear*. Someone has purposely slipped it in my book.' I didn't look at jelais, let alone smile at them.

'Suspect anyone?'

No one, I told him.

'Who is Danny from *Grease*?'

'I don't know.' I asked Khudai for forgiveness for telling a lie, but giving the correct answer could've somehow led to Frishta getting involved.

'Anyone?' His face turned to students.

Everyone sat with downcast eyes, their faces fear-stricken.

'An actor from a film,' Shafih said.

'Ustad, I'll learn it tomorrow. Please,' I said to Rauf Khan, who turned his gaze away to Naqib.

'No one can save you from me.'

The buffalo-headed Mullah Rahmat, to my relief, took a few steps towards the jelai row and asked with a deep-throated voice, 'Who's written the letter?'

Eyes cast down.

'Who do you smile at?' He roared and stormed towards me like a mad buffalo attacking its prey.

A shiver travelled through my back – my body went paralysed, my legs gave way, my thighs felt the warmth around my crotch and my upper legs got soaked. Sighs of *Allahhhh* filled the class. Faces no longer showed fear, but dismay. Sadaf and Laila, in the front seats, clapped their hands over their eyes. Shafih and Jawad squeezed their nostrils with their fingers. My body turned ice-cold when I realised what'd happened.

Mullah Rahmat shook his head. 'You must be ashamed of yourself,' he said, sounding appalled. He ordered Rauf Khan to dry the floor with my jacket. If only I didn't live to see this day; death was much better than this shameful act. Rauf Khan removed my jacket.

'Wetting yourself wouldn't save you. Tell me who wrote it.' He stood right opposite me.

Mahbuba jan took a step, but Mullah Rahmat motioned with his palm. She stayed put.

Mullah Rahmat put his big hands on my ears, twisted my head, and threatened to make me poo this time if I stayed silent, reminding me of his goal to rid the school of immoral behaviour. 'Last warning.'

'I swear I don't know.'

He let go. 'Alright, now you'll confess.' His right hand clutched my bushy hair, and the left one held my belt.

'Name?'

'Please, ustad, tell him to let me go. I'll memorise it tomorrow,' I said to Rauf Khan, who was wiping the floor around my feet.

The giant Mullah Rahmat lifted me.

'Last warning.'

'My hair hurts. Please, mudir saheb.' His sweat odour was equally painful.

'Name?'

'Get away from him.' A jelai's scream. 'One more move, and I'll call my father.'

'Not until he tells me–'

'*I* have written the letter.'

He let go of me and resumed his posture.

Frishta stood on guard. Her eyes were full of tears, her body shivered like the trees in the school gardens outside; trees that hadn't bloomed yet, maybe because they knew what'd befallen me. She looked wild.

'I love Ahmad. By Khuda jan, you touch him again, my father will leave no hair on your head. There's the edara.' She pointed right. 'Go and make a complaint about me, but let Ahmad go. He doesn't know about the letter.'

Mahbuba jan and Rauf Khan looked baffled.

'I'll punish you severely,' he said, kicking the table before the board, which scraped the floor and hit the Afghan flag. The crazy man stormed off, mumbling something to himself. Naqib spat out the paper, put his foot on the floor and hugged me. So did Baktash, whispering I'd be OK and not to pay attention to Shafih and Jawad tittering.

Mahbuba jan rushed to Frishta and whispered something in her ear as Frishta bounced towards me. Whispered if I knew the author. I had no idea. She dashed out.

The school keeper rushed in and collected me and the two ustads to the edara for an 'emergency meeting'. Mullah Rahmat's two armed men with long hair followed from behind.

***

THE BUFFALO-HEADED MUDIR SAT on a swivel recliner. His eyes fixed on the mahogany desk before him. His two bodyguards stood by; two others guarded the door.

The rukhsati bells sounded. Joyful students' chatter, cheers and yells filled the school. Ustads walked in one by one, a few with moistened suits or outfits. Those who knew whispered to the others. Some shook their heads; a few, mainly female, put their hands on their mouths and threw me glances; yet others took a seat and wrote in their notebooks or studied registers.

If only I'd died from measles when I was eight years old.

A panting Frishta rushed in and whispered something to Mahbuba jan, who pointed to Mullah Rahmat and stepped away from Frishta. No one associated themselves with Frishta and took a beating from Mullah Rahmat or his militia. The buffalo-headed man experienced nothing but war over the years. Spoke in the language of violence. As a defector was outside the reach of the law. No way did a helpless ustad square up to him. Hurting ustads was as easy for the hypocrite as drinking water. I was surprised the ugly face had spared Frishta so far. Mullah Rahmat must have known about another bully's fate at Brigadier's hands and, I reckoned, was careful of raising a hand at Frishta. Rumour had it that Rashid was one of his 'trench buddies' from Logar Province. If only Agha was as fearless as Brigadier.

Mullah Rahmat asked for attention as students' chatter quietened. 'I've decided to kick you out of the school.'

'Why?' Frishta said.

'The school can no longer tolerate lundabazi.'

'I object, lundabazi is different from mina.'

'Are you not ashamed to talk about mina?'

'I am not.'

'Today you're in mina; tomorrow you'll fuck each other.'

'At least I won't force him to.'

'Don't give me that look. Or I'll beat you until you have learned decency. Something your father has neglected to teach you.'

'Padar jan's taught me how to stand up to bullies.' She visibly fought against bursting into tears.

He eyed her up and down. 'Wear your headscarf properly.'

Frishta pulled her white headscarf off and tied it around her waist. 'The right place for fighting bullies,' Frishta said, and stood on guard. The front of her moistened black perahan was muddied.

Mullah Rahmat's eyes popped out like a cow being strangled by a rope. You could comprehend that he questioned himself whether he should order his militiamen to beat the shit out of a 16-year-old female student – the sex he scarcely considered a full human being – for challenging his authority. Or should he be patient?

'I blame her father,' he said to the frozen ustads; they didn't even blink. 'She'd be a respectful child if he'd looked after her properly.'

'Padar jan has taught to spit on those elders who abuse their position.'

Frishta considered her ustads as 'second parents'. I never saw her talking back to an ustad.

'He's a coward to let his daughter run riot.'

'Padar jan is a lion. He's on his way for you to know him better. My hero would sacrifice himself for his soldiers' sake. He isn't a hypocrite like you. These female ustads,' Frishta pointed at the fear-stricken faces sitting on chairs behind desks by the walls around the room, 'are sisters, daughters, mothers, yet you're treating them like sex objects. Shame on you.' Frishta's body trembled with rage like the Panjshir River, her hair untangled like a wild woman.

Mullah Rahmat showed no remorse. I didn't think he cared or was even embarrassed. Our physics ustad, Karim Khan, mumbled something to Amrudin Khan and the latter nodded. Karim Khan then limped by the side of the desk and whispered to his superior, half of his face getting hidden behind the bouquet of artificial flowers. Everyone heard what he said in a nervous tone: Mullah Rahmat may have misunderstood Frishta and me, both disciplined students who excelled at our studies. They never had a complaint about us, and Frishta joined all voluntary work at school. None of these good words changed Mullah Rahmat's indignant face, a face I loathed like Satan's.

Mullah Rahmat's bodyguards prevented a female ustad from leaving. Everyone looked at one another in surprise, but no one commented. Their faces looked haunted.

A silence followed. I bet every person in the edara waited for Brigadier's arrival and what he would, or rather could, do to the powerful Mullah Rahmat with an armed militia.

Silence, apart from the sound of the howling wind.

The door opened and a bodyguard rushed in, holding a walkie-talkie.

'The school is surrounded.'

'How many?'

'Hundreds.'

'How many are you?'

'Ten,' the bodyguard said over a muffled crackle spluttering out from the walkie-talkie.

'Where the fuck are the rest?'

'In the base. On leave.'

Mullah Rahmat shook his head. He considered something and slammed the desk, causing pens to drop from the filing tray.

Ustads jumped.

'All ten of you in this room. We fight. Let's die for our religion.'

The bodyguard dashed out.

Ustads begged Mullah Rahmat to reconsider his decision for their and their children's sake.

Armed men in long perahans and waistcoats stormed in, motioned to ustads by the windows to move away, pulled away the grey curtains to reveal a cloudy sky, and placed their guns on the recesses.

Cries, screams and pleas filled the edara when the two bodyguards by the door blocked ustads from leaving. The armed men roared at them to shut up.

'You're surrounded. Give up your weapons,' a voice said on a loudspeaker from the outside.

Ustads with pale faces and tearful eyes begged Mullah Rahmat to use dialogue, and implored Frishta to speak to Brigadier not to fire.

He picked up the handset but hit it back hard, causing the Afghan flag to fall. 'Let them in.'

Sighs of relief and 'thank you, mudir saheb' filled the room.

'I'm doing it for you,' he said to the ustads. 'I'm doing it for you, understand?' he screamed. The ustads flinched.

He was indeed mad.

Silence. Muffled sounds of people tapping against the hard floor.

The door slammed open and armed men with muddy boots stormed in and disarmed Mullah Rahmat's thugs.

Brigadier marched in, followed by Agha, whose presence brightened my world. At last, I received his support. If only he'd come an hour earlier.

Brigadier told the screaming ustads to calm down and ordered the guards to remove 'the puppies' and shut the door.

Agha told me to stop crying. Mahbuba jan put her hands on my shoulders, telling me all was well. Salty tears entered my mouth. I was meant to be in the middle of the edara earlier on, fighting abuse. I was physically stronger and taller than Frishta, yet I couldn't challenge Mullah Rahmat. Stood motionless like a dead body. I was at the mercy of my genetic flaw. I despised my cowardly side. Despised me. If only Khudai had created me as brave as Frishta.

Frishta took a step back and stood by me with her calming jasmine scent. Like me, her eyes were full of tears. We both trembled. A pale Mahbuba jan held my shoulders and told me to relax.

The ustads by the mahogany desk opposite us gave up their seats for Agha and Brigadier. Agha appeared to be fuming.

'Apologies to all ustads for the manner in which we entered. And to you, sir, for stepping in before you,' Brigadier said to Agha, whom he respected like his elder brother.

I didn't think Mullah Rahmat – who stayed motionless throughout – had expected Frishta's father to come down with so many armed guards.

'What have I taught you, Frishta? Leopards fight; they don't cry.' Brigadier's authoritative voice filled the room. 'Mudir saheb, what crime has my princess committed by giving Ahmad a mina letter?' Brigadier went on, his right arm resting on the desk.

To my great relief, Agha showed no reaction when Brigadier mentioned the letter.

'More than a crime – a sin.'

'What's wrong if the two of them are in mina? I can't find a better son-in-law than Ahmad.' Brigadier guffawed, straightening the fallen Afghan flag.

'Lundabazi is forbidden in the school.'

'Speak like a principal. What do you mean by lundabazi?'

'Unreligious sexual relationships.'

'Who says mina is unreligious?'

'Our dear religion.'

'Did you think about Islam when you asked Huma jan for sex? It's not the Red Shorawi but *you* who's the real enemy of Islam, by preaching one thing and doing the opposite.'

Brigadier gestured to Frishta to keep quiet and asked Mullah Rahmat what religion forbade mina.

'Do I have to remind you of your religion?'

'Please.'

'The Holy Religion of Islam.'

'As far as I'm concerned, Islam is a religion of peace, tolerance and mina.'

'Not that type of mina.'

'Not in your distorted interpretation–'

'Because my interpretation is different from a Communist's interpretation.'

119

'We made the April Revolution to get rid of backward people like them,' Brigadier said to Agha. '14 years down the line, and we still get hurt by these hypocrites with one Islam for them and another for us.'

Agha explained to Mullah Rahmat how he did me injustice: he shouldn't have threatened me to the extent that I wet myself, but instead explained my errors.

Mullah Rahmat said it was for my 'good'.

'Beating children teaches them nothing except fear, shame and helplessness,' Agha said, leaning against the wooden chair with cushion seats, adding that these feelings ultimately affected their performance at school, damaged their self-confidence, and prevented them from being who they were likely to become.

'My ustads beat me up. I'm not doing that badly.'

Brigadier told Agha reasoning with a 'bandit' was useless.

'Did it teach you how to behave?' Agha asked.

'Don't worry about me. Your son will never write a mina letter if he remembers today.'

'You likewise won't raise a hand on a helpless child if you remember me.' Brigadier leapt over the desk and threw Mullah Rahmat on the floor. The clay pot tumbled onto the concrete ground, breaking into pieces. Brigadier punched him in the face. Once, twice, thrice. Shouted 'Quick' and armed men rushed in, kicking, punching and elbowing Mullah Rahmat in the stomach, back and even face.

Cries of help filled the room when Brigadier threw Rauf Khan on the ground over the wet mud. Frishta covered Rauf Khan's body and pleaded with her mad father that the ustad wasn't to blame.

'He must've stood by his students,' Brigadier said. Agha told him to calm down.

I now understood Frishta had inherited the loss of temper from her father, or rather stepfather. Brigadier ordered his guards to take Mullah Rahmat away. They held him by the arms and pulled him towards the door, blood flowing from the side of his mouth. Mullah Rahmat guffawed like a mad buffalo, spat skyward a mixture of blood and saliva, and shouted to the ceiling, 'May Khudai keep you away from the venom of the cobra, the jaw of the tiger and the revenge of the Pashtun.'

One of the guards pushed him out. Agha and Brigadier took their seats and told everyone to do so. They apologised again to the ustads for their approach; they saw no other way to deal effectively with an armed Mullah Rahmat. The relieved ustads, now fewer in number, apologised for what'd happened to me. They said Mullah Rahmat behaved like a militia commander, beat them up 'like fatherless children' for refusing his 'unlawful orders', and molested female colleagues at will. The ustads remained helpless because he 'terrified' them. They felt proud of Frishta for facing another bully.

What did I see? Amrudin Khan, standing upright before Frishta, the right-hand palm facing forward and the fingers touching the forehead's right side. 'You remind me of a student I am very proud to have taught years back.' His eyes welled up. 'Nahid Shahid.'

'Na...' Frishta's voice broke. 'I'm nowhere near to one of my heroines.'

In defiance of the Kabul government, the student Nahid participated in the anti-Soviet demonstrations in the first year of the Soviet invasion in Kabul until a bullet from a pro-Communist puppet's gun *shahid*, martyred, her.

'You'd officially be presented with the medal of The True Jelai of Afghanistan.' Everyone clapped. Mahbuba jan hugged Frishta, tears rolling down the ustad's and the student's eyes. Brigadier's lips stretched, his eyes misting over.

Brigadier told the ustads they'd never see Mullah Rahmat again. Agha explained that an investigation would be launched, and he'd be punished in accordance with the rule of law. The ever so diplomatic Agha tried to convey that the proper legal system would be followed. I knew Mullah Rahmat would experience the darkest days of his life in the notorious KHAD prisons. Mullah Rahmat was history, I was sure of this, but my humiliating deed would stay forever.

***

THAT EVENING, leaning against my bedroom door with the light switched off and curtains drawn, I overheard Mour and Agha discussing in the lounge whether wetting myself had any connection with a medical cause. Mour suggested Agha take me to the doctor; Agha saw it as normal to piss out of fear.

'It'll dog him to the end of his life,' Mour went on after a silence. Her voice broke.

'People forget.'

'Not in Afghanistan. Haven't you heard the *tizan* story?'

According to the legend, a man returned after 20 years, thinking the villagers had forgotten about his accidental *tiz*, fart. He asked a village halek if he knew where Ghairat Khan lived. Nobody had seen the tizan, sir fartsalot, for 20 years after his tiz, the halek replied, but his son, known as the son of the tizan, lived by the mosque. The man this time left for good.

I'd carry on the nickname of piss pants. Never see the end of this. It'd hurt even my son, who'd be called the son of piss pants.

'Students will poke fun at him. He won't get into medical school. If only he kept his bladder tight.'

'He must learn to be strong. He must learn from Frishta,' Agha said.

'Frishta is the cause of all this.' She added that no one else would dare to plant the letter in my book. Mour pleaded with Agha to stop the evening visits.

Agha said Mour misunderstood Frishta.

'My judgment is hardly wrong,' Mour said. 'She's ruined my son's future.'

'Your endless lectures on tradition are equally to blame.'

'They're for their good.'

'Are they? A million times today he's told you he hasn't written the letter? You know why? I bet he wet his trousers for fear of your reaction.'

'Children must learn about their religion and culture. I think we should–'

'I have real worries on my mind.'

'Is there any real worry other than our son's future?'

'I fear for my life.'

'Why?' I overheard panic in Mour's voice.

'Najibullah is finished.'

'Na?'

'He tried to flee the country. Dostum's militia didn't let him get on the plane. He's taken refuge in the UN office near the Arg Palace.'

Earlier today, I thanked Khudai for having Agha around me, but his 'other worries' demonstrated he lived with his other wife and her concerns. Even so, the possibility of losing Agha frightened me. The mujahideen would take away our apartment and leave us on the streets. Would Mour survive Agha's death? What'd happen to my sisters' future? What about me? As the only male in the family, I'd have to drop out of school and work to provide for Mour and my sisters.

Chapter Thirteen

Brigadier and Mahjan greeted my parents in the hallway. A knock on the door, to my anxiety. I pulled the blanket over me. A pause. The door opened, stayed for a moment, and then shut. My withdrawal had worried Mour. Thanks, Khudai, she left without bothering me to join them.

I freaked out as I removed the blanket and saw a black figure by my feet.

'I'm sorry. Did I scare you?' she said, sitting by the edge of the bed.

'Why are you here?' Her secret entrance annoyed me. I didn't expect Frishta to come to the apartment, let alone into my room.

She jumped to her feet, turned on the light, whose brightness forced me to close my eyes, pressed the cassette player play button, and sat back on the bed. 'Why haven't you come to school for the last two days?'

I rubbed my eyes, hating the painful light. Loathed school, my classmates, ustads, even myself. I used to love her company, but it strangled me now. I knew she looked down on me for wetting my trousers but acted as if it hadn't mattered; actually, it hadn't occurred to me. Had it been someone else, she'd mention him first thing and go on all evening talking about him, even acting out the moment. Her pretence distressed me more, but she was my guest and melmastia compelled me to make her welcome. I owed her a thank-you and mumbled one.

'Regard others if you want to be regarded; for everyone has a self like you.' Frishta quoted Rahman Baba over Ahmad Zahir.

124

'Why, then, do people do awful things to other people?'

'Because they don't think of you as people. Give them hell, and they would.'

'If only Khudai created me as fearless as you, Frishta.'

'If there was no fear, there'd be no need for courage. I'm afraid, too, but I've learned to conquer my fears.'

'*How?*'

'I guess I'm willing to sacrifice my limb and head for the rights of my sisters.'

'So you *really* fear?'

'Everyone does. Fear is good for you. It warns and protects you. Think: why don't we jump off the fifth floor but walk the stairs?'

'Did your heart beat fast or your body freeze when you challenged Rashid and Mullah Rahmat?'

'I felt afraid, in pain, furious, helpless – all at the same time. That's why I couldn't stop crying. Then I thought, *Khuda jan, You didn't take my life in the biting snow, maybe for today.* I placed my trust in Khuda jan, and my physical well-being no longer mattered.'

'My heart abandons me when it senses danger. My hands and legs freeze... All I wanted was Rashid and Mullah Rahmat to beat me up and get it over with. I'm a coward. I hate my heart.' I told her what I hadn't revealed to anyone and fought against breaking down.

'Take refuge in Khuda jan. Once He protects, no one will overcome you.'

'Will Khudai help a coward?'

'Khuda jan helps those who have a sense of purpose... who are passionate about others.'

'If you want me to tell others how to live their lives, I'm not that sort of a person. But I want to be a doctor, look after my parents when they're old, wed my sisters into decent families... have a wife and kids. Is this not "a sense of purpose"? Am I not "passionate" enough?'

She shrugged.

'But I don't feel like I'll be able to do any of those.' This time, I couldn't stop my tears.

'Don't let bullies shatter your dreams.'

'People will remember last week's... humiliating incident until Qiyamat Day.'

'Fuck what people think about Ahmad. Live for others. Prevent more Ahmads from wetting themselves. Passion and compassion will help you find meaning in your life; inspire you to do extraordinary things. You as Ahmad would no longer matter.'

'I don't know.'

'Those fallen from the mountain will get up again, but those fallen from the hearts will never rise.' Frishta quoted another Rahman Baba. 'You're a proud Ahmadzai. Live like one. Have faith.'

'Faith?'

'You've got the blood of one great Afghan and the name of another.' Frishta reminded me of the reason why Mour had named me Ahmad. My first name traced its origin to the founders of Afghanistan's two largest Pashtun tribes, Ahmad Baba from the Ahmadzai, and Ahmad Shah Durrani from the Durrani.

'Ahmad Shah Massoud wouldn't miss school,' she added.

'Massoud?'

'Another warrior,' Frishta said. 'Anyway, tell me, what have you been up to?'

'Nothing. Just sleeping.' I buried my eyes in my hands. I needed darkness, not light.

'You're coming to school tomorrow. Baktash misses you a lot. We all do.'

I removed my hands and looked into her dark eyes – which showed nothing but an eagerness to please me – and paused for thought: should I say it, or should I not? I did. Baktash was in my room earlier that day and let me know how Shafih increased his compliments for Frishta, how she returned them with smiles, and how she and Shafih at breaks conversed privately in the school's corners. What was going on?

Her face lost colour.

An awkward silence filled our once chatty room, except Ahmad Zahir's song about people with two faces, and the chatter of adults and children from the lounge.

'You do know who put the letter in my book.' My tone sounded more accusatory than I'd intended.

Her face turned darker. She searched for something in my eyes.

'Where do you go every afternoon and come back hours later?'

She still searched as if she'd lost something in them. Shook her head. Her eyes welled up. She stormed out, not just of my room but out of the apartment, without saying goodbye. Never had done this before. Her furtive behaviour awakened my suspicion even more.

According to Baktash, Shafih had authored the letter, and he alleged Frishta had aided him. Baktash wasn't alone; Mour, too, suspected Frishta had somehow been an accomplice. Mour's suspicion would turn into belief if she found out that *Grease* was Frishta's favourite film. Though I hadn't fully bought into Baktash's accusation and Mour's strong suspicion, I believed Frishta was up to something. She hid something from me – probably her relationship with Shafih because he lived in Bimaro, a neighbourhood Frishta lately walked around every afternoon, and he was the one Frishta showed an interest in, and she must've confided in him her likes and dislikes. But were Shafih and Frishta really together? Both Baktash and I believed Shafih to have slipped the love letter in my book. What I didn't understand was how Frishta would benefit from assisting him. Why would she do this to me? Because I'd refused to help her with studies? Or, as Mour told me, to remove me from school so that she got first place? But why would she stand for me if that was the case? No, my other part reasoned that a chaste jelai like Frishta would never get involved in immoral behaviour: a loyal person who lived for others. No matter what, she wouldn't humiliate 'the trusted person' in her life.

I decided to follow her tomorrow to discover once and for all her true character.

Chapter Fourteen

It'd been *two and a half* hours since Frishta had entered a mud house. The day had turned into a moonful night, and, like a fearful shepherd standing on guard for the wolf's arrival, I waited impatiently by the corner of a dirt alleyway with a thin stream dug along it. Open, smelly drains, serving as gutters, came across from each muddy house and joined the narrow stream on the passageway.

Frishta stepped out at last and glanced right and left. Locked the padlock and darted off. Startled as she turned the corner. 'Have you been tailing me?' Her tone conveyed more disappointment than anger.

'What were you doing in that house?' My heart pounded against my chest.

'None of your business.' She shook her head and strode off, holding a bag in her right hand and a red notebook in the left. A woman in a burka, carrying a tray of pleasantly smelling fresh *naans* with one hand and a little jelai with another, passed, staring at me.

'Of course it is,' I said as I caught up with her by the end of the stench-smelling passageway.

She paused and turned around. 'Who are you? My father, mother, brother?'

She had a point. I was nothing to her. We'd formed a trusting relationship, but I just struck another blow to it. I looked deep into her eyes, and they expressed only one message: how badly I'd let her down. In a sick way, hurting her felt good.

'Look, Ahmad, by now you know perfectly well I'm not one of those women who're told what to do. I was born free and will die free.'

'What's the notebook about?'

'Stop asking me bleeping questions.' She adopted a guarded stance – more Taekwondo than judo – staring at me like an angry leopard. She was scary.

I checked around. Thankfully, no one was about apart from an older man holding a toddler's hand walking on the barren land with sporadic thorn bushes. She dropped her guard after a few moments and carried on walking, shaking her head. Guarding against the trusted person in her life pained even more.

I didn't know what to do. Part of me believed she'd betrayed me. The other part, the sensible one, reasoned that she rightly claimed she was a free person and chose where she wanted to go. Couldn't she have informed me about it, though? As one of the closest persons in her life, did I not have the right to know about her relationship? Couldn't she just *say* she wasn't an accomplice in the love letter business if she was innocent?

A fire burned in my stomach for the truth. The anguish of not knowing was unbearable, especially her alleged relationship with Shafih. I knew I couldn't get anything out of the stubborn Frishta, so the red notebook, something I never saw before and over which she became defensive, could offer all the answers. Maybe it was an album of photos of Frishta and her lover.

I ran against the dusty wind and caught her by the barren land closer to Airport Road. 'I'm entitled to know about your business in that house. I'm your mina. Remember you admitted it in front of the whole school,' I heard myself say, to my disgust.

'I don't want a piss pants to be my mina.' She stood on guard again.

The words 'piss pants' went through my heart like a sword. 'I understand, I'm not your mina. Your mina lives in that house. It's the ugly Shafih?'

'He's more handsome than you are.'

'Is that why you helped him with the letter?'

'What can you coward do if I did?'

'I trusted you, Frishta. But you've proved you really are a *harami*,' I said, feeling as if I had thrust the thorny bush behind her into my stomach by calling her 'bastard'.

She froze. Wanted to say something but struggled to open her mouth. Her eyes locked on my eyes. I had no idea what damn thing she sought out in them. She burst into tears as though she discovered both her step-parents had just died. 'Don't ever talk to me again.' She collected herself and carried on walking on the uneven ground.

I had a sudden compulsion to do something but decided against it. Then, to my horror, found myself sprinting and snapping the red notebook. Her bag's content flew and scattered on the dirt ground, making a mixture of clinking and clattering sounds.

I flew off.

The chubby Frishta stayed put. Didn't even utter a negative word. Only pleaded to return the notebook if I had any respect for her.

I carried on sprinting and, after crossing Airport Road, hid behind a muddy shed in the green land from where Mour often dispatched me to get fresh milk and vegetables. Peeked. Frishta froze on the dirt ground, lost in thoughts like a widow with starving children. Crushing her down purified the miserable feelings I'd gone through. She *betrayed* me. The agony of not ascertaining her business in that dirt house, and her connection to the love letter, choked me to death. Poked my head. Still on her knees, picking up the scattered crockery and cutlery.

I headed for a construction site in Makroryan. Climbed over the wall and jumped in. Sat on the cement bags on wooden plates with Russian lettering, situated between two cranes, as high as the sky. In trepidation, flicked open the first page of the red notebook in the full moon and saw the drawing of a white pigeon. Flicked another page and read, 'The Diary of Frishta *Gharibdost*', 'Loving the Poor'. Skimmed through more pages and, to my horror, found everything in

Russian. I recognised the alphabet because Raziq Khan had acquainted us with the letters when he doubled as a Russian ustad. But the letters were all I knew about the Russian language. Turned more pages in desperation, but apart from the few words that introduced Frishta's diary, found nothing else in Dari.

The illuminating moon enfolded my attention. I once read in a book that the moon didn't fight. It attacked no one. Didn't worry and posed no questions. Remained faithful to its nature, and its power never diminished. I envied the moon. I betrayed my nature and bit my loyal friends. Posed questions I had no business with. Questions that ate me from within, especially after she didn't deny Shafih was her halek and hinted at helping him. I'd believed her diary might answer those questions, but it didn't defuse one bit of my anxiety. Wanted to scream but decided against it. I knew our closeness belonged to the past. Three days ago I lost my reputation; today I lost Frishta. This time for good.

I felt more tired than I'd ever been before, as though the two gigantic cranes weighed on my shoulders. Wanted to stay on the rough bags with a mixture of cement and grease odour forever. Didn't want to return to the world where I was known as a piss pants, where people perceived me as a sinful lover; a world which Frishta was no longer going to be a part of. I'd lost a trusted person forever. Or was she trusted anymore? My head was exploding for not learning the truth. I couldn't believe I stole her diary. Worse, I fell to the lowest of the low by calling her a bastard. Taunted her with the very secret she'd shared with me. Did she not mock me, though, calling me a coward? Was she not meant to keep the secret? Yesterday she said people forgot, but today she called me a piss pants. She used words she knew bit me like a snake.

I closed my eyes, wishing Khudai took my life. I loathed myself even more. The place calmed me down somehow. None of these precast concrete walls of flats, balconies and windows recognised me as a piss pants. They had no knowledge about the wicked letter. Didn't know I was a thief, a cowardly one. Had no tongue to taunt me. No soul like Frishta to deceive me.

My eyes opened when the thought of tomorrow crossed my mind. How would Brigadier react to stealing his princess's diary? What about Mour and, of course, Agha, who'd warned me against a complaint from Frishta? Importantly, what about Frishta? I didn't want to think. A few days ago I was the trusted person and a good child whom everyone was proud of; today I became an embarrassment, even a thief, and let everyone down. How years-old reputation could shatter into pieces in a day.

I tucked the diary into my jeans and sprinted home.

Chapter Fifteen

Baktash cheered when he found me waiting in the bright morning under the acacia tree. I thanked Khudai for giving me such a loyal friend, and wished Wazir was also there.

***

STUDENTS PEEKED AT ME, whispered, or shook their heads in the assembly. I must learn to face my new, embarrassing reality. I didn't tell Baktash about yesterday, and awaited Frishta's reaction. She was revengeful, so I had better be prepared for a badal, a beating-up, by Frishta and her halek, the new school gangster, or rather bully, the ugly Shafih.

***

IN CLASS EVERYONE acted like things were normal. But you couldn't miss the 'I'm sorry' feeling behind their masks. I had to be careful with being playful with my classmates, or they'd jeer at me. Anticipated that any moment someone would call me a piss pants. I wasn't wrong.

***

MY HEART FELL as Baktash, Shirullah and I returned from the break and read 'piss pants' on the blackboard. Shafih and Jawad had their arms around each other's shoulders, giggling.

Baktash erased it.

'Why did you touch it?' Shafih pushed Baktash.

'Please don't.'

'Please don't,' Shafih mimicked and kicked me, causing a dull pain in my buttock. Shafih scraped the words again with a piece of chalk. 'You dare to remove it.'

A slap stung me at the back of my head. I turned around. Jawad put his hands on his private part and screamed, 'Oh no, I've pissed in my trousers.'

'Mama, my nappies.' Shafih pretended to do a baby cry.

Both laughed loud.

My heart sank; my body shivered and eyes welled up.

Jelais scolded them. They paid no attention.

'Where's your friend, the murderer?' Shafih pushed me. 'Bring the murderer.'

'He's hidden in his sisters' room,' Jawad said.

'Keep my sisters out of this.'

'Fuck your sisters,' Jawad said.

'And your mother,' Shafih said.

I stayed frozen, thanks to my heart. Kill an Afghan but never swear at his women. I despised even more my cowardly self.

'Frishta's recognised you. You're a fucking coward,' Shafih said.

'A crying one,' Jawad said.

'Leave him alone,' Shirullah said.

Everyone stood up as the art ustad entered the class. Laila told the ustad to get a student to clear the blackboard. She peeped at the word and thankfully asked Laila to clean it. She sat on the chair behind the desk and asked for five minutes' quiet to fill in a form, cursing bureaucracy.

Baktash reiterated that he was 100 per cent sure it was Shafih and Frishta who had engineered the plan for my downfall.

'How many times have we seen Frishta and Shafih together at breaks?' Baktash said in a low voice as he turned back to Shirullah.

'Every day since your absence,' Shirullah whispered.

'I told you so,' Baktash said to me and took his seat.

'They're always alone, usually by the corners of the school,' Shirullah said.

Baktash raised his eyebrows and nodded.

'What do they do?' I wiped my eyes.

'Talk,' Shirullah said.

'And flirt,' Baktash said.

'I haven't seen them flirting,' Shirullah said over the muffled chatter in the class.

'I have,' Baktash said. 'And you heard what Shafih just told you about what she thinks of you.'

Frishta even shared her thoughts about me with him.

'And his reply to Mahbuba jan this morning?' Baktash added.

Earlier that day, in response to Mahbuba jan's inquiry about the uncharacteristic absence of Frishta, which I said I didn't know anything about, Shafih said Frishta told him yesterday she'd be missing the school today. Where did they meet, if not in Bimaro, in that muddy house?

I remembered the night Frishta hinted at needing a soul friend. I gazed back at Shafih's spotty face right at the end of the row, his ears as big as the doors of a rickshaw, and wondered how on earth Frishta and other jelais fancied such an *ugly* block. Which parts of his features looked like a 'model'? He possessed no personality, no beauty, no moral values, yet Frishta had chosen him as a soul friend. Delicious meat indeed ended up being eaten by the ugliest bird.

Frishta was right, though. I lacked courage. Brooded over consequences. Worried about what others thought of me. Had got Wazir and Frishta too many times to fight my corner. Too many times I'd been a liability to them. I prayed to Khudai to help me fulfil a vital Pashtunwali principle, the one I'd neglected: *meraana*, courage. Frishta said yesterday everyone was afraid but they transcended their fears. I must do the same with the help of Khudai; I was an Afghan and must live like one. Shafih had done me wrong, and nothing in Pashtunwali was ever forgotten. Ill treat an Afghan, and he'd make sure you received the same care. If he couldn't take revenge, his sons or even grandsons would have to seek justice. Otherwise, the family would be taunted with acting cowardly.

I wouldn't leave it to my sons or grandsons. I'd take my own revenge. This evening.

Chapter Sixteen

The wooden door, crumbling with age, had no chink to peek inside. Should I knock, or jump over the wall into the house? If I knocked and someone answered, what was I supposed to say? If that person was Shafih, I'd thrust Mour's kitchen knife into his stomach. But then I wouldn't catch the two red-handed. And what if Frishta opened? Or worse, Shafih's mother or sister? The combination of a hot April afternoon and harrowing thoughts soaked me with sweat.

I placed my trust in Khudai and found my right foot on the metal knob, pulled on the upper edge of the wooden door and was on the wall of the one-storey hut. Scanned the yard, and to my relief saw no one. Threw the knife into the dried plants and jumped in, causing a dragonfly to fly away.

The yard's unattended yellow and green plants almost covered the well, with a plastic jug sitting on the wooden cover. Placed the knife in my hip pocket and tiptoed towards two rooms built from mud and clay on the far side. My heart thumped; my forehead broke out in a cold sweat. I stepped on upper ground which led to the entrance hall's wooden door, the only access to the two rooms on its left and right; it was padlocked from the outside. The thick curtains obscured the rooms inside. Their wooden window frames were covered with plastic sheeting. I reckoned nobody lived in the house. It served as a pastime place: invite women, spend the time in total privacy, and nobody, not even the police, would have the slightest doubt the crumbling house was being used for womanising.

Tiptoed to the two mini-sheds in the yard's left corner, and stepped on the mud stairs. Hordes of bees flew as I removed the curtain and peeked through the hole. Cupped my nose and dashed out. Trod into the adjacent shed. A shovel and a saw leaned against the coals and firewood. I placed it on the opposite side, moved some wood and coal, created a hiding space, and through the chink secured a good view of the two rooms.

I'd wait until Frishta and her halek's arrival, allow them to enter one of the rooms, pause and then burst in to catch them on top of each other. The kitchen knife would burst Shafih's belly.

My heart sank to my stomach as I overheard the clanging of a padlock opening. *I seek refuge in You, Khudai*, I prayed in my heart. The door clunked open. Footsteps. I breathed gently, a sharp piece of wood poking my back. *Please, Khudai, help me conquer my fears and fulfil my pledge.*

Frishta came into sight. Placed a bag of dishes outside the doorway, opened the padlock, and disappeared. Any moment now, the door clunks opens and Shafih comes in, I thought. Frishta pulled a straw bed out and walked back in. They chill out outside. Great – it makes my revenge easier. Come on, ugly Shafih, I thought.

The dramatic scene – or not at all dramatic, given her nature – Frishta displayed next created within me a claw with sharp nails like Mour's kitchen knife, squeezing, twisting and cutting my stomach: Frishta pulling a thin corpse, her hands placed underneath its shoulders. She laid the corpse on the straw bed, closed her eyes, inhaled and exhaled a few times, her face breaking into a sweat. Rushed back in, exposing to view a woman in a brown dress and black headscarf. Brought out an Istalifi-sufali pitcher and put it under the bed. Withdrew a nappy, and as she took the woman's trousers off, I closed my eyes. After washing the woman's hands, face and feet, and drying them with a towel, Frishta helped the woman to wear new, dark brown trousers; they belonged to Frishta. The woman prayed throughout for Frishta, and the claw pulled my stomach out, forcing me to throw up the sour liquid on the dirt floor while trying hard to shut out the sound.

The woman started to pray by gestures, and Frishta headed for the sheds with the dirty clothes and a pot. What if she smelled my vomit? Thankfully, she entered the toilet. The sound of bees flying coupled with washing clothes. Sweat rolled down my forehead. *Please don't come in here, Frishta; please Khudai, help.* I thanked Khudai for the wall between us, not the one I'd created through my sick imagination, but for the mud and straw wall which divided the shed and the toilet.

I wiped my sweat and breathed with ease as she walked back. She took the dishes out of her bag and placed them next to the praying woman. Sprang to her feet, apologised and rushed inside. Stepped out with a photo frame, showed it to the woman and giggled. The woman kissed Frishta on the head, considered the photo frame, and felt it with her hand. The look on her face told a long and nostalgic story between the photo in the golden frame and her. Frishta propped the frame right in front of the woman.

Now the photo faced me. I recognised the face in the black tie. Not just me, but our whole school knew him. No longer feared him, though, because Wazir had sent the man to the life of eternity. Everyone would lose it quickly and have constant puffy eyes like Baz Muhammad if they had to care for an invalid wife in such poverty-stricken conditions.

My right hand travelled to my forehead and stayed there. I understood Amrudin Khan's salute was not a pretence. Raziq Khan didn't exaggerate to regard her as the 'True Jelai of Afghanistan'. Their comparison of Frishta to Afghan heroines came from the heart. Frishta genuinely possessed all the qualities that a *true* daughter of Afghanistan like Malalai Anna and Nahid Shahid had displayed: chastity, bravery, loyalty. Above all, integrity. I knew now what the word meant, and Agha was spot on. Malalai Anna and Nahid Shahid sacrificed their lives, but declined to abandon their brothers. Frishta jeopardised her physical and moral safety but refused to desert her sisters – and brothers. Frishta once again showed her true nature.

Instead of helping Frishta with caring for the algebra ustad's invalid wife, I doubted her chastity; instead of thanking her for putting her reputation on the line for me, I accused her of being an accomplice; instead of supporting her with her studies, I stole her diary. I still couldn't work out why she spoke to Shafih, but talking didn't mean dating. We stayed in each other's rooms for hours every evening. Did we date? Did she even once act inappropriately? Her comments about Shafih must've been a prank. My sensible part convinced me I'd made serious errors of judgment about Frishta, and, actually, it was *I* who'd betrayed her. I pinched my flesh. It didn't hurt. Squeezed it again and again. No pain. Pressed Mour's knife against it. My arm was covered in blood, yet I felt no pain.

After my argument with Frishta, I started to crave for her, her jokes, stories, her whole company. A glimpse of Frishta in the school, or corridor, or even on her balcony, quenched my thirst; I felt like I was flying in the air. My heart dreaded the moment she wasn't there. I was physically in my room, but mentally with Frishta. Her thoughts had turned me into an insomniac. Her…

That day in the shed, I confessed to the Almighty – a confession I didn't dare to admit to myself: Khudai, You know *what* I've been through after the damn argument with Frishta. It isn't being used to her, so I must stop trying to convince myself. It isn't Satan who wants to lead me to the wrong path. It's a true mina, which I can't live without, even for a day. No one has the slightest idea about my feelings for Frishta, as You know. I myself noticed the day we stopped the one-to-one classes. You have been a witness to our every meeting. You know throughout the time I've known Frishta, never a dishonourable thought has crossed my mind. But I fear You will punish me for falling in mina before marriage, especially with a jelai whom I've called a *sister*? Punish me for a stain to my Afghanness? For a betrayal of a friendship? Something that'd been eating me from within. I beg You for forgiveness. Please help me find a solution. I promise if we ever get together, we'd go through the Islamic channel – she'll become my wife. Please, Khudai, forgive me. Please help me... please... please.

The claw's sharp nails now burned my stomach, urging me to go to Frishta and beg her for forgiveness. But I knew she'd get furious if she found out I spied on her. Again. I waited until she fed the woman, took her back into the building and left the dirt house.

***

MINUTES LATER I climbed over the wall and sprinted to our local mosque. The mullah in white perahan tunban and white turban, and unlike me, smelling of rose fragrance, inquired whether the jelai's mother had breastfed me, or whether Mour had breastfed the jelai. I answered no to both questions. To my great relief, he confirmed I could marry Frishta, even though I'd called her a sister, elaborating that in Islam all haleks and jelais were considered brothers and sisters to one another unless they got married. He also told me not to be hard on myself, as Khudai sympathised with genuine mina and was merciful.

***

ON THE WAY home, I decided to speak to Frishta in school, hoping she'd come, and *beg* for her forgiveness. Once she forgave me, I'd then find a way to let her know *what* I'd gone through for her after the evening classes ended. I dreaded revealing my feelings for her, though. Had to be very careful how and when to express them, or else I'd lose her forever. If she showed sympathy – I didn't know at this point what I'd do if she got mad – I'd send Mour for khastegari to Brigadier and Mahjan. How to tell Mour about my feelings for Frishta was another hair-raising step to take. I prayed Khudai brought kindness to Mour's heart.

142

But that tomorrow where we'd go to school never came.

Chapter Seventeen

Agha reassured Mour not to worry because the mujahideen had promised not to harm the pro-Communists, as he took off his right sock in the hallway.

It was midday and Agha had just returned home; he'd been away overnight to officially hand over power to Sibghatullah Mojaddedi, the head of the mujahideen *Shura*, what Agha called 'a parcel from Peshawar'. His red eyes showed he hadn't slept all night. He didn't ask how I felt, something he did every day after the school incident. Real worries occupied his mind; wetting my trousers had become an occurrence of the last century.

'Can't trust them. They've vowed to take revenge,' Mour said, standing by the shoe cabinet.

'What's written in destiny won't change,' Agha said, and removed his left sock and passed both to Mour. 'Get me a cup of coffee.'

A knock on the door.

'Must be the neighbours. It is the third time they've come,' Mour said to Agha.

Half a dozen neighbouring men, including Brigadier, stood as I opened the door. Agha invited them into the lounge. They wanted to discuss the dreadful repercussions of the 'bad news': armed men had just abducted, tortured and killed former Chief Justice Abdul Karim Shadan.

I filled cups with tea.

Agha didn't know the details.

'We've been kept in the dark. Everything is so sudden. What's really been happening?' a former Minister of Education from the third corridor said.

'Long or short answer?'

'We have time,' he said, pointing to the steaming cups I placed by the trays of sugar-coated almonds and chocolates on the table.

'Seven Sunni mujahideen groups from Pakistan have flooded Kabul. Another eight Shia groups have stormed the capital from Iran. Russia and India support Ahmad Shah Massoud, who cares about no one and seems to be the kingmaker. Pakistan and Saudi Arabia back Gulbuddin Hekmatyar to minimise Indian and Iranian influence. Every neighbouring country has a favourite group.

'None of the 15 guerrilla groups have any government experience. All they know is how to fight. All are armed to the teeth and, most dangerously, loathe each other with a decades-long history of feuding and infighting. They each want to reclaim their "long-denied" rights. They have conflicting interpretations of Islam, originating from Pakistan, Iran, Saudi Arabia, Egypt and Turkey. The race for which group and their foreign benefactors will have more sway in the Arg has begun,' Agha said.

'They hate us, too.'

'It's a non-violent transfer of power, and the mujahideen have pledged not to hurt us.'

'You buy that?' one of the 'comrades' in pyjamas asked, leaning against the edge of the sofa by the flowerpots.

'I assume Massoud will stick to his words. Not sure of Gulbuddin Hekmatyar,' Agha said.

The second name took the air out of the room. I thought they looked for an assurance from Agha. They pledged to stand up for one another once they discovered Agha was as uncertain about the mujahideen's reaction as they were. The neighbours left. No one had touched their tea.

'They hid like a mouse when ill fate befell Najibullah. They'll do it again,' Agha said to Brigadier.

He nodded. His happy nature had vanished.

Mour came in and passed a cup of coffee to Agha.

***

I BEGGED MOUR to let me stroll to the Makroryan Market with Baktash later that afternoon. I reasoned the fear of compulsory conscription and rockets no longer existed. Mour relented.

I had three pairs of perahan tunbans, which I wore to the Friday Prayer, and put on the white ones. As it turned out later, we still didn't have a *pakol*, a round hat, to be in line with what most mujahideen wore. Baktash had no pair and so slipped into his father's baggy perahan tunban, the size of their 'lounge curtains'. The new dress code troubled him because he didn't look 'handsome'.

***

MAKRORYAN HAD TAKEN on the appearance of my parents' village in Surobi. Like the Surobi Market, piles of Pakistani wheat flour and rice sacks, as well as tins of oil, each the size of a nomad tent, had popped up before the locked-up cooperatives still filled with pockets of macaroni, and their vendors were shouting, 'Half price, half price'.

I grew up listening to music in every social rite, on transport, in shops and hotels, but now the mujahideen seemed to have muted the culture. Music ceased to play for the first time in my life, and in the Makroryan Market's life, and our favourite videocassette shop was shut. The Market resembled a semi-prison without Indian songs being played on loudspeakers. It no longer was the place we'd known. You rarely spotted a jelai or even a woman. Gone were the days of short skirts and scarves; all you saw was perahan tunbans, pakols and turbans supplemented by black and white Arab scarves. Very few brave haleks put on jeans and shirts. You caught no glimpse of middle-aged men. Yesterday's Kabul had already become a dream. We seemed to have gone from one extreme to the other; the mujahideen had taken the clock decades back.

The Market, for the first time, bored me. I prayed that the Islamic government brought Wazir back: he'd be over the moon to see the change. Perhaps he'd make the strolls to the Market enjoyable again. Inshallah, by then, King Zahir Shah would have allowed music and films.

'Let's see them.' I pointed to the crowd gathered around near the mosque.

'Better to ignore them. They don't like flat-nosed people.'

'Come on, we're all brothers,' I insisted and made for the crowd.

Armed with guns, grenades, rockets and other weaponry, the mujahideen in pakols guarded their checkpoint surrounded by bags of sands on Makroryan Road. Frishta had filled me with their heroic stories, struggles and sacrifices, especially about the charismatic Commander Massoud famous as the 'Lion of Panjshir', whose large photo was displayed over the tank. Now we Kabulis saw them in the flesh. They did look like heroes, like the ones in *Rambo III*.

They spoke to us, the fascinated Kabulis, shook our hands, smiled, asked how we were, and even let some haleks talk on their walkie-talkies and climb on their tanks. Some Kabulis handed them flowers. Others tossed chocolates and sugar-coated almonds to them.

We left the 'pakoled Mujahideen' and set off for Old Makroryan to see the 'turbaned Mujahideen' there. I noticed most Russian jeeps and Volgas had vanished from the front of the blocks. So did the women and men sightseeing from balconies. Only haleks strolled, wearing either too baggy or too tight perahan tunbans. You hardly saw someone whose perahan turbans fit them. It really felt like the Surobi Market, except the haleks here had fresh faces. So did our school bushes and trees at the front and the back of the buildings, whose classrooms were now occupied by the armed Mujahideen.

This side's mujahideen equally surrounded themselves with bags of sands and pebbles. Like the turbaned photos of their leader on the walls of the roundabout, they wore turbans and glared at us like we came from a different planet. The rough faces and dusty hair – the part visible outside of their turbans – convinced you that they'd just risen from the grave. We didn't dare to speak with them.

'They're Gulbuddin Hekmatyar's fighters. Thankfully, we aren't under their government,' Baktash said.

'Jawad is.'

'Hopefully, they won't let him come to the school in our country.'

'Shirullah also won't be able to–'

'Look how wild they are,' Baktash said, pointing to a Russian tank full of armed mujahideen in turbans. The tank drove out of Old Makroryan, spun around with a screeching sound, creating dust and chanting *Allahu Akbar*, 'Khudai is great', firing guns into the air in celebration, forcing Baktash and me, like many others, to hold our breaths and block our ears.

'No more hoorah. Get used to Allahu Akbar,' Baktash said as we headed back to *our* country, New Makroryan.

'I hated hoorah. The school forced me to,' I said.

Another caravan of pick-up trucks full of armed mujahideen in pakols turned onto Makroryan Road, equally chanting 'Allahu Akbar', firing *deth-deth-deth* into the air.

Pedestrians echoed their chants.

Baktash and I jumped as cold water splashed over us. A woman with a plastic pot in her hand looked from the balcony in the direction of Makroryan Road, which the seven pick-up trucks disappeared into, and screamed 'Thank you, Khudai' for ending Afghanistan's misery.

We headed back to the Market, to the pakoled Mujahideen's country.

'The mujahideen will turn Kabul into a river of blood,' Baktash said, his left shoulder soaked in water.

'President Najibullah said this. He lies.'

148

'Papa also thinks so. Afghans' joy will soon turn into misery.'

'No bullet will be heard in Kabul from now on. The mujahideen will bring back King Zahir Shah.' I wondered how much Frishta's thinking had influenced me.

'We drove out Shorawi, and instead invited Panjabis and Iranians to occupy us. What is the point of the jihad?' Baktash said, pointing to the stock of food.

'The mujahideen are liberators. Khudai has given them success because they have the prayers of all Afghans.'

'Papa says they're proxies of the regional powers. They fight for their interests, not Islam.'

'Your father is pessimistic because he's lost power.'

'So has yours.'

'Agha never worked for the KHAD.'

Baktash's father led a branch of the KHAD renowned for the torture and unlawful killings of thousands of mujahideen over the past 14 years. Apart from the previous government's high-profile ex-members, the remaining Kabulis treasured the mujahideen's victory. Why shouldn't they? Islam succeeded. Eternal peace and security replaced war and instability. The inflation rate reduced considerably. The King's arrival would make things even better.

'In the past 24 hours, we've lost all the gains of the past decade and a half,' Baktash said.

'Like what?'

'Like education. These bearded people may shut jelais' schools.'

My thoughts raced to Frishta and whether we'd go back to school. School without Frishta would become as dull as a grave. I missed her like I hadn't seen her for years. The feeling of having lost a precious thing was a nagging worry at the back of my mind, but the mujahideen victory had become a form of escapism.

'I can't become an actor either.'

'Why not?'

'They view acting as un-Islamic.'

Will the mujahideen prevent Frishta from going to school? The horrifying question crossed my mind.

'Don't tell anyone, Ahmad. We're going to Moscow.'

'Really?' We arrived back at the place the Khalqi agent had tried to conscript Wazir, where now the seller with a dusty face shouted, 'Half price, half price,' and a crowd of shoppers loaded the 49kg wheat flour bags onto two-wheeled sack trucks or their backs.

'Life's going to become Hell in Kabul.'

'You leaving me?'

'Tell your father to come with us. His life's also in danger.'

I was filled with trepidation when he mentioned Agha. I didn't want to lose him. My sisters and I would beg the mujahideen not to harm my father.

'We'll go to the same college in Moscow and stay friends. We'll get Russian jelais.'

'It's haram,' I said. And I'd never leave Frishta, no matter what.

Baktash said they'd be selling their household goods and the apartment soon. He wanted me to stay out longer, but my thoughts raced home – in case Frishta and her parents drank tea at ours.

I'd have stayed longer had I known what was around the corner. Most Kabulis didn't realise it was the first day of a different life.

Chapter Eighteen

I excitedly told Agha and Mour how the pakoled mujahideen came across as friendly, and how the worries about the mujahideen were unfounded.

Agha, with a smouldering cigarette in his hand, hung on my words but made no comment. Mour passed me a plate of scalding *ashak*, pasta dumplings filled with leeks and topped with tomato sauce and yoghurt, to carry to the mujahideen checkpoint by our block – the one Baktash and I had skipped earlier on. Zarghuna took another container to Frishta's. If only Mour asked me to deliver the second platter. Seeing Frishta, even for a short time, would've alleviated my thirst; except I knew Frishta would throw me and the ashak out of her apartment.

I delivered my plate to the checkpoint – at last, I'd helped my mujahideen brothers and had my share in the jihad against the Red Empire, the kafirs.

The mujahideen, who unusually wore *both* pakols and turbans and dug the ground, received the plate without saying a thank-you. It didn't hurt. Kabulis' dishes of various food were nothing compared to what they'd done for their people and watan. They earned the respect they received.

***

MOUR SPREAD ASHAK ON our plates and placed an extra pot of yoghurt in the middle of the tablecloth. Agha's eyes fixed on the evening news, broadcasting the interim administration head

Mojaddedi calling on Gulbuddin to lay down his arms and help establish national unity. I dipped an ashak in the yoghurt and placed it in my mouth. The sound of an explosion, not in the far distance. I jumped to my feet and looked out of the window, chewing on the ashak. The celebratory shooting sprees now encompassed not only their AK-47s, but also rockets and machine guns. Another massive explosion went off. Zarghuna shrieked and hugged Mour. The electricity went out – a blackout. *Duvvv...* another ear-splitting blast, shattering the glass windows and smashing Mour's flowerpots. Everything quietened, except a clanging sound in my ears.

Agha's muffled shouts to lie down.

Mour's hands pressed on my shoulders. 'My son's injured.'

'I'm OK, Mour,' I said and coughed over my sisters' cries and coughs. Had Mour poured warm water on my right shoulder?

'Get to the hallway,' Agha said and then coughed.

Warm water on my shoulder got hotter as Mour pulled me. Pieces of glass and flowerpot soil fell off me as, feeling the ground, I crawled to the hallway, all the way coughing in the dust or smoke resembling burning leather.

Banging on the door. 'To the basement,' Brigadier's voice. 'Immediately.'

'Move,' Agha said.

Shouts of husbands telling wives to hurry up and leave their valuables behind, mothers screaming children's names and cries of toddlers filled the corridor as everyone rushed down the stairs. My head bumped into the basement door as we sped down the stairs. Someone before us tripped over and rolled down the stairs. A jelai screamed, saying someone stepped on her foot. Mour's head banged against the low ceiling but continued pulling my sisters and me by our hands into the pitch-dark basement with a musty smell, despite Brigadier's shouts to duck our heads and grope our way about. You couldn't see faces, only shadows, rushing to secure a place in the basement.

Cries of children persisted. Like me, they perhaps set foot in the basement to their block for the first time in their lives. Families kept their members close to themselves. Those who'd ended up elsewhere joined their households, using voice, touch and limited vision to reach their families.

As my eyes grew accustomed to the darkness, I spotted the rectangle-shaped basement, with steel pipes, as large as tree trunks, carrying waste and water out of the apartments along the walls. Its concrete floor must have been brushed for it to be as clean as Mour's lounge. All 12 families from our corridor positioned themselves on the damp floor, on the two sides of the wall, half a metre tall, dividing the cellar. My world lit up when I spotted Frishta sitting in between her parents, closer to her father, while Safi lay on his mother's lap. For a brief moment, I thanked Khudai for whatever He'd brought on us, and for my spot, diagonally opposite from Frishta, which enabled me to have her in my view without looking at her: Agha sat next to Brigadier and alongside Agha were my sisters, Mour and me, leaning against the short wall in the middle of the cellar.

A wailing voice in the distance cried out, 'Save my daughter.' The voice cried out again. Everyone quietened, even the children. No one ventured out to help the poor man – not even Agha or Brigadier. Everyone stayed put, as Agha had put it earlier, 'like a mouse'. Close shotguns of a Kalashnikov. The voice died out.

'*Tawba-tawba*, Allah saves us,' Mour said, 'repenting' to Khudai. Mahjan uttered an ameen. Others recited a *sura* from the Quran, and at the same time begged Khudai for protection.

What did I see? Agha and Brigadier, with lowered heads, made their way out despite Mour and Mahjan's pleading. Mour let go of the cloth she pressed against my shoulder. The prospect of losing Agha, however, was more painful than the nagging shoulder pain.

The odd explosions had changed into what sounded like a war; more blasts, more artillery, more machine guns, and plenty of AK-47s.

Our new home, coupled with the lack of electricity, deprived us of listening to the radio or viewing our television to know what was happening. How could they run the channel when the television crew and presenters were stuck in the war, anyway? One of them, television newsreader Nadim Barmak, together with his wife and two little daughters, settled down in the opposite corner.

Thanks, Khudai, Agha and Brigadier ducked their heads and stepped in from the cellar door. They wended their way among the families. Agha held his portable radio in his right hand, and Brigadier carried a burning oil lamp.

'Who was it?' Mour said.

Sweat trickled down Agha's forehead. His eyebrows were close together and his eyes widened. Something serious must have happened. Agha asked about my shoulder. The blood stopped, I told him.

Brigadier put the lamp with the orange light in the middle and asked Frishta if she was alright. She was, once her 'hero padar jan' came back. Brigadier knelt and hugged her. Did he burst into tears?

'What shall we expect from the others if you behave like this?' Agha said. Brigadier tightened his hug, their shadow ducking on the wall. 'You're a military man: behave like one.'

I'd never seen a weak side to Brigadier. I came to know him as a brave man who feared nothing. He'd killed many enemies in the frontline and got injured countless times. Beat the shit out of the villainous Rashid and the bullying Mullah Rahmat not long ago. And I'd never witnessed a brave Agha. I felt proud of him, thanking Khudai for having him around us.

'Children make you a coward,' Brigadier said.

'Frishta is also my daughter. I'd allow no one to stain our honour unless they pass my dead body.'

Brigadier stopped sobbing. Wiped his eyes and apologised to Agha and the other bewildered neighbours, including Frishta, whose eyes widened and ceased to blip, perhaps at learning a new side to her 'lion' padar jan.

Agha's last comment worried me. Was something bad about to happen to Frishta? She positioned herself in such a way that we didn't face each other. She wasn't the jelai I knew. The freshness on her face had given way to dark circles around the eyes; circles which the dim light intensified even more. Her droopy mouth and bleary eyes showed that she'd deprived herself of sleep for nights. Yesterday Mahjan told Mour that over the last few days Frishta kept herself to herself and talked to no one. Mour asked me if anything had happened between us. I disclosed nothing, hoping Frishta and I would resume our private classes. Our parents, I thought, suspected we'd fallen out. It didn't displease Mour, who'd told me to 'keep it that way'.

All the signs indicated she hadn't told her parents about the diary. I didn't know why she kept everything to herself and hadn't taken revenge, given her scornful nature. But in Pashtunwali revenge was a dish best served cold.

Chapter Nineteen

Everyone in the dimly lit basement shushed as the extended BBC Pashto Service broadcast the night news:

This is London. This is the Pashto programme.

Agha told mothers to keep their children's noise down, asking my sisters, and even some adults, to stop flying paper airplanes. I knew the introductory words for the news by heart. Most Afghans did. The BBC had imprisoned Afghans since the Soviet invasion in 1979, and the news in Pashto and Farsi was the only two meals it served its inmates in 24 hours; all eyes and ears fixed on the radio as if it was updating us on the progress of a cure for a deadly pandemic.

After a 14-year-awaited victory, the mujahideen are fighting among themselves. Massoud and Dostum's forces fight against Hekmatyar's armed men. There are fire exchanges between Old Makroryan and New Makroryan, as well as Bala Hissar and areas surrounding Ziarat-i-Ashuqan-o-Arefan... The radio disappeared. Agha tapped it and extended the aerial, but there was no reception; his and the others' faces were as frustrated as patients deprived of heart medication.

Bala Hissar accommodated the former seat of royal power that guarded the south-western approach to Kabul. Its citadel once opened to tourists to hike along its walls.

The two brothers and spiritual leaders, Ashuqan and Arefan, so the legend went, protected Kabul during the 12th century and brought prosperity to the city. Every Thursday, women visited the site to ask Khudai for help, but the two brothers couldn't prevent the mujahideen from turning their tomb into a trench. Baktash was right all along: the turbaned mujahideen and the pakoled Mujahideen's fighting did truncate Kabulis' joyfulness.

'Dostum has got air power. His participation will intensify the war. Kabul will be flattened out. Kabul will be flattened out,' Mr Barmak said from the opposite corner of the basement, half of his face lit by the oil lamp, his daughters sitting on his lap.

Mr Barmak's dishevelled hair and word repetition indicated he was more anxious than everyone else. Everyone knew him in Kabul as a 'Communist'. If the mujahideen ever executed anyone from the block, he, Agha, Baktash's father and Brigadier topped the list. We feared any moment the armed mujahideen could rush in, take them outside, shoot them in cold blood, and leave their bodies lying there. My chest tightened.

***

I CONSIDERED HOW and when to apologise to Frishta throughout the night in the musty basement where everyone, like the homeless in Shahr-e Naw, slept, snored and occasionally farted. Her possible reaction frightened me. She held her face in the opposite direction to the small window, lying on her right side. I didn't know whether she was asleep or awake. Her presence, however, so close, was calming. If only I didn't have the damn argument with Frishta, and she asked me to assess her with the exams. I knew she wouldn't. If only Nowruz or Eid was around. I prayed to Khudai to bring Nowruz in Frishta and my relationship, a moment you forgot and also forgave each other's mistakes and started the New Year with new hopes and new goals.

Knocking on the cellar door raised the adults' heads. Our block representative whispered Agha's name. He knocked again.

'Gently, kids are asleep,' Agha said.

Only Agha and Brigadier groped their way and exited. More whispers outside. Agha poked his head through the door and murmured 'shovel' to Mour.

'Why do you need a shovel at 4 o'clock in the morning?'

'Just tell me where the damn thing is.' Agha turned impatient with the mujahideen victory – he never spoke to Mour rudely before.

'Behind the bin in the kitchen.'

Agha withdrew his head and shut the door. Sounds of footsteps leaving the corridors. *Please, Khudai, keep him safe.*

Every parent had sneaked out to their apartment and got duvets, blankets and pillows. We managed to spend our first night in the cold basement with a damp stench. The first night Kabulis tasted war first hand. We'd seen it in other parts of Afghanistan on television or heard it from the radio, but never in our city.

Nazir from the adjacent corridor peered in, cupped his nose and giggled when his eyes caught mine. *Please, Khudai, don't make him call me a piss pants.* He was two years older than me and wasn't the sort to lose sleep over concerns for obro and ezat, which he demonstrated last year in the circumcision party of the fourth floor's baby son, for which Afghan rugs were spread over the lawn before the block with cushions being laid on top of them. Men and young haleks reclined, smoking *chillums*, and four women dancers danced till early morning accompanied by tabla and harmonium duet music, which loudspeakers the size of our television amplified to the extent that attracted the kind of Nazirs and Shafihs from Bimaro and surrounding villages.

I'd never seen such breathless interest and excitement among men than I witnessed from my room window that night. The whole crowd seemed to devour the dancers with their eyes. They followed and applauded every movement the dancers made. Nazir proved the most shameless of them all. A drunken Nazir danced with the young women, and at their request, even displayed his Taekwondo skills topped with breaking dance moves, to which he received clapping from the crowd. One of the dancers condescended to offer him a bowl of tea; Nazir took it with a profound obeisance and returned it in the same way, addressing her as 'majesty' and adding that she accepted him as a 'slave'. The shameless Shafih likewise danced *parde awal* all night, and the following morning boasted in the class how the two got *jiggy, jiggy* with the female dancers in Nazir's apartment. Wazir used to taunt Nazir with 'jiggy, jiggy' while Baktash and I laughed, but it was a relief he didn't retaliate before the parents and children.

Desperate to know, I brought myself to ask him. He knelt and poked his head, allowing some light to come into the basement through the cellar door. Every adult face turned to Nazir, Frishta's included. She sat up and leaned against the basement wall. Nazir's face brightened, obviously enjoying the attention of so many curious people to what he was about to unfold.

'Everyone's so observed.' He giggled, disregarding the fact that children slept, and some annoyingly chewed. He thankfully carried on. 'The mujahideen from the checkpoint before the block break into Quraish saheb's apartment.' He peeked over his shoulder. 'The thugs shoot dead the brother, father and stepmother. The daughter jumps off the fifth floor to save her obro and ezat.'

'Tawba-tawba, Allah saves us from such cruelty,' Mour said in a hushed tone, pulling the blanket over the sleeping Nazo and Zarghuna.

'May Khudai turn our food into poison for them,' another said.

'They were meant to be Khudai's angels. They'll answer for their sin on Qiyamat Day,' yet another said from the corner under the tiny basement window.

'They were thieves disguised as Mujahideen,' Nazir said, crouching, his white Adidas as clean as the cellar door.

The combination of turbans and pakols at the outpost suggested something fishy about the checkpoint. I knew the jelai. Someone else among this eager audience knew her better. She'd helped the victim gain confidence. To my surprise, Frishta, hands placed around her legs, and whose thighs touched her chest, revealed no emotions at all for her best friend, Roya.

Somebody said the 'thugs' gaped at Roya when she hung clothes on the balcony yesterday afternoon.

Mahjan enquired about Roya's fate. Heads turned to Nazir, who gave a dismissive gesture.

'A dead branch penetrated her stomach: her body hung from it.'

A spontaneous 'Oh' came out from the listeners' mouths.

'No one's alive from the family. Her brother had just become engaged,' Nazir said.

'She was Frishta's best friend. What a lovely jelai,' Mahjan said. She covered herself and her son in a blanket with a portrait of a leopard on it.

'She'll go straight to Janat. She won't be answering questions on Qiyamat Day,' Mour said.

At last, Nazir had to join the others, where he belonged: to dig graves under the same tree behind the block. He pleaded with us to say nothing to our parents, who intended to keep the story secret as 'women unnecessarily get scared'.

Mour rested her hand on the blanket over Nazo and Zarghuna, begging Khudai to save her daughters. Tears trickled from Mahjan's eyes, too. She told Frishta to come under the blanket. Mr Barmak was calming his wife down. Now I understood why Brigadier broke into tears. Guns weren't as dangerous as losing the obro and ezat. I got even more worried for Frishta and my sisters.

The mujahideen had released all prisoners from the Pul-e-Charkhi owing to their National Pardon policy. Thousands of thieves, murderers and rapists loitered on the streets of Kabul. How could we distinguish between the mujahideen and criminals? It was a question many asked.

The mujahideen looked after the female hostages like 'sisters' and safely handed them over to the British in the First Anglo-Afghan War.

I remembered in Surobi men giving up their way to female villagers and making their journey hundreds of metres longer. Your enemy didn't touch you if you had your women with you. All out of respect for the honour of women, something our history was proud of. This damn war in Kabul even challenged that notion. It disgusted me. Unless they pass my dead body, I'd allow no thug to touch a woman from this basement.

Moments later, Frishta, covered in a warm blanket, wrote in a notebook – a black one. As always, she faced away.

Chapter Twenty

I throw a surprise party for my wife's promotion as King Zahir Shah's Advisor for Women's Affairs. Frishta thanks her 'supportive husband', *me*, in her speech, and everyone claps, including Wazir and Baktash, alongside their wives. Our two sons and a daughter play with Wazir and Baktash's kids.

We picnic in the Qargha Lake every Friday. Our wives chat and the kids play ball. Wazir, Afghanistan's national football hero, teaches them football tricks. He sees potential in Baktash's son. Baktash, the next Salam Sangi, the superstar of Afghan cinema, works on a monologue with Wazir's son.

The seasons take us to different provinces for fruit-picking: melons in Kunduz; berries in Panjshir; pomegranates in Kandahar; grapes in the Shomali Valley; apples in Logar.

My best friends and their parents lunch at Agha's flat, and have dinner at Brigadier's place on the first day of Eid. Baktash's parents cook dinner on the second day, and Wazir and his mother's turn comes on the third day. Every Eid evening after dinner, the families drive to Shahr-e Naw for *shiryakh* ice cream.

Wazir holds the spool and Baktash flies a kite in the Makroryan Festival. Wazir has torn up the books; we're all Afghan, not Moguls or Panjabis. The father of the nation and the symbol of unity, our King, loves all Afghans like his own children, and has ensured that bullets and guns are alien to us.

A *Duvvv* sound... The ground shook. Screams of kids and women. Agha and Brigadier's assurance that the explosion 'went off far away'.

My father and Brigadier couldn't mute, though, the sound of the flying shrapnel striking against the block.

Fantasies were as sweet as Helmand's watermelons, but facing reality afterwards was as suffocating as the hopeless basement. Frishta abhorred me. She sat next to her father or mother, writing or reading, and, without fail, facing away. Wazir had disappeared, and there was no news of Baktash since our stroll to the Market a week ago, even though he lived a few corridors down. The dark basement pressed a heavy stone against my chest every time I took a breath.

The vicious war had worsened by the day. Gulbuddin Hekmatyar's fighters fired at random hundreds – or in a sour mood, *thousands* – of rockets daily to Kabul, and Massoud's forces retaliated by dispatching an equal number of weapons to the outskirts of my city. Aerial bombardment added to the constant sound of heavy artillery. Kabul had turned into Mour's heating clay oven, in which she used to bake us fresh naans. Families took a 50-50 chance and abandoned us one by one for Pakistan, Iran, safer provinces, or even for Kabul's relatively peaceful districts in the north. Their mattresses, pillows, blankets, cutlery, crockery and oil lamps lay untouched in the cellar. Five families stayed put from our corridor; those who either weren't fit to face the journey's challenges, or had no relatives elsewhere to support them.

We fed on naans, which Mour baked on a petrol lamp, or sometimes on fires, provided she found fuel materials. Mothers no longer could afford to fry chips or place dough in boiling oil to make *parathas;* Zarghuna and Safi's crying for chips no longer succeeded. Nazo had forgotten 'the smell' of chips. One oil lamp lit the basement, burning at a low level, which prevented us from walking over each other at night. Families were running out of wheat and petrol, however. The fighting died down every day at 4am, which gave us a time window to bring water from a well located behind the block and visit the toilets in our flats. Buckets and jugs replaced the push-button toilet flush. Everyone had turned into a smelly beast; water barely sufficed to drink and cook with.

Adults ate only to survive and left more naans for the children. Families had money to buy basic needs, but you risked a bullet or shrapnel if you ventured out; even a visit to the toilet during the day involved a discussion over the timing and often subjected you to the parents' beratement for missing the right time or urinating too many times.

No shops were open, anyway. According to Agha's multiple news stations, the gunmen owned Kabul. They robbed its treasure. Killed its sons and daughters. Allowed its zoo animals to die of hunger. Looted its Exchange Market. Plundered its National Gallery of Art, National Archives and the Kabul Museum, all of which I'd visited on school trips. I remembered our history teacher pointing at 'Remnants of the British Army', a painting by Lady Elizabeth Butler, showing the last survivor of the British retreat and the document of the British granting Afghanistan sovereignty at those places.

Shukria, the National Gallery of Art's deputy head who lived on the second floor, feared that these historical items had found themselves at auctions in Peshawar. 'The war has stolen our identity,' she repeatedly said.

Everyone fought for their life more than for their identity, nevertheless. Dead bodies lay all over Kabul like berries lying on the ground at the Shewaki farm during the berry seasons. No one dared to take them. Barmak's wife didn't even get the chance to see his body, dead or alive. Four bearded men beat him up and threw him in a pick-up truck two days ago when he put a barrier around his shattered windows. Nobody knew his whereabouts. The wife sat mute: days of sobbing and screaming must have damaged her vocal cords. Barmak wasn't the first and certainly not the last.

***

THE RAIN HIT against the plastic paper which covered the tiny basement window, whose glass a rocket had shattered two days back. I, like most others in the depressing place, buried myself under the blanket. Agha and Brigadier searched for *any* afternoon news on the hissing and crackling portable radio as we overheard a female's screech. Agha switched off the radio.

The voice shrieked again. 'No, for... sake... four little kids,' the half-audible voice said. AK-47 shotguns shut it out.

Agha's mouth opened and his eyes widened. Nazo held Agha's arm. They'll now come after my father: the horrible thought crossed my mind. My heartbeat increased. Frishta pressed her head against her father's upper arm.

The half-broken basement door slammed open and a soaking wet woman like a *shishak,* a witch, rushed in. Children and mothers shrieked. She tripped over the stairs and rolled over. Slapped her invisible cheeks with bloodstained hands as she knelt. Pulled her hair violently, which covered her face, and yelled something I couldn't register. She stormed in my direction to eat me up. I yelled as she grabbed my right hand. Mour hugged me. The shishak pulled me to her blood-smeared hair. I screamed; the vampire was about to tear out my heart with her canine teeth. Mour pushed her. She fell back on Shukria, whose cutlery caused a clattering sound. Cries and shrieks filled the cellar as the screaming Shukria struggled to disentangle herself. The shishak's wet hair drew back and the blood-covered face revealed itself.

'Khala Lailuma,' I cried out. Something horrible must've happened to Baktash's father, I thought, my heart panting against my chest. She sprinted for the basement door, crawling up the stairs like a toddler. I released myself from Mour's hands and accompanied Baktash's mother. Agha and Brigadier followed us.

The machine gunshots and rocket sounds competed against the sound of a heavy shower outside. You spotted no living species as if the Little Moscow of Kabul was located on the moon. Branches of trees and bushes, green leaves and clay like sugar-coated almonds and chocolates at a wedding covered the ground thanks to the rocket impact in the garden. Khala Lailuma slipped on the concrete floor and fell over. Sprang up and rushed towards the lawn.

I counted two bodies lying on top of each other on the grass under the acacia tree. My stomach turned over and I fell. Khala Lailuma shouted to hurry up because Baktash 'won't go to Moscow without me'. The next few steps to the tree proved the hardest. Baktash, in a baggy perahan tunban, placed his cheek on his father's chest and grabbed his father's jacket with his right hand. The gun smoke and powder had burned the father's face unrecognisably. The bullets had created holes in the cheeks, forehead and neck. Agha covered his comrade's face and the blood pool mixed with grey and black materials like walnuts' nutmeat around the head with his jacket.

My stomach turned over again, and I threw up

'Wake your best friend up,' khala Lailuma said to me. 'He's getting dirty.' She grabbed my jacket and shook me. 'My Shahzada hates dirt. Wake him up.'

Baktash's nickname at home was Shahzada: Prince.

I knelt on the muddy grass and took a deep breath. Moved the fringe soaked with a mixture of mud and blood to the side. Fresh blood flowed from the eye-like hole in the forehead, joining the puddle of blood on the father's chest and under Baktash's neck.

'Oh, Khuda jan, he's bleeding. Stop the blood.' Khala Lailuma threw herself on them, removed dirt from Baktash's face and pressed her hand against the hole. Nutmeat patties-like things flowed from the bushy hair at the back and joined more of the same material and blood on the father's chest and the grass.

'It's OK. Martyrs never stop bleeding,' Brigadier said.

She smiled, let the hand go and planted a kiss on her son's cheek. 'Congratulations on your martyrdom, my Shahzada.'

Agha told Brigadier to take the bodies back to the basement and bury them in the early morning; no one would venture out when the fighting continued. She screamed, saying to dig graves for her and the three daughters, too, because they had no men left to provide bread and butter for them. Agha and Brigadier pleaded with khala Lailuma to calm down. Agha reasoned that once Khudai closed one door, He'd open many others. Like brothers, Agha and Brigadier would support her and the kids. *Dow, dow, dow* cannons fired from Bimaro Hill towards eastern Kabul, forcing us to duck.

Apparently, once the heart stopped, bodyparts wouldn't straighten when they cooled. Baktash wouldn't let go of his grasp, even though Agha and Brigadier asked him to.

Agha told 'the mother' to speak to Baktash and ask him to loosen his fist. She wanted his 'best friend' to do it.

'Baktash,' I heard myself say, part of me confused as to why they wanted me to speak to the dead.

'You're again late for school.'

No movement. *Karss, karss, karss* of Gulbuddin's rockets blasting somewhere in Bimaro.

'Remember, we're going to the same college in Moscow.' The other part of me disbelieved that a few bullets would take Baktash forever from me.

'I heard Moscow has the best acting school in the world.'

Quietness, apart from raindrops hitting against his left cheek and the incessant firings of Kalashnikovs.

'You'll be the next Bruce Lee, inshallah. I should get your autograph now, man.'

May Khudai strike me blind should I tell lies. As the last sentence finished in my mouth, his face turned to me, his lips stretched and fist loosened. I took his hand and put it against his side. My fingers entered a hole twice bigger than the one in his forehead as I held his head with

Agha and Brigadier's assistance to turn him over. Blood and the nutmeat bits stained my left hand.

My body began to shiver as if someone threw ice cubes in my stomach. 'He's left me. My best friend's gone forever.'

Brigadier tapped on my shoulder.

'He planned to study in Moscow, not to enter a grave behind the block.'

'Ahmad?' Agha said, pointing to the dazed khala Lailuma.

'Agha, Baktash has gone. All my friends have left me.'

Agha told me to have patience; his pale blue perahan tunban was drenched.

'Why did they martyr him? He'd harmed no one.'

'Patience, zoya.'

'Under this very acacia tree, he pleaded with me not to disown him.'

'Ahmad?' Agha said.

'I'm sinful, Agha.'

'Zoya, you didn't mean it.'

'Baktash, I'm sorry. I'm deeply sorry.'

'Ahmad.'

'Actually, you've always been a hero, Baktash. I sided with the villain. I'm not a good halek, Agha. I betrayed my friends.'

'You didn't mean to.'

'Yes, I did. Frishta is right, I don't have an Afghan heart.'

'You've earned her respect,' Brigadier said.

'Khudai's created me Afghan but has denied me the heart. Why am I a coward?'

'You're not a bad person, nephew,' Brigadier said.

'I let Frishta down, too, aka Brigadier.'

'It's OK.'

'Accused her of bad things. Stole her diary. I'm a thief.'

'We all make mistakes. Learn from them,' Brigadier said. Pointing to the bodies in the heavy rain, he whispered, 'Time to make it up to friends.'

'My best friend did live like a shahzada, a happy one.'

'Pray for him. Let's help the rest of the family,' Agha said.

'I didn't stay longer in the Market last week when he wanted me to.'

'You didn't know,' Agha said.

'I would have if–'

'Ahmad, he needs your help now.'

'I miss my friends. My school. My old life.'

Brigadier planted a kiss on my head and echoed Agha's words about patience, his grey hair and baggy pyjamas soaked in the rain. He reiterated that it was time I made it up for Baktash, adding to stop crying, or I'd make it worse for khala Lailuma.

Agha hugged me and told me it was time to help the family.

'What if they hurt you, Agha?'

'They won't.'

'Who would I say farewell to in the morning and greet in the evening?'

'I'll always be around, zoya.'

'Promise me.'

'I promise.'

Agha said something three times today that he hadn't said a single time in the whole of 15 years: he called me zoya. I hugged him, as tight as Baktash's grabbing of his father's jacket. 'I love you, Agha.'

He kissed my head – several times – and told me to let go, but I wouldn't. His hug, the sweaty, fatherly scent, was what I'd been craving all my life. He said again to let go as we heard sounds of 'papa' from behind.

Baktash's sisters in pink nightwear stood next to each other, rain and tears coming down their faces. The two youngest wanted to know why Papa and Shahzada stayed out in the rain: why didn't they come home?

Brigadier stroked their hair and told them that Papa and Shahzada were preparing for their 'real home' journey. 'Khudai has invited them.'

'Where's Khudai's home?' the youngest said.

'I'm also coming,' the one in the middle said.

'Only I get to sit on Papa's lap,' the youngest said.

'Khudai only invited Papa and Shahzada,' Agha said.

'He won't go without his princess,' the youngest said, pointing to herself.

'*I* am his princess,' the one in the middle said.

'Stop it,' the eldest said to the siblings.

Brigadier's eyes welled up and looked skyward. 'Oh, Khudai.'

Agha told him to collect himself.

'Are Papa and Shahzada dead, Mama?' the eldest sister said.

Khala Lailuma slapped her face and pulled her hair. She hugged her daughters. All four wept, as loud as the weeping sky of Makroryan.

We carried the bodies into Baktash's apartment and laid them next to each other after Agha and Brigadier managed to persuade khala Lailuma to move inside. Khala Lailuma screamed and slapped herself. I prayed to Khudai to look after the family and keep the mother sane for her children.

All the families from their corridor had vanished as I peeped into the basement, leaving their belongings in the living quarters untouched. She and the daughters refused to come to our cellar. They stayed in, wanting to have one more night together with their loved ones before sending them on a lone journey forever in the early morning.

Chapter Twenty-One

Baktash and his father's killings shocked everyone. Shukria, who worried more about Afghanistan losing its identity than her losing her life, supposed 'high-profile Communists' who stayed put at their addresses, or rather in the basements of their flat, would meet the same fates as Baktash's father and Mr Barmak, because the mujahideen longed for revenge. She endured the basement, what she called 'the homeless shelter', because her elderly parents couldn't walk long distances, but wasn't sure why those who could 'fly' still stuck around. Her words captivated Agha and Brigadier. Both kept nodding.

Frishta covered herself in a blanket, her head resting on Brigadier's right arm. The face revealed no expression, and the eyes shed no tears over Roya and Baktash's deaths. Perhaps she didn't believe she'd never see them both again. Or maybe those she'd trusted the most let her down. I knew, though, that she worried for Baz Muhammad's wife, as I overheard Brigadier on several occasions over the past week reasoning with her how dangerous it was to go to Bimaro.

***

LATER IN THE SAME AFTERNOON, Agha spoke *the* few agonising words that were about to separate me from Frishta: we were to leave tomorrow morning for the peaceful Mazar-e-Sharif where Dostum reigned with an iron first and defended ex-pro-Communists, including Agha's friends. The offer extended to Brigadier, but everyone knew it was impossible for a wife who was nearly eight months pregnant to duck, dodge or walk – not to mention run for miles. Brigadier was 'tired of running'; he was 'born' in Kabul and would 'die' in Kabul.

Wazir's disappearance, the humiliation in school, the stealing of the diary, Roya's death, the shooting of Baktash and his father all appeared to have taken place decades back when destiny was about to separate me from Frishta. I gulped for breath as the stone that was stuck to my chest from day one in this stinking cage pressed. I asked for toilet permission from Agha and, before Mour realised, sneaked out. Turned the key in the door and tiptoed among the shattered glass to the kitchen to turn the generator on. Entered the lounge. Rain showered through the glassless windows over the scattered potting soil and pieces of broken glass, having turned Mour's Jalalabad into a muddy Bimaro. Switched on the satellite TV, a rare gift from Agha after the school's incident, and flicked through a few channels. Men and women in long hair and black undershirts played guitars and drums like crazy. Thousands of teenagers clapped, danced and sang together with them. It wasn't real. Could there be such a world where there was no bombing, no fighting, no hiding in a basement? Where you didn't collect your best friend's brain with your own hands? Where you were forced to separate from your mina? The teenagers on the screen lived on another planet. I switched the television and the generator off and got into my room.

Glass window pieces and rainwater rolled down as I lifted the corner of my mattress and pulled out the red diary. Leaned against my bed, pushed the books with my feet to stretch out and flicked the pages, but wasn't able to read the damn Russian language. If only Raziq Khan were around to translate Frishta's writing. Everyone seemed to have abandoned Kabul; even its sunny days had turned into depressingly grey ones like today. I kissed her handwriting. Held it closer to my heart. The harder I pressed the vinyl cover, the lighter the stone's weight became. Opened the diary again and read the dates below Frishta's notes. The first entry dated back to nearly nine weeks ago, the first day of year nine, the day I first met Frishta. She offered me her friendship. What did I give her in return? I kissed her handwriting. Once. Twice. Thrice. Kept kissing it. No one saw me. No one heard me above the sound of the artillery and explosions, a sound which, like the Surobi mill, hardly stopped. *Khudai, please give me another chance.* Shockingly, it was becoming less likely.

Time to make it up to friends, a voice whispered Brigadier's words from this morning. *Stop being a coward*, the voice went on. *Place your trust in Khudai and go for it.*

I put the red diary under the mattress, tiptoed to the bathroom, performed ablutions, then to the kitchen, filled a bottle with water, got two dried naans, removed the mould from them, placed both in a carrier bag, locked the apartment door, rushed down the stairs, opened the main block door and off into the ghost town where you'd think a plague had claimed the lives of everyone. The muffled sounds of *deth-deth-deth*, *devv... devv*, *tak-tak-tak* filled Kabul. *Khudai, I'm in Your hands, please keep me safe*, I prayed and carried on with my journey, dodging and ducking through the block gardens whose chopped shrubs covered the ground like glitter on the hall floor of the InterContinental Hotel at Baktash's birthday party. The sound of the *chew-chew* of bullets above my head persisted, some hitting and deflecting off the walls of the block.

A bomb had created a hole in the playing ground, the size of the Russian truck Brigadier had filled with guards to get Rashid, and in the middle of it lay a leg half-buried in the water. Next to it, a dirt-smeared pink baby doll leaned against a wet dirt clod. I hastened, my head ducking by the side of the nursery wall. Even the stray dogs had disappeared. They might've gone into the basement or emigrated to safer provinces. I covered my nose from the smell of rotting flesh. My foot stepped on soft ground as I turned around Block 8. Scores of flies flew with a buzzing sound. I cupped my nose and screamed, jumping over the decomposed dog body with its tummy exposed to the air. Breathed in and out, my legs trembling. A hole as huge as a garage had appeared in the side of a bedroom; its carpet and furniture had disappeared. *Khudai, I seek refuge in You; may You save me from bullets and shrapnel.* I carried on with the journey, trying to pay no attention to my legs trembling. The ground-floor flat of Block 11 had become blackened, and its windows shattered. Below the windows, four fresh graves, two of which were tiny, had been dug by the backyard lawn.

The front of the block allowed me to view the spectral Bimaro. The barren ground on the other side of Airport Road, where I'd snatched Frishta's diary, was full of with sporadic, 'half-price' wheat flour sacks covered with white cloths. *Khudai, give me the courage to help Frishta. Help me suppress my fears like Frishta.* I darted across the road and raced through the wheat sacks and the thorny shrubs, but my foot tripped on a flour sack and I fell over. Froze as I removed the white cloth from my foot, feeling a tingle of goose bumps over my body. The fabric now pulled at the hips of a bald man with a long moustache holding a cigarette in his mouth and with a piece of paper was stuck to his chest with writing in blood: 'Food, Clothing and Shelter for the Poor'.

I raced on with my journey as a heavy shower broke out. Khudai must've been angry this year on the warring mujahideen for the rain to come down so forcefully that I feared it might wash away the Bimaro huts. I climbed up the hill and footslogged along the stench-smelling passageway of the ghostly neighbourhood.

I hurled the plastic bag over the wall, put my right foot on the metal knob, pulled on the upper edge of the wooden door, but my trembling foot slipped on the knob. Succeeded at the second attempt and jumped into the yard. Tore the plastic and climbed over the window. Blocked my nose and stuck out my neck for air. Inhaled. Exhaled. Repeated it again and again. Flies buzzed as I got closer to the corner. Her face had turned yellow, her eyes closed and the mouth was open to the right as if someone had punched her on the left side of her chin. I was too late to nurse her.

Frishta worried for this woman; laying her to rest reduced Frishta's concerns. Khudai may have given me the opportunity to make it up to Frishta – and to Khudai. Accusations without proof were a sin.

The grave horribly mangles the body, crushes its bones and robs the soul for the call on Qiyamat Day if it is buried without proper Muslim rites, we conversed as children. I distrusted the accuracy of kid conversations and tried to remember the teachings from our mullahs and religious books. I knew Islam demanded ritual purity in death, as in life. Understood female relatives washed a woman's body in the female quarters, but had to give this a miss. Was sure graves should be about six feet deep and have an L shape called *lahad*. Unsure whether the feet pointed towards Mecca, so on Qiyamat Day the body sat up facing the Holy City, or the feet pointed towards the south, the head to the north and the face to Mecca to allow the dead person to sit up at the Last Judgment. Went for the position where she faced the Holy City on Qiyamat Day.

He was the most Gracious and Merciful, and I begged for His forgiveness, if I got the Islamic procedures wrong. I prayed for His help and began digging. Afghans believed that when you had no one, you had Khudai. I witnessed this in the case of the poor woman. The rain had turned the soil as soft as Mour's dough, but it miraculously stopped during the excruciating hours of digging. One shovel clobber dislocated the padlock and the chain. Khudai gave me the physical strength to pull her heavy body to the grave, throw dirt, or rather wet soil, on her.

I luckily found a small stone in the shed and installed it parallel; inshallah, I got that right as men's feet and headstones sat perpendicular to the body line. Her body remained above the ground. But Khudai knew that was the best I did in the situation. I read a few suras I knew from the Quran. That day I also prayed to Khudai not to make me die on a rainy day and get buried in the cold, wet soil.

175

The mouldy naans with the water tasted like Mazar-e-Sharif's *quabili* palaw, rice palaw, and boosted my energy to head for my second destination amidst the muffled gunshots. *Khudai, I seek refuge in the perfect words of You from the evil of that which You have created. You say no harm affects us without your permission; please let me safely reach my next stop.*

I came across no other living species as I hurried down the muddy passageway in the middle of the huts, at times touching the walls to avoid skipping. From the corner, I saw the grey blocks. You'd say Genghis Khan had risen from his grave and once more annihilated the entire population of the Little Moscow of Kabul. *There is no god but Allah, Muhammad is the messenger of Allah*: I read the *Shahada* and sprinted like a deer being chased by a cheetah across the barren land, but lay flat behind a burned-out Volga as four red Mitsubishi Pajeros sped along Airport Road and turned onto Makroryan Road.

A carrier bag-shaped object in a brown perahan tunban on the ground grabbed my attention. Had I seen the colourful embroidery? Using my sports classes training, I crawled on my chest and cupped my hand over my nose when I got to the body. All the neighbours' assurances that Mr Barmak was alive and they'd do their best to have him released had been in vain. His body lay curled up on the dirt ground with holes in his forehead. I couldn't do anything but get the white cloth by his feet, cover his body, pray for him and continue my journey.

Read my Shahada and shot across Airport Road. Two male bodies were stretched out with their heads tilted back; next to them lay dogs' bodies with large bullet holes, one holding bloody flesh in its mouth. Scores of flies fed on the decaying corpses. I jumped as a dog leapt out of a window from the lounge of a ground-floor flat and disappeared into the trees on the lawn. Nipping by the sidewall of Block 1, I crossed the road and rushed inside the mosque whose red carpet was buried in shattered window glass, broken ceiling panels and white plaster.

Why did You humiliate me? Put a sick mind in me? Turn me into a thief? Take my friends away? What were Baktash's faults? And Roya's faults? The invalid woman's faults? Did Mr Barmak's kids deserve what happened to their father? Was it because they were born in Afghanistan? Why did You give one life to those teenagers at the concert and another to us? And *why* were You about to separate me from Frishta? The main 'why' my body and soul had brought me to the House of Khudai.

No reply. Broken plaster poked against my knees.

I shouted, 'Answers.' All my life I heard about His miracles to save His subjects in need. A lot of crimes had been committed in Kabul today, and yet He was silent.

Why?

No reply.

Why? Answer me.

Silence.

My goose bumps prickled. I sensed that Khudai watched me from above, and any moment might punish me, or worse, take Frishta's life, if I wasn't careful. The mullah of this very mosque once said Khudai tested us with hardship to wash away our sins, replace a worse misfortune or strengthen our faith. We had to show faith by reacting with patience and contentment. Khudai knew best. We had to have trust in Him. He tested, the mullah continued with raised eyebrows, those Whom he loved the most.

I prostrated myself and begged Him to forgive me for questioning His decisions. May You send the dead to Janat and take care of the living, I prayed, begging Him to love Frishta but make the test easier on her, and help her fulfil her dreams.

Mour believed that if you wanted anything from Khudai with all your soul, He'd grant you the wish. My face still touching the mosque floor, I prayed from the bottom of my heart, *Save Frishta from the monsters who fought in Kabul; save her for me. Purify her heart from all the hatred*

*she holds for me and bring her back into my life. Make her my wife. Before that,
though, help me be worthy of her; assist me in succeeding over my weakling heart.
Please, please, please.* Tears pricked my eyes and made their way down
my nose and onto the carpet.

A sharp object pressed against the back of my head. The sound
of a slide moving backwards. Men in camouflage outfits and pakols
with guns in their hands stood as I turned around. Their barrels were
pointed at me.

'Looting the mosque?' His tone showed dismay.

'I'm not one of you.' My stomach lurched at the thought of
robbing the House of Khudai. I rose to my feet, holding my hands up
in the air.

He hit me with the barrel. 'This is a PK.' He waved a machine
gun as long as the size of him. 'It'll create so many holes in you. You
won't know from where to piss and from where to poo.'

Everyone laughed.

'You've let down your jihad and the mujahideen who'd sacrificed
their lives for their watan.' Was this me talking?

'What are you doing here?'

'You saw me.'

'Weeping like a woman.'

'Have we got any other choice except to weep to Khudai to
punish your kind?' I said, surprising myself again. Had Khudai
accepted my prayers?

His eyes flicked to my bloodstained perahan tunban and jacket.
'Have you murdered anyone?'

'They're smeared with my best friend's blood.'

'And then both of you swam in the mud?'

'The one you've dug in. Khudai's punishing us for your deeds.'
The sunny May had turned into rainy days and the trees remained
bloomless. Kabul did resemble a muddy grave.

'Take him to *Amir* saheb,' a man from behind said and poked my
back with a Kalashnikov barrel.

178

About two dozen armed men in camouflage outfits guarded near red Mitsubishi Pajeros by the side of the block damaged with holes; the same Pajeros I hid from earlier. A man in a light cream military outfit with a pakol and a short beard talked on a walkie-talkie inside one of the vehicles. I recognised him. His photos were displayed on most vehicles and checkpoints of the mujahideen with pakols; one on the checkpoints Baktash and I had visited on our last stroll to the Makroryan Market. I'd heard about his triumphs over the Red Shorawi all my life; most lately from Frishta. He jumped out of the vehicle – his military boots as polished as his Pajero. The charismatic 'Commander-in-Chief' stood before me like a mountain in the flesh and inquired what'd happened. The soldiers accused me of looting.

His sharp eyes flicked to me. 'Is it true?'

'I've come to pray for Frishta's life.' I didn't tell him about Baktash and the burial in Bimaro because I doubted his help. After all, they'd brought all the misery on Kabulis.

'Who's Frishta?'

'Inshallah, my future wife.'

'His Lyla,' another said, holding an RPG-7 launcher and rockets. 'He's in mina like Majnun.'

Everyone sniggered. Majnun and Lyla were the equivalents of Romeo and Juliet.

'We die for our watan. He worries for love?' yet another said.

More sniggers over the continuous gun fire and explosions.

Amir saheb's face stayed unchanged. He took a step closer and put his stony hands on my shoulders. 'Gulbuddin Hekmatyar saheb's shelling hasn't given me the chance to see Kabulies' true spirit until today. You give me hope. Inshallah, Khudai will help you with your mina.'

Everyone fell quiet. Their leader gave me his blessing. Turned me from a thief into a hero.

'Say ameen,' Amir saheb said.

Everyone stroked their cheeks and beards and echoed ameen.

He shook my shoulders gently and hugged me, his pleasantly strong-scented smell entering my nostrils.

He ordered a mujahid to walkie-talkie for more mujahideen to come and guard the mosque. Drove me to the block and promised to do his best to defend Kabulis and bring back our old way of life. *Films* and *music* as well as *jelais' schools* included, he confirmed with a broad smile when I asked him. Told me to contact him if I required his help, explaining where to go and how to find him.

I rushed into my apartment and dared to do one last thing.

Frishta jan,

I'm really sorry for writing in your diary without your permission. But I have no choice – you don't talk to me, and as you know, we're leaving Kabul tomorrow for Mazar-e-Sharif, and I need to tell you something very important.

Before that, though, Frishta, Baz Muhammad Khan's wife sadly passed away. Don't worry, I managed today to put her in a temporary grave in her yard. We'll inshallah bury her with all the Islamic procedures once the war ends. Also, Mr Barmak is dead. His body lies where we argued over the diary. Please say nothing to his wife, or else she'd put her and the children's lives at risk. Wait until peace. I've just been to the mosque to pray for them and, importantly, for you. I begged Khudai to *save* you from these horrible people and help you achieve your goals. I'd be a liar if I claim I didn't beg Him, too... I'm nervous to say it. Please let me explain before I tell you what I asked for myself...

That evening you told me about having chosen Shafih as your 'soul friend', I got angry because it contradicted the Frishta I'd known. You called it a prank but refused to stop mingling with him. I got mad, but couldn't do anything, so I ceased to assess you with your exams – something I'm now very ashamed of; I'll never forgive myself for abandoning you in times of need. If only you'd asked me for lessons. I knew you wouldn't.

I started to crave for you, your jokes, stories, your whole company. A glimpse of you in the school, or corridor, or even on your balcony, quenched my thirst. I stood by the window in case you popped out on your balcony. When you did appear – sometimes with a cup of tea in your hand – I felt like I was flying in the air. My world brightened and my senses worked. Conscious of every second you were there, I wanted the time to stop. My heart dreaded the moment you walked back in. I thought of when I'd see you next. Sometimes you didn't come out at all, so I thought of the precious moments we'd spent together, or daydreamed about the future where we'd have our classes, tell jokes to each other and watch movies.

I was physically in my room, but mentally with you. Your presence, or the lack of it, turned me into an insomniac. Thanks to Habib from the next block, his rubab's percussive sound put me to sleep every night. I tossed and turned the night he didn't play the lion of instruments. Words that didn't come from your mouth or didn't go into your ears had no importance. Food without you lost its taste. Movies without you turned into the BBC News. Your face was the only drug that... awakened my senses. Talking to you in the class or corridor, even for a brief moment, completed my world. No one else – not even my friends – gave me that sense of completeness.

What's happening to me? I questioned myself. I thought it was me being used to you. As the days passed, I became more... how to explain... like a drug addict. It's infatuation, I tried to convince myself. I had to struggle not to admire your bravery to stand up against cruelty. Your willingness to call a spade a spade. Passion for your watan. Dedication to your sisters. Religiousness to wear the hijab. Chastity. Honesty. Caring. Hard work. Logicality. She *is* the true jelai of Afghanistan, I eventually conceded in Baz Muhammad's shed. In the same place, I surrendered to my true feelings.

I agonised that I'd betrayed our friendship and committed a sin. But what could I do? I tried hard to feel different but failed. Failed to forget about you. Failed to suppress my feelings.

Those feelings eventually compelled my worst side to emerge. When I saw you leaving in the late afternoon and coming back hours later, I felt panicky. Jealous. Mad. Betrayed. All at the same time, especially as your destination turned out to be Bimaro, where Shafih lived. Shafih had snatched the drug that cured me. I stole the diary because I thought you were with Shafih.

I now know why you visited the house in Bimaro (I'm sorry for having followed you again). Couldn't you have told me the truth when I asked you in front of Baz Muhammad's house? It would've made things much easier. After all, I was the trusted person in your life, a person who felt vulnerable in those days, a person who craved your sympathy.

I'm not defending my action. I'm deeply sorry for what I did. I know I let you down, so I don't deserve your forgiveness but I beg you for compassion.

Now you know the cause of my action. I've been to the mosque to pray to Khudai to make you my wife. Yes, Frishta, I admit it today to you, and the whole world if need be, that I'm in mina with you, and madly so. You bring strength to my character. Peace to my life. Hope for my future. I want to spend time with you, not just the two hours a day, but every hour of every day for the rest of my life.

181

Your mind isn't on mina, I know. I fear you'll get mad at seeing this entry but I've had to tell you the truth. I'm really... sorry for feeling this way for you. Have never planned for it. Swear to Khudai during our one-to-one lessons, *never* a filthy thought crossed my mind.

Frishta, I can wait for you as long as it takes before you're ready to marry. It'd be OK if you didn't love me. I'll do my best to make you fall in mina with me. I'll never distrust you. Will try to make things easier and happier (I'm sorry for having distressed you; you won't understand how much I grieved to see you down). Support you to fight your sisters' rights (even if it means we fight the whole of Afghanistan). I vow I'll no longer turn a blind eye to the wrongs. I won't care what people say about Ahmad from now on. Develop compassion. You're right, once you put your trust in Khudai, *really* do so, nothing can overcome you; and the feeling of the inner peace like a toddler in a mother's arms once you help someone... The feeling of flying overcloud like Superman once you see results... The feeling of removing the weight of the whole world from your shoulders once you speak your mind!

Last thing: Frishta, I promise I'll come back immediately from Mazar-e-Sharif as the war ends (the charismatic Amir saheb met me today and pledged to bring peace and security. I told him you were worried about jelais' schools, and he said he'd allow them to open. I'll tell you everything when we come back...), so please wait for me.

Frishta, please don't get mad. Think with a cool head.

Ahmad,

7:47pm., 6 May 1992

***

MOUR WENT BALLISTIC for having 'burned the family alive'. Her and my sisters' eyes had turned red. When I told them I'd ventured out, Agha slapped me for the first time in my life, warning never to leave their side again.

***

I CONTEMPLATED how to give the diary to Frishta. Every night she fell asleep at 11 at the latest, but that night she was awake.

Hours later, she turned around, her eyes shut. My hands shook as I withdrew the diary from out of my jeans. My heart beat against my chest as I crawled by the legs of a snoring Brigadier and Mahjan, touching the blanket gently in the dimly lit cellar and praying I didn't press a leg or hand. Lifted the lower part of Frishta's blanket and put the diary in her jacket pocket, feeling as if I had climbed the Pamir Mountains.

Chapter Twenty-Two

'Zoya, wake up. We're going,' Mour's voice said.

'Where?' I asked.

'We're leaving.'

'I'm not coming.'

'Ahmad, it's 3pm. We're leaving now.' Agha's voice again.

I rubbed my eyes and opened them to see a sack by Agha's legs next to the burning lamb. I realised and jumped to my feet, hitting my head against the steel pipe. Even time wasn't on our side. The fighting had died down an hour earlier.

Brigadier told Agha and me to stop worrying about Baktash and his father – anytime the war could escalate. Last night I insisted on taking part in Baktash and his father's burials.

Mour gave the keys to Mahjan. 'It's taken me 20 years to build it. Please look after my home until we return.' I never imagined Mour abandoning her mosque one day.

'I'll take care of it like my own home,' Mahjan said, leaning against the wall by the stairs.

'No crying please. Don't make me emotional,' Brigadier said.

Mahjan and Mour hugged, both sobbing.

'It's only a few weeks before the UN brokers a peace settlement,' Brigadier added.

Mour reiterated that Mahjan checked on her apartment every day.

'Think that you're here yourself.'

'I thought I'd bring Ahmad's bride to this flat. Wed Nazo and Zarghuna from here.'

'Khuda jan is merciful.'

Mour pointed to Mahjan's round baby belly. 'I'm concerned about you.'

'Don't worry. By then, the war will be long over. You'll be here, cooking us delicious ashak,' Brigadier chipped in.

'They'll help,' Mahjan said, pointing to the tearful Shukria and Barmak's wife, both standing by the stairs.

They nodded.

'We'll continue to pray for Barmak saheb,' Mour said.

'My heart says he's well,' Mahjan said.

Fresh tears came to Mr Barmak's wife's eyes. She nodded.

I feared she'd break down when she found out about her husband's fate.

'You've filled in the space of the brother I never had,' Brigadier said.

'The feeling is mutual,' Agha said.

They hugged. Their eyes welled up.

Every neighbour's eyes misted. We lived most, if not all, of our lives in this block and shared the sweetness and bitterness of life together.

'Princess, you haven't said goodbye to your aka jan and tror jan,' Brigadier said.

Frishta leaned against the wall in her usual place. Still refused to look at me. Still denied tears to her eyes.

'Frishta jan, goodbye for now,' Agha said, stroking her white headscarf. Throughout the war she put on her school uniform.

A scream, as loud as a hurricane, filled the basement.

'Frishta?' Mahjan said.

Brigadier gestured to leave her alone. Perhaps he wanted Frishta to release the emotions she'd built up over many days.

'Aka Azizullah, why does every wall we lean against fall to pieces like sand?' Tears flooded her eyes.

185

'Human greed,' Agha said.

'I don't know how much longer Khuda jan will punish us.'

'Patience, zoya,' Agha said.

'Roya and Baktash are no more.'

'Pray for them,' Brigadier said.

'I'll miss you, aka jan.' She jumped to her feet, hugged Agha and kissed his hands. 'And you, tror jan.' She embraced Mour and pecked her hands. Mour planted a kiss on her head. Tears poured down Mour's cheeks.

She hugged Nazo. Both sobbed. 'You eventually managed to take her away from me,' Frishta said to Mour and chuckled. She picked up the sleepy Zarghuna from Mour's arms and kissed her on her cheeks. She hugged Agha again, carrying on weeping. 'So you're leaving us, too.'

'Frishta jan, we'll be back as soon as the war ends,' Agha said, and stroked her head.

'It'll end soon, princess,' Brigadier said.

'Look after Nazo and Zarghuna,' she said to Agha and kissed Zarghuna.

'Don't worry, they'll be playing with you soon,' Agha said.

'Aka Azizullah, you're very fortunate to have a loyal wife. Cherish her.'

Agha's eyes wandered; so did Mour's. Mahjan frowned and told Frishta to let us go. Both sobbed. Frishta passed Zarghuna to Mour.

During all this, she never looked at me or uttered a word.

We left.

***

WITH THE SLEEPY Zarghuna on my back in the heavy showers, I turned around and had a final peep at the basement buried in bushes, and mumbled a goodbye to Frishta, to Baktash, who'd soon enter a wet hole behind his flat forever without his best friend being there, to the bloomless acacia tree – wet, cold and weeping like me – and to the block, whose heart must've ached like me to see one child dead, the other abandoning it, and the third broken.

Goodbye, my sweet Makroryan, I said. You know, I love you. I'll soon be back. Look after my Frishta.

***

AFTER STAYING FOR A night in a camp in a relatively safe Khair Khana, we took a coach to Mazar-e-Sharif, almost a day-long trip, to Agha's friend's three-storey house.

I horrifyingly found the red diary on the first day in Mazar-e-Sharif. Frishta had given her jacket to Nazo, who'd worn it under the raincoat. To my astonishment, I was about to find out Frishta's greatest secret.

Chapter Twenty-Three

The middle-aged translator, who had a haircut like Raziq Khan, required a week. After doubling the money he asked for up-front, the man agreed to translate the diary on the spot.

Opposite my wobbly chair on the wall had been stuck a photo of the Shrine of Ali; beneath it read:

A local mullah in the 12th century dreams of the secret site where Ali ibn Abi Talib, the Prophet's cousin and the fourth caliph of Islam, is buried. The locals find the Shrine. Later the Blue Mosque is constructed on the site and the town of Mazar grows around it.

'Shut the door and turn round the sign.'

I hesitatingly did and the sign now read 'Closed', not knowing why he wanted to shut the place. Pedestrians strolled up and down on the pavement in front of the shop, as small as Baz Muhammad's shed. Above the pedway, a gigantic billboard featured General Dostum in military uniform.

'Where's Frishta now?' the translator said, leaning on the enclosed glass table full of books, with a sign on the other side of the glass reading: 'Translations and Interpreting Services'.

'Kabul,' I said. Moved my chair to by the glass window and sat closer to him. My eyes were locked on his writing hand while listening to his nose whistling. He continued to write the translation in small writing underneath each line. At times he paused, contemplated and shook his head. Twice wiped his eyes.

He stopped translating after some two hours. 'Took longer than I expected. Had to pay really hard attention.'

'Thank you.'

'Are you Ahmad?'

'Yes.'

'Wait.' He took my notes out of the cashier and put them in the diary. 'No charge for the true jelai of Afghanistan.' He passed me over the diary.

'Take it. You deserve it.'

'Na,' he pointed with his palm. 'When you next see Frishta, tell her she has a brother in Mazar-e-Sharif who'd be proud to put her and the entire family up.'

'Inshallah, peace will soon come to Kabul.'

'Give this to Frishta as my gift for her answer to the Russian colonel.' He performed what many others and I had executed before: stood straight and raised his right hand to his forehead, his eyes welling up.

I crossed by the side of the glass table and hugged him.

As I was leaving his shop, he told me that Frishta had written Dari in Russian script.

I touched the diary every second step in the ten-minute sprint between the translating shop and the Shrine of Ali. Never was I as excited about reading something as reading the diary. I sat on the grass among dozens of families with children who chilled about, snacking on *shornakhud*, salty chickpeas, ice creams or grapes with pleasantly smelling Uzbaki naans while the white pigeons flew around the half-lit Shrine. Read the translator's neat handwriting with apprehension. Frishta wrote about women's issues; their inferior status in Afghanistan; Baz Muhammad's invalid wife; her efforts to persuade Roya to stand for herself; making peace between Sadaf and Roya; the 'coward' Rashid; the villainous Mullah Rahmat; books she started or finished reading; and Wazir and Baktash. She thought Baktash lacked courage. Disagreed with his criticism of religious principles. Worse, Baktash had got his father to dispatch the man with the long moustache to enlist Wazir. Frishta chastised him for the 'cowardly'

189

act. She saw Wazir as a 'courageous brother' who possessed typical Afghan qualities, and he earned her 'trust' and 'respect'.

She threw her shoe at a Russian ustad – and hit him in the face – when he, in a drunken state, told his students of having 'touched' an Afghan woman in a village in Kandahar. The college expelled Frishta from Moscow. I now ascertained why Raziq Khan's eyes teared up on the day he introduced Frishta to us, and why the translator saluted earlier.

The Shrine became darker with the flicking of each page that offered nothing about me. I skimmed more pages but no mention of me. I felt betrayed.

A toddler screamed. The parents told him not to throw grapes on the white marble floor, on which Mazaris sauntered, enjoying the sight of the blue and turquoise Shrine as well as the spring breeze.

Hang on... How did the translator know my name? I remembered him writing on the other side of the notebook, too. Turned around the diary and found the description of our first encounter:

A separate section for my cousin, Ahmad.

Met my shy cousin this morning. How startled he was when I introduced him as my cousin. Wanted to kill me. Can't wait to meet him tonight. He shall know I was right, ha, ha.

4:31pm, 8 March 1992

The next page read:

Wow, the staggering expression on his face as he opened the door, ha, ha... As if I was there to take his life. My Khuda jan, how I stunned him when I changed his room's disorderly layout. He was awkward tonight but will inshallah be a good cousin. Aka jan is so knowledgeable, so lovely. Tror jan upset me. She has no idea what's good for Nazo and Zarghuna.

9:59pm, 8 March 1992

On another page, she recorded:

Today, we started mathematics. Thanks to aka jan, Ahmad agreed... but with a stupid condition.

Aka jan and tror jan were in our house for the first time. Aka jan enjoyed himself; not sure of her. Do your best to avoid quarrelling with her – not for his stupid condition, but for padar jan and madar jan.

Must go to bed; already 10:04pm.

190

9 March 1992

I read more inserts. They were on what I said or did on a particular day and what she thought of it. She thought I gave my '100 per cent' to ensure she got the highest grades, even in Science, and never gave up on her. Talked about how my Indian music and action movies grew on her, how she liked my 'gentle Kabuli accent', and how she loved it when I laughed at her mimicking ustads and no longer took myself 'so seriously'. I likewise brought the 'kid Frishta' out in her.

A hand touched my shoulder, giving me a scare. A young jelai, holding a straw tray and an Istalifi-sufali pitcher, asked if I wanted warm bolanis with cold doogh. I shook my head. She rushed to a family of grandparents, children and grandchildren, each adult holding the hand of a child, all smiling, giggling and licking their ice creams. My eyes turned to the diary. I skipped a few pages and read something that made my hair stand on end:

What's happening to me? Can't get him off my mind. Don't see him for a few hours, I miss him... like I've lost something. When he's there, I feel I don't want anything else but his company. I even enjoy action movies with him. Oh, Khuda jan, I'm losing control of my heart. Please forgive me. Need to concentrate on my studies. We're the luckiest to have the opportunity of an education. Most of us right now get bombarded by Russian puppets' jets.

10:31pm, 27 March 1992

We both suffered from the same disease, missed each other and denied our feelings. The only difference was she'd caught the disease weeks earlier. A man touched my shoulder, asking if I bought 'natural, genuine Mazar-e-Sharif's kohl kajal powder'.

I shook my head. In desperation, I read another passage about me:

Intelligent, honourable, dignified, sincere, Islamic... respectful of his elders. All the qualities a true Afghan man can have. Plus, he's such an attentive listener and fun to be around. Say nothing about his appearance... his fair skin, brown-thick hair...thin body in baggy T-shirt tucked in jeans (especially with his jean jackets)... force you to look at him all day long. His soft skin and long eyelashes give him a

191

perfect face. His lips, as red as the tulips of Mazar-e-Sharif, add to the perfection. Maybe Khuda jan has made him especially for me... that's why He's turned us into the best of friends. Please, Khuda jan, forgive me for thinking about him in this way... My heart's taken the better of me. Can't I become both a good wife and a good servant to my dear Afghanistan?

9:38pm, 3 April 1992

It became clear she struggled as I read more and more. Her heart ached if she didn't meet 'her Ahmad'. She was cross with Khudai for making this happen to her, 'because it weakens my determination' and 'creates an obstacle to my commitments to my watan and sisters'.

Frishta also had a question about me:

Why can't he understand that his pros and cons approach can turn him into a coward... a selfish one? He must learn to confront injustice even if it doesn't concern him. Must stop fearing what others think. Stop sacrificing his life for his mother and do what he loves and is good at, history. He's so hard-working, so committed. Will definitely become a prominent historian. Every kid wants to be a doctor. Afghanistan cries out for another Abdul Hai Habibi.

9:12pm, 5 April 1992

A page later read:

His backward views on traditions are upsetting. He blindly follows his mother. How can he deny university to Nazo and Zarghuna? How can he take away their rights?

9:41pm, 6 April 1992

My eyes caught the word 'murderer' three pages later. A splashing sound followed by cold water drops hitting against my right cheek. A man with a four-wheeled cart full of carrots and a juicer on the other side of the fence surrounding the Shrine threw another pot of water on the grass. My attention shifted back to the notebook whose vinyl cover my hands grabbed as tightly as the mujahideen leaders held on to the Arg Palace.

I don't know why I told him. Why do I want to share everything with him? Why would I drink poison from your hand? Your face dropped like I told you I was dying of a disease. I am sorry, Ahmad jan. But you must know your future wife is the daughter of a murderer. I told you lies; I do need your sympathy.

9:48pm, 15 April 1992

I searched for her comment on the night we had the argument over Shafih and found it:

His ingrained beliefs have blinded him to get a tease. Thanks, Khuda jan, I didn't disclose my feelings for him – would've lost him forever. Never make such a prank, Frishta. Why did I return his notebooks? A stupid decision. But he hurt me. He knows I hate being bossed around. Would rather die husbandless than allow myself to be controlled. Worse, how did he dare to imagine I was such a jelai? Stop crying, Frishta.

10:39pm, 17 April 1992

I skipped to her thoughts on the school incident:

Have this terrible feeling the ugly mudir punished you for getting to me... I'll never forget the look on your face until the day I die. Why did I not act earlier...? Was I scared of the ugly beast...? How would I know you'd... come on... he must've stood for himself. Fight his own fights. Please, Khuda jan, help my Ahmad; this can destroy him. I'll find out who's written the mina letter. I'll clear your name. I promise you, Ahmad jan.

7:22pm, 24 April 1992

Mullah Rahmat's jumping from the bottom of the register to the top justified Frishta's suspicion. A scream: a child behind me throwing a tantrum, stomping his feet. The parents' soothing strategy – that they couldn't buy any more seeds to feed the pigeons as it was dark and all the pigeons rested – proved as ineffective as Benon Sevan's plan to end the Afghanistan war.

In the next pages she recorded her conversations with Shafih, who told on Jawad. Frishta suspected it was Jawad's handwriting, but the actual engineer was Shafih, though he continuously swore to Frishta that he had nothing to do with the letter and had no knowledge of *Grease* being Frishta's favourite film. He blamed my cowardly heart. Frishta warned him never to call me a coward because I loathed the word. He asked Frishta if she was in mina with me: 'I'll sacrifice my life for Ahmad' was her reply.

In the last conversation Shafih revealed his 'true mina' and readiness to marry her. Frishta's heart had no place for a 'pervert', giving him one more day to profess the truth voluntarily in the edara,

193

or she'd get him sent to his boss, Rashid. That day never came as she was absent from school, an absence caused by the very person she tried to protect.

After the pages on Shafih, she jotted down that it had been the second night she hadn't met Ahmad, and she missed me. She begged Khudai to look after me. After meeting me, she'd put down:

I'd lay my life before him, yet he thinks... If only he burned me alive but hadn't accused me of an accomplice. What's been happening to him lately? – he's never been like this before. Where is my logical, reasonable, supportive Ahmad? Where's this sick... arghh?... Don't explode. Please stop crying, Frishta, and sleep.

11:49pm, 26 April 1992

Frishta's search in my eyes and her abrupt leaving without goodbye now made sense. Following her the next day, accusing her again, naming her harami, and stealing the diary... Damn Satan. If only I had the power to change the past, I'd have cut my tongue off rather than pronounce the word. I loathed myself for it.

The Maghrib *azan,* call to prayer, brought me back to a fully lit Blue Mosque, as bright as a Kabuli day. Stars had filled the sky: time to go home. Instead of joining the worshippers walking in hundreds towards the mosque, my eyes went back to the diary. Flicked a page and came across a long passage in which I noticed the word 'khastegari'. It read:

It is 1:12am and I can't sleep. Why am I thinking of the day tror jan and aka jan (Khuda jan, I'll tell them who I am and You'll help change their minds to accept a 'harami' as a daughter-in-law) accompanied by their kinfolk come khastegari? Padar jan and madar jan hand them a lump of sugar buried in chocolates and sugar-coated almonds. I'm in my room, waiting. Stop it, Frishta. Oh, Khuda jan, what am I supposed to do with my heart? To Hell with everything else, let's just dream, Frishta.

I overhear tror jan and other women singing and drumming the dayereh with jingles. I pop out and see you standing on your balcony, not as Ahmad but as *my* fiancés. Forever. Why does my heart skip a beat when I think of you as a fiancée? That's mina, jelai. Yes, I love you. Love you more than anything, anyone.

It's our *shirini-khori,* a bigger engagement party. I've got the traditional Afghani dress on with a golden necklace, and Ahmad is in a black perahan tunban. Jelais and haleks go round and round in a circle to the beat, clapping, turning, twisting and snapping heads side to side. They ask us to join them. We both aren't good attan dancers. I wobble in my long dress. He catches me. Everyone claps.

Our *khina* night, the night of henna, arrives. Zarghuna and Nazo, along with another five jelais dressed in traditional Afghani clothes, come through the door, holding a silver tray with candles and assortments of fresh flowers with little henna containers, dancing and turning to the throne of bride and groom. Tror jan places a teaspoonful of henna onto my palm and shields it with a triangular cloth made of shiny fabric. Madar jan puts the henna on Ahmad's palm and covers it with the same fabric. Tror jan tries to open my hand but fails. She must now give me an expensive gift. I decline any present – she's already gifted me a rare diamond.

It's our *wadah*, the wedding ceremony. Stop it, Frishta... No, to hell with it. I'm in green clothes with a golden crown and Ahmad in a suit. Nowhere but in Kabul Hotel, no one but Farhad Darya sings *walk slowly my light of night go slowly*. Everyone inside the hall stands up with smiles on their faces as we make our entrance. Padar jan holds the Quran over our heads. We take our place at the throne because we're the King and Queen of the night. In front of us stands the decorative table with candles and flowers. The sound of Casio keyboard and tabla resonate in the air, and a mass of jelais and haleks spin around, shimmy and twirl on the dance floor.

A mullah and two witnesses ask Ahmad and me if we accept each other as wife and husband. I accepted him, I accept him and I will accept him as my husband, I reply. Ahmad jan says the same words. The nikah is complete. We're officially wife and husband. Darya's *bring henna and place it on their hands* fills the hall. I get into a white dress, and Ahmad into a dashing, dark blue suit. Guests one by one take pictures with us and then join the dance on the floor.

Veiled by a decorative shawl, the husband and wife open the mirror to see each other in it, recite verses of the Quran, and pray. I ask for eternal peace for Afghanistan, where my husband and I live a happy life alongside my countrymen and women. The King and Queen of the night then cut the two-tier cake, exchange glasses of home-made sherbet and spoons of *malida*, my favourite dessert. He smiles and puts some in my mouth. Cake and malida get distributed among the guests. Darya sings, *congratulations, I gave you my heart, now I leave it to Khuda jan*.

The peak of the hours of enjoyment comes as Darya plays fast-beat songs, and the dance floor fills up with people who dance and attan till the end of the ceremony at dawn.

Safi jan ties a green cloth around my waist to prepare me for my new home.

We arrive at Ahmad's flat. I won't come out of the wedding car until I receive a promise of a property. The property I demand from tror jan is to *accept* me as her daughter-in-law. She plants a kiss on my head, and I kiss her hands. I step on the ground but won't allow a sheep to be sacrificed under my foot. Want to stay at my husband's home forever, so I hammer the biggest nail into the doorway and step into my new home.

I wake up the following morning and see Ahmad's face lying on the pillow opposite me. Plant a kiss on his cheek. No, two. No, more. Thousands. Millions. Stop it, Frishta, time to go to bed. I can't, dream, jelai. Dream more.

We have a son and two daughters, Malalai, Nahid and Amanullah. I feed Amanullah, and Ahmad plays with Malalai and Nahid. Stop it, Frishta. It's too late.

1:39am, 27 April 1992

We both lived in the opposite apartments, both on the same side rooms, both deeply in mina with each other, both denied it to each other and both daydreamed about each other in which both wanted three children, with the only difference being I fathered two sons and a daughter, while she mothered two daughters and a son. If only I had revealed my feelings, she could've been here with me in Mazar-e-Sharif. I'd never have left Kabul without Frishta. If only Frishta had told me. After all, she was courageous. She defended everyone else's rights but failed to reveal her feelings for me. Everyone feared when it came to losing something dear to them. Even Frishta.

But we were where we were. I decided to take a bus tomorrow to Kabul and tell Frishta, louder than the mujahideen's guns' sound, 'Will you marry me?' Nobody could stop me, not even my parents or tradition. We'd stay in Kabul in Khair Khana or, if she wanted, return to Mazar-e-Sharif.

***

MOUR AND AGHA to my relief paid no attention to my lateness. Mour's eyes were puffed up. Our host, Agha's friend, a pro-Communist Parchami who worked for Dostum, and had Dostum and Babrak Karmal's faces painted across the wall of the vast lounge we sat in, told Agha that what had happened was the wish of Khudai. A woman in a long headscarf echoed her husband. I thought some other pro-Communist comrades had been killed, or Mour worried about her house getting looted. But then Agha dried his tears with a white tissue.

I'd never seen Agha crying over losing a comrade or the flat. What had happened?

'I wish they'd left with us,' Agha said, his left hand resting on the black leather sofa. Farhad Darya sang on the television at a low volume.

My heart sank. 'Who?'

'Brigadier and his family have been martyred, zoya,' Mour said, breaking into fresh tears.

'Frishta, too?'

'Woh, a rocket struck in the tablecloth as they sat at dinner,' Agha confirmed.

'Their flesh spattered across the walls. Tawba-tawba,' Mour said and burst again into tears.

Frishta wasn't dead; it was a bad dream. She hadn't worn the green dress yet. Cut the wedding cake. Hit the nail. Why did Mour scream? Why did Agha shake me? Did he ask me to move my eyes? Why did Mour want me to talk? Had something happened to someone? What was Frishta's connection to all this? Darya sang, *You want to come to Kabul jan, love? You know about me? I'm dying from your parting, You want to come and see me, love?*

Blackout.

Chapter Twenty-Four

For weeks, my only companions were insomnia, nightmares and regrets. I mulled over my response in the past few days leading to our departure from Kabul and wondered if I could've done anything to stop Frishta's death from happening. If only I told her I loved her. She would've been with us. Or I would've died together with her. If only Khudai accepted my prayers in the Makroryan Mosque. Frishta wasn't going to be part of tomorrow, or the day after, or forever thereafter. Frishta was dead; the civil war in Kabul took her away from me. Never let her wear the white wedding dress. Farhad Darya reminded me of this every single hour of every day when he sang, *Frishta was a memory; Frishta was a dream; Frishta was a fond remembrance; Frishta was gone and gone.*

To Agha's disappointment, the situation in Kabul worsened. Turning Shia against Sunni and vice versa, setting Afghanistan's main ethnic groups of Pashtun, Tajik, Hazara and Uzbek against each other, and accusing each other of uniting with the remnants of pro-Communist members and thus not being Islamic enough, the 15 or so mujahideen groups fought each other, killing tens of thousands of innocent Kabulis, displacing hundreds of thousands, and turning half of Kabul into mudbrick rubble with bombs, rockets and cannon fire. The conflicting interests of Pakistan and India, Iran and Saudi Arabia, not to mention Russia and America, as Agha said and Baktash had predicted, were fought on the streets of Kabul. To my disgust, I, too, had played a part in that conflict.

After my psychiatrist gave me the OK following months of support and advice, and after Agha was certain that peace and security were not in sight, and Mour discovered that entire neighbourhoods in Kabul had been looted and their doors and windows sold on the open market, her apartment included, we left for Moscow where his other friends ran import-export businesses. I learned in Moscow that once you lost power in Afghanistan, you lost dignity. Agha's rich friends hid, as you did from a pandemic, in case Agha asked for favours. Agha never showed his face to them. 'My honour is not for sale,' he said.

Life was such we both travelled to the same workplace, the Soviet-era Sevastopol Hotel now transformed into a business centre; Agha worked part-time as a porter and spoke full-time about current Afghan affairs. I sold milk and home-cooked palaw rice, which Mour prepared.

The hotel accommodated hundreds of Afghan firms that imported and sold various goods from China and Turkey. You also found Afghan food, from palaw to ashak; Afghan baked products, from baklava to cream rolls; Afghan poetry books, music, movies with celebrities, from actors to singers; and plenty of posters for Afghan concerts. We'd emigrated from the Little Moscow of Kabul to Moscow's Little Afghanistan.

Agha likewise found what he cherished: politics. Like Afghanistan, the place witnessed debates among the different camps: Islamists, pro-Communists, Liberal Traditionalists. These camps further subdivided themselves into the pro-Taliban Islamists versus the pro-Mujahideen ones. The Khalqi comrades versus the Parchami comrades. Both versus the Maoists. The parliamentary system defenders who favoured King Zahir Shah versus the presidential system who favoured Daoud Khan. Worse, these subgroups divided themselves into further categories who defended different mujahideen commanders. Even worse, Pashtun, Tajik, Hazara and Uzbek disagreed on what percentage of the population they constituted and how they had violated one another's rights in past centuries. Plenty to debate on Afghanistan, and plenty of historical examples to invoke to blame each other for Afghanistan's ills. These discussions often ended up in fights. Agha was frequently beaten up in those debates.

After about six months, Ali Hussain, a Hazara Shia Afghan businessman, told me, his 'Afghan brother', that I could do better than sell milk. He gave me shoes on credit from his firm in Sevastopol, and I sold them in the Cherkizovsky Market, as vast as Makroryan. His every kindness reminded me of what Wazir and I had done to Baktash, and put me to shame.

Over time, I bought a store. Like tens of thousands of other Afghans, Chinese and Central Asians I employed two Ukrainian women – but unlike most employers of the marketplace, my saleswomen were in their sixties. Soon I supplied shoes to two dozen small stalls, whose owners were Afghan men and a couple of women. They paid me once they sold the goods. I told Agha not to worry about my sisters' school fees and apartment rent, and pleaded with him not to work; he daily got verbal abuse from Afghans for his part in the pro-Communist government. He gave up his job as a porter and his full-time job now constituted talking about politics – and drinking. He drank at least a bottle of vodka every day with his comrades in Sevastopol, and returned home in a state of perpetual intoxication. There was no time when Agha's mouth didn't smell of alcohol, but Mour's respect hadn't diminished one bit; my father was still a minister for Mour.

I disagreed with the notion that time healed. Life was never the same without Frishta. I never managed to fix my grief, but succeeded in coping with my feelings and focused on my caring responsibilities for my parents and sisters, as well as Baktash and Mr Barmak's families who were now based in Pakistan, until one day in Moscow they called to plead for a large sum to apply for 'a widow visa' to America. After receiving the money, both families never spoke to me; my father's relative, Shujah, told me he'd never seen them and their flats were 'grabbed' by warlords. I prayed they made it to their destination and forgot about them – not about Frishta. At times little things like Ahmad Zahir's or Farhad Darya's songs or Schwarzenegger's movies overwhelmed me with grief. But then I'd hear Frishta's voice, *Don't allow bullies to shatter your dreams.* I'd perform ablutions, pray *nafl*-prayers, supererogatory prayers, read the Quran, pray for Frishta, and carry on concentrating on my responsibilities: something Frishta would have wanted me to do if she was around. Every time I faced a situation where another person or I was unfairly treated and my heart wanted to abandon me, Frishta's voice whispered in my ear: *Take refuge in Khuda jan. Once He protects you, no one will overcome you.*

While Afghans in their debates in the Sevastopol Hotel blamed each other for their ills, I blamed Afghanistan and all those who lived in it and vowed to cease all my connections to my watan. Nothing was left to connect with, anyway, and the time had come to journey further away in search of what our watan had taken away from us: peace, security and dignity. Whereas some enjoyed the kebab-drink-and-women aspect of life, most Afghans saw Moscow as a platform to the West and toiled from 4am to 9pm to save up. I hated both the political debates and Moscow's liberal life. As I made enough money for the human traffickers, Mour and I began to persuade Agha to leave for the West where Agha could get help for his alcohol addiction, and where I could restart education and my sisters further theirs; years of coaxing resulted in Mour agreeing to send her daughters to university. Once the Taliban hanged Najibullah and dashed Agha's hopes of serving as an advisor or minister, Agha gave in.

After working for three years and eight months in Moscow – three years and eight months of humiliation, indignation and random Moscow Police checks when you either had to pay a bribe or get a beating – we left for England. I was filled with trepidation on the day the human trafficker placed us on the train to Ukraine; I feared something bad was about to happen.

The unbelievers want to turn our *watan* into their 'Little America'...

PART TWO

Summer 2013

Chapter Twenty-Five

My sisters flailed their hands, screaming 'Mour'.

'Please save my daughters!' Mour cried above the deafening outboard motor noise. She banged her head against a man to the right; her headscarf had slipped to her shoulders. The man wouldn't release his grabbing of Mour's arms. Another asylum seeker held the man's belt with both hands.

'Ahmad, tell the godless people in their language,' Mour told me, the rain hitting against her face.

'Stop the boat,' I said to the smuggler in Russian. My body had already half sunk into the ice-cold water because the son of a bitch had squeezed 23 asylum seekers in a dinghy designed to fit eight.

The smuggler carried on grappling with the trolling motor in the torrent shadowed by trees as formidable as the Hindu Kush mountains. They shut off the stream from everything and everyone, even from the dark sky of the early morning.

Zarghuna let go of Nazo's shirt and went motionless as though she had given up hope and accepted her fate without a fight. The current swallowed her in a tiny mouthful.

'My sister's drowned. Stop the damn boat,' I said and kicked the rubber edge, water splashing on my face and into my mouth.

The man next to me tightened his arm around me, squeezing me against his sweaty chest.

Nazo shouted 'Agha', her throat contracting.

The dinghy wobbled. The sound of someone jumping overboard. To my horror, it was Agha.

'He can't swim. He's drunk. Stop the bloody boat,' I said and caught my breath.

The inflatable dinghy drifted away.

I bit the hairy arm and untangled my right hand. Threw my fist against the smuggler's face, feeling his teeth and lips with my middle knuckle.

He shouted something in Hungarian to the man next to me.

'Have you gone mad?' the man said in broken Russian and secured his grip. Another arm, as large as an electricity pole, placed itself against my throat and pressed it against his sweaty chest. I threw kicks, the cutting water raising my belly button. I felt my oesophagus closing. Agha, with flailing hands pushing towards his daughter, blacked out. I was relaxed. Peaceful.

Chapter Twenty-Six

'Ahmad, pay attention,' Mour said.

'Seat belt,' a Turkish air stewardess said.

'Sorry, miles away.' Traumatic memories rippled through me and I hadn't even set foot on its soil. I pulled out the strap from underneath Mour and pushed it into the buckle.

'Don't forget why we named you Ahmad,' Mour said.

'Stop worrying. It isn't good for you.'

'You're a pure Pashtun.'

'Mour, relax. Breathe in.' Mour's anxiety had forced her to step up her lessons in who my ancestors were and what values they held dear in case I said or did things in my khastegari that would contradict 'Pashtunwali'.

I pulled Mour's hijab shawl over her white, thinning scalp and wiped with it the beads of sweat from her pale face.

'Call Shujah aka and don't forget to kiss his hand,' Mour said, tightening her seat belt over her white, calf-length dress with navy dots like the seats of the airplane we were on.

'It shows you've been brought up well.'

'Mour, respectfully, I grew up in Afghanistan.'

'And you've been away for 21 years.'

'So?'

Kate Winslet, rushing up the stairs, froze on the seat-back screen in the front when the pilot announced something in Turkish.

'Akanai Nazigul is like a mother to you. She deserves a lot of respect.' Mour raised her voice to compensate for the announcement and crying babies. 'Call her akanai.'

'I already call her Nazigul on Skype.'

'I thought you grew up in Afghanistan?'

'Mour, *hila kawom*,' I said, 'please.'

Kate Winslet came back into motion.

'You disrespect your elders if you refer to them by their first names.'

'But Nazigul is the nickname the in-laws have given her.'

'An ill-mannered son wouldn't count for proper Pashtun.'

'Proper *Afghan*,' I said and pressed my thumb against the front seat's torn leather. It unfolded once I released the pressure.

'Akanai has taken all the trouble to dig you out the jelais. One of them will become your wife if you don't spoil it,' Mour went on, raising her henna-dyed palms in prayer and wiping her face with them.

'Inshallah,' I said, my thoughts racing to the moment when Mour would place a gigantic lump of sugar surrounded by chocolates and sugar-coated almonds before me, breaking out the news that the jelai and her parents accepted me as 'their servant', and thus I got engaged. I wondered which jelai would turn out to be my future wife. Latifa, Nazia, Kubra or Humaira?

My ears got a feeling of fullness as though a roller coaster was going down a steep slope. I took a deep breath. Everyone else looked undisturbed. Two men in perahan tunban wore their turbans. A woman plodded up and down the aisle, soothing her crying baby. They were all meant to have been seated with their seat belts fastened. Same old Afghans: they cherished their customs but resisted foreign-imposed rules.

Mour's eyes were closed, her lips moving and her body rocking from side to side. As she finished a Quranic verse, she prayed to Khudai to support my khastegari.

'I've had two wishes – giving you a good education and finding you a decent wife. My first wish is fulfilled and may Khudai help me with the second,' Mour said to me, looking skyward.

'Ameen.' I wiped my beard. 'What about the other two?' I referred to 'seeing my children' and 'purchasing our own property'.

Mour went back into pleading with Khudai without acknowledging my tease.

Khudai must've heard a thousand times Mour's four wishes, and, inshallah, He'd grant us them all.

'Your presence in the khastegari makes things complicated.'

'With due respect, we've already discussed this,' I said.

'Spell it out: we don't own the flat.'

'It's true. The housing association does.'

'It's permanent.'

'"Permanent" is different from owning.'

'Do as you wish; it's your khastegari,' Mour said with a resigned sigh. 'Is this a plane or a nursery?'

Afghan families poured into Kabul during summer holidays, and it appeared that kids didn't like flights.

'What's the smell?'

'Pampers,' I said.

'You never stank. Someone needs to teach her the importance of changing nappies quickly. Her own nose will thank her.'

'Mour, hila kawom.' The woman with heavy make-up and a crying baby now sat on the aisle seat, a metre away from us.

'I'll say it to her face. You think I'm scared of her?' Mour shook her head and glared at the woman. 'All today's mothers think about is make-up.'

'She may be passionate about make-up. Why should we judge if it makes her happy?' I said.

With a sudden bump the plane touched down. Mour put her hands to her ears, swaying from side to side, her lips moving.

AN ANCIENT blue and white bus ferried us to the only building in Kabul International Airport, as large as a medium-size train station, and dropped us beneath the smiling photo of the beleaguered Afghan President with his traditional Afghan *qaraqul* hat and tribal *chapan*.

***

A MAN IN A BLUE uniform tapped on my back and gestured to follow him as I waited for the luggage. He led me into a windowless room with one desk and three chairs. The man left.

My heart beat faster. Why was I in this tiny room? Would they bring Mour, too, from the Prayer Room? *Khudai, I take refuge in You. When You protect, no one will overcome me,* I prayed in my heart.

A man in a faded suit and thin tie entered. 'What're you doing in Kabul?' He sat at the edge of the metal desk with a wooden top, his broad shoulders covering Hamid Karzai's photo on the grey wall.

'This's my watan.'

'Was.' He stood straight. 'Hold up your arms.'

'Who are you?'

'The NDS.'

'Can I see a proof?'

He looked me in the eye: his bushy brows covered the corners of his scleras. Withdrew a card from the breast pocket. I read 'The National Directory of Security' in bold above his frowning photo. He reinserted the card and gestured at my arms.

His touch pushed the notebook against my chest. 'What's this?'

'My diary.'

He removed it from my suit jacket. He raised his bushy eyebrows, revealing the blue pupils behind them. 'A red colour diary for a man?' He shook his head.

'And this?'

'My money.'

208

'Take it out.'

My heartbeat increased. According to Shujah, mafia gangs killed you for £100 in Kabul, and the security forces turned a blind eye. Like a drug dealer caught by the police, I brought out the three envelopes.

He tore them open under the overhead fluorescent light the size of a car bumper, whose brightness filtered through his full hair, giving it a blue-grey colour.

'How much?' He felt the Queen's head with his thumb.

'£6,000.'

'For your bearded brothers?'

'It's for my wedding.' My legs trembled, realising why I was being interrogated.

'Enjoy the honeymoon and then tell the poor jelai you've already got a wife in the fucking West?'

'I've got obro and ezat.'

'And yet you ran away from your watan?'

'People like you forced me to.'

'Beghairat.'

'At least I don't spy for the infidel occupiers.' Did my forehead have 'coward' written on it in Pashto, which everyone read in Afghanistan but no one could in England? With time, I loathed the word even more, the worst kind in Pashto, someone who lacked 'self-honour'. Proved an Afghan a coward, you left him stripped of character.

'Does your mother know his son's planning to be a jihadist doctor?'

'I'm not–' Hold on... 'How do you know I'll be a doctor?'

'I know plenty. Just finished university. Live in Durham. A member of Hezb-e-Tahrir. We work closely with our colleagues from MI5.' His blue eyes beneath bushy eyebrows were fixed on me.

'I'm a member of no Hezb.' What the hell? Did MI5 spy on me?

209

The door clicked open. The man in the blue uniform dashed in. 'Downstairs at once. Ten KG.' His eyes travelled to the notes in his colleague's hand.

'As though the world didn't suffice, they now fucking want to supply Mars?' the man with the bushy brows said to his colleague. His face turned to me. 'Listen, son of a whore. I don't want any trouble in my city. Understood?'

'Don't dishonour me.'

A bang against my right ear, causing a 'binging' sound. Calling Mour a whore hurt more than the slap.

'So what?' He pointed to the desk. 'Want me to shove its leg up your backside?'

'You're abusing your power.'

'Another word and I'll hang you by the beard.'

'And violating my civil liberties.'

'Chup.'

'I want to speak to your superiors.'

'I said fucking chup.' His eyes popped out like a mad dog.

He took half a step closer, his shoulders level against my head, reminding me of the evil Mullah Rahmat. *No, it won't happen again.* My legs trembled, and my heart beat fast. *In the Name of Khudai, with His name nothing can cause harm in the earth nor in the heavens, and He is the All-Hearing, the All-Knowing,* I recited a dua in my heart. The cigarette smell entered my nostrils as he put the money in its rightful place and pushed me towards the door. 'The sooner you leave my city, the better.'

'My diary?'

'It stays here.'

I took a deep breath. 'I won't go without it.' It belonged to Frishta's grave.

He slapped it into my hand and told the other man to throw me out.

As I stepped outside, he made a *cheesht* sound. 'I'm watching you.'

AFTER COLLECTING OUR luggage, consisting of bargain clothes from Primark as gifts for Shujah's family, and taking Mour from the Prayer Room, an old-aged porter dawdled with us amidst a strong wind to Section C of the airport; Sections A and B served the elite.

The fenced-in section in the open air felt like a half-empty car park surrounded by billboards: Afghan cricketers in blue and red uniforms advertising 4G Internet; a young woman in an Afghani dress with gold threading detail and gold beads held a metal can, saying, *My energy source to rap*; and three young men and a woman in suits and ties inviting Afghans to their concert for the coming Eid. I'd been away from Afghanistan for more than two decades and recognised none of these faces. All my knowledge about post-invasion Afghanistan came from Nadir, a former lecturer at Kabul University and now a PhD student at Durham University, and Shujah. According to them, new Afghan singers, predominantly female, had blossomed since the American intervention in Afghanistan. Afghan TV channels invited indigenous and foreign singers from abroad to give concerts in the hundreds of newly built wedding halls in Kabul during Afghan festivals. Warlords owned many of those channels and halls. They'd once fought for Islam and now entertained Afghans, Nadir would say.

Beneath the fresh-faced celebrities on the billboards, however, in the blowing wind of a sunny mid-morning, waited men, women and children with weather-stricken faces. To the right, outside Section C, some dozen concrete barriers stood on either side of the road, leaving a narrow entrance for vehicles. Blue-uniformed policemen with Kalashnikovs manned it, one holding a German Shepherd searching a Toyota boot. A fine layer of dust covered their faces.

Deth-deth-deth-deth-deth shots of an AK-47 grabbed my attention. A jeep with tinted windows braked, making a screeching noise. A 16-

or 17-year-old halek in a pakol hat jumped out of the vehicle, slapped, kicked and punched a policeman.

'Please forgive him,' a colleague of the policeman said.

'He won't stop your vehicle again,' another said.

'He didn't recognise that you're the Minister's son,' another colleague said, holding the dog leash.

'He'll fucking recognise me once he's transferred to the frontline,' the halek said and jumped into his jeep, revved the engine and drove off.

The victim policeman stood numb. A colleague picked up a hat from the ground and placed it over the beaten man's dishevelled hair.

'Salaam alaikum,' a voice said. 'Don't worry. You'll see plenty of such cinemas here.' A man bowed and pecked Mour's right hand. 'Salaam alaikum, zoya.' He embraced me, his pot belly getting in the way.

We greeted, and I planted a kiss on his hand with a strong, alcohol-smelling aftershave.

The clean-shaven, thick-haired Shujah of no more than 5 foot 3, who looked shorter in real life than on Skype, took the luggage from the porter and handed him a banknote; the man showed no gratitude. Instead, he looked at me, pointing to his white beard.

'Fuck off,' Shujah snapped, his small eyes disappearing into his wrinkled face.

Cursing Shujah under his breath, the porter walked off. I paced up, and placed a £5 note in his hand.

'Leave me to deal with them; I know their language better,' Shujah said once I caught up with him and Mour heading out.

'They've swallowed billions of US dollars, yet they complain America has done nothing.'

'America has stolen our mineral riches a hundred times more,' Mour said.

'Invaders rob; they don't give,' I said. A strong gust of wind lifted some dust, and particles of sand entered my mouth. 'Why is it so dusty?'

'Combination of the dry weather over the last few years and an influx in population,' Shujah said, pulling the luggage.

I shielded my mouth and nose with my hand. His eyes narrowed. 'What're you grinning at?'

'You so-called foreign Afghans have become a little delicate abroad. You all moan too much whenever you come back to Kabul.'

'I didn't mean to sound snobbish. Kabul was nowhere near as grey as when I was growing up.' I recalled summers being hot and often windless. Even autumns brought both wind and rain, but hardly pollution.

Duvvv... The ground shook as if a colossal hand had shoved it. Everyone dropped face-down like trained soldiers, objects raining down on us. Mour and I ducked behind our suitcase above which a blood-flowing arm in blue uniform holding a silver dog chain landed. Bodyparts and debris had filled the ground. A thick, black pillar of smoke filled the air. My ears felt like someone had rung them with a sledgehammer. The smoke-like burning rubber tightened the muscles around my nose and throat, and compelled me to cough black mucus. Muffled cries, wails, screams of pain and coughs. A male scream topped everyone else's: 'My whole body's burning, Khudai. My whole body's burning.'

Mour and I dropped face-down following Shujah's shouts to lie flat and not to move as there was often a further bomb. I checked on my hands and legs – thanks, Khudai, they weren't missing; Mour and Shujah seemed OK. 'Thanks, Khudai. Thanks, Khudai,' I kept saying. I could've just died if I was a little closer to the blast. Writhing and yelping, all in either Pashto or Dari, continued on the other side. Blood kept gushing from the chopped arm onto the ground. Goose bumps pricked my skin, and I looked away. My heart pounded and my body shivered: the two physical sensations that'd become alien to me in England. The enormity of my decision sank in. I was in Kabul, even though I'd decided never to step back on its soil.

Earlier on, I spared Mour the unnecessary worries and myself timeless interrogations and hushed up everything about the windowless room. I knew what to do with MI5 or 6 – I couldn't distinguish between the two once I returned to England. But what about Afghanistan, the ocean of troubles? What if the next blast wiped me out, or the NDS arrested me? If you got blown away by chance to an Afghan prison, Shujah often said, it'd take six months before they gave you a pen and paper to jot down your details. Worse, what if kidnappers...?

Shouts of blue-uniformed men and women like ants scattering from pick-ups and ordering us, the uninjured, to shift to the far corner until further notice, adding to keep a vigilant eye open for signs of a second attack.

I leaned against a concrete wall as events in the aftermath of the bomb attack unfolded. Men in white overalls picked up the dead bodies and the injured, removed the bodyparts and placed them in ambulances. Men in orange overalls swept together the shards of the broken windows and car parts and washed the streets, including our bloodstained, eight-wheel spinner suitcase.

Voices of the police shouted, 'All's normal'. Indeed, normal life continued after a 70-minute wait, as though nothing had just happened, when we drove through the blast-site where a *fedayi*, a suicide bomber, had slammed his vehicle into the entrance. New faces in blue uniforms searched the incoming vehicles; without the German Shepherd, though – unlike indigenous lives, foreign lives, human or otherwise, had real blood flowing in them, and the loss was investigated before a replacement was provided. But life would never be normal for those families who just lost their loved ones. My heart ached for them. We continued to die in wars that were never ours. I didn't know when Khudai would have mercy on this land.

Mour thanked Khudai for having saved us all once Shujah drove his 1980s Russian Volga out of the airport, drifting amidst the strong wind blowing against us, at times making the air so thick with dust that we almost lost sight of the slow-moving vehicle in front.

'Imagine it never happened: don't think or talk about it. Otherwise, it'll drive you crazy,' Shujah said to Mour.

'Best approach. Life must carry on,' I said, finding myself sighing.

'And don't use up all of your prayers. You'll need them,' Shujah went on, looking at Mour in the rear-view mirror.

'I told Ahmad we'll find a suitable wife in England. But he won't listen,' Mour said.

'Now you're here, I've got to tell you the truth. I didn't want you to come either,' Shujah said.

Mour reiterated that she knew and told me so. '"Don't let fear define you", he'd say,' Mour added in a deep voice, pointing at me.

Shujah sighed. 'Kabul's turned into a valley of the wolves.'

'What Khudai wills happen, Inshallah, he'll keep us safe,' I said. My heart had dropped to my stomach, and my legs trembled. I'd experienced these symptoms at the start of year nine in school, and in Moscow, days before we set out for England. Would something horrible strike again? Mour wouldn't be able to take it this time... *Damn Satan. Khudai, I put my trust in You; may You look after us and take us in one piece back to England. Save us from all the evil of fedayi bombings, windowless rooms and kidnappings; please accept our prayers and help us find an honourable bride from a decent family.*

Chapter Twenty-Seven

The unpredictable life of the airport gave way to the safety of Shujah's home and his family: Nazigul, her 13-year-old, and four-year-old daughters and the six-year-old twin sons.

After freshening up and exchanging news about the fedayi bomber, and after I implored Mour, Nazigul and Shujah to stop discussing the horrifying experience, Nazigul – a few inches taller and much slimmer than her husband, and in a calf-length brown dress with white trousers – led us to the lounge, furnished with machine-made red and beige Turkish kilims.

You'd say Nazigul washed, ironed, polished and repolished every launderable item in the room. The brown mattresses around the walls and brown pillows for backrests shone. The brown curtains blocked out the sun and gave the impression that a giant floor lamp stood up behind the curtains. The walls looked as white as the snow of Salang. A vanilla scent and rotating fan added a sense of freshness to the room. The corners of Mour's mouth stretched towards her cheeks, I thought, at seeing her apartment having been kept in good order. Inshallah, from now on, a smile would replace Mour's constant headaches.

Shujah answered his mobile. His forehead wrinkled, and he left.

Nazigul and Amina brought in one type of food after the other – *sabzi challaw* or spinach palaw, *kofta* kebab or chopped meat kebab, *mantu* or meat-filled dumplings, yoghurt, salad, Coke, lemon juice, melon cut in slices like crescents and *Hussaini* grapes – and spread them out over a tablecloth on the floor. The steaming quabili palaw smell took over the room.

'How can you afford such riches?' Mour said, pointing to the food. Shujah taught my once-favourite subject, History, in a high school for a monthly salary of £80 and worked as a taxi driver in his free time, yet struggled to cope with rising inflation.

'It's nothing. You've travelled over from London,' Nazigul said, sitting next to Amina in the left corner near the door.

'I'll decide the menus going forward from now on,' Mour said.

Mour's announcement relieved me because, according to melmastia, Shujah and Nazigul would borrow, or worse, see their children go to bed hungry, but ensure that Mour and I received such delicious food.

Shujah entered, and the twins sprinted to him. 'Excited your tror has come?' Shujah, who'd changed into a black perahan tunban, asked his twins about Mour. The twins jumped up and down and hugged Shujah. Like him and Amina, they were short in stature with shaved heads.

As I put the first mouthful of rice, raisins and sliced carrots and sipped my lemon juice, the twins sat cross-legged near their mother, staring at their father. Shujah, Nazigul and the twins had already eaten; they motioned for us to carry on.

'I'm hungry,' one of the twins said, pulling at Nazigul's white silk headscarf.

'Shut your face,' Amina said, glaring at her brother. She was old enough to know that the guests ate the most supreme portions of food in Afghan culture.

Mour and I insisted on them joining us. The twins didn't need to be asked twice after Shujah nodded, but Amina kept shaking her head. Using their bare hands, the twins ate like they'd never tasted quabili palaw before, especially raisins and carrots. Every time we asked if

217

they wanted more food, they nodded, pointing towards their plates – and cups: they drank Coke like water.

'We've finished,' they finally said in unison, dusting the crumbs off their laps.

Nazigul told them to wash their hands and dry their Coke-stained perahans. They exchanged looks, did a succession of backward rolls across the floor and exited the door next to the muted 32-inch flat-screen TV stuck to the wall.

My eyes caught the words *Sitara*-e-Afghan. Three men and a woman with a bare head and a traditional Afghan chapan of black, red and green, sat behind a large desk while a teenage jelai with a microphone sang. Amina confirmed it to be Afghanistan's equivalent of *Pop Idol*. She told an amazed Mour and me, as we chewed on grapes and melon slices, how Afghans now watched nearly 100 Afghan channels which aired their versions of famous Western programmes; not to mention the hundreds of international stations through satellite. In the 1990s Afghanistan broadcast only one TV channel. I recalled neighbours queuing to use our home telephone: now '20 million' Afghans owned mobile phones. Afghanistan wasn't what I'd envisioned: an old acquaintance that I'd left in a crippled state.

***

NAZIGUL BROUGHT IN TWO thermos flasks of green tea with three glass trays of sugar-coated almonds and chocolates, and placed the trays before me, Mour and Shujah. Amina entered with three more trays, passing the one full of cups to Nazigul, and putting the other two in front of Mour and me. She left.

'Your watan's dried fruits,' Shujah said to me, nodding at Amina's tray (divided into six), holding almonds, walnuts, pistachios, dried blackberries, green raisins and fried peas. Tea and dried fruits signified teatime – a time for discussion. And for once, it wouldn't ensue around politics, but rather around a business which pulled Mour and me to our watan.

Sitting cross-legged at the top end of the room on a mattress and with the fan blowing air against her face, Mour asked when we'd meet the jelais and their families. Shujah and I sat diagonal to Mour's right and left on mattresses alongside the wall, leaning against cushions. It looked like Mour chairing a meeting.

'Tomorrow,' Nazigul said. She poured tea into one of the cups and placed it before Mour.

'The sooner, the better,' Mour said. Steam came out of the cup and made its way towards the closed curtains.

I conveyed my gratitude to Nazigul for searching to find me the necessary stone and mortar to construct my home: a decent wife, healthy children in time and, inshallah, an increased sense of purpose to Mour's and my lives.

'It's no trouble whatsoever for a nephew. Inshallah, your wife will soon be here sipping tea with us,' Nazigul said, blushing. She put a cup of tea before me.

I said manana and drew in the cardamom flavour.

Nazigul filled a black cup and placed it in front of Shujah. 'By the way, Nazia turns out not to have finished her school.' Nazigul gazed at the ground, her face blushing.

'I thought they had all finished their education.' I confirmed the facts Nazigul had told us. Over the years, Mour and I Skyped Nazigul, sometimes Shujah, in our pursuit of finding me a suitable jelai in Kabul. Nazigul and Shujah did the background checks. Impropriety, bad reputation and incomplete education were red signs in a khastegari: the latter delayed the wedding for years.

'May Khudai strike me blind for having believed her mother,' Nazigul said, blushing again. 'The mother lied because she didn't want to lose us. The jelai's willing to abandon her studies should she get engaged to Ahmad jan.'

'Good. A woman can't be both a wife and a student.' Mour ate a sugar-coated almond and sipped her tea. 'Education isn't important for a woman, anyway.'

'With due respect, education is empowerment.' I wouldn't let Nazia drop out; I'd wait until she finished her education. Years back, I learned my lesson from Frishta and made a pledge. National honour compelled you never to break a promise.

'Both you and I aren't educated. Have we both not been suitable wives?' Mour said to Nazigul, who glanced at Shujah. 'And suitable mothers? Haven't I succeeded in giving you an outstanding upbringing?'

'You *are* educated, Mour,' I said.

'Why do you insist on education? I fear you might even send her to work?' Shujah said.

'What's wrong with a woman working?' I said.

'Women are created to be home ministers.'

'They can be foreign ministers, too, under the right circumstances.'

'Would you allow your wife to be a Naghma?'

'You jump from one extreme to another, aka Shujah. Teaching's what I have in mind.'

'I'm surprised, given your Islamic views.'

'Islam doesn't prevent women from working, provided certain conditions are met.'

'Those won't be met unless the Taliban take over England,' Mour said.

'They already exist in Islamic schools in London and Birmingham,' I said.

'Well, for us Pashtuns, husbands living on wives' salaries are considered... "brave".'

'I've already told him,' Mour said to Shujah.

I forced a smile. 'Is imprisoning them courageous?'

'Whichever jelai you choose will inshallah become your daughter-in-law. They're all willing to marry Ahmad jan,' Nazigul chipped in, her face blushing.

'They don't want to marry him, really. All they want is a ticket to England,' Shujah said with a wink in my direction, his right hand counting prayer beads. 'Who in their right mind would want to marry Ahmad?'

'Correct,' I said and took a mouthful of almonds and green raisins.

Everyone laughed.

I sipped my tea.

'Appearance isn't important for a halek. Education, skills and decency matter, and mashallah Ahmad jan has all of them.' Nazigul sounded like my defence lawyer.

'So you are confirming he's ugly.'

Everyone broke into laughter again, apart from Nazigul. She blushed, swearing on Khudai that she didn't mean the connotation Shujah ascribed to her sentence.

I got some walnuts and dried blackberries. Chewed on them. Thanked Khudai for the arrival of the moment I'd prayed for for years.

'Visit first those who've finished school,' Mour said to Nazigul.

'Latifa.'

'The Tajik one?'

'No, it's Humaira,' Nazigul said.

'Mour, respectfully, Tajik, Pashtun, Hazara: they're all Afghan.'

'Mour's insistence makes sense.'

'Why's a Pashtun better than a Tajik, aka Shujah?'

'Hawks fly with hawks, not with crows.'

'Latifa's Pashtun,' Nazigul chipped in, glaring at Shujah.

'Those racist views have ruined nations,' I said.

'Ignore him, brother. He's been brainwashed.'

'So have our brainwashing stamp,' I added. 'Anyway, is Latifa confirmed?'

'Whoever you choose,' Mour said without looking at me.

'OK, it's Latifa... Thanks, Nazigul.'

Children screamed. Amina slammed open the door and poked her head through it to complain that the twins had misbehaved. Shujah shouted to keep it quiet. Asked Amina to shut the door and carry on babysitting. Sat upright, slipped the prayer beads into an inside pocket of his brown jacket, and asked for our attention. I sat up straight with my hands in my lap. Shujah closed his eyes and recited a verse from the Quran. After the verse's completion, we held our hands up before our faces and prayed to Khudai for forgiveness and blessing on Agha and my sisters.

Had we lived in Afghanistan when the tragedy took place, we'd have had *fateha* on the third day after the burial, where friends and relatives would've brought in foods. For the next 40 days, they'd gather in our home every Thursday evening, read the Quran, visit the graveside to pray for the souls of Agha and my sisters, and return home to a quabili palaw. On the fortieth day, we'd hold another *khatm*, read the entire Quran, where all friends and relatives would join us. Last, we'd have the first anniversary, where friends and relatives would drop in for a final memorial ceremony and perform a khatm.

But we knew no Afghans based in Durham or even Newcastle. Only a handful of Afghan families lived in England then, mostly in London. We kept in contact with no family even after Afghans began to pour into England post-1998, after they ascertained the Taliban didn't intend to bring King Zahir Shah out of exile, but pursued a radical agenda. Shujah's fateha was the first we received, and it was as soothing as the sound of the blowing fan.

'How did it happen?' Shujah asked, taking his prayer beads out of his jacket pocket.

'My sisters slipped off the boat between Slovakia and Hungary. Agha tried to save them, but they all drowned.'

Shujah shook his head and motioned to Nazigul to serve tea. 'No one to save them?'

'Like the Day of Reckoning, nobody cared about anyone except themselves,' I said.

Nazigul emptied my cup and filled it with fresh tea. I uttered manana.

'Did you tell the police?'

'Illegal asylum seekers have no existence. Plus, the smugglers broke your legs if you stepped outside.'

'The bastards themselves didn't help?'

'They chained me like a dog because I'd put their colleagues in danger.'

Shujah shook his head once more while Nazigul, who refilled Mour's cup, appealed to Khudai to blind the human traffickers and their family members.

I scarcely discussed personal matters. Not once mentioned anything to anybody about our journey to England. No idea why I opened up to Shujah. He called me 'son' at the airport and I saw Agha in him. Or guilt didn't trickle through me for overburdening him and Nazigul with the painful details of our past lives? Or perhaps I opened up because Shujah and Nazigul cared and let us grieve? Whatever the cause, it lifted a heavy weight from my chest.

'I remembered the day Agha and I spoke to the Afghan smuggler, Qadir, in Moscow,' I said to Shujah. '"$5000 per person. Leave the money in the firm next door and within two weeks you'll be in London," Qadir said. "Living next door to Princess Diana." He winked at Agha and laughed. "Don't forget to release the money once you reach London, though. A telephone call will suffice," Qadir went on.'

'May Khudai put in a grave his long ponytail,' Mour said.

'You know, aka Shujah, before we reached Hungary, we were sold like slaves four times between smugglers. They shoved 30 people into a stinking room where they pressurised us to defecate and urinate, all in one bucket. Feed us with just enough food and water to survive. Threw 15 in seat-less Audi A4s like sheep. Squeezed dozens into the back of lorries for hours without food or drink. You didn't know whether the lorries would end up in England or back in Ukraine or Turkey. Gave toddlers "sleep medication" to shut them up. Parents had no clue that their kids were intoxicated.'

Nazigul put her hands on her cheeks in shock, saying how the alcohol impurified the poor kids' blood.

'People died from heart attacks, strokes and suffocation because we weren't allowed to see a doctor.'

Nazigul prayed to Khudai to never show such a day to anyone.

'A family abandoned their grandmother in bitter snow because she couldn't keep up the pace.'

Nazigul asked for forgiveness, making another prayer to keep all Muslims from such an experience.

'The searing sun turned you round and round and dropped you dead.' Knowing it was disrespectful to sit with legs outstretched before the elders, I adjusted my position on the bumped-up mattress to unlock my knees and relieve the pain. 'After spending five months in Ukraine and Lithuania's prisons, Mour and I arrived in England. A "two-week" journey took 15 months.'

'Getting to Europe is like passing through the Seven Labours of Rustam,' Shujah said.

'Rustam at least made it in one piece to Sohrab,' Mour said.

'Agha and your sisters weren't the first ones to perish on the voyage, and won't be the last.'

'Europe's like heroin. Flies you in the sky as you discover it; pulls you under the ground once you live with it.'

'Still, we see it as the easiest solution to escape despair. There's no future for our kids here.' Shujah sipped his tea. Nazigul withdrew a container from his side pocket and sprayed the room with more vanilla scent.

'If only we found Agha and my sisters' bodies.'

'I'll have to go to my grave knowing we haven't fulfilled our obligations,' Mour said, rocking from side to side while the fan blew against her face.

Mour went on telling Shujah what she'd been telling me over the years, how Agha and her daughters never got the relatives to wash their bodies, sprinkle rose water on them, wrap them in a white cloth and transport them on a straw bed to a mosque where a mullah would recite their *Janazah* prayers, the prayers for the dead. They never had their friends and relatives gathered at the graveside intoning, *We come from Khudai, to Khudai we return*. In fact, no graves were dug for them. 'We let the fish eat their flesh...' Mour's voice broke.

Nazigul sat by Mour's feet, putting her hands on my mother's knees.

'Nazo wanted to be a doctor. Zarghuna loved journalism,' Mour said.

'That was their destiny. You could've done nothing to prevent their fate,' Shujah said. 'You have your son to be thankful for.'

'Thanks, Khudai, a hundred times over. He's a hard-working halek with no bad habits. Focuses on his studies. Hardly misses a prayer. Always respectful to his mother. He's a diamond,' Mour said.

'I'm aware,' Shujah said.

I didn't think I was as good as a 'diamond', but I did my best never to forget for a moment who I was, where I came from, what I believed in and why I did so.

'Pull open the curtains, Nazigul. We're all vitamin D-deficient in England,' Mour said.

The sun's rays came through the tree branches as Nazigul drew the curtains aside and opened the windows. The trees were filled with birds; their tweets sounded as calming as Ahmad Zahir.

Mour held out a £20 note to Nazigul to get Amina to exchange it and bring some watermelon for me. Nazigul took it after Mour insisted. I asked Mour if Shujah could keep the rest. Mour thanked me for reminding her, and asked Shujah to look after our money and passports. With relief, we handed the three bundles and our passports to Shujah.

'Can't you keep them yourselves?'

'Going out with so much money is an invitation to death, stupid woman,' Shujah said to Nazigul. Nazigul blushed, gazing at the kilim. 'With a pointy nose, ferret-like eyes and a long neck, she not only looks like an ostrich but also acts like one,' Shujah added.

Nazigul blushed again. I bet she'd have concealed her entire body if she could. She dashed out.

The unnecessary assault upset me, but telling an Afghan how to treat his woman equalled a declaration of war.

Shujah put the bundles in his pocket.

'Brother, haven't you heard? Count the money even if you find it on the street.'

Shujah yielded after Mour insisted and confirmed each bundle was £2,000.

'This is our life savings for Ahmad jan's wedding,' Mour said.

'Consider it locked in the safe of the Afghanistan Bank,' Shujah said, indicating to us to drink our teas.

I opened cow candy and put it in my mouth.

'Zoya, Mour's sacrificed plenty for you. You'd agree she's got more rights over your life than you do yourself,' Shujah said.

'Sorry.' Sipped my tea to swallow the melting candy stuck in my throat. 'The Quran and the Prophet, peace be upon him, emphasise that children show kindness, respect and obedience to parents,' I said.

'Especially the mother.'

'Woh.'

'You know why?'

'Mothers go through the problems of pregnancy, pain of delivery, sleepless nights of feeding, raising and educating,' I said, thinking who'd spend 36 years of her life in full service of another person? Only a precious mother made such a sacrifice.

Amina entered, followed by Nazigul with puffy eyes, the daughter holding a watermelon half her size. She placed it before Shujah.

'Listen to what your brother said about parents,' Shujah said to Amina. She ignored him. Sat against the wall, closed her eyes and took deep breaths.

Shujah looked at me and pointed at the door with his eyes.

***

I FOLLOWED SHUJAH INTO what was once my bedroom, furnished with red Afghan handmade rugs, red mattresses and pillows. He shut the door.

'What are you *really* here for?' he whispered, still smelling of strong aftershave.

'In Kabul?'

He nodded.

'You know it... the khastegari.'

'That's not what the NDS thinks.'

I was filled with trepidation. 'What does it think?'

'You're planning to travel to Miranshah to join the Taliban.'

'How do you know this?'

'The phone call before lunch... was from the NDS.'

I took a deep breath. A child outside counted numbers, and others shouted to hide.

'You shouldn't have come to my house. I have a wife and four kids to look after.' His chevron moustache and upper lip trembled.

'Aka Shujah, relax. I won't do such a thing to put your family in harm's way.'

His forehead wrinkled. 'These jihadists are good to no one. You saw it at the airport. They nearly killed us all. Don't get brainwashed by them.'

'The American puppets tell lies.'

'They're our lions, you know. Fucking true patriots. You live in peace in Europe owing to *their* sacrifices,' he said, drops of saliva landing on my neck.

'Let's agree to disagree.'

'Have you thought of your mother?'

'Aka Shujah... don't worry. I'm *not* what they suspect I am.' I pleaded with the half-convinced Shujah to keep it away from Mour. 'Let's have the watermelon.'

***

LYING ON MY MATTRESS with my head on a pillow, viewing the starry sky like blue water filled with white marbles, hearing neighbours' talk and laughs over Ustad Mohammad Hussain Sarahang calming ghazal, accompanied with harmonium and tabla in the distance, and feeling the Kabuli breeze wafting into the room through the open windows, I couldn't sleep. Saw Frishta everywhere in the room but didn't let her memories shatter my dreams, just as she'd want me to. Having not seen the jelai likewise occupied my thoughts as the imminence of the khastegari, as early as 'tomorrow', dawned on me.

Back in England, the eyebrows of my fellow student doctor, a psychiatrist, rose and his mouth dropped when he learned I'd marry a jelai I hadn't seen or known. I told him, inshallah, marrying a traditional jelai from Kabul would address his common diagnosis of consistent fights among partners: different reference points, blurring responsibilities, trust deficit and unwillingness to make a sacrifice because 'life's too short'.

He nodded and his mouth stretched. Behind the smile hid a question: where*'s mina in an arranged marriage?*

I trusted mina would develop, I told him, if I took his prescribed medications to fighting couples: mutual respect, care and appreciation.

He smiled and uttered an inshallah.

'Inshallah,' I heard myself mutter over Sarahang's *Oh Yaar*.

I knew my future wife would be leaving her entire family behind in Kabul. Her parents would be giving me a piece of their hearts, and I could envisage pleading in her father's eyes to look after his princess. I'd be there for her not only as a husband, but also as a best friend. I'd appreciate her. Listen to her concerns. According to the Prophet Muhammad, peace be upon him, the best of us were those who were good to their women. I'd show her as much respect as King Amanullah had given to Queen Soraya.

Would Latifa emerge to be my Queen Soraya? Ahmad and Latifa. The names sounded good together. Would she give me her hand tomorrow or say salaam from a distance? What would she talk about? How long would we have to spend together to get to know each other? I prayed I wasn't sleeping alone this time next year.

To hell with it: I let myself envisage next year and the years after... Open my eyes in the morning and it is Latifa I see first. She's the woman whom I kiss for the first time in my life. I come home, and she says salaam and kisses me on the cheeks. I return the gesture and hug her because Mour is upstairs. The three of us eat dinner together. Soon the number increases to five. I'm different from Agha. I give Latifa and my kids all the time and attention in the world. I drop my son and daughter at school and help them with their schoolwork. We go shopping for food and clothes on Saturdays. I take them to different cities in England on Sundays. Latifa hugs me and kisses me when I reveal I've just become a threshold consultant. She's proud of me. I say I can't wait for the day she completes her degree. We watch movies together. Cook together. Clean up together. Mour and my loving wife drink tea in the living room while her grandchildren sit in Mour's lap. Mour feeds them with walnuts and dried blackberries.

They call Mour 'Anay' – Grandma. I see a smile on Mour's face, as vast as the sky of Afghanistan.

Chapter Twenty-Eight

We parked Shujah's Volga at the bottom of a concrete road in Khair Khana. Under the blazing sun of mid-afternoon climbed up a hill you'd say had been drawn by a nursery student with fancy colours: the hill accommodated hundreds of detached and semi-detached houses: some mud and others concrete; some single-storeyed and others two- or three-storeyed; some with purple and others with blue-, brown- and yellow-coloured exteriors and doors.

We stopped three times for Mour to catch her breath and for me to wipe the beads of sweat from Mour's forehead before arriving outside a two-storeyed mud house with a three-foot-tall wooden gate. Nazigul, in a head-to-toe black hijab, knocked. Shujah and I positioned ourselves in the shadows, alongside the wall.

Would the tiny house turn out to be the one that accommodated my future wife? Would Latifa emerge as the loving wife destined to fill my empty home? Would...

'How on earth is she going to look after my son's house if she can't clean her own?' Mour said, pointing towards a cigarette box, a few empty cans and a banana skin lying around.

'Mour, hila kawom.'

Nazigul knocked again.

'Surely they must know we're here,' Mour said and leaned against the wall. Her face had turned pale.

'Perhaps they're taking their time ensuring the house is in good order,' Shujah said to Mour.

'They must learn from Nazigul,' Mour said. This morning, Mour called Nazigul a 'true Pashtun' for having good hygiene, and wished we found a jelai like her.

'Never go wrong with praising a woman,' Shujah said, gesturing with his head at Nazigul's beaming face.

'Anybody home?' Mour raised her voice. 'Knock harder, Nazigul. Or I'll die from the sewage stench.'

'Mour, hila kawom, keep it down.' Mour behaved like she'd grown up in Switzerland.

Nazigul's face flushed, asking for a few more minutes.

'Make you look like Grandpa,' Mour said, eyeing me up and down. She'd wanted everyone to put on their 'full khastegari gear'. She wore a black jacket, a grey, calf-length dress, loose white trousers, a long shawl draped elegantly around her head and shoulders, and high-heeled shoes. Instead of a tie and suit, I wore my navy trousers, russet shirt and light brown brogues.

'I'd put a padlock on the door of M&S if I had the power,' Mour said.

'What's M&S?' Shujah said.

'A store standing for quality over fashion,' I said.

'Afghans won't see you as modest; they assume you have no money to buy fashionable clothes,' Mour said.

'She'll see Ahmad as he is,' I said.

We heard footsteps from behind the closed gate, followed by the sound of a padlock being turned. Mour abandoned her leaning position and stood upright.

The gate parted to reveal the face of a 14- or 15-year-old jelai with a white headscarf and a black skirt. She said salaam, extending her head to steal a quick peek at me. She led us to the first floor and a square-shaped lounge almost twice the size of Shujah's Volga, and left us.

'Latifa would keep not only your home spotless, but also the household goods in new condition,' Shujah whispered to Mour.

Indeed, like the giant 1980s Russian TV set on the wooden table, the two-seater black leather couches must have lived through both the Russian and the American invasions. You'd assume the owner treated the room like a museum where you could look but not touch.

Mour wondered when Latifa would show up.

The door opened, revealing a woman in a black skirt and jacket with a grey and white shawl around her shoulders and a black silk headscarf over her grey hair. We all stood up. She performed the usual right, left, right touching of cheeks with Mour and Nazigul, while with the non-mahram men she covered her right hand with her shawl and shook our hands. The tired-face woman sat on the leather armchair next to the door.

The women exchanged the usual pleasantries, which revealed that she whom Nazigul called Qandigul was my future mother-in-law – provided we liked her daughter and the family approved of our family and me. The jelai who answered the door earlier was her youngest daughter.

'I take it he's your husband?' Qandigul pointed to Shujah in an old, faded suit with an open-necked, white shirt. 'I didn't recognise him.' She nodded at me.

'Mother-in-law will be your first patient. A high blood cholesterol level and high blood pressure,' Shujah whispered, smelling of the alcohol-based aftershave.

I looked at my hands. Pretended I heard nothing.

'Mour and Ahmad jan have come from London,' Nazigul said. She sat next to Mour on the opposite two-seater couch. Everyone acted as if they spoke about me for the first time.

The same young jelai from earlier opened the door, peeped in to glance at me and dashed off, shouting, 'I told you he's the halek.'

Qandigul's forehead wrinkled; she stood up and closed the door. 'What do you do in London?'

'Just finished university.'

'What did you study?'

'Medicine.'

'He's a doctor,' Mour chipped in, her eyes widening.

I wouldn't forget the day I broke to Mour the news of a place at Durham Medical School. The sense of accomplishment within me equalled King Amanullah's triumph over the British Empire. Mour planted a kiss on my head and I pecked her hands, grateful to Khudai for having given me Mour as a mother. Throughout that night she stayed up to perform nafl-prayers and read the Quran to thank Khudai for granting us one of her years-long wishes, while I watched *The Godfather Part One* for the third time.

'He's got a first-class degree. His thesis will be published in reputable medical journals.'

'The department has only predicted a First,' I said, dreading contradicting Mour and simultaneously wishing she didn't show off.

Qandigul nodded, her hand letting go of the door handle. 'You speak fluent Pashto. Nowadays, we need an interpreter for foreign Afghans.'

'I grew up in Kabul,' I said.

'Have you not found work yet?' Her intense gaze fixed on me.

'I haven't sought employment.'

'Why not?' Qandigul sat down.

'Because I was planning to travel to Kabul soon after my studies... I didn't want to start somewhere and have to ask for time off straight away,' I said and took a deep breath, nervous of the fact that I embroiled myself in my khastegari as much as America involved itself in Afghan affairs, and both violated traditional Afghan values; something Mour had recently been warning me against.

The marriage process in Kabul required months, if not years. It took weeks for the elders of the two families to get to know each other and to discuss and agree on things like a *walwar*, bride price, gold jewellery, expenses of numerous ceremonies and other necessities; which we hoped the family didn't ask for beyond our financial capacity. Once both families agreed on everything – an accord which at times proved as difficult as passing a UN resolution, since every paternal and maternal aka and tror had the power of veto – they'd fix a date for the *namzadi*, a small engagement party. It'd be at least another two weeks before we threw the shirini-khori. We'd wait for a month or so before the jelai's family agreed to hold the wadah, followed a week later by the *taqjami*, wrapping up.

Mour and I had set off for Kabul the day after I sat my final exam, hoping to complete everything within a month. I anticipated, though, that we'd end up extending our stay in Kabul far beyond.

'Plenty of jobs waiting for my son in England.' Mour was exaggerating again.

'I've got an unofficial job offer from a hospital,' I interfered. The hospital was in Newcastle, where last year I undertook my clinical training as a student doctor.

'Latifa jan would have a comfortable life in England,' Mour added.

I looked down at my hands.

'I thought they lived in London?' Qandigul said, her gaze turning from Mour to Nazigul, with a blank look on her face.

'London's England,' Mour said with stretched lips.

In our first months in England, Mour, too, referred to the UK as London, and the UK population as 'London people', so she should hardly have been surprised at Qandigul's lack of knowledge.

Qandigul deepened her eyes into Nazigul's, her forehead scrunching up.

'I didn't know they lived in a different country,' Nazigul said, her voice visibly trembling.

'London's the capital city of England, as Kabul is the capital of Afghanistan,' I said.

Qandigul raised her eyebrows. Mour nodded, and both colour and smile returned to Nazigul's face.

'We'll invite you to England if Latifa jan becomes my daughter-in-law – even pay for your tickets. It's a beautiful country worth visiting.'

I counted four black hardwood tables sitting against each other alongside the wall between the two windows.

'Where's Latifa jan?' Mour asked.

'It's not the done thing for the halek to see the jelai. Nazigul and you may meet her, but not the men,' Qandigul said.

'But Ahmad and Latifa are marrying each other, not us,' Mour said, her jaw dropped. 'Tell Latifa jan my son doesn't bite.'

I counted three squares in the Afghan rug.

'Maybe they do things that way in the West. Here we haven't forgotten our Pashtunwali,' Qandigul said.

Mour's face reddened. I didn't remember anyone accusing Mour of being non-traditional, especially of a lesser Pashtun.

A female voice outside cursed those tossing banana peels on the ground. I glanced through a chink in the white curtains with hand-embroidered flowers and noticed with a sinking heart a woman in a burka on the ground, her legs pointing to the sky. Qandigul must've overheard Mour's earlier comments because we sat in the room right above the main wooden gate, where, beside Shujah's strong aftershave, I smelled the sewage stench.

'My elder daughter saw her husband for the first time on the *aina mosaf*. It bestows purity.'

Qandigul wanted me to see Latifa no earlier than the *aina mosaf* when Latifa and I, as a bride and a groom veiled by a shawl, would 'open the mirror to see one another in it' and to read a few lines of the Quran.

Turning her accusing gaze to Nazigul, Qandigul continued. 'We can excuse their ignorance because they're "foreign Afghans", but you should've known better. How come you've brought the halek to my house? What would my husband say if he saw a non-mahram halek sitting in the lounge, waiting to see his daughter? You think we're no better than pimps.' Qandigul trembled.

Nazigul's initial spontaneous smile had vanished. Shujah covered his left hand with the right, as if in prayer. Did he breathe? Woh, he glared at Nazigul. Everyone sat there as though we'd just buried a loved one. A man in his late fifties with a beard and a grey and black turban from the photo on the television peered at me.

'The men must leave if you want to see my daughter,' Qandigul said after an awkward silence.

Shujah and I made our way out, his dark brown face turning darker and his small eyes disappearing into the face.

'She spoke of the Afghan culture and yet lacked melmastia,' Shujah said as we stepped away from the house.

I put my finger on my lips and pointed upwards.

'I bloody want her to hear.'

We stood before a mud wall a couple of houses away from Latifa's.

'Mour could've been more diplomatic.'

'I'd break your Qandigul's mouth if she was a man.'

'Aka Shujah, we're not a warlord.' The mujahideen ruined our watan because of the tendency to use violence instead of logic.

'You're a guest.'

'It doesn't mean we have to smash her face.'

Shujah wiped the sweat from his forehead with a handkerchief. 'If Qandigul is such a whore, how's her daughter meant to behave with such a role model? The second she arrives in England, she'll kick Mour out, you watch,' Shujah said about Latifa, whom I'd last night built a home with.

'Let's not sin by swearing at an honourable woman.'

'I can't for the life of me work out why they stayed to see the fatherless whore.'

'Mour has waited a long time for this day. She wouldn't miss out on the chance to see the first jelai,' I said. Did I speak for myself? Qandigul's insistence on tradition indicated the family's decency. Only an honourable woman behaved like this. Losing it upset me, so did Shujah's use of that particular swear word. Shujah excused himself into the secluded corner; his bladder was 'exploding'.

A piece of straw poked against my back as I squatted against the wall.

'Salaam alaikum, aka,' two barefoot haleks, each carrying a bucket of water in their hands, said in unison, and I acknowledged their salaam. They put down the buckets and took deep breaths. The climate had roughened their dust-covered faces. Unsurprisingly, they were oblivious of the burning sun, which had forced me to put my hands above my eyes.

Thud, thud, thud sound came from overhead as if someone was splashing mud against the dirt wall.

'Aka, *bullets*,' one of the haleks screamed. They dropped face-down. I followed suit. Shujah shouted from the other side, 'Come across.' Using the sports teacher's training from school, I pushed down on my chest like a snake and got to the haleks. Told them to get to the wall where we'd be invisible from the top of the hill, where the bullets came from.

'I think I've been fired at.'

'I heard the sounds,' Shujah said, pushing against his chest to get alongside the wall.

'Who wants to kill me?' My heart raced as fast as the bullets.

'Wrong time, wrong place.' He leaned against the wall.

'What does that mean?'

'You've been a victim of betting.'

'Bet on human lives?'

'Unfortunately. A punter's just lost a bet.'

'By missing me?'

'Woh.'

238

'Fuck, fuck, fuck.'

'Thanks, Khudai, you're safe.'

'Who are these crazy punters?'

'Thugs. Warlords. Militiamen. Their teenage sons.'

'My Khudai. Does the government really exist here?'

The haleks whispered that their mothers waited for water. They got up.

'Wait,' I told them.

'Don't, it's dangerous,' Shujah said.

'More so for them.' *I put my trust in You, Khudai. Please shield me from harm and bless me with Your protection.* I sprinted to the buckets with a racing heart, picked them up and dashed back. Told the haleks to walk alongside the wall. They plodded up the hill, chatting away as if nothing had happened.

The gates creaked open; Mour and Nazigul came out. I shouted that they should get to the other side of the road by the wall. Pleaded with Shujah not to tell Mour about me having been turned into a betting horse. If only he listened.

Chapter Twenty-Nine

It'd been half an hour since we'd departed from Qandigul's, and I'd heard nothing except discussions on the horror of the random bullets and yesterday's fedayi attack, coupled with Mour blaming me for having thrown ourselves into a 'burning fire' and Nazigul's gratefulness to Khudai that Shujah and I were safe and sound.

I asked Mour what she thought of Latifa.

'She laughs with a *qah-qah*. Qandigul's taught her no Pashtun manners,' Mour said after a short silence.

A Toyota pulled out of a side road in front of us, forcing Shujah to jam on the brakes with a screeching noise. Mour and Nazigul screamed for Khudai's help.

'Have you gone mad?' I shouted at the driver.

'Donkeymen have become drivers in Kabul.' Shujah didn't exaggerate.

On our way to Latifa's earlier on, vehicles carved, cut out, cut in, turned left from the right lane and right from the left lane, turned off a 'no entry' sign, and crossed red lights. Yet, no one raised an eyebrow as if it was the norm, not even the white-hat traffic policemen manning crossroads in the blazing heat.

We now drove smoothly. Nashenas sang at low volume from the cassette deck in Shujah's Volga, or what Nazigul called yesterday 'a portable carpet shop', because every interior part was covered with Afghan handmade carpet.

Allowed to study with haleks in the same class but disallowed to hold a five-minute talk, in the *presence* of her parents, with someone she'd be spending the rest of her life with, I said after a silence. 'Qandigul has taken tradition too far.'

'She'll have to keep the daughter forever if she isn't willing to show her to the halek,' Nazigul said from the rear seat.

Helicopters flew overhead as we drove past a green and white multistorey shopping mall on our left.

'Islam encourages haleks and jelais to meet each other under supervision before they get engaged.' It felt like I was talking to myself. I reckoned Mour saw me as the cause of today's humiliation.

'Do you see Chaman-e-Babrak anywhere?' Shujah asked. Chaman-e-Babrak was where my classmate, Shafih, and his father used to bring their 'champion' dog to the dog-fighting tournament.

I didn't.

'This is it.' Shujah pointed to four- or five-storey mansions and monstrous wedding halls lit with bright neon lights and mirrored glass, and surrounded by large concrete barriers. Armed men guarded them. Foreigners nicknamed this and the forty-metre street, which we drove on to Latifa's, 'Las Vegas'.

'How on earth can we reduce pollution in Kabul if all land planned to be green townships is grabbed?' Shujah dried his forehead with a handkerchief and stopped behind a line of cars, as long as the Soviet tanks going to Panjshir Valley to fight the mujahideen. The taxi driver from the front told us that the escort of a high-profile foreign 'donkey' to the Arg Palace had caused the traffic jam.

'Here parents don't put their daughters on display. They don't want them to get stigmatised if they're rejected. Other suitors may not come forward, thinking there was something wrong with the jelai. The rejection can even damage the jelai's self-respect,' Mour said. 'In language colleges or universities, Jelais don't chat with haleks to get chosen for wives. Students behave like brothers and sisters.'

A woman with a year-old sun-stricken-faced child begged for *khairat*, money. She pointed to the left, a makeshift camp made up of tents, saying they were war-displaced families from Helmand.

'They'll swarm if you give her money,' Shujah said when he detected my hands moving into my pocket. He swore at the 'fatherless' beggar. She disappeared.

'And here children listen to their parents. They don't contradict them publicly.' Mour got to the point.

Mour boiled; best to let her cool down.

Tilting herself to Mour's side and fanning Mour with her purse, like a farmer trying to please his Khan, Nazigul told Mour not to worry, since we'd choose from the remaining three jelais. Nazigul hoped their families would allow their daughters to speak to me when I asked her about the possibility.

'Confirm this before you take us next time,' Shujah snapped at Nazigul over the drivers' annoying showcase of their horns and a helicopter's thumping.

Nazigul blushed, swearing she'd notified Qandigul of my presence. Qandigul's sudden outburst had baffled Nazigul.

'Why are you so insistent on seeing the jelai? Look at all the trouble it's causing,' Mour said after the beeps had died down.

I took a tissue paper from the heated metal box on the carpet-covered dashboard, leaned to the left and wiped beads of sweat from Mour's forehead. The shawl and jacket were too much for the heat, but I knew Mour wouldn't remove them if I asked.

'Ahmad zoya, if you want a good wife, listen to your parents. We look at the overall beauty of the match. A young man, under the pressures of sexual desire, only judges exterior looks. What would you do if she was as beautiful as a *pari* but had a sharp tongue?' Shujah said, his face rotating from me to Mour and vice versa like a fan. He took off her jacket and passed it to Nazigul.

The Prophet Muhammad, peace be upon him, said parents made the best choice, I told Shujah. And the inner beauty indeed mattered,

242

more so in my case because England practised a different way of life, of which Mour and especially Shujah had limited knowledge. Nowadays, couples didn't think twice before they moved on. 'It's therefore important I get to know the jelai,' I went on.

'That's only possible if she's your colleague or classmate. You won't get to know her in a short meeting.'

'We can still learn about each other.'

'What is it you want to learn about?'

Personality, beliefs, outlook on marriage and children; what we expected of each other as a husband and wife, and if we could fulfil each other's requirements; what we liked and disliked and, importantly, whether we got on. 'The same values make up the backbone for a stable marriage,' I added.

'I'm aware you want a woman who possesses the highest moral values and the least argumentative personality. We'll make sure–' A deafening horn like a train beep from behind cut off Shujah.

'Move the fucking car away,' a gunman with long hair said and banged his Kalashnikov against the bonnet of Shujah's white and yellow taxi.

'Why do you jump off the queue?' I stuck my head out and said.

'Don't argue with them,' Shujah shouted and switched off Nashenas.

A hand slapped against my face. Mour and Nazigul screamed.

'Come out, a Kabuli coward.' One of them pulled me by the collar.

Mour poked her head out and begged for forgiveness.

'For that mother's sake, or else we'd show you the queue.' He let go of my collar.

Shujah drove to the side to let the pick-up pass, followed by two jeeps with tinted windows, and another pick-up full of armed men in brown and green camouflage uniforms.

'Have you lost your mind?' Mour said.

'Six million Kabulis can't stand up to 60 warlords?' I said, my left cheek tingling and heart beating fast. The bizarreness of the khastegari, yesterday's cold-blooded massacre, the random bullets, Mour's behaviour and the militiamen's abuse of power had tightened the muscles around the walls of my airways.

'They can hang you from that electricity pole, and no one will ask why. This isn't your Racial Equality Centre,' Mour said.

'Focus on what you've come for, don't create us extra trouble,' Shujah said, sounding like Agha.

'He doesn't. We're happy to have them,' Nazigul said.

'What do you know, stupid woman?' Shujah snapped at Nazigul.

The armed men waved their hands. The vehicles in the front gave way. The carts parked on both sides and pavements, carrying watermelons, apples, grapes, bananas and cherries, likewise obeyed. Pedestrians, who strolled in opposite directions on the pavements and in between the vehicles, cleared off as though the armed men possessed venom.

'Americans have tasked those wolves to defend our human rights,' Shujah said, pointing to the jeeps, which drove over a curb and decelerated on the one-way road along with the tents, the militiamen jumping in.

'They're leeches who sucked the blood of Afghanistan,' Mour said.

'No surprise, young haleks join the Taliban to take revenge,' I said.

'The country had optimism and hope when America overthrew the Taliban regime, but look now,' Shujah said, sighing. 'Khudai knows what'll happen after America withdraws?'

'They won't leave,' Mour said.

'At least it isn't as windy and dusty as yesterday,' I said. We'd never get the chance to discuss the real subject if Mour joined the political discussion.

'What does America *really* want in Afghanistan?' Shujah's gaze shifted to me, eager to know my thoughts.

'I stay away from politics as I do from the guns and bombs of the mujahideen.'

'Good decision.' Nazigul complimented me.

Except for Nadir's doctoral thesis on America's Afghanistan War, which a month ago, at his pleading, I read and reread to check for grammatical errors, I hadn't read a single piece of paper or watched the news on the history or politics of my watan for the past 21 years. Part of me wanted to quote Nadir's thesis in reply to Shujah's earlier question but I abstained; a small comment led to more comments and turned into a heated debate.

'You mustn't lose interest in your watan,' Shujah said.

'My watan gave me everything with one hand and took away with the other,' I said and mopped away beads of sweat from my face with a tissue. I'd never forget the rainy day we abandoned Makroryan; my sisters' pleas for help; and Mour's words, Frishta's *flesh spattered across the walls*.

'They all tell lies,' Nazigul said.

'Chup, what do women know about politics?' Shujah said.

'Afghanistan would've been Switzerland if women had been in charge of political affairs. They're intelligent, compassionate and, importantly, honest. We men have fucked up our watan,' I said.

'Mind your language. What's happened to you today?' Mour said.

Shutting up anyone's mouth insulted me. Really, Nazigul was spot on: one party used Islam as a pretext and the other democracy to achieve their ulterior objectives.

'We need another Abdur Rahman Khan in this watan,' Shujah said after a silence. 'You know who he is?'

King Abdur Rahman Khan took power in 1893 and made towers from the strongmen's skulls until he established an efficient central government, I told him. 'I know the history of my watan.'

'Good.'

'We've been discussing how to see the jelai, aka Shujah,' I said, being desperate to return to the main topic, the one he wanted me to 'focus on'.

'Let Mour choose. My parents chose Nazigul, and I'm a happy man,' Shujah said.

'His father and I didn't "get to know" each other before marriage – weren't we happy together?' Mour said, pushing her shawl forward a little.

'You knew Agha from childhood,' I said. 'The problem is parents don't show us the jelai; let's discuss it and find a solution.'

'I've grown tired of his analysis-solution nonsense,' Mour said.

'Nazigul's already made sure they're tall and slim,' Shujah said.

'The appearance doesn't bother me.' I remembered Nazigul insisting she wouldn't hang up if I didn't say what the jelai should look like. 'Tall and slim' formed my reply. Shujah supposedly had this in mind, falsely assuming my insistence was about looks. Moderate physical attractiveness was more than I had hoped for, and actually deserved, given my age and looks. After all, I no longer had the freshness of a *zwan*, a young halek; my hair was thinning. Personality was what mattered to me. When Nazigul described Kubra and Humaira as 'chaste and honourable' a few months ago, I insisted on Mour and Nazigul easing their unfair beauty-judging criteria. I also insisted Humaira's Tajik background should form no obstacle.

The taxi from the front switched on the engine and revved. Black exhaust smoke entered our vehicle. I placed a tissue over my nose; rather breathe the black exhaust than close the window of the overheated interior.

'I can't understand why men today are after tall, zero-size women with large lips like sausages,' Mour said, rolling up her window. 'They're shallow. A beautiful woman must have a small mouth and tiny lips. It's a bonus if she has a round body. Such women are fit enough to do the household chores and produce healthy children.'

Mour lectured on one of her several chief topics, which filled our over-dinner conversations in previous years.

Topic one: how not to blame Islam but Muslims, especially the mujahideen, for using religion for their vested interests.

Topic two: how America turned Muslim politicians into puppets who cared less about their people, and more about staying in power.

Topic three: US motives in Afghanistan. Mour and Nadir's heated debate over US goals back in Durham never ended. US national security required not only a peaceful Afghanistan, but also a peaceful world, Nadir would say and then sip his tea. For Mour, Nadir knew 'nothing' about politics since all these were 'excuses'. 'If America decides, Afghanistan would be peaceful like that.' Mour would snap her thumb and middle finger. 'America has other ulterior motives. So she's given the power to traitors. It's called divide and rule.' Mour never moved an inch on her views, and when the talks didn't go Mour's way, she'd ask to 'change the page', but minutes later she'd mention the same subject again.

Topic four: the importance of keeping one's culture and religion. She praised the Pashtun, especially the 'brave Taliban', for having stuck to 'Pashtunwali'. For Mour, the Pashtun made up the majority in Afghanistan and had ruled the country since its birth. 'No one will ever be able to govern Afghanistan except the Pashtuns, the true Afghans.' If only Mour knew.

Topic five: freedom eroded respect and led to corruption. Less respect for the police, less respect for the teachers, and, most frighteningly, less respect for parents, she'd say. It all boiled down to discipline, but neither parents nor teachers could discipline because this or that right was violated.

Topic six: how Afghanistan's neighbours received Afghan migrants. 'Iran, Pakistan and Russia treated us worse than we treat our dogs in Afghanistan. The British made us their equals. Never forget this, zoya.'

Topic seven: how parents, in my case, Mour, *knew* how best to make the right 'bride choice', in terms of both beauty and decency.

At the end of each topic, she forged a personal connection. 'Agha would've been over the moon if he saw his daughter-in-law and grandchildren,' she'd say after the lecture on my wife. 'Agha never touched a penny but look at the thieves in the Karzai Government,' she'd add after the lecture over pervasive corruption in the Afghan Administration. 'Nazo would've been 31 this year if the mujahideen hadn't let us down.' Every year since the deaths of my sisters, Mour unfailingly mentioned how old Nazo and Zarghuna would've been; what careers my sisters would have had; what they'd have looked like; whether they'd have been married; if so, whether they'd have had children; and that if only we hadn't left for the West, everyone would have been alive...

I reasoned it must have been Khudai's will; Mour mustn't let the past take over her future; grieving could neither change the past nor solve future problems. She would nod but the following day mention my sisters and Agha again. I diagnosed listening as her prescription: telling her story over and over lessened Mour's grief. I heard everything she said, comforted her, switched on the Jadoo box and searched for Afghan comedians such as Asif Jalali or Zalmai Araa. Their nostalgic jokes on the good old days in Kabul and the difficulties foreign Afghans faced in the West, as well as their political satires, relaxed Mour. Sometimes she even smiled. Her smile turned my day into Eid.

I'd tell lies if I claimed dealing with Mour was always as exciting as Eids. Listening to her repetitive advice equalled reading a maths book over and over again. Her populist views subjected me to waterboarding. Other races in Afghanistan were as great as Pashtun, and like any other Afghan, had every right to govern their watan, I'd say. Never convinced her. Her repetition of the same topics sent me into a deep hole with little oxygen. Her being wrong on facts subjugated me to prolonged hooding – many Pashtuns had adopted Western values for better or worse.

The life cycle had turned Mour into a child and me into a parent. Mour's inability to speak English and the introduction of new technology made many things alien to her and left her no one to talk with, except me. Two mini-strokes in the past few years had worsened things. I drove to Newcastle bus station twice last year to pick up Mour, who'd mistaken the Newcastle bus for Durham. A two-hour cleaning job at college now took three hours. The constant blood pressure reading warned of the inevitability of the third stroke, and I feared that one would take her away from me.

I hardly created a situation that stressed Mour or triggered her anxiety, especially when I knew it was impossible to alter her ingrained views, and, importantly, when most of the time they didn't interfere with the way I lived – the exception period was the last few months before our trip to Afghanistan. If mothers were patient with children, I often reasoned with myself, why should it not be the other way around? I'd never forgive myself if my disobedience caused another stroke. The Afghan way of life would shun a weak son. Khudai wouldn't forgive me. The Quran warned children not to say so much as an 'uff' to parents. So every day was a struggle not to show even a slight expression of irritation or disapproval.

The traffic began to move.

'I'll tell you why he wants to meet the jelai,' Mour said to Shujah. She looked at me with an accusing expression.

To my relief, Shujah, whose underarms and belly in the white shirt were drenched in sweat, turned the engine. The sun had turned the Volga into a sauna. You'd say the carpet-covered seat I sat on produced heat. The sweat smell had now dominated Shujah's aftershave and my Giorgio Armani.

'He's going to prove what an honest person he is. He'll disclose how he was in mina with a whore.'

'Relationships must start out with nothing hidden between the couple,' I said.

'If the jelai's parents find out about your shameful past, they'd kick you out of their house. This is Afghanistan,' Mour said.

'Mour, with due respect, I want to get to know the person I'll have for my wife.'

'We meet her – is that not enough?' she said, her pitch rising.

'No, it is *not*. And I won't be forced into marrying a jelai I haven't met.' Mour calling Frishta a whore angered me.

'In my youth, children didn't dare to speak back to their parents,' Mour said, her body muscles tensing. I hit her with a mujahideen rocket if I talked back. It was then that her emotions took over her senses. It was then that I disturbed her nest, and she'd launch an attack. Damn Satan, I knew Mour couldn't force it on me: why did I snap?

'Mour, I didn't mean to back talk. I–'

'What am I supposed to do with him? He'll be your age before too long and he isn't even married,' Mour complained to Shujah, who then answered his Samsung mobile.

I hoped he spoke long, so that Mour cooled down. A delicious smell of melon wafted in from the pavement carts as we drove ten miles per hour on Kolola Pushta Road.

'I know men who've been intimate with half of the world's women, but their wives don't know. You can surely hide having a girlfriend decades back?' Shujah said after he hung up.

Did his eyes reflect disappointment that a son, as good as a diamond, not only spoke back to the parent, but also had committed an immoral act? If he did, he was wrong; I told him I never had a girlfriend.

'He was melancholic for years like Romeo in mina with Juliet. Didn't mourn as much for his sisters' deaths as he did for the death of a whore named Frishta.'

'Please keep the dead out of this.'

'She was a mad dog who bit everyone, *including* him. Thanks, Khudai, they murdered her.'

'Mour, bringing up the past to hurt me solves none of our problems.' Next she'd mention the school incident.

'For years, I had to endure his longing. Now he wants to see the jelai in person so that he can ruin the entire khastegari. His stubbornness will put me in an early grave.' She slapped the back of Shujah's seat, kicking up dust.

Shujah pleaded for patience.

'Other parents' sons his age have children. He doesn't even have a wife. Is that not shameful?' Mour said. 'Parents don't show their daughters to him. He won't marry unless he has an MOT check on them. How will that work out?'

'There *are* other ways Ahmad jan can see the jelai.'

'Don't give me false comfort, Nazigul,' Mour said.

Shujah glared at his wife in the rear-view mirror.

'Once you liked the jelai and the family, it can be arranged for Ahmad jan to see her.'

'How?' I said.

We waited until an oncoming Carina drove past, a qataghani song blaring out.

'When she's on her way out to school or a language course, ask her a question... about an address, or the time. Then talk to her.'

'See, Mour, inshallah, problem solved,' I said with some relief. If necessary, I added, we'd extend our stay until we found the right jelai.

A halek jumped and shot the ball over the volleyball net but missed and it banged against Shujah's Volga. The halek dashed off and passed from sight behind a beauty parlour with a massive photo of Angelina Jolie. Shujah shook his head but, thankfully, uttered no foul words.

Mour contemplated. Perhaps she found the new strategy effective, and it turned the talk towards visiting the second jelai, the student, Nazia. Shujah cursed and pulled over behind another queue of stationary cars half a mile away from Kabul city centre in Shahr-e Naw. A currency exchanger with a bundle of Afghan and US notes in his hands pulled down his mask and shouted 'Dollars', 'Afghanis', 'Telephone cards'. Above him, a woman washed clothes on the balcony of a white block of flats.

'Ahmad Zahir lived here. Right?' I asked.

Hands like shovels hit against my cheeks and pulled my head out of the window, holding it an inch away from a penetrating gaze. He growled like a mad wolf, his bushy eyebrows moving upward and droplets of spit landing on my face. 'Al-Qaeda, I'm watching you.'

I let out a scream.

Shujah pulled me in. The hands let go as Mour and Nazigul shrieked. He dashed off into the crowd of pedestrians and carts.

'He's gone crazy,' I said and dried the saliva from my face.

'What did he say?' Mour asked.

'Nothing. He's mental,' I said. My heart beat hard against my chest, and my legs and hands trembled, ashamed of screaming like a baby.

Shujah's face was as pale as his shirt. He caught the word 'Al-Qaeda' and wanted to ascertain why the man mentioned it.

'Perhaps he referred to my beard.'

'You must go back to England.'

'I'm going nowhere until I get married.'

'I'm a mere teacher. I can't save you if they throw you in prison.'

'We have Khudai, aka Shujah.'

Shujah stared into my eyes and shook his head. The Afghan rug steering wheel cover had come off in his hands.

'I've grown tired of telling him to shorten the beard,' Mour said.

'Mour, not everyone with a beard is Al-Qaeda.'

'See?' Mour said to Shujah.

'Don't fear the King if you aren't a thief,' Nazigul said.

'Well said, Nazigul.' Except I was afraid. My hair stood on end when I recognised the broad-shouldered man in rugged clothes and with artificial hair. Mour would suffer the third stroke if they locked me up. *Khudai, please protect us. Take us back in one piece to England. Help me get married before, though. Importantly, please, please... help me avoid playing a coward again.*

***

THE PISTACHIO SHIRYAKH and kebab smell brought me back from the fearful world of the broad-shouldered man to the Shahr-e Naw Park, the New City, the only place in Kabul with such a mixed scent, as we queued behind slow-moving traffic. Mir Maftoon sang with much banging and scratching music out of half a metre-long loudspeakers at a restaurant. Beneath them, white-aproned waiters prepared shiryakh, grilled sikh kebabs, juiced carrots, pomegranates and mangos. Young men and women, standing hand in hand, enjoyed the taste of mango juice and shiryakh, while young children washed their Corollas or Mitsubishis on the other side of the road in shadows of the trees of the Shahr-e Naw Park.

A woman in a burka, holding a teenage jelai in school uniform, stood behind my window, pleading for someone to help her for Khudai's sake; her children starved, forcing her 17-year-old daughter to drop out of the final school year and join her.

Shujah told them off.

What if Nazia is 17? The thought crossed my mind. Jelais and haleks generally started school at seven in Afghanistan, so seven plus 12 school years made Nazia 19. I shared my concern with Nazigul.

Nazigul replied not to go by the school, explaining that the gap in education between the Taliban's closure of jelais' schools and the opening of school after the American intervention, and then the late start by some students made it difficult to find the correct age of a jelai.

'It'll still make her 24,' I said, assuming Nazia joined the year she'd left off after the five-year-old Taliban regime.

'You want to marry a grandma?' Mour said.

I sensed more disappointment than anger in her voice.

'My father used to say that a woman's ready to be a wife if she doesn't fall when you hit her with a hat,' Mour said with such conviction, as if Grandpa's words were a binding law. She carried on explaining one of her topics, that women aged quicker than men, so the jelai needed to be a few years younger. She warned me to stop messing around as I was getting on, and, given a few more years, nobody would give their daughter to me.

'You know my health is deteriorating. If I were to die, there'd be no one to do the khastegari. Please let me die in peace.'

'You'll live long, inshallah. We're making the Hajj pilgrimage next year.'

'You see, our worries are out of care, not control,' Shujah said.

'They shouldn't push me to the extent that you forget it's me getting married.'

Mour went onto another topic of hers, that she interfered in the khastegari to ensure I didn't end up marrying a jelai who had a long tongue and spoke back to her husband; who refused to 'make me a cup of tea' or cook dinner when I came home from work. Worse, the jelai might say no to getting pregnant as it'd 'ruin her body'. There'd be constant arguments between 'my son and her', and she'd eventually divorce me. Such a stigmatic act would bring shame on our family and make it a source of gossip among friends and relatives. The family played an important part, Mour said, jumping onto another topic. A jelai from a decent family thought thrice before committing an unvirtuous act – the jelai thought of her parents, me and her tribe. Jelais with no family lines resembled wild creatures. They cared less about their reputation, let alone others. Didn't appreciate the importance of obro and ezat. A simple telling-off about a trivial matter was good enough to ask for a divorce, Mour concluded.

The importance of family wasn't part of our discussion. Normally, the main topic got lost or barely discussed because Mour tended to go on and on with her lectures, jumping from one subject to another and another. Sometimes she got lost herself and asked what it was we discussed. By then, I was already in the oxygenless hole. This was another reason I avoided arguments with Mour.

I told Mour that I knew she put her heart and soul into finding someone like herself. But those people had gone. The world had changed. We were in the 21st century. We must ensure, I added, that the jelai's parents didn't force her into marriage, just because the proposal came from 'London'. The jelai had the right to get to know the person with whom she intended to spend her entire life. I could've told her: Mour, I got married, not you. It's none of your business. Hurting Mour's feelings wasn't the right answer; it was the laziest solution. In fact, defiance never worked as a strategy to iron out differences with Mour – lately, though, frustration had forced me to forget this hard-learned fact. The remedy lay in addressing her fears and providing her with reasons.

'Be careful, though, zoya,' Nazigul said. The *ta-ta-ta-ta* sound of ISAF helicopters vibrated Shujah's Volga as we approached Kabul Bank manned by armed guards near Shahr-e Naw Market. Nazigul wouldn't read too much into what the jelai or parents claimed, she added. Most weren't willing to make their daughters older than 18, even though she could be 25. $20 got you a birth certificate showing a date of birth of your choice. Nazia was at least in her mid-twenties, and it would be proven to me once I saw her for myself. Nazigul, however, suggested that she and Mour went alone to visit the family tomorrow afternoon, and once Mour saw her and the family, they'd arrange a way for me to see the jelai.

Looking for my future wife had turned Nazigul into a khastegari expert.

'Don't tell me our Kabul is less advanced than your London,' Shujah said, pointing to the Shahr-e Naw Market brimming with stores selling Western jeans and skirts, white and green Afghan wedding dresses, Turkish men's suits, 60-inch flat-screen TVs, iPhones and iPads.

I smelled kulcha. 'Is the Kulcha-e-Azizi still open?'

'Inshallah, soon we'd be queuing here for your *eidi* and *nowruzi*,' Nazigul said.

At Nowruzes, Eids and Barats, the fiancée's family received nowruzi, eidi and *barrati* – kulcha, fried fish, jalebi, along with gold, clothing and sweets – and the fiancé's household did the future daughter-in-law proud if the kulcha came from the Kulcha-e-Azizi.

Shujah's eyes narrowed as he turned left into Kocha-e-Murgha or Chicken Street.

'What's the matter?'

'Why do you foreign Afghans marry so late?' Shujah said, shouting a 'Hi, mister' to a Western man and woman in traditional Afghan clothes entering a shop that displayed Afghan-made jewellery, teapots, old coins and traditional costumes.

'Education first; marriage second.'

'By then, you risk your father-in-law turning up as your classmate,' Shujah said, the wrinkles on his face widening.

Nazigul laughed, telling Mour in a high-pitched voice how a halek, a bold American-Afghan, turned out to have been in the same school class as the jelai's father, how the astounded father explained to his 19-year-old daughter that the khastegari was off because her would-be husband happened to be her uncle, how she greeted the uncle and kissed his hand, and how humiliated the bold American-Afghan was. Everyone laughed, Mour included. Nazigul's face beamed in her hijab.

***

THE HALF-HOUR journey from Khair Khana to Makroryan took us three hours, and it gave me a clear picture of Kabul, or at least half of Kabul. Kabul had both changed and not changed.

You saw too many beggars; too many multistorey shopping malls; too many dirt huts with small shops squeezed into them built on mountains, hills and empty pieces of land; too many beauty parlours; too many tents; too many luxury blocks of flats; too many carts; too many vehicles; too many beeps; too much heat; too much dust; too much population; and consequently, too much pollution.

Everywhere you looked you saw a maze of concrete barriers surrounding government or mafia buildings, with armed men also guarding in front of them. With all its percussive sounds of *ghichak*, tambur and rubab, the garden city of the 1960s had turned into a maze of concrete walls, which resembled the Pul-e-Charkhi Prison. Nine times through our journey today the *ta-ta-ta-ta-ta-ta* of helicopters filled the sky of Kabul. I counted 22 Mi-17 Russian helicopters in front of gigantic military hangars at the airport yesterday, with the American soldiers either loading or unloading. With all its liveliness and the pleasant smell of shiryakh ice cream and sikh kebab, Kabul looked like a battleground.

But Kabul hadn't changed. My birthplace remained a *qurbani*, sacrificial, lamb where the Taliban daily slaughtered its sons and daughters, the punters turned them into betting objects, and the government neglected them. It awaited another Taliban takeover. The insurgents hung on for the withdrawal of American forces. Kabulis hoped their security forces, what Shujah called 'lions', some of whom kept me on their radar, would save them.

Yesterday's horrible fedayi attack, as well as today's bullet firing and assault by the broad-shouldered man, had shaken me, no matter how much I tried not to think about them. My heart had dropped to my stomach. My mind was disturbed. Kabul did feel like a valley of wolves; several of them had already snarled at me. What if they attacked the next time? Mour wouldn't be able to take it. The sooner we found the wife and left, the better.

Chapter Thirty

I put a mantu with a piece of naan in my mouth and chewed on them. Shujah praised me for following the habitual practice of the Prophet, peace be upon him. I told him that I hadn't abandoned my traditions, including using my hands to eat, thanking Frishta in my heart for her contribution to my life.

Mour and Nazigul entered the lounge.

'Her round face was like a Persian queen's. Her soft baby skin. Her huge, black eyes. Long eyelashes. Smile. Shyness. Cleverness. Housekeeping skills. Hygiene. Khudai must've had a whole day available to spend so much effort into making Nazia,' Mour said, her face beaming with pleasure.

'Mour loved the jelai,' a smiley-faced Nazigul said to Shujah, taking her hijab off.

They forgot to say salaam. Mour sat in her usual place, leaning on a cushion against the wall at the top of the room. She didn't join us when Shujah invited her to the tablecloth to eat mantu with lintel *korma* and fresh naan.

'And what an honourable family,' Mour said.

How could I see this perfect jelai?

Her friend, Najiba, would help, said Nazigul and sat cross-legged on the mattress by Mour.

'Everyone's happy with Nazia. We all wait for your consent,' Mour said.

'You'll go crazy when you see her.' Nazigul's face beamed with excitement, delighted to have finally found me a wife.

259

'Khudai's blessings on you, Nazigul. I'll never forget your and aka Shujah's help and sacrifices,' I said. *Please, Khudai, make it easy for us if Nazia is the person we are looking for.*

Nazigul was 'happy' to have assisted the son of his 'late brother'. She pressed the button to turn the fan, but her face dropped. 'One hour of electricity then no electricity the whole day. Do they call this electricity?' She wiped sweat patches from her face with her headscarf. Pulled out the black container from her side pocket and sprayed the vanilla scent into the air. She preferred to keep the curtains and windows of the sunless lounge closed. Mour asked Shujah if I hadn't ventured out again after finishing a lecture on what curtains Nazigul required to prevent extra warmth from getting into the heated lounge. Shujah said he'd kept an eye on me.

In the early morning I slipped out of the apartment and travelled to parts of Kabul I'd craved to visit as a young halek, without telling Mour and Shujah knowing they'd invoke the threats of fedayis, kidnappings and the NDS, and thus disagree. I left a letter in my room to reassure them I'd be back by the afternoon, well before the visit to Nazia. Mour and Shujah boiled with rage when I returned. Shujah suspected another motive behind my disappearance. He wasn't wrong; the events of the past days had obliged me to take action.

'Visit the Qargha Lake finally?' Mour said.

I nodded and put a spoon of home-made yoghurt in my mouth.

'Was the risk worth taking?'

'Captivating.' Hundreds of Kabuli families did what Agha had never given us the chance to do: sipped green tea in cafes with free Wi-Fi; munched on sikh and chapli kebabs in restaurants; smoked shisha; went boating; played golf; took rides; went horse riding; swam in the lake; and, like me and my elderly taxi driver, ambled along the road adjacent to the lake and enjoyed the scenery. Contrary to what Mour and I'd assumed, Kabulis lived, or pretended to live, a normal life.

I told the taxi driver to drive to two more places I longed to visit back in the days: the Paghman District and Shomali Valley, the latter famous for remaining green during Afghanistan's long summers, where also hundreds of families on Fridays, a day off, went to munch fresh berries and drink doogh, and where you once found King Zahir Shah during holidays. But the taxi driver said we'd be unable to return by the afternoon for the khastegari, even if we visited just one of those holiday hot spots.

To compensate, however, we drove through Sarachowk, whose buildings had burned down to rubble. Trolleybuses and their overhead copper wires had vanished: looted and sold to the scrap dealers.

Chaman-e-Hozori's green lawn, where back in the days we played football on Fridays, and where Afghan and Iranian singers gave concerts to tens of thousands of Kabulis during the King Zahir Shah era, had turned into dirt, full of tiny tents: drug addicts sat in groups with headscarves, perhaps to smoke in privacy or to escape the blazing sun. Next to it, the Kabul Nandari Theatre, Afghanistan's only national theatre, had burned down.

I regretted telling the driver to journey to Chaman-e-Hozori – it now clicked why Agha used to say ignorance was bliss.

***

LATER THAT AFTERNOON, after Shujah and Mour had discussed politics, and after Shujah told us about Kabulis, their lives and the difficulties they went through, I inquired about my childhood friends – something I'd asked him about many times but never got a clear answer to. Sitting in the lounge and eating a Kunduzi watermelon while the sunshine came through the open windows and the birds sang, Shujah repeated that he hadn't seen them and that most 'Muscovites' were either killed in the mujahideen civil war or the Taliban-American conflict, or emigrated abroad. Some sold their apartments to feed their children. Others lost them to the mujahideen, and later to the Taliban, because the Muscovites had committed a 'crime' of having worked for a pro-Communist government or 'run away' to the West.

'I visited every government department and court to save this flat,' Shujah said for the hundredth time, ordering Nazigul to put a cushion on the window recess to cover Mour from the sun's rays.

Mour said Shujah's bravery enabled us to afford the wedding, and skilfully broke the news we dreaded: the intention to sell the apartment. Shujah's forehead wrinkled: he had 'a feeling' we'd sell the flat. Nazigul's face darkened as she placed the cushion on the recess; she didn't know how they'd be able to afford $300 per month in rent for the affluent Makroryan, and pleaded that we should find an alternative. It wasn't easy for Mour and me to sell a flat with sentimental value and make kids homeless, Mour told them, but we saw no other option.

Our £6,000 would go nowhere to cover the costs of an Afghan wedding. In addition to the hundreds of relatives, family friends, neighbours and colleagues, you got a few hundred wedding-crushers whom you fed to stay committed to melmastia, or else you'd be dishonoured. Young haleks remained wifeless for years; the lucky ones sought work abroad days after their nuptials to pay off their debts, but many came back as drug addicts or didn't return at all.

I'd spent no money on the wedding and instead gave out the expenses to the needy in Kabul, if it was down to me. But no jelai family would consider such an 'insulting' proposal.

Chapter Thirty-One

In the bright early morning of the following day, on the way to school, Najiba, who had thin lips and a headscarf covering her forehead down to the bridge of her nose, popped in to explain the plan. We thanked Najiba for her invaluable help. She did this because Khudai loved those who assisted two young people to 'build a future'. Plus, Nazia, 'a quiet and hard-working student', deserved to marry a 'doctor' from a 'decent family' fortunate enough to live in 'London'.

Afghans considered a jelai lucky if she married in the West because scarce proposals of a khastegari came from there. She'd have a peaceful future in an environment where sorrow, stress and depression had no existence. After all, what did Western Afghans have to worry about? They had three meals a day, clothes to wear, a place to live and, most importantly, the certainty to return home in one piece after a day's work.

Maybe foreign Afghans' concerns about marital relationships, their children losing Afghan traditions, struggling to find a suitable person for their sons or daughters, and getting buried thousands of miles away from your ancestors in the wet soil of a foreign country weren't worth stressing over in the eyes of local Afghans.

***

MY HEART POUNDED as though everyone glared at me for the shameful deed of loitering in front of a jelais' school. I looked at my watch: 10:52. My Khudai, another eight minutes to linger around in the unbearable sun; maybe more before Najiba and Nazia walked out.

263

I preoccupied myself with the make-up items and pointed to a pair of earrings for Farzana, Nazigul's younger daughter, in the corner of the four-wheeled cart. A 12- or 13-year-old jelai priced it at 20 Afghani. I paid a 100 note and told her to keep the change. She glanced at a shaven, middle-aged man who uttered an 'OK' to his 'daughter'. She took the earrings out of their plastic case, cleaned them with a cloth, which appeared dirtier than the earrings, put them back in, and passed me the plastic case.

A row of white and yellow taxis near the metal school gate and carts bursting with leek bolanis, pakoras and shornakhud on both sides of the road squeezed in and their drivers abandoned their transports, as American soldiers in military helmets gestured to stay away from the three Humvees beeping their ear-splitting trumpets. A woman relinquished her crossed-leg posture and sprinted away from the road, leaving – like the rest – her circular straw tray full of samosas unattended. I followed the father and daughter and sat under a tree. The road bustling with traffic a moment ago went empty as if a Bollywood villain had made an entrance. The Humvees flew past.

'*Alhamdulillah*, a fedayi didn't explode himself,' the shaven man 'thanked Khudai' as he shifted his cart back closer to the street. His neatly organised departments of stationery, biscuits and chewing gum had scattered messily.

'And didn't get run over,' the daughter said.

The cart next to us opened his steaming pot and served a halek with a plate of shornakhud. The whiff of boiled chickpeas and potato salad, coupled with hot sauces, took me back to my schooldays.

'...Standing close to Americans in Afghanistan equals committing suicide,' the father said and put blue, red and green packs of crisps back in their place.

A tall man with bushy eyebrows covered his face with his turban and jumped into a red Carina as my eyes caught him. He drove off in the opposite direction to which the Humvees had vanished from sight. I was filled with trepidation. What the hell did the broad-shouldered man want from me? *Khudai, You're my strength and my support. Please help me go forward and win my fight. I don't want to chicken out, not anymore.*

I tuned into the father talking as I grappled with my heart beating against my chest.

'How would they protect us if they don't step down from their vehicles? They see every single passer-by as a detonating bomb,' the father said.

'They're even scared of a little jelai,' the daughter said and laughed.

'Tell him the story,' the father said.

She hesitated.

He encouraged her, informing me how she wanted to be a journalist.

'A school jelai runs towards the American. He shouts, "Stop, stop," but she doesn't know what "stop" means. He fires by her feet. She freezes – her schoolbag drops. The Afghan soldier finds nothing in the backpack but books, notebooks and pens, telling the American she raced because she was late for school. The American collapses, his body trembling, saying, "Same-age daughter, same-age daughter". Another American walks out of a Humvee, gives the crying jelai chocolates, and tells her to rush for her class. He drags his weeping friend in.'

'You can't secure Afghanistan with cry-babies,' the father said.

Enlisted in the military service to make some kind of difference, but a trivial mistake could've turned him into a monster in his own eyes and made the man hate himself all his life. I identified with the feeling. At least the American soldier had been lucky; some of us hadn't.

'China's now roaring as the world tiger,' the father said.

'A giant one,' I said.

'It'd be soon China's turn to invade Afghanistan. Like the Red Shorawi and the kafir America, we'd tame China, too,' the father said.

This time, I also joined the father and daughter's laughter and checked around for the bushy-browed man. No sign of him, thankfully.

He carried on speaking about how Karzai's disagreements with America were showy. Realising I showed no interest in politics, he discussed how today's students preoccupied themselves with games and mobile phones, and how ill-mannered they'd become, especially 'Kabuli haleks' who had nothing else to do except to 'harass' women. He sighed. 'Where have those honourable men gone?'

'Is this why she isn't in school?' I said.

He required the daughter's companionship to look after her section because his department alone failed to support his family unless he sold 'mobile accessories', which he didn't have the capital for. Some people were 'bad': they paid a double or triple price but asked for 'dirty things', he added, shaking his head. I realised why she glanced at the father earlier on when I said to keep the change.

'You're different, of course. You're a good man.'

'What makes you say that?' The corners of my mouth stretched.

'Your manners.'

'Thank you.' Politeness wasn't a habit. You had to make an effort. It felt good when someone appreciated it.

'Importantly, you haven't looked at a single female passer-by.'

'Women have an honoured position. They're mothers and sisters.'

He nodded. 'You're a man of integrity.' His eyes watered. 'My trust has been restored in humanity.'

'*Integrity*,' I found myself saying, thinking how desperately I had once wanted to discover what the word meant. 'I'm nowhere near what you think,' I said to the man. I indeed was nowhere near my hero, Frishta. My phone rang, and I excused myself. Nazigul was at the other end, saying to mention *nothing* about the khastegari to Nazia; we'd meet today, and Nazia would be told later on about me, and if we liked each other, then we'd move to the next phase. This wasn't part of the plan, I annoyingly told Nazigul. She apologised, adding that

Najiba and Nazia's mother had just phoned to say that Nazia was 'shy' and would 'lose confidence', and might 'refuse to walk out' with the teacher if she found out about the meeting. Unlike Qandigul, Nazia's mother favoured that the halek and jelai sit together under supervision, but believed her husband and sons would disagree. I took a deep sigh and uttered an *OK*, discouraged by the meeting's woulds, mights and ifs.

I heard the school bell in trepidation. Jelais in black dresses and white headscarves covered the school's front like ants coming out of their anthill, chatting, giggling and screaming. How to spot Najiba and Nazia among hundreds of jelais? One excited jelai of around 15 or 16 ran past me, shouting after another that she had some cake left. None of the jelais looked older than mid-teens. How come Nazia was at least in 'her mid-twenties'? The question concerned me. Ustads in light green overalls and coloured headscarves now walked out in twos and threes. Where was Najiba? What if... A hand waved. To my relief, it was Najiba in emerald-green overalls. 'For the mobile accessories,' I placed pound notes in the father's hand. 'Send my niece to school.'

He gasped, his eyes widening. 'Thank you, brother.'

'I'll take the money back if she doesn't start attending school.'

As a university graduate, the father understood the importance of education.

'You'll make a talented journalist, inshallah.' I told the jelai what I'd said years back to Zarghuna.

I said goodbye to its owners and strode towards Najiba and a medium-sized figure in a black dress and white headscarf.

Najiba took a step forward. We greeted.

'Oh, I forgot to bring your book,' Najiba said.

'Enjoy it?'

'Loved it. So proud of Khaled Hosseini.'

The name rang a bell.

'This's my student, Nazia, by the way. My cousin, Ahmad jan.' Najiba pointed with her eyes to the jelai.

Nazia's gaze fixed on her feet, the searing sunshine reflected in her hair clip.

'Salaam alaikum,' I said, my mouth getting dry and heart pounding harder.

'Salaam brother.' Her voice was barely audible. She didn't even put her eyes up for greeting. Nazia's wavy hair favoured her: it covered half her face. She did possess Mour's wow factor, but to me, she wasn't more than 20.

'Back in seconds,' Najiba said and rushed off in the direction where cheering jelais sprang out.

'Don't need it now. Bring it home,' I said. Najiba rushed inside the school, anyway. I made up my mind. Despite all the wow factors, I'd never make Nazia my wife. Would've got a daughter her age had I married earlier on. I didn't know what convinced Mour and Nazigul to estimate Nazia's age at over 25?

My heart beat faster; I was clueless about what to say. Nazigul's solution proved humiliating, even cruel.

Sweat erupted on her forehead. Her left hand trembled. Najiba's decision to leave her with a man, I reckoned, confused Nazia. A man she'd never seen before. A man and the situation she'd known nothing of.

'Is my cousin a good ustad?' I broke the awkward silence, praying in my heart for Najiba's swift return. The back of my neck started to itch. The sun was right overhead.

She nodded, her face blushing. She pulled her white headscarf forward. I bet she had a heart as tiny as a warbler. No wonder she'd grown on Mour. She appeared as if I was about to take her to the gallows. I decided to stop torturing her and leave at once.

'Tell Najiba I've gone home. She can bring the book—'

Bang. A whack stung my face, the force of which made me lose my balance. Another smack. I fell to the floor. Legs flew around me in a circle. My ears rang. What was happening? Did a hand hit across Nazia's face, too? Another one grab her ponytail and pull her onto the dirt floor?

'You whore. Instead of studying, you bring your lunda to the school,' a rough voice said.

A kick hit me in the thighs. A hard object against my head. A kick in the stomach. Another knocked the wind out of me. Attempted desperately at breaths.

Fists, slaps and kicks came from all directions. I curled up and covered my head with the hands and elbows. Noticed some from the crowd wore dark green uniforms.

'Our daughters cannot go to school because of people like him,' a voice said. Did I know the voice?

'Hit the bastard,' another said. 'He's got no obro or ezat.'

'Give the son of the dog a lesson, so he never lundabazi in front of the jelais' school,' said another voice among many more.

The words obro, ezat and lundabazi struck me like the airport fedayi attack, eating into my sense of honour.

'Beat the fatherless whore. She's brought shame on the whole school.' Another voice.

A couple of hands shoved dried biscuits into my mouth, but as they squeezed against my teeth and tongue, they tasted like dried leaves having gone bad. Their odour rang the alarm. I spat out the dried faeces, spat again and again until no saliva remained in my mouth.

A figure in dark green uniform shouted, '*Bas.*' Enough. 'No more beating. No more laughing,' the voice added. Two dark green-uniformed men pushed the mob away.

'Tffff.' Saliva landed on my face. The green-uniformed men shoved away the spitter. I wiped my face. 'How dare he speak to my daughter? I'd have killed him had I known the hypocrite's business,' he said. 'Take your haram money with you.' He hurled the folded £20 notes at my feet and spat in my direction again.

The green-uniformed men placed Nazia and me in a dark green pick-up with the word 'POLICE' written on it.

Chapter Thirty-Two

A green-uniformed man, sitting in between Nazia and me, warned that each word earned us a slap. He held the rose flower design earrings I'd bought for my cousin sister. Glanced at them, glared at me and shook his head. Abstained from battering me, perhaps, because his boss in the front passenger seat received walkie-talkie reports of how another child fedayi surrendered to the authority, and how the child's handler had promised the child that Khudai would spare him from the flame and shrapnel, and only obliterate the 'American infidels'.

The pick-up truck drove into a metal gate above which read 'District Nine Police Headquarters', and pulled over in front of a white building. The policeman, with the earrings in his hand, escorted us inside the building, down the stairs to a basement and shoved me into a urine-smelling concrete cell, as narrow as my shoulders' width and as high as my neck. I sat on the rough floor and leaned against the wall. Orange bulb light fell through the square-shaped food hatch.

As my eyes became acquainted with the dark, I read on the unpainted walls, *Fuck the police chief's wife*. Another one wanted *pussy*. A topless woman with enormous breasts was drawn beneath the writing. Was what happened before the school real? Was I locked in a cell? Did I feel like Khudai had taken off my and Nazia's clothes and stood us nude in the Makroryan Market?

Khudai had taken Frishta, my father, sisters, friends, watan from me, and the one thing He hadn't fully denied me was my obro and ezat. He confiscated what'd been left today. Dishonoured me and, more distressingly, Nazia. My action defamed her before the entire school. Destroyed her future. Who'd marry a jelai who had a lunda? Nothing restored your obro and ezat once you lost them in Kabul. Khudai, why do You keep punishing me? What sins have I committed that You don't let go of? If You're angry with me, why did You stigmatise an innocent jelai? How can she take all this with a tiny heart? You could've broken my legs and smashed my face but spared Nazia the humiliation. I'd have gladly swallowed all the poop before the school if only it spared Nazia. My eyes welled up, and I let Ahmad loose. Let him scream as loud as yesterday's fedayi bomb. Let him bang the walls with his fists, heads and legs, as hard as the mob beat me. Let him sleep, as comfortable as the Chaman-e-Hozori's addicts high on heroin.

**

WHO'S SOBBING? And why? Why am I distressed? My eyes opened. My senses came to me and my heart fell – thunder had hit Nazia and me in front of the school.

The sound of footsteps followed by a key turning in a padlock, and the metal door opened. A darker-faced officer in a uniform spat. Saliva mixed with hard fluids bombarded my face. I knew it from its pungent smell, like a fresh bundle of coastal hay, to be *naswar*. I wiped the grains of naswar with my sleeve.

'Out.'

I stepped out in the dim orange light, suffering pain in my thighs and arms.

'Jot down your details,' he said, his mouth still full of naswar. He extended a file. Half of his jumper buttons were undone, allowing his many-sizes-larger shirt to come out.

'There's a misunderstanding,' I said.

He punched me in the stomach.

I folded and sat on my knees, unable to breathe.

'Must be ashamed of yourself, a *chatal* womaniser.' It stung when he accused me of being a 'dirty' womaniser: an accusation I tried to avoid all my life. I remembered from time to time Satan tempting me in England to have a girlfriend, especially when I discovered jelais had developed feelings for me. Every time the urge came, I'd perform ablutions, pray nafl-prayers, and ask Khudai for a halal relationship – a righteous wife.

'Stop acting pain.' He kicked me with the heel of his military boot.

'You're breaking the law. You have no power to raise your hand.'

He shadowed over me, smelling of hashish. 'Tonight I'll tear your balls off. You'll no longer be man enough to harass jelais.'

I didn't doubt him, given he was high at work and had already violated my civil liberties. 'Please let the jelai go. For her obro and ezat.'

'Did you think of them when you loitered before the school?'

'Why don't you like a man say the real reason why I'm here–'

'Chup. One more word and I'll kick you in the face,' he said, raising his right boot. He clenched the jaws and his joined eyebrows lowered, which turned the dark circle around his eyes darker. He looked mad.

I believed in the power of reason. In logic. He lacked it, so I couldn't win with him.

After a pause, he put his leg down, passed me the file with a pen stuck to the side.

'You're old enough to be her father. Where are your principles?'

Like the suffocating cell, principles had caged me and compelled me to go through plenty of trouble and humiliation, those of today included, or else I could've been long married. Still on my knees on the damp concrete, I jotted down my details in the shadow as his head covered the pear-shaped light bulb. He took the file, locked me up and stepped away. The sound of a key turning in a padlock from two cells away.

'Name?' I overheard him asking.

Nazia burst into sobbing.

'You should've thought of the consequences.'

Nazia sobbed.

'Don't waste my time. Write.'

'I'm not such a jelai.'

'Yeah? Was I doing lundabazi?'

'I swear on Khuda jan I don't know him.' She burst into tears.

'Details.' He raised his voice. A *taqq* sound.

'Khudai, damn you for raising your hand on a woman,' I screamed, and punched the door.

'Chup, bastard.'

'I won't let you get away with this. My first complaint will be to the Independent Human Rights Commission as I step out from this damn place. I'll leave no stone unturned.' Yesterday, besides travelling to the Qargha Lake and popping into the state-owned Jamhuriat Hospital to say I could provide free online advice from England if they needed it, I visited the Commission, the main motive for my disappearance, and told them how I felt threatened by the NDS. For 15 years, I explained, I'd been volunteering to the Racial Equality Council in Durham and produced reports when human rights organisations required them. Was I a terrorist because I criticised the government's policies? Or did MI5 or MI6 suspect I planned a terrorist plot because I prayed in the same mosque with people who possessed extreme views and, on occasion, supported their racial discrimination claims? The Commission reassured me of their support, took my phone number and address in Kabul, and told me to let them know if anything happened to me. I reckoned the mad officer followed the broad-shouldered man's orders. Nazia paid for whatever wrong I'd committed.

Quietness. A couple of minutes passed.

'Makroryan? The centre of lundabazi.' Hearing Makroryan being a centre of corrupt behaviour wasn't a first – or fair. The sound of a cell getting locked, footsteps up the stairs, and a door shutting.

For the next few lingering hours, Nazia wept silently, went quiet, and wept again. I did nothing; couldn't even comfort her. Hoped Najiba had informed Shujah, or someone from Nazia's family, about our arrests – our uncertain fates. I'd known getting married in Kabul was not straightforward, but I'd never foreseen that my khastegari would lead to dishonouring a jelai. Mour and I failed to find an Afghan jelai from the thousands of Afghan families who lived in England, mostly in London. Perhaps we had nobody like Nazigul to look for a suitable family, or maybe many families found us too backward. One Afghan jelai told me she had no intention of marrying a 'Pashtun from the Rahman Baba period'. Another took a lenient approach and made me feel I belonged to two centuries later, 'the 19th century', and expressed shock that I held to its 'backward values'. Yet another wanted me to give up my 'radical Islamic views' and shave my beard on the day we got married. For many others, we never got to the discussion stage since, as they kindly confided in me, they already found their future husbands without their parents' knowledge, but would inform the parents at the right time when I opined that the relationship might not be solid without the parents' blessing.

Mour and I liked a jelai, the only one who wore a hijab and taught in an Islamic madrasa, but she and her family wanted me to move in with them. 'She wears the hijab and is an ustad. She does so without you forcing her. All your conditions met. Go ahead, you won't find such a jelai,' Mour said. 'Don't worry about me. Khudai will look after me,' Mour added. I refused to trade my mother for a wife. 'How would you feel if your son cherishes you until he needs you, and then throws you away in your days of need?' I remembered telling the jelai.

'I don't need a son to babysit me.'

'Your demand violates both Islam and Afghan tradition,' I added. We never returned to the family.

Finding an Afghan jelai from a traditional family who'd know a daughter-in-law's responsibilities and give me a hand in looking after

Mour if need be proved as difficult in England as discovering a solution for the US-Taliban conflict. Afghanistan presented itself as the obvious choice.

Nazia was silent. She might have run out of tears. How worried would Nazia's parents be about her sudden disappearance? What would they think of a daughter imprisoned for having a 'lunda'? According to Najiba, Nazia was a punctual student. Always did her homework. Scarcely discussed anything else apart from her studies. How would her classmates view her now, though? How would she keep people's mouths shut? Or repair her obro and ezat? What if they kept her overnight? People would gossip about how the policemen 'touched' her. The thought of it turned my stomach.

I did dry ablutions. Clueless of the time of prayer, I performed nafl-prayers. Dropped on my knees, pressed my face to the urine-smelling concrete, and begged Khudai to save Nazia. I pleaded He heard me this time. My face pressed to the ground. Please. Please. Please...

***

THE SOUND OF footsteps, lots of them. I sat up and, through the food hatch, caught a glimpse of a figure in black between policemen. A key turned in a padlock. Green-uniformed men filled the tiny, orange-lit corridor and obscured my service hatch. The door of the parallel cell clink opened. A woman's voice asked if Nazia was OK. Nazia burst into tears. The woman reassured Nazia. The person before the food hatch stepped off and followed Nazia and a figure in black – I reckoned, the woman – surrounded by policemen and people in black suits and ties walking upstairs. The woman's voice troubled me. Had I been listening to it for years? It sounded like... Mour. No, like Zarghuna. Or Nazo? Were they here to save their brother from the wolves? Did Khudai send them? Or was I losing it?

More footsteps. My service hatch opened, and a hand entered, holding a disposable plate full of white rice and a small piece of meat in the corner with a buttery odour. The plate travelled back out when I didn't take it. I had no clue whether Khudai heard me or there was some plot. Where did they take Nazia? Who did the familiar voice belong to? Sound of steps rushing down the stairs. Key turned in my padlock, plate *qeghgh* moved to the side, and the door opened, revealing the mad officer, holding a teapot and a towel. He'd buttoned up and combed his side-parted hair.

'Can you step out, please?'

Was he the same person?

He passed me my iPhone, the folded notes and the earrings. 'The school constantly complains about bad haleks. We have to be strict.'

'Where is the jelai?' I stepped outside.

'*Wakil* saheb's taking her home.'

'Which Member of Parliament?'

'She's for... Kunduz.'

'Dr saheb, please don't complain to Wakil saheb.'

'What about Khudai? You fear a Wakil saheb but not the entity Who's created her?' I suppressed the urge to punch him in the face. I remembered once kicking someone and the next time pushing another person. Apart from those two incidents, I'd never laid a finger on anyone in my life and wouldn't do so even if I had the power to break the nose of this cocky plus mad officer. What good would have come of it? It wouldn't mend Nazia's obro and ezat. She'd forever carry the social stigma. 'You can't punish prisoners before they're proven guilty; it's the job of the court to pass judgments.'

He nodded. 'Please freshen up.'

Maybe he didn't want Wakil saheb to see my broken head and bloody hands. He held the teapot and poured the cool water. Under the dimmed light, blood mixed with water made its way on the concrete floor as I washed my face and hair, feeling the stiffness in my knuckles. Completed the ablutions. Drank from my cupped hands the water, as pure as that of Paghman, once he confirmed its cleanliness. He passed me a 'clean' towel, which I also used as a praying mat.

**

AS MY EYESIGHT became accustomed to the reddened sunlight, I noticed five white Mitsubishi jeeps parked behind one another, and two or so dozen armed guards in black suits and black glasses scattered around them.

'We'll take Dr saheb home,' a neatly trimmed bearded man in black suit and tie said to the mad officer. With a muscular physique like one of the security guards from the CIA, the middle-aged man shook my hand, introducing himself as Ashraf, the chief head of Wakil saheb's security detail. His hairy hand with long fingers buried mine. He'd fixed his eyes on me from the time he'd introduced himself as if I was some expensive goods and he was interested in purchasing me. It was unsettling. Did he plan to kidnap me? Or he worked for the NDS, for the broad-shouldered man, the director of every single scene of today's drama?

'Which Member of Parliament?' I tried to suppress my fear.

'Wakil saheb Afghan. She's representing the courageous people of Kunduz.'

The mad policeman thanked Ashraf, whispered another apology to me before disappearing.

Agha was right, if you had money, power, or connection to power in Afghanistan, everyone respected you. No one hindered your business. Everything flew. No matter what crime you committed, you got away with it if you had one of the above three magical weapons. Apart from Khudai, I knew no one with power in Kabul. I reckoned Nazia had the last one: connection to the woman who owned the polished Japanese jeeps, the woman whom all those bodyguards protected and the mad policeman feared. But I had faith in Khudai and believed my prayer must've played a part.

The mad officer reappeared – they required me in the office of the police chief. The broad-shouldered man won't let me go, I thought with a sinking heart. *Khudai, I take refuge in You. When You protect, no one will overcome me.* Carrying pain with every step, I followed Ashraf and the mad officer walking to a long corridor on the first floor and into a large room with the photos of President Karzai and someone who once gave me his blessing, the legendary Northern Alliance leader, Ahmad Shah Massoud, sitting up above the giant desk.

I remembered writing an A-Level assignment one midnight when Mour knocked on my door and broke the news that two Al-Qaeda terrorists posing as journalists exploded their bomb hidden in a camera, killing the charismatic leader. 'They'll inshallah capture the entire country,' Mour said. The Taliban held 90 per cent of Afghanistan, and with Massoud's death, everyone believed the Taliban would capture the remaining 10 per cent. Two days later, 9/11 occurred and America, to Mour's disappointment, re-energised the Northern Alliance to overthrow the Taliban and their benefactor, Al-Qaeda.

Security guards in black suits and ties, and policemen and women, stood before the desk. No sign of the broad-shouldered man, thankfully. I caught a glimpse of Wakil saheb and Nazia standing with their faces towards the mahogany desk as the mad officer guided me to the back of the room. Ashraf made his way to Wakil saheb and whispered. Wakil saheb nodded and jotted down something on a piece of white paper over the desk. The police chief behind the maroon desk saluted Wakil saheb and they shook hands. Wakil saheb touched the rotating world global map with his right hand, touched the eyes with the same hand, and then kissed the hand.

Four guards in black suits rushed and held the door open. Three more and Ashraf marched behind, and the two sides of Wakil saheb and Nazia; they looked like the CIA agents around President Obama. The entourage stopped by the door, bodyguards squeezed to opposite sides, revealing Wakil saheb's glaring face. She held the penetrating glare and shook her head, and out she went. Thunder struck. The ceiling fell. The room and its maroon sofas turned round and round. My hands shivered, my body trembled, and my legs collapsed.

'You OK, Dr saheb?' a voice asked. 'The floor's dirty: sit up.' The police chief held my left arm and sat me on a soft object. 'What's happened?' He rested my head against the squashy thing like a pillow.

The police chief's iPhone rang. 'Me and another officer,' he answered. He ordered the mad officer to leave. Extended his Hugo Boss-smelling hand.

'Still a thief?' the familiar voice from the basement said with a relaxed tone.

My gaze fixed on the police chief's hairy hand holding the iPhone. Perhaps he sensed my hands didn't have the nerve to hold a mobile.

'Stole Nazia's peace of mind, too?'

My mouth lacked the strength to utter any words.

'Since when have you become a pervert?'

My lips remained sealed.

'Do you know who you're speaking to?'

My heartbeats elevated.

'Think hard.'

My body shivered.

'Scared?'

Was I scared? Actually, the ceiling had just fallen on my head, causing such concussion that I didn't know what to make of everything I saw or heard.

Silence, except for my heart's fast beats.

'Have you gone mute?'

Like my body, my lips had no energy to move.

'I'm Frishta.'

The brain blocked the word 'Frishta' from entering my head. How come the dead turned up alive? Frishta had been killed, buried, dusted.

'Already forgotten about me?'

My brain remained paralysed.

'Frishta? Your neighbour, the daughter of Brigadier?'

Did I dream of a voice telling me on the phone she was Frishta? Did Frishta turn around and look me in the eye earlier on?

'The Leopard, remember?'

The Leopard, my lips moved to repeat the words without a sound.

'Hello,' she said, raising her voice. 'Chief, can he hear me?'

The police chief brought the handset closer to his right ear, saying I heard everything. She asked him to pass the handset back to me. He held it close to my right ear; the Hugo Boss scent got stronger.

'Stay away from jelais' schools. I don't want to hear another complaint. Understood?'

The police chief's fresh bouquet at the corner of the desk containing red, pink and orange flowers kept getting blurry.

'I'd have left you to rot in those urine-smelling cells if it wasn't for Nazia. I won't allow you to destroy the life of another woman.' She cut off. Seconds later, the mobile rang and the police chief answered.

He took a few steps, pushed away the three-tier filing tray with his backside with a scratching sound and sat on his desk. 'I can give him a lesson if you–' I overheard. His face changed colour. His right hand moved to the back and brought out a black pistol with a dark orange hand. He pointed the handgun at me. Revenge, a voice whispered. *Please, Khudai, don't punish Frishta for my death; I deserve it after what I've done to her*, I prayed and read Shahada, *There is no god but Allah, Muhammad is the messenger of Allah*. He shook his head and pressed a bell with the pistol. The mad officer stepped in. 'Throw the coward out,' the police chief said, waving his head towards me.

Chapter Thirty-Three

Mour planted a kiss on my head and thanked Khudai. I pulled my head away as she aimed to kiss me again. Hobbled to my place in the lounge, heavy with freshly sprayed vanilla, and sat on the mattress. Shujah and Mour took their places. The wrinkles on Shujah's forehead had increased in number.

'It's all my doing, I'm sorry,' Nazigul said. She didn't sit by Mour. Perhaps she sensed I wasn't in the right frame of mind, so kept a distance. Her eyes had turned red, and since I'd stepped into the apartment, she'd kept thanking Khudai.

I chose not to say anything, thinking whether she was also an accomplice to Mour's lies.

One of the twins shrieked in the parallel room and Amina threw open the door, warning that she wouldn't babysit her little siblings anymore if they interfered with her studies. Shujah raised his voice, telling the 'fatherless' children to behave or else he'd throw them off the balcony. Amina darted off.

'Getting married into a Pashtun family involves going through pain,' Shujah said to me.

I wondered if he might've given Mour the news on Frishta's rebirth. Mour might've silenced them. Shujah and Nazigul abided because they didn't want Mour to throw them out of the apartment, or, at the very least, impose a rent. They endured mother-and-son arguments, confined their children to one room, so their noises didn't cause Mour a headache, and took time off work to do my khastegari to be able to live rent-free. Or perhaps, to please Mour further, they –

282

more likely Shujah – might've given Mour the idea not to reveal to me Frishta's revival. Mour normally wasn't that imaginative.

'What did you think of the jelai?' Instead of thinking about Nazia and her obro and ezat and feeling guilty for having faked Frishta's death, my selfish Mour sought to know my opinion on the jelai. I wanted to smash the window panes, punch the radiant crystal light dangling from the ceiling, and tear the kilims to pieces. But furiousness doesn't justify a destructive response: things get worse when you react in the heat of the moment, my psychiatrist colleague used to say.

'If you mean Nazia, she's a child. I can't marry a child.'

'In this case, don't ever get married. Age wifeless,' Mour said, telling Nazigul to open the door to let the evening breeze in through the window.

I cursed Satan. I avoided people with emotions; today I struggled to control mine. The woman in the brown dress sitting at the top of the room by the open windows reminded me of the misery, pain and sleepless nights I'd gone through for Frishta's death. All but for Mour's lies.

Every time Mour talked of Nazo and Zarghuna, or Agha, or whenever someone mentioned war, Mujahideen, the Taliban, mina, or anything on Afghanistan, my thoughts raced to Frishta. What would Frishta have looked like if she was alive? What would've she done for work? How many children would we have? Some nights, Frishta came into my dreams, sometimes smiling, sometimes crying, and most of the time wandering around. I'd shout I was there for her, but she wouldn't hear me, and vanish. I'd wake up, perform ablutions, pray nafl-prayers, read the Quran, and pray for her. Mour said the dead needed prayers when they came into your dreams. I spent most of the nights praying for Frishta in Ramadans. I didn't remember a day I missed a prayer in the past 21 years, or a prayer in which I didn't pray for Frishta.

After Frishta, I looked up to Mour as my role model. She had taught me that Islam prohibited lies, but she hated Frishta to the extent she let herself be guided by lies. Like Afghanistan, Mour gave me everything with one hand and took it away with another.

'Did you ask for Frishta's help?'

'Amina phoned her,' Shujah said.

'Did you speak to her, Mour?'

'Actually—'

'Aka Shujah, I'm asking Mour.'

'Yes, I did. What do you want to prove?'

'When did you find out Frishta was alive?'

Silence, save the rustling of leaves outside the windows.

'I asked you a question.'

Silence. Amina's muffled voice pleading with the siblings not to touch her books.

'Why have you been feeding me lies all these years, Mour?'

'Mour thinks about your well-being,' Shujah said.

'I almost lost my health because of her lies. Was that for my fucking well-being?'

'Mour protected your family name. Frishta wasn't the sort of jelai one could recommend as a wife.'

'What was wrong with her?'

Shujah wanted to say something but hesitated.

'I'll tell you, brother,' Mour said to Shujah. 'She spent a year in Moscow *alone*, and Khudai knows how many Russians she slept with, yet he quite happily saw her as my daughter-in-law.'

'Did you see her sleeping with Russians? Baseless defamation is a sin.'

'An actor's daughter only becomes a whore. A harami—'

'Bas,' I said as the slanderous word 'harami' hit me like a bullet. 'Fuck family name. Fuck obro and ezat. Fuck parents' respect.' I hated the serial swearers and the bad-tempered, but today I had turned into one.

Shujah scowled. Mour glanced at me, then averted her gaze to the kilim. Nazigul flinched and rushed out of the room.

'I won't tolerate anything bad being said about Frishta.' Mour should've known her place. So did Shujah. 'If I find out you've helped Mour to hide Frishta from me, aka Shujah, I'd ask you to fuck off from my flat.' I could no longer try to sound reasonable on the outside.

Mour had the right to advise me on Frishta's suitability as a wife; she had no right to steal her from me. I didn't know what to do with Mour, or what to think of her anymore. I tried to shut out what was on my mind, but it burst through. 'Until this morning I thought of you as a caring mother. You turned out to be a poisonous snake. You've been biting me all these years and I didn't even know it.'

Her eyes didn't move; they sat on the kilim.

'I feel like a child whose mother purposely turned him into a drug addict so that she had control over his life,' I said as if to myself, and my voice broke.

I'd hardly seen Mour shed tears since Agha and my sisters' deaths. She was a worrying type except with no tears. Perhaps her limitless sorrow had drained her fluid. Not today – tears seeped down her cheeks. Her son's shocking behaviour compelled her eyes to dig in and produce the last reserved fluid. A son who used a crane to demolish a castle he'd spent every hour of every day of the past 36 years building.

'As good as a diamond?' Shujah muttered and shook his head.

His mocking stung. 'It's nothing to do with you.'

'If you swear one more time in my house, I'll break your mouth. Had enough of you, piss pants.'

Shujah's outburst increased my heartbeat. The words 'piss pants' felt like a mujahideen rocket, but Frishta's voice whispered, *Fuck what people think about Ahmad. Live for others.*

'Brother, he's my son.'

'And you failed to teach the coward manners. The result of a fatherless upbringing.'

'Leave my husband out of this, please.'

Nazigul burst in and rushed to Shujah, 'Please, don't make a scene. They're all I've got.'

Shujah's hand travelled backwards and forward and banged against Nazigul's face, forcing her head to bump into the wall.

'Whore, chup.'

'Are you not ashamed of raising your hand to a woman?' I said.

Kids' cries filled the hallway.

'You're supposed to be a man, piss pants. Come on,' Shujah said and jumped on me like a venomous spider. My body unashamedly froze. He put his hands around my neck and squeezed me against the wall. His palms compressed my throat; I could feel my oesophagus closing. Mour and Nazigul pulled his hands, begging him to let go.

He released his grip, uttering coward.

I gasped for breath.

'I don't want to see your face again in this house,' he said and made for the door.

'This is our flat,' I said breathlessly, my voice faltering to my disgust.

'It's mine now. I spent money refurbishing it.' He stood by the door.

Nazigul burst into tears.

'*We* sent you the money. How is it yours?' I said.

'This's my husband's,' Mour said, her muscles tensing.

'Your alcoholic husband should've come out of the fish stomach and saved it from the Mujahid commander.' He slammed the door and dashed off.

'The proverb is right: don't stretch a helping hand and you won't meet problems,' Mour said.

I remembered Shujah imploring Agha, his 'elder brother', on the phone more than two decades ago to let him move into our apartment in Makroryan. Shujah, Nazigul and her mother, Agha's aunt, had just returned from Pakistan after ten years and had no place to live. Mour told Agha to help them. Neither of my parents had any siblings, so Shujah and Nazigul were the only close relatives as such. I heard Mour many times refer to him as the brother she never had. Every time I transferred money to Baktash and Mr Barmak's families from Moscow, I also sent some to him. Mour and I carried on helping him out from England. One clarification, though: you'd hardly find an Afghan with no relatives. We used to visit many trors and akas on Eids and Nowruzes back in Kabul, but we'd lost touch, partly because Mour as 'a Pashtun widow' kept herself to herself, and partly, I realised now, because Shujah kept them from us.

Nazigul wept.

Amina entered and sat by her mother. 'Didn't take even three days before he showed his true colours,' Amina said.

'I wish I died the day I got engaged to him,' Nazigul said.

'He's gone gambling,' Amina said.

'What? We've given him £6,000 and our passports,' Mour said. Like me, she sounded stunned.

'The minute you gave him the pounds, he's itching to gamble them,' Amina said.

'Na?' Mour slapped her face in shock.

'He'll probably sell the passports to human traffickers,' continued Amina.

'You should've told me,' Mour said to Nazigul.

'He would've killed Mum,' Amina said.

'Oh, my Khudai. How do we get back to England?'

'I'm sorry.' Nazigul burst into tears. A neighbour played Indian music as loud as my heart's palpitations.

'He doesn't give us a penny you send,' Amina said.

'Tawba-tawba,' Mour said, repenting to Khudai for Shujah's sins.

'He wanted to wed me with an old man for a fatty walwar, but Mum warned she'd throw herself from the balcony if he went ahead.'

Mour slapped her face, this time with both hands, and uttered another tawba-tawba. The last revelation shocked me even more. Amina was just a kid.

'Has he transferred the ownership of the flat?' I asked Nazigul.

'He's been visiting the court in Surobi; he might have. He won't tell me,' Nazigul said, asking for forgiveness.

I remembered Mour and me travelling to the Afghan Embassy in London to give him a power of attorney so that he fought the Mujahid commander, who later defected to the Taliban. He must have used the document to transfer ownership.

'Ahmad brother. Please don't fight with him. He's so bad he can hurt you,' Amina said.

'Over my dead body,' Mour said. My mother had more courage than me.

'Don't worry for tonight. He won't come back. He'll be in the orchard in Bagrami, drinking, womanising and gambling until morning,' Amina said, disclosing other shocking revelations about Shujah.

Mour slapped her face, again with two hands; Nazigul broke into fresh tears. Amina put her head on her mother's lap, her eyes welling up. The Indian song played at high volume.

I slipped out.

***

BOTH PHYSICAL AND MENTAL pain had overwhelmed – actually concussed – me, but the mental one was more excruciating. I didn't know why I had the urge to scream and swear. Was it for the rebirth of Frishta? The humiliation of Nazia? Discovering a new side of Shujah? My cowardice? Or for Mour's betrayal?

How wrong I'd been all these years about Mour. I still couldn't believe Mour was capable of such deception. Shujah likewise. Given his consistent advice on Skype about the importance of Pashtunwali, his lectures on Afghan history and his good-natured jokes, I'd have never suspected Shujah of committing such grave sins. Every time we spoke on Skype, when he sat on the Afghan rug behind the iPad camera in this very room I was now in, he'd temporarily excuse himself for a few minutes to pray. We thought we'd been supporting the family all these years, but Shujah gambled our money and starved his children. And had Frishta helped only to insult me? She knew too well I hated womanising, so why did she sting me with the word 'pervert'? Given Frishta's unpredictable nature, our unsettled account, and the police chief's fierce eyes, I lost heart when he pointed his gun at me. Mind you, powerful people in Afghanistan did have the licence to kill.

And, importantly, what of my cowardice? Shujah had taken my property, my naamus, by force. I decided to pluck up my courage and stand up to Shujah earlier on, but my body trembled, heart pounding as loud as the dhol, and I froze like a coward. I knew why? After two decades of trying repeatedly to stand up for myself, it still happened to my body when it discerned violence. Damn it. Millions of Afghans sacrificed their lives to claim back their national honour from invaders, but I chickened out to defend mine. *If there was no fear, there'd be no need for courage*, Frishta's voice whispered. I took a deep breath and swore that, like my ancestors, I'd give up my head but wouldn't allow Shujah to grab my property.

A thud sound, followed by Nazigul's scream. Mour has had a stroke, I thought, and rushed out of my room to witness a moment I'd never forget. Nazigul in the hallway with a Nokia handset in her right hand, her face as ashen as the Salang Mountains' snow.

'Khuda jan, forgive me. Tawba-tawba, forgive me,' Nazigul said, tears coming down her cheeks. She tilted backwards. Amina and Mour held Nazigul against the concrete wall, but her legs were bent forward, her back pushing down against the wall heater. Her brown headscarf collapsed onto her shoulders. I, a non-mahram, couldn't touch her.

'What's happened?' Mour asked, pulling the headscarf over her hair.

'She's dead.'

'Who?' Mour said, her face as pale as Nazigul.

'Nazia's just hanged herself. Her mother cried her heart out. Khudai–' Nazigul's eyes closed.

'Mum's dead,' one of the twins said.

Mour told them off, ordering them to go back into their room. Nazigul breathed. I told Amina to position her on her back and loosen her dress around the neck. Rushed to the kitchen, filled a cup with water and offered it to Nazigul. She opened her eyes. Took a few sips.

'She wanted to prove... she was as chaste as the daughter of the Prophet, peace be upon him,' Nazigul said, and a tear made its way from the corner of her left eye. She looked as if she'd cried and screamed all day.

Mour wiped Nazigul's tears, telling her it was Nazia's fate.

'And she *was* as virtuous. I'm a witness to this. Khudai, please forgive me. I'm the engineer of all this.' Nazigul went on begging for Khudai's forgiveness.

I, more than Nazigul, felt responsible for Nazia's death but shed no tears. The immensity of the painful events in the past days had baffled me. Frishta failed. I did destroy Nazia's life, but Nazia didn't allow me to stain her honour. Khushal Baba once said:

Let the head be gone, wealth be gone, but the honour must not go because the whole of the dignity of a man is due to this honour.

Nazia was courageous enough to prove her dignity. But I... A hand held my throat and pressed against it. Shujah's apartment felt as small as District Nine's cells.

***

I TOOK A DEEP breath and hobbled, letting the warm breeze touch my cheeks. Like the lit Makroryan flats, bright stars and a half-moon shone out of the sky. A star twinkled and dropped. Maybe Nazia's star said its goodbyes from this world of lies and betrayals. I took a stroll the same way I'd taken one 21 years ago with Baktash. Our last stroll. What an innocent time it was. I'd urged no one to commit suicide.

Men played cards on the grass in front of their block. Young haleks sat cross-legged in a circle, and two wrestled each other in a brightly lit lawn before the next block. Senior men with white hats, pakols and turbans perambulated, perhaps waiting for the Isha Prayer. Teenaged haleks and some jelais wandered in twos and threes, licking ice creams, sipping juice or carrying shopping bags. Muffled beats of Afghan, Indian and even English music thumped through flats and passing vehicles. Makroryanis lived their everyday lives without Nazia. She'd lived last night this time; maybe she prepared her homework for school, working hard for a future she'd never have. My khastegari played the leading part in stopping her from seeing that future.

The Makroryan Market arrived. Even the fluorescent lights in its shops, which made the place as bright as a summer morning, and the smell of the freshly made mango and banana juice couldn't brighten up one of my darkest days. My feet took me to the mini-restaurant where my childhood friends and I used to eat burgers and ice creams. It had turned into an estate agent's, and a man with a large moustache sat behind a desk. Like the ice cream shop, my best friends had vanished. They weren't around to help their friend. The hand tightened against my throat. I wandered back down.

My eyes drifted to the barefoot young haleks playing *khusai* on the dimly lit lawn before Shujah's block. They held their right feet with their left hands at the back, hobbled with their left feet, and wrestled with their right hands, panting, puffing and yelling. It brought back memories from the old days. We'd divide into two teams of three or more, and push, pull and wrestle each other until one side let go of his holding leg or fell on the ground. Wazir alone wrestled three players. Whoever had Wazir on his team won the tournament. The very same play on the very same lawn, but different players, I thought. I was ready to pay half of what I possessed to relive those childhood moments; pay the other half to suspend them until death. At least Nazia's life could've been spared. And I'd have not emigrated to England.

England felt like a golden cage. From the outside, life looked as if days were Eid and nights Barat; but, from the inside, it tasted like a cucumber: neither sweet nor bitter. The English had their weekends to go to nightclubs or pubs. They celebrated Christmas and Easter. Went on holiday and visited their relatives and friends. We neither had relatives, nor celebrated Christmas or Easter. It didn't make sense to celebrate our festivals without families and friends. At times I didn't even realise the arrival of Nowruz. During Eids, I offered the Eid Prayer in the mosque, and off I went to the workplace or university. During all those years I never heard the sound of azan from the mosque, but from my phone.

There was no *Khana Takani*, cleaning home. No queuing for hours in Mandawi to buy kulcha-e-Eid or kulcha-e-Nowruz. No new clothes to put on. No Agha to give me eidi money. No Wazir and Baktash to accompany me to neighbours to '*Eid Mubarak*' them, Happy Eid, and ask for eidi. No Wazir's mother to offer us home-made khajor. No Makroryan Market to spend all the eidi money on shornakhud, egg tapping and fanfares. No trors and akas to visit and hide-and-seek with their children over the rooftops. No fancy dinners in their houses. No lounges full of trays of baklava, cream rolls and half a dozen dried fruits. No sisters to fight with over trors and akas' eidis. I envied my ancestors; they were the most fortunate people. They were born, grew up and died in the same country; never had to go through the humiliation of emigrating to another country where everything felt foreign and, importantly, never traded their identity for their security.

London had a sizable Afghan community, and during our special holidays it organised Afghan concerts with Afghan comedians from Europe and America. Mour and I neither approved of concerts nor could afford to buy train fares, let alone concert tickets. A few times we travelled to London for our passports and asylum applications or my khastegari during our 16 years in England; otherwise, we stayed put in Durham and, like a machine, worked, studied and slept.

England was the Amazon jungle where no species had any idea about me or my past, however. I didn't know the next-door neighbours by their proper names, even though we'd lived next to one another for years. No one interfered in my business or told me how to live my life. No one taunted me with coward or, worse, piss pants. Conversely, they perceived me, to my pleasant shock, as 'courageous'. They saw me as courageous, in large part, because of Frishta and perhaps, in small part, owing to the nature of the struggle to fight for racial equality in a non-violent way. There you didn't have to physically fight your war to take revenge, anyway; everyone was allocated a powerful bodyguard: the rule of law. It always – well, almost always – stood by the victim. I lived a new life.

My eyes drifted to the half-open basement door of the block, the very door Frishta retreated to in my dreams. I'd taken the basement as a grave. But why would Frishta wander there if she was alive? I found myself passing through the metre-long door and stepping down a couple of stairs. No sign of Frishta, but the musty place had a calmness to it. The hand around my neck eased its grip. I leaned against the hard concrete, placed my hands on the warm floor and wept like a young halek, asking Khudai for forgiveness for Nazia's death. The hand around my neck released its grip and my eyes closed.

***

I OPENED MY EYES and they were acquainted with the darkness. I saw the empty place in the middle where once the young Frishta sat, her head on her father's arm, her brother and Zarghuna playing marbles. Ironically, I sat in the exact place where young Ahmad used to sit, eating chips, while Mour talked to Frishta's mother. Agha and Brigadier listened to the BBC News on the portable radio. 11 more families from our corridor squeezed themselves into that little section of the basement: the cries of children, the conversation of women, the smell of chips and the smoke of small fires. I saw my past, even though more than two decades had elapsed.

Faith, if you believed in it, united me again with my past. Khudai indeed had accepted my prayers for Frishta in the Makroryan Mosque. The time had come to disclose to each other what we hadn't dared to do then.

Chapter Thirty-Four

The jeep drove through Afghanistan's green zone, Sherpur, or what Nadir called 'Sher-chur' (lion's loot) in his thesis. Nouveau riche warlords, drug lords and bureaucrats grabbed the barren patch of hillsides near Wazir Akbar Khan District in the first years of America's invasion and turned them into the Beverly Hills of Kabul, each mansion with skyscraper glass windows worth millions of US dollars. We turned into a street, and four times vehicle barriers were raised up before pulling over on the driveway of one of the luxury mansions, surrounded by gigantic blast walls. Two guards in military uniform jumped out of the concrete room by the metal gate and let our vehicle in.

A guard in a black suit gestured to me to raise my hands as I stepped out of the jeep with pain all over my body.

'Apologies, Dr saheb. We're ordered to search everyone,' Ashraf said after the man moved a metal object like a cricket bat from my head to feet.

'Don't be sorry for implementing rules,' I said and followed Ashraf along a lawn, which solar night lights illuminated like a bright day in the otherwise blackout of Kabul. According to Nadir, one-third of Afghans benefited from the Central Asian-imported electricity. Frishta made up one of the lucky ones.

'The house seems huge,' I said.

'Four floors with 22 rooms, a rooftop fountain and two heated indoor pools.' Ashraf looked up at the villa with the cream and brown exterior. 'Each room has its own bathroom and toilet. The construction map is designed in Dubai.' Ashraf sounded like he owned the villa. Sacks of sand were placed on the front of the multistorey building roof; a man guarded behind them. The flapping flag of Afghanistan and several tall aerials stood nearby.

'Frishta own it?'

'Of course.'

'How many months' salaries get you a mansion like this?'

Ashraf's lips stretched. 'She can buy ten villas like this from her business.' He handed me over to a woman, who introduced herself as Nahima and led me into a room as large as Chaman-e-Hozori, and as full as the Ghazi Stadium staging an Afghan Premier League football match.

The strong perfume-scented Nahima muttered for me to take a seat. She sat on a chair next to a desk in the corner.

I found myself sitting at the end of the room with high windows and grey leather sofas, right by the door where two guards in black uniforms and black glasses stood alert. My heart beat hard and my legs shook. Held the sofa and took deep breaths. Peeped to the corner over the coffee tables arranged before the couches. A small figure sat behind the working desk and, to my relief, was busy talking to two senior men. Two guards stood by her side. Took more deep breaths. Stole another glance at the figure on the swivel leather chair; her head, to my relief, was down, writing. She wore a black headscarf. The black, red and green Afghan flag was embedded on the top-left pocket of her black jacket. Beneath the jacket was a white shirt. Frishta's face had shrunk, the eyes had got smaller – though she still seemed younger than her mid-thirties.

A variety of emotions overwhelmed me seeing Frishta in the flesh, but disappointment took over. Selfishly, I expected a good reception from her. She didn't even greet me. Why did she abandon melmastia?

I counted six guards and 27 visitors in the room, a Western male and a female included. Women constituted most of the visitors, all in their burkas. No one had taken their shoes off; I didn't know where the foot stink came from.

The two senior men stood up, placed their right hands over their hearts and walked towards the door. Frishta followed them. 'Don't worry, I'll personally speak with Karzai saheb,' I overheard Frishta in faultless Pashto say near the door.

I remembered Brigadier's words, *One day you'll make history, princess. I'm sure of this.* She was making history, right there in that gigantic lounge, right in front of my eyes. How wrong Mour had been to predict Frishta's destiny: *The daughter of Brigadier will bring shame on her family. Remember my words.*

Not even in my daydreaming had I imagined her to grow into such an important person whose security detail comprised dozens of armed guards, and I *thanked* Khudai for this.

'Salaam Azizi saheb.' A voice gave me the shakes; Frishta stretching out her right hand while keeping a distance, her two guards standing by her with fingers on the triggers of their Kalashnikovs. We shook hands. Surprisingly, her hand trembled, too.

'I was busy talking to the constituents.'

Did she read my mind? In the corner, behind her right shoulder, I read Bathroom, and Prayer Room with its door wide open and guarded by a man in black uniform. Stop trembling, it's only Frishta, I said to myself.

Frishta turned to the Westerners sitting opposite her desk in the top corner. 'This is Mr Ahmad Azizi. We used to be neighbours, and... good neighbours. He now lives in London. Don't you, Mr Azizi?' Frishta said in a raised voice and, without waiting for my reply, limped back to her place, followed by the guards. Had she twisted her ankle? And why the formal tone?

The couple smiled. The woman in a knee-length dress over a pair of black jeans and a black scarf gestured to the empty place on the three-seater sofa next to her and the Western man. She introduced herself and the man, her husband, as Naomi and John in an American accent as we shook hands.

They loved London and wanted to know whereabouts I lived. Durham, I told them. They worked for a human rights NGO. Admired Frishta's work for Afghan women. Frishta was a 'courageous woman', the kind any country would wish to give birth to; a voice nobody could 'afford to ignore', Naomi said, and John, in dark blue trousers with a light blue shirt, nodded.

Clueless about what to say or how to start a conversation on the way to Frishta, the Americans thankfully broke the ice. John and Naomi, who seemed somehow interested in my personal life, appeared impressed to hear I'd just completed my medical degree. Constituents had visited Frishta on the wrong evening because she evidently eavesdropped on my conversation with the Americans more than listened to their worries. She was at a loss for words to a visitor on the occasion that I mentioned my medical degree.

Frishta saw the constituents one by one and told Nahima and the guards, one of whom stood behind us in our corner by the closed door with an Exit sign above it, to go and eat.

'I've just been saying, Ahmad jan, how much work you've done for the women of this country,' Naomi said as the guards marched out.

'I shall thank you for helping us find our place in society. Afghanistan's women today aren't the women of ten years ago. Our rights are now enshrined in the Constitution. We enter education and the workplace. We freely express our views. We should build on this and take Afghanistan a step further to a new era of freedom, equality and democracy.'

The couple promised to maintain their efforts to build a secure Afghanistan. A woman in a white cooking apron walked in, carrying a tray with four glasses.

'She's the master of mango juice,' John said to me and thanked the woman, who smiled and put the glasses before us. 'Delicious,' John added after sipping the juice, his face beaming.

'Though I'm not so sure now. While America entered Afghanistan championing our rights, she's silent on our fate as she exits,' Frishta said over the buzzing sound of air-conditioners from the wall behind.

'What's happened to the peace talks?' Naomi asked.

I took a sip of the ice-cold mango and crunched on the pieces of almonds.

'Nobody gives away anything. The Afghan government seemingly has no clue. I fear a US-Taliban political deal would trade away our hard-earned rights.'

'Afghan women have the right to choose their roles. They must be included in the negotiations.'

'I've warned the American officials that Afghanistan can't have national security if its women can't have security. It can't have peace if its women are denied their rights to be full citizens.'

'Let's hope the talks are conducted responsibly.'

'One US official told me women rights are one of their "red lines". I said how could I trust him when one of his colleagues described us as "pet rocks" in their rucksack that were "taking us down".'

'That was shocking.'

'It really was,' John said.

John's constant confirmations of Naomi's statements reminded me of my patients in Newcastle, the 'darling-honey couple' whose warm conversation brought a smile to my face, except Noemi and John were younger, in their mid- to late fifties.

'I told him that instead of talking about forming an interim government with them, they should bring terrorists to justice.'

'What did he say?'

'The usual, "every conflict eventually ends with a political solution". But this conflict is very complicated. Would the Taliban cut ties with Al-Qaeda, stop violence against the Afghan state and accept a constitution that defends liberal values and women's rights? Would they give up their Emirate for a Republic? Would Pakistan, Russia and Iran stop assisting the Taliban?'

'Plenty of woulds and hows,' Naomi said. The bright electricity dipped and burned on the crystal chandelier, as large as a truck tyre.

'Precisely,' Frishta said.

'America set the mujahideen up in the 80s against the pro-Communist regime; now Pakistan uses the American technique against America,' John said.

'Precisely.'

'I don't believe the talks with the Taliban will get anywhere, anyway,' Naomi said.

'America longs for a graceful exit. I fear she'd give control of Afghanistan back to Pakistan by gradually empowering the Taliban, who'd subjugate us once again.'

'For Pakistan's guarantee that Afghanistan won't be used as a terrorist base against America and the allies,' John chipped in.

'Precisely.'

'A repeat of Iraq,' John added.

I sipped my mango juice.

'India and NATO won't accept that outcome.' Naomi stood up. John followed suit.

The couple said goodbye to me and stepped outside together with Frishta.

What to say next once she's back? Calm down, she's the same Frishta. I pinched my thigh, but the photo up on the wall behind her told a different story: Laura Bush and Colin Powell stood at a younger Frishta's sides, all smiling while Frishta held a rectangular glass. Underneath the frame read *The International Women of Courage Award*.

My heart raced as the door creaked open and Frishta entered. Thankfully, she spoke. 'These are my days. Start 7am; finish 10pm, sometimes even midnight.'

She sat opposite me on her swivel recliner, her hands shaking.

'Afghan women have deservedly made progress. I'm sure they're grateful to you.'

Her eyes beamed with joy. 'We have a long way to go.' She wiped her forehead with a tissue.

I nodded, clueless about what to say next. Preoccupied myself with the dirt-stained Afghan rugs.

'Our law favours women. But it isn't implemented. Despite the constitutional equality, our justice system regards women as half-human beings.'

I nodded, sensing maybe Frishta, like me, didn't know what to talk about. I pressed my hands together to steady them. Did my evil action of decades back towards Frishta cause the nervousness or her charismatic presence? Or the fact that I no longer spoke to my friend Frishta?

'Even the parliament has approved a marriageable age for a halek of 18, and a jelai 16.'

'Gender-based discrimination.'

'Precisely. This new law would turn the clock back hundreds of years. It's important we annul it,' she said. 'In Afghanistan, you have to grab your rights by force,' she added as an afterthought.

My mind raced to the moment I snatched the diary. Did she still remember it? Had she forgiven me? If only I had the power to read her mind.

'The parliament is full of warlords, religious conservatives and foreign agents. They don't give a damn about Afghanistan or its women,' she went on.

I was desperate to learn about Frishta and her life; desperate to reveal *my* mina to her, let her know how much I loved her, and, importantly, determine whether she still had feelings for me and would marry me. Craved to tell her she'd been dead for me until the day before yesterday, the reason I hadn't come back for her all these years. Talking about politics didn't grip me, even if it came out of the very person's mouth I dearly loved. Only one thing captivated me in Afghanistan: the woman sitting in front of me. I wanted to know how she'd spent the two decades we'd been apart. Her political discussion, though initially welcoming escapism, disallowed the opportunity to raise the subject.

'We view women like children's toys: mindless, soulless, heartless with no talent or ambition. We must change our outlook.'

'Harassment of women on the streets of Kabul is disgusting.'

'Precisely. But what has the government done about it? Nothing. Why should they? Their women are either locked in or chilling out abroad. Karzai's the educated. His wife is a doctor. But we haven't seen her in public,' Frishta said.

Silence, apart from the air-conditioners buzzing and humming. Eight pieces of dried mud lay around my feet.

'Anyway, enough of politics. It was good to see Mour.'

'Today?'

'Woh.'

'*Really?*'

'After I dropped Nazia off. Why?'

'Nothing. She hasn't told me.'

'She almost fainted when she saw me.'

'Yeah?'

'She'd thought I was dead. She kissed me all over.'

Did Mour not know?

'She was mad at your aka for having turned me into the dead.'

Why did Mour act like she'd been aware? Why didn't she tell me she hadn't known? Why did people do this to me? First Frishta. Now Mour. And me? Why hadn't I investigated before making up my mind? I committed the same error. Again.

'She told me about your father and sisters. May Khuda jan bless them.'

'Ameen. It was a hard blow. Mour hasn't recovered from it.' The time was right to tell her how saddened I'd been for her loss. Losing Mahjan and Brigadier did feel then like losing a real tror and aka.

'Life's been a long battle. Overcoming my parents' and Safi jan's deaths was the hardest part.'

I was glad she showed no sentiment or went on talking about her loved ones. No Afghan had escaped unaffected by the nearly four-decade-long war. I didn't know a family who hadn't had a loved one injured or killed. War and death formed a normal part of Afghan life, so we didn't go on mourning it.

'Is Shujah your real aka?'

'Agha's cousin's husband. Apparently, he's transferred our flat ownership and won't give back our money and passports.'

Frishta's face darkened. 'He said he bought the property through an attorney and didn't know your family.'

'It's a lie.'

'You know he almost gambled his daughter?'

'Amina told me,' I said, feeling embarrassed about what Frishta might think of our family.

'He was mad at Amina today for having telephoned me about you and Mour.'

'He'll get even madder if he finds out that Amina got me in touch with you.'

'I told him I'd throw him off your lounge window if he touched her.'

'He's... unbelievable. He wasn't home now. I fear he may gamble our money and passports.'

'I know where he is.' She took her iPhone out and dialled a number.

'How much money?'

'£6,000,' I whispered. Her phone was on loudspeaker.

'Hello,' Shujah said.

'Give the phone to your boss.'

'Hello Wakil saheb.' A deep voice after a pause.

'Listen carefully, no ifs or buts. Mour and Ahmad's money, their passports and the flat must be returned immediately. I swear on Khuda jan if a penny's lost, I'll burn you and your entire gang alive.'

'Leave it with me, Wakil saheb.'

'I said immediately. Now.'

'Understood.'

Frishta hung up, her face still dark. 'Your aka is worse than you think.'

What else? My heart fell.

'He's involved in armed robberies and kidnapping.'

'Na?'

'Really. I know their gang.'

'Why can't the security forces stop all this?'

'Our law enforcement agencies work tirelessly to establish security. Unfortunately, some let their colleagues down.'

'Somehow, the NDS believe I work with the terrorists.'

Her black eyebrows were raised, wanting to know why I assumed so. I told her about the airport incident.

'Bushy brows?' she said.

'Woh.'

'Works for the same gang.' She called a telephone number, but no one answered; she told me I'd no longer get hassled.

The woman in the white cooking apron poked her head around and told us dinner was ready. Frishta required five minutes to pray. She remained seated on the chair under the switched-off 50-inch smart TV stuck on a wall mount. Did she have a bad knee for not doing prayers standing up but in sitting-down positions?

She limped and pointed to the door. I refused to lead.

'It's considered feminine here.' Her lips stretched.

'The gates to the city can be shut, but people's mouths cannot be.'

She raised her eyebrows. 'Your wife is lucky to have a well-mannered husband.' Her smile broadened. Many lines appeared on her forehead. I gauged she was tired and exhausted, even lonely. The hard and long 'battle' had indeed taken its toll, a battle she hadn't fought only for herself, but also for her Afghan sisters.

After walking up the marble stairs, I followed Frishta into a medium-sized room furnished with Afghan rugs and pumped-up mattresses, scenting of quabili palaw. They must be her daughters, I dishearteningly thought as I saw three little jelais sitting at the tablecloth. The woman in the apron spread out the home-made bread. Frishta named her, but I didn't catch it. My mind preoccupied itself with the possibility of having lost Frishta forever to these jelais' father. Where was he, though?

We sat on the tablecloth, and the woman left.

'I hope the food is good?' Frishta said, referring to the variety of food ranging from quabili palaw to kebab to different drinks and a selection of fruits.

The three jelais ruined my appetite – though out of courtesy, I said there was no need for having taken the trouble to prepare so much food.

It was time to clarify facts; no time for nervousness; couldn't afford to spend another two decades regretting. The jelais would have been our children had I dared to express my feelings.

'I have to straighten my leg.' She broke the silence, sitting on the cherry mattress.

'Have you hurt it?'

'A gift from the rocket.'

'What do you mean?'

'The rocket took half of it.'

The room, with windows as high up as in a prison, suffocated me. Frishta without a leg? All these years? How could she have managed? I wanted to hug her tiny body and keep it in my arms forever. Tell her how sorry I was. Reassure her not to worry as I was there for her from then on. I shut up. The jelais' father had already taken my role. Plus, what hung behind her answered my questions: three black gold canvases of Allah, Muhammad and *Dua-e-Qunoot* were stuck to the wall and in golden handwriting read, *Those who have no one have Allah. Those who have Allah have everything.*

'I eat on the tablecloth, like Padar jan. I hope it isn't uncomfortable.' She broke the long-developed silence.

'I prefer eating on the floor.'

Frishta gave a mouthful of rice to one of the jelais, complimenting her for eating solid foods. Frishta preoccupied herself with them as if I didn't exist. She hadn't even looked up. She'd made a home in which she seemed happy – happy, even though I wasn't part of it.

'Has Kabul changed?' she said after another silence.

'Yes, it has. To start with, you can't find a decent jelai.' I turned the conversation to personal matters. Should've done so earlier when she commented on my wife, which had me lost for words.

'A decent jelai for what?'

'To get married.' Did her face darken?

She gave a spoonful of yoghurt to one of the daughters, not the previous one. I couldn't work out who was the youngest or oldest; they resembled each other. All had short hair and wore black dresses from the same fabric.

'How come you haven't been married yet?' Did I hear a sense of eagerness beneath her balanced tone?

'Education.' Ached for asking a personal question but swallowed the urge. I got a mouthful of rice with raisins and sliced carrots.

'Haven't fallen in mina with an English jelai? They're beautiful.'

'English jelais are for English haleks,' I said, excited by how the conversation flew. Took a sip of the tangy-flavoured lemon water.

'Never had an English jelai?' Frishta's personal question saddened me. I suspected she also yearned to discover about my personal life.

'Ignore the silly question. I'm sorry.' I detected a glitter of the old Frishta.

'No need to apologise, Frishta. I never had an English jelai. I need an Afghan wife who understands my language, culture, religion. Help me look after Mour if need be.'

She took a mouthful of rice with a piece of meat and chewed it for what seemed to be forever. Unlike me, Frishta didn't leave the teeth's job to the stomach. 'Have you found one?'

I found my jelai years back. She sat right in front of me, but all the signs revealed she'd gone far away. 'Mour and Nazigul are looking into it.'

Her eyes widened. 'Did you not like any of the four jelais?'

Mour must have told her.

'Haven't met them all.'

'You've remained a dutiful son, Ahmad jan.'

'Thanks, Frishta jan.' My spontaneous reply wasn't for the compliment, but for calling me by my first name. Hearing it from her mouth after all these years took me back to the young Frishta and Ahmad. 'You seem to have settled down.'

She blushed. The bright light dimmed and then brightened again.

'Where's he now?'

'Away.' She blushed again.

'Where?'

'On business.' She blushed yet again.

It wasn't easy for Frishta to talk about her husband, given her feelings for me in the past, no matter how hard she tried to downplay them, so I changed the subject, certain now I'd lost her to her fortunate husband. I praised her 'three daughters'. One of them gazed at me. Frishta gushed 'thanks' and planted a kiss on the daughter's head.

I lived a life outside of the deep hole for the first time in years. Treasured its every moment, despite its nervy, awkward and disappointing moments. Sadly, it'd soon end. She'd moved on without clinging to the past. The woman wearing *J'adore* wasn't the Frishta who'd dedicated one side of her diary to me. She was a wife to someone and a mother to three lovely daughters. I must respect this and mention nothing about my mina. But must clarify I hadn't been loitering in front of Nazia's school. I deliberately focused the conversation on the difficulty of finding a wife in Kabul because parents wouldn't show their daughters to haleks.

'They'd rather sell them for walwar, give them in *baad* or payment to settle a dispute like they're lambs,' she said and shook her head. 'How does a 12-year-old know what's good or bad for her?'

'Not much.'

'Their own parents deprive them of their education, their childish lives. The poor jelais spend all their lives in misery. Eventually burn themselves to death because divorce is against the culture.'

'That's why I went to the school to get to know Nazia, to ensure she wasn't forced into marriage. The police thought otherwise.' It wasn't the police alone; someone else likewise called me a pervert.

One of the daughters stopped eating, and Frishta asked her to go and wash her hands. The daughter took the cloth off her lap and toddled towards the door.

'When I tell husbands and parents about human rights abuses, they react with anger. "Violence against women is a Western idea," they say.' Frishta mimicked them in a deep voice.

I found my mouth stretch: typical Frishta.

'They don't understand human rights are human ideas. They don't see that violence against women is violence against the national law... against Islamic principles.'

She made no comment on Nazia's fate, and I left it there – at least she knew why I'd been in front of the school, something which Mour and Nazigul must've also told her. As always, her head was down on the tablecloth, feeding the daughters. I thought they ate a little too much for their age, especially at that time of night.

The daughter toddled back in, said salaam and sat in her place. Frishta stroked her hair, praising her for cleaning her hands and uttering salaam. Same old Frishta: a sympathetic sister to Afghan women, and a caring mother to her three children.

'I feel today's democratic Afghanistan is like my little princess daughter who's learning to toddle.' Frishta again stroked her hair. 'She needs a responsible adult to hold her hand and help her until she can walk steadily and discover her own way. My wish is that the international community doesn't forget Afghanistan this time until we find our way. I hope our friends don't forget the women of Afghanistan. Women's failure in this country is the international community's failure.'

'I agree.' Every word she said felt as if it was direct from her heart.

'It's equally essential Afghans learn quickly how to look after their own watan; we shouldn't leave everything to foreigners.'

'Agha said we tend to blame others for the ills of our watan. We hardly take responsibility.'

'Aka Azizullah was a wise man. I never forget his words: *Afghans will one day find out who really has crippled Afghanistan: Pakistan or the Soviet Union?* I'd say Pakistan if he asked me today.'

'And America.'

'Unlike most Afghans, I don't blame America.'

'I see no difference between the American and the Soviet occupation.'

'America's intervention is authorised by the UN. But it doesn't mean I'm happy with her footprint. Think: if US forces leave irresponsibly, Pakistan will take over. We don't want to terminate one occupation and end up with another, a much worse one where everyone would die from hunger. We must this time use our common sense, not emotions.'

'What about the invasion on our values? Do those so-called celebrities with bare heads, short sleeves and plumped-up lips represent Afghan women?'

Frishta looked up, her gaze as sharp as a snow leopard's.

'Go and knock on each Afghan house and see who answers the door. Mour, Nazigul, yourself, or plumped-up lips with tons of make-up?'

'Myself?'

'You do; always did, Frishta.'

'Let's not bore ourselves with depressing lectures. I hope you find the right jelai.'

'Is your husband the right person for you?' I asked before thinking it over. All evening she tried to avoid talking about herself and our past.

Silence. The air-conditioners hummed, producing cool air.

'Frishta, I asked you a question.'

'I don't answer personal questions.' She peered down, her large eyelashes covering her black eyes.

'I answered yours.'

One of the daughters reported the other for spilling juice on her sleeve. The culprit denied it. Frishta cleaned the sleeve and told her it was as good as new.

'Frishta, you know well when I want something, I get it.'

Her face turned darker. 'You won't this time, Mr Azizi. I've been fighting all these years to ensure men like you don't get "something" they want.' Her voice wasn't as deep as before, her veins under the white shirt popping out. The sudden outburst shook me.

'You've misunderstood me.' I used the phrase many times in our old days. Though I knew she didn't rationalise when it came to gender equality.

'You're right. You still are a coward.'

'Your anger problem has worsened.'

'Evil men like you have driven me mad.'

'You seem to have done well out of it.'

'How dare you, murderer?'

'I hope you haven't compromised your "purpose",' I blurted out and meant it.

'Fuck you.'

'I'd lose faith in humanity if the solid stone I've leaned against most of my life falls to pieces like sand.'

'You men give us nothing but evil.'

'Misandry isn't the answer.'

'Pissing in your pants is.'

'You need treatment, Frishta.'

'Leave my house at once.' She got up, her hand pointing to the door. On the glass table under the smart television behind her, a long-moustached Brigadier and Mahjan with a seven- or eight-year-old Frishta sitting in the middle. Brigadier peered at me.

I should've controlled my temper and my mouth. But I wouldn't play a coward. I'd clarify all matters and then depart. First, I was to return what belonged to her. I took it from my jacket pocket and passed it to her.

'I don't need it.' She averted her eyes.

'I know you've already forgotten about it, but it's yours.'

'I buried that life when I buried my parents.'

'How easily you've buried your childhood dreams, Frishta.' I sounded more sarcastic than I'd intended. But why did I complain? She had no clue about my mina for her. The young Frishta saw me as a friend – the young Ahmad even denied that status. I put the red diary on the mattress, parting with it after 21 years and some three months, thanking Khudai it was eventually united with a living Frishta.

'I said I don't need it.' Her eyes glued onto mine with a murderous intent – the same leopardine look she'd confronted Rashid and later the bullying Mullah Rahmat with.

'I made a mistake to release you. Now leave before I... and I don't want to hear from you again. Run away like a coward.' She limped towards the door, opened it and gestured to the hallway furnished with Afghan rugs.

What I intended to do next was suicidal, but I must: I pushed on the mattress and rose on my feet with pain in my body and told her I wouldn't leave until she heard me – afterwards, she could have her bodyguards shoot me if she wanted.

Her face turned darker.

'First, I sincerely apologise for the diary–'

'I'll never forgive you.'

'You've got every right not to... but at least listen to me for five minutes. There are things you *need* to know.' I paused. Should I say it in front of the little daughters, who sat with blank expressions, or should I not? I knew the stubborn Frishta wouldn't go to another room. I'd better tell her before I regretted it for another two decades.

'I snatched the diary because I thought you were with Shafih. I felt jealous because I was in mina with you,' I said and took a deep breath. 'After the home classes ended, I realised my feelings for you. I know it's too late, and there's no point telling you now. When it was, I chickened out – something I'll regret all my life. I wrote it in your diary, though, and placed it in your jacket in the basement, but you gave the jacket to Nazo. Anyway, you know now... and I believe you have the right to do so.

'Second, you might wonder why I didn't come all these years to tell you all this. I didn't know you were alive until yesterday. I was told you'd been killed together with your parents. I'd have come for you had I known, even if that meant fighting the entire world. Would've never left Mazar-e-Sharif without you.

312

'But we can't change the past. Maybe we were not fated to. I'm very thankful to Khudai to see you have built a happy family for yourself. May Khudai look after you all.

'Finally, thank *you* for this afternoon; you saved me once more. You won't have to again. I'm going to leave soon after I sorted out the apartment, and you'll never hear from me again.'

She looked down, her face still dark.

'Have you finished?'

'One more thing, all I wanted to say was... sometimes in attempting to fight the evils, one becomes evil. I had *no* intention to hurt you.'

'Finished now?'

'Woh.'

'Leave.' She pointed with her right hand to the corridor, holding the door with her left hand.

'I'm sorry... and goodbye,' I said to the daughters sitting in front of the full tablecloth. I looked at my three-quarters-full plate. We hadn't discussed our friends and classmates. Where had Baktash's family vanished to? Wazir? Frishta's magic spell always turned me into an Ahmad who forgot about anybody else in his life. As I reached the door, I stopped opposite her. 'Frishta jan, thank you for coming into my life and teaching me how to unclip my wings.' I could no longer fight my tears; let them prick my eyes.

The meeting with Frishta ended. She wasn't dead. She was alive, so close to me earlier on that I heard her breath and smelled her perfume, yet it felt we were never further apart. But she was as good as dead to me. I'd never have her. I *lost* her to her husband. As a true Afghan, I *had* to honour this; as a true lover, I *had* the right to let her know about my mina. And I was glad I did.

Chapter Thirty-Five

Nazigul whispered that there were 'people' waiting in the lounge. A man in a qaraqul hat with two armed men greeted me as I entered, introducing himself as Haji Pahlawan.

'Your passports.' He passed them to me.

I checked the personal details pages and Mour's settlement visa on the Afghan passport.

'This is $5,000. Give me 24 hours, I'll return you the rest.'

'Ours were pounds,' I said and looked at Shujah standing by the open window with his head down.

'I'm sorry, we've invested the money. We'll give you dollars by the exchange rate.'

I counted 50 notes.

'What about the apartment?'

'Shujah will sort it out tomorrow in Surobi,' he said.

'Surobi?'

'Your mother and Wakil saheb have just arranged it,' Haji Pahlawan said, his perahan getting dented by the rotating fan. 'Shujah, I don't want to hear a complaint from Ahmad jan.' He asked Shujah to check that 'the way is clear'.

Melmastia compelled me to ask him for tea.

He thanked me. 'Please say you've received your money in full if Wakil saheb asks.'

'I won't tell lies.'

His face changed colour but forced a smile. 'It's OK, I'll speak to her myself,' he said. Shujah gave a clearance of no non-mahrams on the way. He asked me if I followed him downstairs. I hesitated but told him I'd see him shortly. Handed Mour the dollars and passports in the kitchen and, despite Mour's concerns, rushed down the stairs, feeling the ache in my body and reading the All-Hearing, the All-Knowing dua.

The door of a red Carina opened, and the broad-shouldered man got out, the exterior bright corridor light shining on his face. He extended his right hand and uttered a 'salaam alaikum'. Melmastia once more prevailed: I shook his hand.

'He insisted on apologising in person,' Haji Pahlawan said, with armed men standing behind him.

'We've been fed wrong information about you,' the broad-shouldered man said, raising his bushy eyebrows and revealing the blue pupils behind them.

'By who?'

'It doesn't matter. You're now our brother. Anything you want to get done in Kabul, I mean *anything*, give your servant a shout,' Haji Pahlawan said, putting his hands over his chest.

'I don't want a bandit for a brother. I'll pursue my claim against him at the Human Rights Commission.'

Haji Pahlawan's lips stretched as if I threatened him with a snooker club.

'I want my money back by tomorrow,' I said and made for the corridor, seeing Mour and Nazigul's heads poking out from the balcony above.

***

SHUJAH, MOUR AND NAZIGUL discussed going to Surobi in the lounge as I entered. Mour asked me what Haji Pahlawan wanted; nothing important, I said. Amina followed in, telling Nazigul that the twins were asleep. The kids and the family would've gone to bed hours before midnight had it not been for my late coming from Frishta's.

I asked for the timing and details of Mour and Frishta's arrangement, which I found surprising given our argument half an hour ago. But Frishta's helping nature never stopped astonishing me. Frishta had talked to Mour while I was driven back by Ashraf. Mour added that Frishta had just spoken to someone in the court in Surobi, and they'd complete the transfer of ownership in a day. The exact process took up weeks in Kabul. Frishta would handle the paperwork and send the title deeds to Mour in England. What would happen to Nazigul and the children? The question bothered me.

'We'll be back by the evening,' Mour said.

'I'm coming.'

Power went down and came back up again, forcing Nazigul to say 'Na'.

'It isn't safe.'

'I'm not better than you.'

'You're *not* needed.'

'I am. I fight my own battle.' It was disturbing to be a liability to others. I felt ashamed that Frishta kept rescuing us.

'I'm tired of hearing this.'

'Respectfully, Mour, I'm coming. I want to see that all the paperwork is done correctly. Plus, I miss Surobi.' I really did. I no longer wanted the fear of this or that to stop me from visiting the birthplace of my ancestors. And no longer trusted Shujah; he could easily deceive Mour in court.

'You'll go once there's peace.'

'There'll be no peace in my lifetime.' I sounded like Agha.

'Your stubbornness will put me in an early grave,' Mour said.

'Nazigul, did Frishta ever inquire about me?'

Nazigul looked at Shujah, who sat opposite me on the mattress with a wrinkled face.

'Never, once we told her we didn't know you,' Amina said, pointing with her eyes to Shujah.

'Not everyone's like you,' Mour said.

'Thanks, Khuda jan, you didn't marry Frishta. She's the sort to stay away from,' Nazigul said, her eyes swollen from earlier today.

I'd already decided to do so – albeit for a different reason. It was time to forget about her. *Really* forget about her. The old Frishta was mine, killed with a heart full of love for me. The new Frishta belonged to somebody else. I hadn't touched a woman all those years, while she'd shared a warm bed with her husband and produced three daughters. I thanked Khudai I didn't see him. If also I didn't witness Frishta having compromised what Agha admired her for: that absolute integrity.

'I'll bring the flight dates earlier,' I said.

'We haven't seen all the jelais?' Mour said.

'I don't want to marry for now.'

'Why?'

'Things are more complicated than I thought.' Frishta's rebirth and Nazia's suicide, like the devastating airport fedayi, had hit me hard; they pained me more than the crowd punching and kicking me before school. Those destructive blows coupled with the complexities of khastegari concussed my will to get married in Kabul.

'Didn't I tell you in England?'

'It'd be a waste of money to leave before seeing the other two jelais,' Nazigul said.

'In England, he was insistent on getting married in Kabul. "Traditional jelai" was what was on his lips. Now he abandons the traditional jelai in Kabul and gets married in England. I don't understand the logic of this,' Mour said.

'I've made my decision.'

'We–'

'Don't force him. *It's his life.* I'm too tired to care anymore,' Mour cut Nazigul short.

I'd never heard this from Mour. She deserved that I kissed her hands and told her how sorry I was for having wrongly accused her, but decided against it. I'd do it in our *own* home in England. If only I'd known.

Chapter Thirty-Six

Another reality grabbed my attention. As we drove outside of Kabul, I noticed my watan and my people had picked up the colour of dust: the giant mountains, the tunnels, the mud houses; the lone shops covered in piles of green and yellow melons as well as plastic bags of apples; the solitary mansions and supermarkets with photos of ice cream and fresh juice; the dried soil; the sporadic greenery; the advertisements for firms and hospitals on the mountains in blue, green, red and yellow colours; the faces who sold goods on both sides of the road oblivious of how close the traffic passed by; the kids who nonchalantly played around the burned-out Soviet tank in Naghlu; the oncoming vehicles; the air; and even the burning sun. The dust was such that careful drivers, unlike ours, had to turn their fog lights on. My white perahan tunban had turned grey like my waistcoat.

A deafening horn like the warlord from the other day. Our driver pulled over to let a Toyota Hilux overtake us. Half a dozen haleks clapped, sang and danced at its loading bay. A Sardar in a Panjabi turban and white perahan and tunban from the back seat said the haleks, sons to the powerful syndicate, travelled in their zero-miles cars to Darunta Dam to eat fresh fish in its restaurants, swim in the deep water, and stay the nights in its hotels. They acquired their whisky, Chivas Regal and Johnnie Walker bottles from the thriving black market in Kabul and drank them on the way. There was no day when a traffic accident didn't occur on this route. He pointed to kids washing cars, adding that they made $5 a day, if lucky. The children to the elite spent $300 on 'a woman and whisky' in a night. How could we expect peace and security in Afghanistan? he questioned.

'We may see them provided the driver takes us in one piece, Sardar,' Mour said, her left arm resting on the ledge of the coaster minibus window.

'That won't happen, sister. The earlier the driver reaches the destination, the more rewards he gets,' Sardar said. 'Drivers resort to hashish to enhance their performance.'

'So, we pay with our lives for employers' greed,' I said.

'Driver, please take it easy. We all have families,' Mour raised her voice.

'What will happen, will happen: it is Khudai's will.' He touched Khudai's name dangling from his back mirror, kissed his hand, increased the volume of Naghma and Mangal, and carried on driving the minibus like a maniac. Thanks to Khudai, we were in one piece 40 minutes into our journey; only another 20 minutes to Surobi, inshallah.

'Brother, thank you for earlier on,' Sardar said to me after a silence.

'It was my duty, Sardar.'

'What happened to the ethics and morals we inherited from our elders?' he asked and wiped his sweaty face with a handkerchief.

Earlier on, a passenger inappropriately touched his wife, and I lost it. I told him our ancestors used the title of nobility, 'Sardar', to refer to our Sikh and Hindu brothers. Everyone turned on the shameful man who sneaked away.

'We used to buy fabric from sardars for Eids and Barats,' I said to Sardar.

'All is gone.'

'The civil war?'

'They attacked our temples, stoned our cremations, grabbed our land and harassed our women. There's only so much we could tolerate. Ninety-nine per cent of our community have left their watan.'

'I'm saddened and ashamed. I'm sorry,' I said, asking in my heart for Khudai's forgiveness for having caused my own share of harm.

'We've lived here for centuries. We're first Afghan and then Sikh.'

'Of course.'

'If we had businesses, we worked for them from dawn to dusk.'

'Truly deserved.'

'God willing, things will get better one day, and everyone will return to a better Afghanistan.'

'God willing,' his wife uttered under her breath.

Naghma and Mangal were muted. The transport in front of us pulled over, and our minibus followed suit.

'They've popped up even here,' the driver said and detoured onto a dirt track towards the mountain, tilting to one side and then another, chasing other minibuses and the dust storm they kicked up. Armed people on motorcycles with flapping white flags escorted us from behind.

'The Taliban want to search the minibus,' the driver announced as if we were taking a morning tea break.

Coldness chilled my spine.

'Want your property?' Shujah said and sneered. His face had turned dark.

Sardar had never heard of the Taliban having appeared here.

'This's a first,' the driver said. Another man next to the driver agreed.

'Countryman, are you Afghan?' the driver asked, looking in the rear-view mirror.

'Woh,' I found myself snap.

'Foreign Afghan?'

I hesitated but found myself nodding.

'Do you work for the government?' the driver asked.

'Na.'

Sardar told me not to get scared then, adding that the Taliban were fairer than the mujahideen.

'They look for fresh faces. Don't sit next to tror. Move to another chair. Put your head on your hands and pretend you're asleep–'

'Eyes on the road,' a nervous passenger cut the driver short.

'I'm a dutiful Muslim. Harmed no one. Why do I have to hide?'

'Please, do as they say,' Mour pleaded and coughed out the dust drifting in through the windows.

'Mour, nothing will change death if it's written in my fate.'

'Do it for me, I beg you.'

The driver agreed with Mour.

Sardar gave up his seat and moved right to the back, suggesting I move away from the door and sit next to him, as his navy turban often attracted more attention.

I carried out the instruction but wouldn't pretend to sleep. Part of me reasoned I'd been a dutiful Muslim and worked with no government, so shouldn't fear the Taliban. The other part was convinced the Taliban wouldn't spare a foreign Afghan. Against my will, the fearful part had overwhelmed my heart. It beat like a drum. I tried to breathe quietly. Overheard Mour pleading with Khudai how untimely He'd taken her husband and daughters away and if He'd save me from the Taliban.

After a ten-minute drive that lingered as if for ten years, the minibus stopped in between bare hills. A deathly hush filled the minibus, apart from my heart's loud thumps. The door opened with a hissing sound. A bearded figure with a white turban and thick *kohl-* rimmed eyes stepped in, followed by another wearing a white headband saying the Shahada. I couldn't dare to look at them, so cast my eyes down.

'Any hypocrites?' the turbaned Taliban asked in a rough voice.

'Everyone's poor and helpless, Talib brother,' the driver said in a calm voice.

'Where are you going?' It was the rough voice.

'Jalalabad.'

'What's your job?'

'Shopkeeper. I've been to Kabul to do some shopping.' His voice visibly trembled.

'Where's the shopping?'

'My son brings it tomorrow.'

'A lie,' yelled the rough voice, towering over him. The Taliban's intelligence revealed he worked for the Afghan National Army in Laghman.

The driver said the interrogatee did own a store.

A slap hit the driver's face.

The Talib behind at the back dragged the self-proclaimed shopkeeper off the minibus. Quietness followed as the Talib's eyes inspected around. *In the Name of Khudai, with His name nothing can cause harm in the earth nor in the heavens, and He is the All-Hearing, the All-Knowing.* I recited the dua.

Shujah's finger pointed at me. 'Spy,' the scum whispered.

My heart sank. The Talib's forehead wrinkled and *teq, teq, teq* lumbered towards me.

'He's ill,' Sardar said.

'What's wrong with you?' The smell of *reshqa*, a green plant, assailed my nostrils as he towered over me.

'Talib zoya, my son's very ill.' Mour disobeyed the driver's early instruction.

His hand touched my hair and pulled it back.

'You aren't Afghan,' the Talib said in a dismayed tone.

'I *am* Afghan.'

'Alhamdulillah, he's Pashtun like you, zoya. An Ahmadzai Pashtun. A proper Afghan,' Mour said.

'Am I an improper Afghan, then?' the reshqa-smelling Talib said. His forehead wrinkled as he sniffed and covered his nose with his hand. The eyes averted from me to the person behind him. 'Aren't you scared of Allah to wear perfume?'

My heart plummeted. Mour had just got herself into trouble.

'Where's your burka?'

'Zoya, I'm an old woman. I don't need it.'

323

'Both son and mother, out,' he said.

'Mullah saheb, he's a man of dignity. Let him go,' Sardar said.

A slap banged against his cheek; his turban loosened. 'Try to defend anyone again, and I'll give you such a beating as to make you poo in your tunban.'

The Talib who stood by the door waved his Kalashnikov at me.

Shall I do it or shall I not? I thought, as I reached Shujah's seat. My body tilted to the side; my right hand swung back and bashed Shujah's face, and I felt both the softness of Shujah's nose and the hardness of the bone. A Kalashnikov stock hit against my left shoulder. Mour screamed 'Na'. Hands grabbed my shoulders and threw me out.

At least two dozen long-bearded Taliban in perahan tunbans and waistcoats or combat jackets covered with scarves guarded outside, their motorcycles and two pick-up trucks parked around. A stout figure darted like an ape and hit me on the shoulder with the gunstock. He ordered me to hold my hands behind me and kneel next to three men they'd dragged from the other coaster minibuses at the front, adding that I'd pay for gangstering. To my horror they dragged Mour out and instructed her to do the same, facing the opposite side. Turbaned Taliban's muzzle brakes poked against the back of my head and the other two men.

The stout Talib towered over me, covering the burning sun. I read the Shahada written in blood on his headband, tied up around a maroon Sindhi hat. 'Your name, her name, and the nature of your relationship? Quickly, without thinking,' he said, spraying my face with spit.

'Ahmad. Bibi Karima. My mother.'

The stout Talib, who looked and dribbled like an ape, hobbled to Mour and repeated the same question.

'What sort of Islam is this to disrespect an elderly woman?' I overheard Mour say.

'We'll punish you for being with a non-mahram man if you don't answer,' the dribbler said.

'She's my mother, for Khudai's sake. How can you imagine that?' His sick suspicion turned my stomach.

Thankfully, I overheard Mour's answers, and they matched mine.

Like a moving cinema, everyone watched from the three minibuses as the Taliban implemented Sharia law in between the outskirts of light brown hills full of indentations like acne scars.

'Whisper the answers: names of the woman's brothers and sisters, and where they live.'

'You're sick.'

'Cooperate, or we'll publicly lash you both for the sin of–'

'My mother has no brother and sister,' I said, cutting him short of pronouncing the repulsive sin's name.

The dribbler hobbled back to Mour, whose answers I couldn't overhear. Mour pleaded that the dirty ground burned her knees. The stony heart disregarded her and instead accused Mour of being a hypocrite.

Mour pleaded she wasn't a hypocrite but a practising Muslim.

'Don't tell me you're Muslim. Because of women like you, Allah's been punishing us all. You've polluted our society.'

'Mullah saheb, please fear Khudai. She's your mother's age. She can't take all this; she'll have a stroke. I swear to Khudai she's my mother.' I'd seen every possible misery and Mour's humiliation was the last thing Khudai had in stock for me.

A foot struck my back and I landed on my chest, my face hitting against the trainer of a Talib. 'Keep quiet. We're investigating.' The dribbler's voice. He ordered someone from the minibus to search Mour. The reshqa-smelling Talib pulled my shoulders back and ordered me to place my hands on the back of my head.

A widow had two choices in Afghanistan: either stay husbandless, or remarry someone from her immediate family, preferably a brother-in-law. Mour was 45 when Agha vanished, and she had the choice to remarry. She never uttered a single word about another spouse, however. It was too vulgar a subject. It'd have dishonoured Agha, her parents and even her son. I remembered Agha saying, 'If Mour remained a thousand nights among men, I'm certain she'd stay as chaste as she's ever been.' Shujah often told me on Skype how Mour was an inspiration for other Afghan women for the way she'd conducted herself after Agha's passing away. Ironically, the dribbler today accused her of polluting society.

'You act like a child being forced to do homework. I'll have another woman search you – we'd lash you for perverting Allah's Sharia law if she found anything,' the dribbler said.

'Na, it's nothing,' Mour cried.

'Take it out?' the dribbler said.

'Don't please,' Mour shouted.

I peeped back with a sinking heart. A woman in a blue burka pulled something from Mour's pocket and shoved my mother to the ground. Mour's shawl came off. I pleaded for mercy. The dribbler ordered the woman to put the shawl back on as he grabbed a black leather holder and A4-size papers in a plastic cover. These are the last moments of my life, I thought. The dribbler flicked the pages. Looked at me and then the photo. Shouted 'Master'. A Talib stood by the dribbler.

I put my trust in You, Khudai. Once You protect, no one will overcome Mour and me.

'It's an English passport,' said the literate Talib.

'It's my passport; it's got nothing to do with my mother. She lives with my aka in Kabul. Please let her go,' I shouted, loud enough that Mour overheard me, but Shujah hopefully didn't. I knew it belonged to me; the Home Office had never issued Mour a British passport. Passing the Life in the UK Test for Mour was like climbing the Hindu Kush Mountains.

All hell broke loose. A kick in my stomach, followed by a series of punches and a solid gunstock strike. The hills turned black and white with flashes of colour. My ears sounded like I was going through an echoing tube. A blackout.

**

A FUZZY SKY, as blue as the woman's burka who pulled out the documents from Mour's pocket, peered down. A blurry vision spoke over me, drops of spit landing on my face. He told me he knew I lived in England and Mour was my mother because they saw Mour's birth certificate. I recognised the voice. He'd just struck me with the back of an AK-47.

The Indefinite Leave to Remain visa stamped in Mour's passport would've easily given Mour away, but, to my relief, Mour had brought her birth certificate as proof of identity. Shujah had sent the birth certificate from Kabul, which the Afghan Embassy in London required to issue Mour with the passport.

'Are you a spy?'

'I live in England, but I'm not a spy.'

'You're lying. Your beard indicates you are.'

I repeated I was not a spy and pleaded that they should let Mour go. 'She's ill – her heart can't take all this.'

'We will. After Sharia law is implemented,' he said and made a movement with his right palm. The burning sun stung into my face as he rose. We were turned around to face the minibuses, all four of us kneeling.

'Those women who disregard the Islamic hijab and wear make-up or high heels will receive the same punishment,' he said to the frightened passengers on the minibuses in the middle of the Khudai-forsaken hills.

He took a lash from a Talib standing by and flogged Mour with a whipping sound.

'Na, fear Khudai,' I said and rose to my feet. Four Taliban grabbed my arms.

Another lash and Mour let out a sigh of anguish.

'I beg of you to let her go. She can't take this. For the sake of Khudai.'

She dropped to the ground on the third whip. The dribbler ordered the woman in the blue burka to pick my mother up.

Mour heaved a sigh of anguish as he whipped her again.

'Khudai, damn you all. KHUDAI, DAMN YOU ALL.' The Taliban crushed me to the ground, holding my face against the burning soil, and dirt entered my mouth.

Every lash felt like the thorns from the scattered wild shrubs on the hills penetrating my flesh. But I could do nothing except close my eyes and pray to Khudai to give Mour strength. Pleading and begging were what we ordinary Afghans could do.

I remembered Mour calling me to watch how the Taliban was executing a woman in the Ghazi Stadium in Kabul. I refused to watch; I'd already had my share of misery in Afghanistan. Mour defended the Taliban's action for cleansing society of immoral behaviour. Little Mour knew years later she'd be in a similar spotlight.

Mour was on the ground by the final lashes. The searing heat like a burning clay oven single-handedly sufficed to drain your energy.

The woman in the blue burka with two female passengers dragged Mour's motionless body like a sack of turnips onto the minibus. The hands were let loose on the back of my head.

'Let other Muslims learn this will be their fate if they join the security forces of the kafir Karzai Government,' the dribbler said to the audience on the dusty minibuses. Their fear-stricken faces looked as if the Taliban were about to push their Bowie knives into their stomachs and take their intestines out.

A *deth* sound of AK-47. I flinched. Next to me, the man's body swung to the left and hit the ground, kicking up dust. More gunshots and the remaining two men dropped down, joining the first one.

Blood covered the dirt ground. The dribbler tore up a fake hundred-dollar note and put a piece on the head of each body.

Was I in Moscow, walking to the market on a freezing winter morning? Did my body freeze on the snow? I closed my eyes and declared my Shahada, *There is no god but Allah, Muhammad is the messenger of Allah.* My body shivered with cold, thinking a bullet would smash my skull any moment now for spying for England – a country the Taliban saw as one of the occupying forces in Afghanistan. Worse, the British Empire had invaded three times my watan and stole Afghanistan's Pashtun territories on the other side of the Durand Line. *I wholeheartedly accept if this is what You want, Khudai. But please look after Mour. Without me, she has no one but You.*

Hands picked me up and threw me onto the loading bay of a pick-up. To my astonishment, the dribbler ordered the minibuses to move off and the turbaned Taliban to blindfold my eyes.

Chapter Thirty-Seven

After almost an hour's drive on an uneven and bumpy surface, the vehicles and motorcycles stopped. A pair of hands pulled me off. I spat out pieces of dirt and sand. The hands kept pushing me, and a few minutes into the dart, picked me up and threw me onto soft land. Try to escape, and I'd meet the young interpreter's fate, the dribbler's voice said as he opened my blindfold. Blurry men with guns surrounded him. He roped my hands at the back.

'Why didn't you kill me?'

'Meshar Mullah will decide this evening,' he said about the 'Big Mullah' and left, locking a padlock from the outside, leaving me in the dirt (and dark) room with no windows; apart from some tiny light, and air, coming through a chink in the wooden door.

I felt the wall with my hands and adjusted my position to distance myself from the poking saddle in the dried-dung, foul-smelling corner. My wrists hurt. My right shoulder hurt. My head and body hurt. Last night I kept changing sides to relieve the pain. Painful questions came over and over again. Have they spared me for Meshar Mullah? Am I going to be executed today? Is this my last day? Yesterday at this time I looked forward to seeing Nazia: death never crossed my mind. Now it was as imminent as the evening.

I thought of the years I'd lived. How I avoided junk food and coffee; the weekend jogging. All would prove fruitless. What'd happen to my graduation? Everyone would hold a minute's silence for Ahmad's barbaric execution. Mour would receive my medical degree, one of her life's wishes if she lived to see the day. Her heart might have taken the lashes today but it would fail if the only person she lived for was no longer around. All these years I'd been careful not to cause her grief, even when she was unreasonable. If only I had been cautious for a few more days. What had she done for me and what had I given her in return?

Mour woke up at 5.00 every morning for the past 15 years, toasted bread, warmed milk, made a sandwich to take with me to university, and herself left our two-bed council flat to clean rooms and windows in a nearby college. I set off several hours later for the comfortable university rooms. She came back in mid-afternoon, hoovered all the rooms, cleaned the bath and basins, washed the cutlery, cooked dinner and laid it on the table for my return in the evening in case she was late from her afternoon shift.

Mour didn't want me to work in case it interfered with my studies. She'd managed to save up the three bundles for my wedding; those Shujah had almost gambled away, and now Nazigul, together with my iPhone, held onto them without Shujah's knowledge. I delivered pizzas on weekends to ease the financial pressure on Mour. Got home at midnight and, despite my insistence not to, Mour stayed awake. She put the quabili palaw with meat sauce on the table, pushed across the salad plate, poured home-made yoghurt, filled my cup with tea, and went up to her room. She reminded me not to wash up afterwards. 'Pashtunwali' considered it 'shameful' for men to take part in domestic chores. A few times I cleaned up, and Mour warned me not to. So I removed all excess food from the cutlery and left it in the basin full of hot water mixed with washing up liquid. This way, I left light work for Mour.

Yesterday, though, I dropped a heavy weight on her chest, as heavy as the hills from this morning. She'd have willingly accepted the Taliban calling her 'a hypocrite', but not her son referring to her as a 'snake'. Khudai, what sin did I commit in the last days of my life? I prayed that Nazigul or Amina would take Mour to the doctor's. From now on, Mour would have to book her GP appointments herself and ask them to arrange for an interpreter, provided she returned to a country where there was nothing left to go back to.

Shujah must be relieved to see the back of us. On the minibus I gave him what he deserved. But refrained from telling on him. Wanted him to be safe and sound for his children. Children needed a father's love, no matter how many shortcomings he might have. I feared Shujah and his gang might harm Mour if they found out the Taliban had killed me. Shujah might already... stop it... *Please, Khudai, shield Mour from harm and bless her with Your protection.* I read the All-Hearing, the All-Knowing, the Seek Refuge and Ayat Al-Kursi duas. Kept repeating them...

Chapter Thirty-Eight

The sound of vehicles pulling over alerted me. Voices spoke; lots of them. I spotted nothing apart from darkness through the chink. No one had asked if I needed food or the toilet all day long. Nobody had even opened the door. My stomach was as empty as the dried dung fuel-smelling stable, and my lips as dry as this morning's hills.

A key twisted in the padlock, the wooden door opened and in burst armed men, two holding oil lamps. They weren't the Taliban from the morning. These men wore military outfits with AK-47s, RPG-7 launchers, rockets, PK machine guns, chattering walkie-talkies in their hands, magazine pouches around their waists, and black hip hop trainers on their feet. Except for two, they all had long beards, and white, black and combat scarves covered their faces and heads. The two trim-bearded ones preoccupied themselves with setting up a video camera and electrical lines. Two Taliban stood on the opposite side of the room, holding the lamps. Another four in the corners, their guns pointed at me.

The presence of the video equipment made me tremble. I could envisage my beheading in the stable shortly. I read the All-Hearing, the All-Knowing dua.

A gangling, scary figure lowered his head at the door and stepped in. Rose fragrance filled the stable. The dribbler camouflaged himself behind the gigantic figure. Four Taliban carried in a bedraggled skeleton with his hands roped at the back, and then left.

'Delighted to have you, at last, Professor Shafiq Nabizada,' the gigantic figure said to the dishevelled professor in a thunderous voice.

The gaunt man's left eye socket, the one lit with the orange oil lamplight, appeared black.

'I'll shortly grant your wish,' the gigantic figure said to the grey, thick-haired professor.

'Is he the rat?' the gigantic figure said.

The dribbler confirmed.

Heads turned to me with lowered eyebrows and wrinkled noses. The two trim-bearded stopped setting up and took me in.

'Meshar Mullah saheb, it's true I live in England, but I'm *not* a spy. I'm a good Muslim. I harmed nobody.'

His penetrating eyes fixed on me. He must have been six feet three inches, and his high military boots increased the height by another three inches. Had a chest-long beard, and long, bushy hair came out of his turban. The black beard covered his upper cheeks, half his forehead, even his ears. His tall, pointy nose and small, deep-socket eyes made him resemble an eagle. Even though they were covered with a bushy beard, you couldn't miss the conspicuous cheekbones. Only he could carry a turban as big as a round dish over Frishta's vila, with its tail touching his upper legs. He brimmed over with authority. No wonder the Taliban called him Meshar Mullah.

His eyes wandered off. 'He's a good Muslim and yet harmed no one in England?' he said to the camera crew, hands in his plain combat jacket.

Everyone laughed.

'Violence is not the answer,' the professor said.

'No. The rat should've given the British flowers for invading his watan.'

Everybody burst into laughter again. One of the trim-bearded men stuck a white cloth to the wall with the Shahada written on it in black.

'The media's right. The professor does talk like Mahatma Gandhi, non-violence rubbish,' Meshar Mullah said to his entourage. A vibrating generator from the outside started, and one of the trim-bearded men gave Meshar Mullah the thumbs-up. Meshar Mullah towered over the professor, grabbed the poor man, and stood him up against the white Taliban flag next to me, the one they'd just nailed to the wall. The professor staggered but held his balance. Meshar Mullah took a few steps back to reach the dirt wall on the opposite side. 'Now we can have that face-to-face debate you demand from the "terrorists".'

'The Americans would have no pretext to stay in Afghanistan if you took flowers to them,' the professor said.

'Is that so?'

'It is, if you stopped committing the un-Islamic act of killing innocent people and joined elections.'

'Democracy is hypocrisy. It's haram.'

'The origin of democracy lies in Islam. For the first time in Medina the Muslims elected caliphs in free elections.'

'The two Greek words, *demos* and *kratos,* mean "people's rule". In Islam, Allah rules, not man. Allah decides a man's destiny, not man. Only Allah's the legislator, not the majority. What if the majority say we don't want Islam?' Meshar Mullah said.

Heads nodded and turned to the professor, as did the camera and the dimmed light.

'The Constitution forbids any action that contravenes Islam.'

'The kafir Constitution written by the Americans? A constitution that accepts the UN Charter which perceives Sharia law as violent?'

'Nothing is Islamic unless done by the Taliban,' the professor said. 'Afghans want peace. Security. Education. Employment. Infrastructure. Your fanatical interpretation of Islam gets them none of them, except to put Afghanistan decades back,' the professor added. He sounded more frustrated than angry.

'Afghans want us to jihad. Defeat the invaders and the showy Kabul regime where drinking, womanising, corruption and half-naked Indian movies are permanent features of society.'

'You brand the six million Kabulis as deviant from Islam?'

'Our knowledge and actions differentiate us from the kafirs. Western kafirs don't know about Islam, so don't practise it. The inactions of the ignorant Afghans equally amount to being a kafir.'

'Khudai decides one's faith, not fanatical extremists like you.'

'Allah's given us clear Sharia law to decide.'

Quietness, apart from the muffled generator sound and static, and occasional chatter on the walkie-talkies.

'Suppose you took over Kabul. How would you establish a government if you shut schools for half of the population?'

'The Taliban from the madrasas will assist.'

'How would a mullah look after a woman in need of a midwife?'

'Allah would assist her like He'd helped billions of women in the past.'

'Run the government without the outside help, given Afghanistan is mostly dependent on foreign aid?'

'Afghanistan can become the Saudi Arabia of lithium. The $3 trillion worth of mineral resources in Afghanistan alone removes poverty in the Muslim world. We have the oil money from the Gulf. Two billion Muslims to build up an effective army. But lack powerful leadership.'

'And where do you get the powerful leadership from?'

'The Amir of the Faithful.'

'Big dreams, little heads. If you believe all the sophisticated Muslim men and women from around the world would come under the leadership of an Amir they haven't seen or heard of, you truly are a fool.'

I believed Meshar Mullah would blow away the professor's head if he didn't like a point of view, but he appeared calm and seemingly enjoyed a civilised discussion. Perhaps the professor knew they'd slaughter him anyway, so he spoke his mind. Once you accepted death was inevitable, especially when the moment of death lingered, you either spoke your mind or stopped thinking; stopped feeling. You sat there with a lifeless body and were compelled, once again, to allow someone else to fight your battle, and instead listened to a debate you'd escaped all your life.

'You're also a fool if you believe you fight for Islam. The Afghanistan War is a drama written and directed by strong powers. You play the villain, Karzai the hero, or vice versa, depending on which angle you see it from, and ordinary Afghans are the sacrificial lamb.'

Meshar Mullah went into thought.

A Talib sneezed, saying 'Alhamdulillah'. Others said almost in unison, '*Yarhamukallah*,' or 'Khudai have mercy upon you'.

'I'm not a fool if I believe the Kabul government and people like you have sold Afghanistan to 49 countries. True Muslims like the Taliban have stood in the way.'

Meshar Mullah took a few steps with a crunching sound and gently walked the professor to the middle of the room, his legs in the tunban shivering as Meshar Mullah pushed his shoulders to kneel him down. The professor went with the flow and showed no resistance. Everyone stared at him as if he was a piece of dirt.

Meshar Mullah spoke to the camera. 'At the kafir invaders' orders, the professor preaches democracy and human rights at the expense of Sharia law. We've warned him several times, but he won't listen. He's betrayed his watan and religion and will rot in Hell.'

A knife *sss-ice* pulled on the professor's throat, his blood spurting over his neck and shoulders. Something cold ripped up my spine. I lost balance and collapsed to the floor at the feet of a Talib, his AK-47 pointing at my forehead.

A cheerful shout of 'Allahu Akbar' filled the air. The professor's body and its hanging head collapsed onto the wheat straw once Meshar Mullah's hands let go.

'Anyone who collaborates with the invaders or their puppets will join the professor,' Meshar Mullah said to the camera.

'Allahu Akbar,' said the Taliban in unison.

The two trim-bearded men pressed a button and joined the cheers. Everyone hugged one another as if they'd just scored a decisive goal. The dribbler congratulated 'the worrier', Meshar Mullah, for having just gained 'another major' reward.

Afghanistan lost its 'Mahatma Gandhi'.

Meshar Mullah asked the crewmen not to film his face; they were mindful of that, they replied. One of the trim-bearded men said 'rat' in Urdu to Meshar Mullah, whose barbaric eyes turned to me, ordering his men to stand me next to the professor's bloody body.

As hands tugged me off the straw and raised me to my feet, I turned cold like someone had dropped a piece of ice into my stomach. 'Khudai, I take refuge in you. When You protect, no one will overcome me,' I screamed as hands pressed against my shoulders to kneel me down. I won't chicken out in the last moments of my life; I'll stand up for myself and won't allow my cowardly part to win, I resolved. 'There's no god but Allah, Muhammad is the messenger of Allah.' I declared my faith. 'I perform my five daily prayers as you do. Abstain from food and drink from dawn to dusk in Ramadans as you do. Donate a portion of my wealth to the needy as you might do. Why am I a lesser Muslim than you are?' I said.

Meshar Mullah's eyes locked onto me. The burning oil lamp stayed close to my face.

'All my life I've followed the teachings of Islam. Refrained from violence, envy, greed, lust, profane language, gossip. Got along with fellow human beings. Why am I a lesser Muslim?' I said.

His eyes were still fixed on me.

'My feet never stepped into nightclubs. My mouth never tasted the alcohol. My eyes never saw women as sexual objects. Why am I a lesser Muslim?'

His face stayed unchanged.

338

'Honour my mother as Khudai has instructed me. But my promise will be dishonoured and I won't remain a dutiful son if you kill me.'

'Why's that?'

'I've pledged to take my mother to Saudi Arabia for the performance of the fifth pillar of Islam next year.'

His eyes narrowed.

'I *am* a practising Muslim like the three million Muslims living in Britain.'

He examined me, his right cheek lit by the lamp, and the left as dark as night.

'I emigrated as a minor with my parents. It wasn't my choice.' I spoke at a fast pace, trying to enlighten him with as much information as I could. Everything I said was the truth.

'How old were you?' he said.

'15.'

'Even worse, young haleks are better brainwashed.'

The sons of shit in the sky have disappeared, right? someone shouted on a walkie-talkie.

'Far from it; I was in the Hizb ut-Tahrir at university. I've come here to support my Taliban brothers.' I unbelievably heard myself telling a lie. I didn't know if my cowardly side had forced me to lie, or if the courageous side, the one I'd been working for two decades to create, made up things in desperation to save me. No matter which part was responsible, I felt as fake as those two-faced politicians who'd betrayed their watan and people.

'How?'

'I'm a medical doctor.'

He considered me carefully.

'What is Hizb ut-Tahrir?'

'A party of liberation. We stood for the implementation of Sharia law in England and did jihad to change England from a *Dar al-Kufr* into *Dar al-Islam,* a caliphate.' I made up the last part of my remark to compare Hizb ut-Tahrir's aim with the Taliban's objective.

In reality, some students at college, a few of whom I'd helped with their cases at the Racial Equality Council, had attempted to persuade me to join them in Hizb ut-Tahrir, but I told them the mujahideen civil war had convinced me that whoever fought under the name of Islam used the religion as a means, not a goal. What hadn't they done to Kabulis under the name of Islam? Because of them, I'd lost my friends, family, watan, and the most precious person in my life, Frishta. Because of them, I was in the captivity of the Taliban, or else I'd have been married long ago to Frishta. Hizb ut-Tahrir gave up on me eventually.

'What proof do you have?'

'See my passport photo.'

I grew a long beard in the first year of university, which was when I took the photo. Although the bearded photo compelled the anti-terror police at Heathrow Airport to bombard me with questions, it postponed my death by a few minutes. Meshar Mullah inquired as to the passport's whereabouts.

Everyone waited in silence, like spectators waiting for the referee to decide if the winning goal was scored, until the passport found itself in the hands of Meshar Mullah. He opened it. Took a glance. Flicked. Went back to the early pages. Brought the side closer to his eyes and himself closed to the dimmed light. His pupils went up and down the page. Did he read my details? In English?

'Born in Makroryan?' Meshar Mullah confirmed.

'Woh.'

'Which one?'

'The Third Makroryan.' Was he aware of the Little Moscow's liberal environment?

'It was full of Russian puppets. Was your father one of them?'

'He was in the Arg Palace with President Najibullah.'

'His name?'

340

'Azizullah Azizi.'

'Yours?'

'Ahmad Azizi.'

He shifted his gaze to me as though he read every single expression on my face. His penetrating eyes got bigger and bigger. Did his mind travel elsewhere? What was he thinking about? What if he took out the knife from the shoulder strap and slit my throat? At least I wouldn't die a coward if he decided so. I prayed Khudai would bring kindness to his stony heart.

'What happened to the beard?'

'Had to shorten it for the labs.'

'Pack up,' he said to the camera crew.

They exchanged looks.

'I'll inquire about you,' he said and rushed out. His bodyguards from the four corners and the dribbler followed him out. The dimmed light was switched off, followed by the generator. Two Taliban carried the professor's body, leaving untouched the pool of blood on the straw.

The crewmen shut their aluminium case and exited together with the two Taliban holding the burning oil lamps. The dribbler reappeared and locked the door.

Silence, apart from muffled chatter of walkie-talkies outside.

***

I TOOK A DEEP breath in the pitch-black stable and uttered a heartfelt thank-You to Khudai. Simultaneously, I asked for forgiveness. And tried to fight against the feeling of a disloyal politician, a traitor who betrayed himself.

Chapter Thirty-Nine

That's it, I thought earlier on when Meshar Mullah's gaze shifted to me after killing the professor. Why did he spare me? Because of Hizb ut-Tahrir? How would he 'inquire' about me? And how long would it take? What... A key twisted in the padlock. The door opened and four armed Taliban entered, carrying a burning oil lamp. Put a black cloth over my face. My heart palpitated. Fresh air hit me as I stepped outside. They pushed me into what felt like an enclosed space after a minute-long journey. Removed the blindfold and told me to wait in the dimly lit room. They departed. Why did they bring me here? To change the setting and slit my throat in a room furnished with a faded kilim? Where are the crewmen and, importantly, Masher Mullah?

'Salaam alaikum,' Meshar Mullah said in a booming voice and lumbered in, holding a thermos, two cups and two Afghan chapati naans. He put down what he held in his hands, unfastened my shivering hands and gestured to the thin mattress. I felt blood flow in my wrists. We both sat.

Had Hizb ut-Tahrir cast its magic on him, or did he play a game?

'How are you feeling?'

'Like the qurbani lamb.'

'What do you mean?'

I told him that on the first day of Eid al-Adha Nurrullah butchered our neighbours' lambs before the block for *qurbani*, the feast of the sacrifice, which honoured the willingness of Ibrahim to sacrifice his promised son, Ismail, as an act of submission to Khudai's command, but Khudai intervened to inform Ibrahim that Khudai had already accepted his prophet's sacrifice. The eyes of the neighbours' lambs jerked in fear when they witnessed Nurrullah slaughtering their fellow lamb. I bet they knew they'd be next. Like those lambs, all I felt, despite my inner struggle to fight it, was fear; my other senses stopped functioning, even the early hunger sensation.

He poured the tea into a dirty glass cup and put it before me. Gave me a chapati. Filled his own cup. In the light of the oil lamp hanging on the old, paint-peeling wall, his eyes appeared red as if they'd witnessed the slaughter of hundreds of Afghans.

'The mujahideen don't get ready-made foods. Ordinary households cook whatever they can. Tonight's host can't afford sugar,' he said, referring to the Taliban as 'mujahideen'.

'We must be grateful for whatever foods Khudai provides. Right now, millions go to bed hungry.'

'When did you leave Afghanistan?'

'In 1992. After the mujahideen came into power.'

I'd never imagined I'd meet a Talib, I now conversed with a top-ranking one – an extraordinary human being adept at acting ordinarily.

'You should've informed us before you set off.' He put a piece of bread into his mouth and sipped his tea.

'I didn't know any of the brothers here.'

'Who was the woman who got lashed?'

'My mother.'

'Why did you bring your mother with you?'

'British intelligence and the NDS kept me under surveillance. Had to bring Mour along under the pretence of khastegari.'

A Talib chuckled outside.

'She knows about your plan?'

'The only plan she knows is the khastegari.'

'Not married yet?' Meshar Mullah asked over Taliban chatter outside the windows covered with white curtains containing hand-embroidered flowers.

'Na.'

He raised his eyebrows. He pointed at my tea. 'Drink before it gets cold.'

I put in a large piece of chapati and sipped my tea. Felt no taste. Maybe all my senses were focused on ascertaining what he wanted from me.

'What're you thinking?'

'I'm worried about what you'll do with me.'

'Lean back, make yourself comfortable.'

Leaning back was the last thing I thought about, but tipped towards the white pillow with hand-embroidered flowers. Noticed piles of large, wooden boxes from the curtain's side on my left, the curtain splitting the room into two.

'Tell me about your life in England.'

'Consisted of praying, studying, working and jogging.'

'In detail.'

I woke up early in the morning, performed my prayer, had breakfast, went to university, returned home in the evening, had dinner, revised, prayed and went to bed. Jogged for two hours each day on Saturdays and Sundays, ate lunch, started work at midday, came back at midnight, dinner, praying and bed, I told him.

'When do you get the time to watch films?'

The question baffled me. 'What films?'

'Indian. American. Jackie Chan.'

What sort of a game was this? Films had nothing to do with my connection to Hizb ut-Tahrir. Or was he a hypocrite? According to Nadir, some Taliban watched international television yet forbade ordinary Afghans. Or maybe he played the good cop? I had to tread carefully with what I said.

'I watched films before joining Hizb ut-Tahrir.'

'What kind?'

'Both Hollywood and Bollywood.'

'Bollywood is the Indian cinema?'

344

'Woh.' I noticed he had a Pashto accent from the other side of the border – Pakistan's side – where more than 30 million Pashtuns lived. I took another piece of chapati and sipped the cold tea.

'See American films?'

I just told him Hollywood. Didn't he know Hollywood meant American movies? 'I used to watch American movies but stopped ever since I joined Hizb ut-Tahrir.'

'What kind of American films?'

'Mostly starring Al Pacino and Robert De Niro,' I blurted out.

Thankfully, his blank expression demonstrated he recognised neither.

'Does Schwarzenegger make films?'

'I think he hasn't since he's been a governor.'

He raised his eyebrow. 'Was he a politician?'

'The Governor of California. He's in the same party as Bush. Could've run for the presidency had he been born in America.' I went with the flow. The game was getting too clever for me to comprehend.

'Is he not American?'

'He's Austrian.'

'Yet they made him a governor?'

I abstained from displaying surprise or excitement like him.

'Schwarzenegger was the best actor, wasn't he?'

'Afghans like him because he does action movies.' I doubted my first perception of him; the subject genuinely intrigued him. Though I quickly reminded myself that he'd just butchered the professor with whom he held a supposedly genuine political debate. He surely tested me to discover my religious commitments. I only watched films *until* I'd joined the Hizb ut-Tahrir, I'd clarified, thankfully. I must be careful to talk only about films released before my participation in Hizb ut-Tahrir. Luckily, I hadn't even specified the year I'd joined Hizb ut-Tahrir. On the good side, though, discussing movies gave me a great deal of pleasure, even in this extreme circumstance.

His eyes were fixated on the piles of folded mattresses and pillows alongside the wall by the oil lamp; he was thinking. What was it? I spoke about films? Or did he think I was lying? Or he listened to the chatter on walkie-talkies outside the window behind him.

'Is Rambo a governor?'

'I don't think so.'

'He journeyed to Panjshir to make a film. Right?'

'I don't know.' Continuously deceiving him hurt, but once you tell one lie, you had to keep telling lies to avoid being found out. I did know. My English friends corrected me in England: Sylvester Stallone had filmed the movie in Israel in the 80s rather than Afghanistan. I decided not to embark on the matter with Meshar Mullah. I'd already come across as knowledgeable on movies – more was a gamble.

A silence developed. A thought crossed my mind: does he watch films? My voice faltered when I asked him.

Na, he snapped; it was haram.

He did play a game, after all. For me, it was halal; for him, haram. I went through my replies in case I'd blurted out something controversial that raised his suspicion. But time was running out, so in a sudden panic, I made a statement to clarify things: the only television I'd been watching since I'd become a jihadist was the Afghan news channels and Al Jazeera. No films, no music.

'No music?'

'Na.' I prayed Khudai forgave me for the lie – and the sin. Music was my life. I didn't remember a day I missed listening to Afghan and Indian music. Though I'd abstained from songs mentioning nudity.

'Alcohol?'

'Never tasted it.' Didn't he believe me earlier?

'*Zina*?'

'Never had sex with a non-mahram. I swear to Khudai. I'm clean.'

'Never committed it?'

'Never.'

He withdrew his AK-47 knife out of the case, stuck on his bullet shoulder strap, put it against my throat, pulled my hand and placed it over a hard thing in his chest pocket. 'Swear on the Quran you've never committed zina or drunk alcohol.'

'I swear.'

'Committed...'

'Committed the two sins of zina and drinking alcohol.'

'Not even with Frishta?'

'Not even with Frishta.'

'I would've cut your throat if you had,' he said and removed the knife.

Thanks, Khudai, he... Hold on... Did he mention Frishta? How did he know about our relationship?

'How do you know Frishta?'

'Still haven't recognised me?'

'Na.'

'You stupid man, I'm Wazir.'

I went numb... *You stupid man, I'm Wazir...* The statement sank in and my body convulsed. I saw the first glimpse of hope.

'Is it you, Wazir?'

'You OK?'

I'm going to stay alive. I embraced him.

'Stop crying.'

I'm going to see Mour again and say sorry.

'Ahmad, stop it, man.'

I'm going to go back to England.

'Ahmad, calm down.' He restrained my shoulders.

'I'm sorry, I'm scared.' My body convulsed, streams of tears flowing down my face.

'You're safe. You're with your brother.'

'Thanks, Khudai, a thousand times. I missed you, Wazir. Where you suddenly disappeared?' Tears entered my mouth.

'Where I was meant to be.'

'I knocked every day on your door.'

'I had gone far away.'

I hugged him again, his rose fragrance giving off nothing but reassurance. Wanted to tell him to get me out of there... Wait, he'd known all along I was Ahmad, yet he cross-examined me. He'd have slit my throat like the professor if I hadn't sworn. Worse, would have done so without telling me who he was. I flinched, coming to my senses. It wasn't the best friend I'd known – a friend who'd lay down his life for me, for his brother – but some murderous Talib who cared about nothing except his extreme ideas.

He placed his hands like a pair of shovels on my shoulders and hugged. 'Stop behaving like a woman. Be a man.'

'Emotions aren't under my control.'

'You're a man. Act like one.' He went on saying how my face had contracted and hair thinned, and how he'd never have recognised me had I bumped into him. I wouldn't either. His bushy beard had distorted the face I knew as an adolescent.

Chapter Forty

Wazir recited his Shahada, turned the ignition key on, and we set off under the moonless sky for my unknown fate, leaving the half-bombed-out muddy castle situating in the middle of orchards and dirt houses, most of them battered with missing ceilings like empty human ribs. Wazir drove in the dark without the headlights on.

Earlier, after eating melons with dozens of the Taliban and then hitting each other with their skins, Wazir told me not to call him by his first name, but instead Meshar Mullah, or Mullah Ghazi Haqqani. My hair stood on end. Nadir's thesis reported Mullah Ghazi Haqqani's atrocities, the 'right hand' of the Haqqani network. Wazir had managed to have his name on the blacklist with a crazy US dollars price on his head, dead or alive. Mullah Ghazi turned out to be my once best friend.

'The brothers can't wait to see you,' Wazir said after a silence.

'The feeling is mutual.'

'A snake bothers us,' Wazir said after another silence.

'Who?'

'Frishta.' His gaze on the road. 'She's become a headache for the jihad.'

I remained silent, letting him elaborate.

'It's handy she still trusts you.'

'How?'

The truck drove into a pothole. A wood cut-out of Allah hanging from the rear window moved from side to side. I held onto the scratched dashboard as the handle was missing. Only Khudai knew how overused the white pick-up truck was.

'I bumped into her when we were in power. She asked after you.'

These words awakened joyous curiosity in me; with the first few I listened to Wazir with interest. *No birds fly in the sky: all clear. Watch for the snakes on the ground*, a voice spoke on the walkie-talkie from the back seat, whose antenna poked between Wazir and me.

'Keep your eyes open,' the man from the back said into the walkie-talkie.

'What did she ask for?'

'Your whereabouts.'

'You knew?'

'Knew nothing about you. Nor was I interested in a coward who'd run away to a kafir country and changed his religion. But, alhamdulillah, you've proved me wrong.'

'How did you bump into her?' The vehicle tilted from one side to another.

'She was there to get back her father's apartment.'

'What makes you think she trusts me?'

'You were close, weren't you?' He gave me a look.

I averted my gaze to the side mirror full of reflections of black figures whose faces were wrapped up in white scarves, white flags flapping by the sides of their pick-ups and motorcycles amidst the clouds of dust.

'She isn't the Frishta we knew.'

I coughed; the dust caught up inside me.

'Did you visit her?'

'Woh. I didn't know she was what you describe.' Did his face darken?

'I would've cut the snake's head had I known she'd turn into such a hindrance to the jihad,' he said and changed gear.

I decided against backing him up. He indeed wasn't the Wazir who stood in for his friends to fight the school bully. The Taliban had brainwashed him to the extent that he wouldn't spare his 'sister'. I thanked Khudai I didn't confide in him. He'd have sent me to the professor.

'What does Agha do?'

'He's dead.'

'To Allah we belong and to Him we shall return,' he said. 'How?'

'Agha and my sisters drowned on the way to England.'

He showed no remorse, except to connect it to fate.

When incidents happened to you in Afghanistan, we considered it written in your destiny and bound to happen. Back in England, there'd be a public outcry, generating dozens of inquiries to detect what had gone wrong and how to prevent recurrences. For nearly four decades Afghans had been suffering from all kinds of disasters, most preventable, but nobody did anything about it because it was fated to befall us. Nobody inquired why Wazir had become a murderer Talib instead of a footballer, why Baktash didn't make it as an actor, and why I was in the captivity of the Taliban. I sometimes wondered if we chose the easy option.

A dog barked from the muddy huts.

The combination of dust and darkness turned the huts and trees into black shapes, but Wazir carried on driving on the snaky dirt road like it was daylight. Curiosity won over and I asked him where he'd gone after the accident with the algebra ustad.

'Paktia. Then Miranshah.'

'Married?'

'Alhamdulillah. Four children. Three haleks and a jelai. The haleks, mashallah, attend a madrassa.'

'The jelai?'

'Gets an Islamic education at home.'

'Have you told them about me?'

'Na.'

The reply disappointed me. 'Will I see them?'

'They live in Miranshah.'

Silence, apart from the non-stop chatter on the walkie-talkie.

'How's Aday?'

'She passed away.'

'To Khudai we belong and to Him we shall return,' I said. 'I'm sorry. What happened?'

'Stroke.'

'May Khudai bless her.'

'May *Allah* bless her.' Wazir raised his voice. Touched Allah swinging from the rear window and kissed his hand.

I saw no difference in the two words because in Pashto it was Khudai, and in Arabic Allah.

'Did she see your wedding?'

'Saw my first two sons' births. Saw me deputising the Supreme Court. Got her back the apartment.'

I thanked Khudai for having enabled Wazir to bring back richness into Aday's life. Nothing, though, could've changed what Wazir had experienced as a child: the deaths of aka Iqbal and his brother, the constant sorrow of Aday, the poverty, the hopelessness and the longing for a father. Perhaps Wazir's past had formed his future.

'We had a dignified life in Kabul. The kafir Americans took it away.'

'Americans poke their noses into everyone's business.'

'It was a choice between handing over our guest, Sheikh Osama bin Laden, or giving up the power.'

'Turning him over to the kafirs would have done away with melmastia,' I said.

'That was the dilemma.'

'Milmastia doesn't even allow you to harm a foe when they seek refuge in your house. Right?' I said.

'Because melmastia takes precedence over revenge.'

'Is it called *nanawatai*?'

He nodded. 'He did deserve our melmastia. We're proud to have protected him.'

'Have you met the Sheikh?'

'A couple of times... briefly... He was a brave Mujahid.'

'Indeed.'

The car now drifted along a concrete road in a desert, as endless as the starless sky. I remembered Wazir's words, *You stupid man, I'm Wazir.* How simply he pronounced them and how enormously they had an impact on me. I saw *life* in that brief moment. But my hopes were fading away. He drove me to an unknown place for 'an important meeting with the brothers'. I had to continue playing the game to stay alive, even though every lie felt like I chewed on a rock.

Guns fired in the distance. Wazir's eyes didn't shift from the road; his hands pressed upon the steering wheel. I wondered how many innocent lives those hands must have ended.

'Play football now?' I said.

'Na, you?'

'Na.'

'England's crazy about it.'

'It's like religion for the English people,' I said.

Wazir hit a hole and I jumped up, hitting the ceiling. The walkie-talkie man swore at the Americans and their bombardment.

'Were your best friends English?'

'My only friends and my classmates since A-Levels were Abdul Zafar and Muhammad Mustafa. They were from Pakistan and India, and both had Pashtun origins.'

'Good Muslims?'

'They were like my double. Socialising was alien to us. We viewed it as a waste of time. We didn't have the time, anyway. We had to study, study and study, spending our entire day in the library or lecture rooms. But we'd leave a lesson and head for the university mosque if it clashed with a prayer time.' I didn't feel guilty for once, as every piece of information about my friends and me was true, though I chose not to tell him how we all liked movies and laughed over Bollywood comedies.

His eyes were on the road ahead, thinking.

'Who are your friends?' I asked after a silence.

'Many brothers.'

'Where are they?'

'Some martyred. Some in the jihad. Some in Pakistan.'

'How long did you stay in Pakistan?'

'Five years?'

'Did you work?'

'Completed my education.'

'In what?'

'Islamic Studies from a madrassa in South Waziristan.'

I nodded. His last statement answered all of my questions. Nadir, in his thesis, wrote that hundreds of madrassas in Pakistan brainwashed their students, their Taliban or 'knowledge seekers', and dispatched them to jihad in Afghanistan. Wazir was one of those fanatics. Full stop. No need to ask more questions about his beliefs. In fact, his aka's books had already done half of the job. They'd even managed to create cracks in my friendship with Baktash.

'The mujahideen killed Baktash and his father in front of the block.'

Wazir gave an exasperated look. He didn't want to talk about the time of Jahili. Wasn't interested in our 'ignorant' classmates. He'd begged Khudai for forgiveness. According to Wazir, there'd been a clear duty on us to fight the Soviets and their puppets, but instead we'd enjoyed our lives in Makroryan. Wazir concerned himself with nothing but religion, something he limited to the jihad and nothing else. I wouldn't have spent a moment with him if I had the choice. My childhood time formed the most precious part of my life for me.

'I'm looking forward to the other world. There's nothing meaningful in this life,' Wazir said after a silence.

'This world is full of lies, deceit and deception,' I said.

It may have been my inability to speak my mind or the amount of beating I'd received and fear I'd gone through since yesterday, or perhaps the overwhelming tiredness coupled with a smooth drive: extreme sleepiness overcame me.

***

A HAND SHOOK my left shoulder. A ray of bright sunlight from above the mountains and through the trees beat down on my eyes. Believe it or not, I'd fallen asleep the entire journey. Wazir had pulled over in front of another enormous muddy castle surrounded by mountains and manned by armed Taliban.

I got out of the pick-up. The fresh air of early morning hit my face. Wazir put his hand on my right shoulder, the same way he used to do in school, and reiterated how the 'brothers' couldn't wait to meet me. 'Inshallah, your jihad would change the course of history.'

'Inshallah.' He didn't know that his once best friend had planned his own mission: to flee at the earliest opportunity.

Chapter Forty-One

We climbed the steps, bursting with trainers and shoes, and walked into a prayer hall as enormous as a community mosque. Green carpet with hundreds of prayer rug-like shapes lay on the floor. Some two dozen men prayed nafl-prayers or recited the Quran, swaying back and forth. Those who didn't rushed to Wazir and hugged their commander and me. No one had shaved their natural beard. They all looked at least ten years younger than me, except one. The middle-aged man with a black and white beard read the Quran by the minbar and mihrab at the top. We sat closer to him.

What next? I wondered.

The man prayed, inserted the Quran into a cover, placed it on an x-shaped foldable book rest before him and rose to his feet. We got up and he embraced me like a father who hadn't met his son for years. Fragrant rose scent emanated from his black perahan tunban. Embraced Wazir and gestured to the isolated corner. He took the lead.

'Welcome to Afghanistan, Ahmad brother, the *asli* Afghanistan.' The 'genuine' Afghanistan.

I thanked him.

We sat cross-legged near the bookcases full of the Quran and other books with Arabic titles. He introduced himself as Hanif in perfect Pashto. Questioned whether I knew there once lived a warrior called Ahmad.

The founder of contemporary Afghanistan was one of my heroes, I told him, adding how Mour often reminded me of him.

'Ahmad Shah Baba is equally our inspiration. Baba not only asserted the Durrani Empire, but also expanded it to Delhi.'

'Indeed.'

'But we can't drag him out of the grave to save his dear watan. Afghanistan needs living Ahmad Shah Babas.'

I nodded.

'Have you got the warrior's heart?' he said, his lips stretched.

My heart fell and my eyes travelled to Wazir's grinning face.

'Of course he does if he travels all the way from England to join the jihad,' Wazir said.

I took a breath. A Talib by the mihrab increased his volume of reading the Quran and the back and forth swinging.

Like Wazir, a Pashtun from the Eastern province, Hanif had joined the jihad at 23, first against the Soviet invasion and now against the invasion of '50 countries'. Had six sons. The two eldest had been martyred in the jihad. Another two participated in the active jihad. The two youngest studied in madrasas, being prepared for the jihad.

Wazir chipped in and said the dribbler was one of the sons.

'Yes, he whipped my mother,' I said.

A Talib pulled the curtains, opened the windows and allowed the sun's rays to peek in, creating arched shapes on the carpet.

In recent years, bad knees had compelled Hanif to stay away from the active jihad and be a 'mullah' and a 'servant' to the Taliban. Excited to have seen me and wanted to know about me. He and Wazir acted like they hadn't heard my comment on his son.

I emigrated to England as a teenager with my parents. Obtained a medical degree. Was furious about the US invasion of my watan and the invasion of Iraq. Joined Hizb ut-Tahrir but it didn't quench my thirst, so decided joining an active jihad was the answer.

'Alhamdulillah. Ahmad brother, this world is a bus stop, not the final destination. We must concentrate on the life awaiting us. A permanent life. A meaningful life. Ahmad brother, I agree with you.

Until the Muslim lands are occupied, there's a clear duty upon us to jihad. I've been here for 30 years and have witnessed many brothers martyr themselves in the jihad against the godless Russians and the infidel Americans. But what you're about to do will shake the world, inshallah.'

'Inshallah,' I said. Hundreds from the West joined violent groups in the Middle East every year; I wasn't sure why Wazir and Hanif assumed my participation would 'change the course of history' or 'shake the world'. Was it impactful because I was a medical doctor?

'I envy you and your place in Janat, Ahmad brother.' Hanif sounded like he'd just signed a binding contract with Khudai to allocate me a special place in Janat. On the contrary, the Quran said that killing one innocent person was akin to killing all mankind.

The charming Hanif kept mentioning my name and referring to me as a brother like we'd been the best of friends since childhood. He offered me a pair of black perahan tunban to wear instead of my melon-stained ones, adding that every Talib washed their own clothes.

***

LATER THAT DAY, after eating rice mixed with raisins and hard chapati naan for lunch, and after the afternoon prayer, the imam, Hanif, in a black turban, standing on the minbar, asked one of the Taliban to tell us what'd befallen him.

The Talib, who had dried lips like the rest, narrated: Americans ambushed their village. Pressed them against the ground, which made him choke. Took off their trousers in front of the villagers and fingered their backsides. Got the dog to smell their private areas. Mocked them and then took their pictures to show them to 'the whole world.' American women treated the female villagers in the same way.

'What sort of life is this?' Hanif asked the attentive listeners, who sat cross-legged around Hanif like hungry children waiting for parents to ration food.

'The Americans and the British have occupied our watan. Oppressed our brothers and sisters. Insulted our religion. Stained our honour. Snatched our independence. Undermined our dignity. The unbelievers want to turn our watan into their "Little America"! Would Wazir Akbar Khan have accepted such a shameful life?'

All heads shook.

'What would Ahmad Shah Baba or Mirwais Baba have done against such un-Islamic acts?'

'Jihad,' everyone shouted in unison, their faces and necks breaking into a sweat. The sun beamed down on us through the open windows of the *qubba*, the dome.

'That's what we'll do, inshallah,' Hanif said. 'We won't be the puppet Karzai,' Hanif added over the birds chirping in the young trees in the yard.

'Death to America and its puppets,' everyone said in unison.

'Our proud history compels us to defend our land against the tyrants, or else we deserve our heads to be cut like Shah Shujah and Karmal.' Shah Shujah Durrani 'invited' (to invade) Great Britain in 1839, and Babrak Karmal the Soviet Union in 1979.

'We have faith in one Creator, Allah. He'll help us win, inshallah.'

'Inshallah,' everyone shouted.

'The infidel British and Americans have the watches, we have the time,' Hanif said.

'Death to the British,' everyone said in unison.

'Why are you quiet, Ahmad brother?' Hanif caught me off guard.

'I agree with everything you said, Hanif brother.' I sounded more eager than I'd intended.

'Alhamdulillah.'

'I've joined the lion Meshar Mullah to take revenge and then get shahid,' the victim Talib said, his eyes welling up. The 'lion' Wazir had left to attend 'some court work'.

'You will, inshallah,' Hanif said, shouting 'Allahu Akbar.'

359

'Allahu Akbar,' said the rest, me included, in unison.

I'd guessed it right: the 'servant' Hanif wasn't a mullah but a mentor, and a skilful one, who mentally prepared me for the jihad. I suspected Hanif, one of the 'brothers', had had me in his gaze since he'd met me. It was unsettling.

I didn't show a spontaneous reaction earlier because I was busy working out what'd happened to the victim Talib and the villagers. I didn't think the victim Talib or Hanif concocted the story. Americans hadn't learned from the experience of previous invading empires. They didn't get the simple fact that searching a private part was trivial in America but suicidal in Afghanistan. Afghans valued their traditions. Cherished their independence. Gave their heads for their religion. Anyone who disrespected those values met Afghan fury. An Afghan who didn't show bravery offended the Afghan way of life and deserved death; Afghans must stay loyal to their values, their history. The British had 'disrespected' our women in the First Anglo-Afghan War, and only one British person made it out alive out of thousands. I agreed with Mour once more today that the Afghanistan War was as much about 'protecting Pashtunwali' as it was about Islam.

Chapter Forty-Two

After travelling in a pick-up truck full of RPG warheads and with religious music playing out loud, after driving past some mud and a few stone huts in the middle of sporadic pine nut trees on the hills and mountains, after seeing the Taliban's white flag on the left wrapping over concrete mansions and Pakistan's white and green flag on the right, I, along with some 20 armed Taliban, arrived in the centre of a 'market' somewhere in 'Khost', Wazir and his aka's headquarters.

Wazir broke from a crowd of some 50 men and haleks and greeted me by the butcher's shop. The combination of the bright sun and the white perahan tunban and turban had brought out Wazir's distinctive black beard.

'Ready for a stoning?' Wazir said. The butcher hit a hanging lamb leg with a cleaver and chopped it off.

'What stoning?'

'Should have thought before committing zina,' he roared and pushed against my forehead, a bandolier slung over his midriff.

My knees buckled. 'I swear to Khudai I haven't touched a woman, let alone committed zina.' Had Wazir not believed me? Was it why he'd let me live? Was it why the Taliban sped 'to get me on time'?

'Everything ready?' Wazir asked a Talib holding a walkie-talkie with a static sound.

'I'm telling the truth.'

He pushed me again. 'Chup.'

'Please, Wazir–'

'I'm joking, man.' He burst into laughter. 'Stop panicking.' He put his hands on my shoulders and repeated that I should calm down, his Makarov pistol hanging under his left armpit.

My eyes caught four Taliban carrying a 20-or-so-year-old man. The young man's presence, selfishly, allayed my anxiety. I loathed Wazir even more. I'd forget I once had a friend named Wazir when I escaped. You didn't joke about a matter of life and death.

Wazir asked if the young man had performed ablutions.

A Talib in turban replied yes.

Wazir ordered for his blindfold and handcuffs to be removed.

The Talib carried out the instructions. The young man's behaviour took me back to the first day of Eid al-Adha, to the lambs Nurrullah butchered. Like those lambs, the young man's eyes flicked from one Talib to the other, to the crowd and back to the Taliban.

Wazir ordered the young man to pray his afternoon prayer, whose time was running out, and shouted at the shop assistants to join us in the 'field'. They rushed to the centre, leaving their fuel, fabric and plastic pot shops.

The young man collapsed as the Taliban released his hands. Wazir instructed to let him pray sitting.

The young man's feet weren't willing to take the last few steps of his life when they stood him up after finishing the prayer to reach his final position: the lower ground dug in by a bomb in the centre of the so-called market consisting of six or seven scattered shops like empty sheds with roller shutter doors.

'Move,' the eager crowd said, many of whom were young haleks who wore taqiyah skullcaps and torn slippers, their faces and feet as dry and dusty as the ground around us.

Wazir scolded the young man to be brave and deal with it like 'a man'. He put the black cloth around the young man's eyes and tightened it. Tapped his shoulders and commanded him to stand firm on his feet. His thin legs behind his tunban shook and he collapsed again. A cackle from the crowd. Wazir ordered the four Taliban to carry him.

Wazir and the four joined the crowd. He stood next to me and passed me two stones. 'Mubarak on your first major reward.'

'I'm a medical doctor, I can't do this,' I said.

'Afghanistan is in dying need of the implementation of Sharia law,' Wazir said angrily. He commanded everyone in the crowd to follow the instruction, which he also repeated in Pashto, Dari, Urdu, Arabic, Panjabi and Russian, mainly how large a stone should be.

'Allahu Akbar,' Wazir said.

The crowd echoed.

He threw his stone and hit the young man on his chin. Wazir motioned with his eyes to my hand.

Khudai forgive me, I prayed. *Save my watan, people and religion from these fanatics.* My throw missed the young man, from whose face blood flew.

Wazir threw another stone and caught the young man's neck, and the young man closed his eyes.

My next stone was also a miss.

Wazir gave me a stare. So did the man standing by my left, stinking of diesel.

The young man reacted to the first stones, but as they rained down on him like sleet, his reaction became less and less until Wazir ordered a stop.

'Hand the body to the family,' Wazir instructed the four Taliban, pointing to the young man with a fractured skull covered in blood.

The crowd dismantled, and my eyes caught an unsettling scene: Hanif with two other men – men I'd never seen before – read me. Their faces showed no expression. They must've observed me throughout the stoning. Wazir approached them. They spoke for a good five minutes. Wazir nodded all the way through. They left with Hanif.

Did they discuss me? Were they the big 'brothers' who called the shots? Was the stoning a test to see my commitment? I must've failed both of today's tests.

Wazir walked back and pointed to the faded kilims circled by straw beds under the trees for the Asr Prayer.

***

AFTER THE PRAYER in the open on the kilims, the imam, Wazir, stood up.

'Don't confine Islam to just worship,' Wazir opened the sermon. 'Islam isn't just about performing the daily five prayers or reading the Quran. It's about a jihad against non-believers. About sacrificing your lives and properties for Allah's sake.'

Sitting cross-legged under the quietly creaking tree branches, worshippers maintained eye contact with Wazir and didn't even blink.

'I blame the religious scholars for limiting Islam to a mere religion – Islam is a way of life. I blame them for reducing a jihad to only fighting one's personal desires.'

Everyone listened eagerly. Nobody questioned his interpretation of Islam. I didn't think they had the education to do so. One had, but Wazir beheaded him last night.

'We jihad for an Islamic state with Sharia law as its constitution. We aim to protect Islam through the power of the state. Shoot anyone who says religion and politics are separate in Islam.' Standing like one of the surrounding trees over us, he said it with such fury that it frightened me. 'Point blank in here.' Wazir pointed to his forehead.

Silence, apart from insects buzzing or trilling, and tree branches creaking. The sounds reminded me of our summer holidays in Surobi. Just 100 metres away behind the straw beds was a flowing stream where the worshippers and I earlier did ablutions. You could holiday all your life by that stream.

'Just as Islam teaches you how to pray, fast and give alms, Islam gives you the law whereby you run a state, establish a government, administer foreign affairs and conduct treaties. It's a complete system.'

'Allahu Akbar,' a Talib standing by Wazir shouted.

'Allahu Akbar,' the worshippers and Wazir's security detail guarding our surroundings followed.

'Any law which puts man in power over another man is un-Islamic. Only Allah's law is Islamic. We reject democracy.'

'Allahu Akbar,' everyone screamed.

'We oppose the occupation.'

'Allahu Akbar.'

'We want to transfer Islam from madrasa to mosques, home and into all aspects of our lives – implement Allah's law in Allah's land.'

'Allahu Akbar.'

'Remember Prophet Ibrahim's parents opposed their son. His family rejected him, and, in turn, he rejected his father. I'm *not* suggesting you reject your parents. On the contrary, respect them because the Prophet of Islam, peace be upon him, emphasised that the key to Janat is under parents' feet. But make your parents understand we're invaded by the Western kafirs, and so there's an obligatory duty upon us to liberate our watan. The only way to do so is to join us in the active jihad,' Wazir got to the point.

'Does my family not want me to be by their side?' he questioned the worshippers that he mesmerised with his words. 'Instead, I'm here to defend my people, my watan and, crucially, my religion.

'This brother in black perahan tunban,' he pointed to me, 'has commendably left his mother, job and comfortable life in England, and come here to participate in the active jihad.' He motioned to me.

I received a spontaneous 'mashallah' as I stood next to him. Cheers of repeated 'Allahu Akbar' filled the air. I joined them, knowing I'd done poorly in the previous two assessments.

Everyone tried to hug Wazir, or at least touch their hero, their celebrity, who'd come to their tiny village to meet them as they returned to their business. I got a few taps on my shoulders, too.

Some worshippers stayed behind and shared their issues with Wazir: the Taliban fired from the middle of their houses and the Americans bombarded them and their families; their children continued to study under trees and their books no longer come from the Kabul government; hospitals lacked basic facilities and no female doctor existed – the male doctors were self-taught pharmacists; only those with male relatives in Dubai or Saudi Arabia could afford walwar and the poor parents' ageing sons (who had no one abroad) 'wander around like crazy'; no one accepted Afghani but Pakistani rupees; their sons were imprisoned for using a mobile phone or watching a Bollywood movie; and plenty of complaints about the mountains 'not belonging' to this or that tribe, and hence this or that tribe had no right to cut the trees. Sitting cross-legged on the faded green kilim with paper and a notebook, Wazir listened, jotted down sometimes, and promised to address their concerns, warning he'd 'drown' anyone killing another over the ownership of mountains. He invited the elders of two tribes over for a jirga next week. They thanked him for meeting them today, adding it'd been months since they'd been looking for him.

***

ESTABLISHING A LEGAL SYSTEM based on Sharia law was their first imperative, Wazir said after a few minutes' drive in his pick-up truck followed by his usual PSD. According to him, it was transparent, quick and effective; and no one would ever dare to commit zina in that village again.

The requirements for stoning to death were rigorous in Islamic law. Only the court or religious scholars, whom he'd scolded in the open mosque, delivered the judgment – not a radical jihadist like Wazir. How my people's lives had become cheap. How today's

Afghanistan turned good people into villains, and bad ones into heroes.

'We need Sharia law to bring security to Afghanistan, not democracy.'

'Security is imperative,' I said. My eyes flicked to young haleks jumping from trees into the river one after the other, swimming with their clothes on.

'Only Sharia law can clean Kabul from drinking, womanising and *Bacha-bazi*.'

'I agree.'

'The local police won't fight without a *bacha* on their side.'

'Na.'

'We outlawed the practice as we got into power and executed the perpetrators.'

'A great decision,' I said and meant it. To my disgust, I'd kept telling lies to support the first lie. It felt great when occasionally you spoke your mind. For centuries, prepubescent and adolescent haleks were forcefully sold to wealthy or powerful men for 'boy play': entertainment, mainly dancing, and sexual activities. For decades, the practice of dancing haleks had been illegal under Afghan law, but they were hardly enforced against powerful offenders.

'The man was the father of the scum we stoned,' Wazir said, referring to an elderly man with a henna-dyed beard who earlier on pleaded with Wazir for a private talk when he finished the jirga.

'He wouldn't take the body because the son dishonoured him. I told him to give him a proper Islamic burial and leave it to Allah,' Wazir said over the static sound of the walkie-talkie from the back seat.

'No doubt. Who did he zina with?'

'Let's say a militia commander, a scum, who preyed on young haleks, is one fewer on the earth.'

I nodded. My eyes caught a herd of sheep and goats eating plants under the pine nut trees on the mountains, as high as the sky.

'This's how the Amir of the Faithful founded the Taliban movement back in the 90s,' Wazir said, driving through the water of a stream, making a bow wave.

'How so?'

'The villagers come to Mullah Omar Mujahid with a complaint about how their two daughters had been kidnapped and raped by a Mujahideen commander. The Amir takes two dozen men, releases the victims, and hangs the thugs from a tank barrel.'

'Good for him.' The Taliban makers took us for fools as if it was a Bollywood movie. You couldn't financially support a small family in Afghanistan, let alone establish a movement and then involve it in war with 49 countries. 'We should also outlaw opium and punish the criminals,' I said.

'We did it in 2001. The opium production dropped to 180 tons a year. Now it's risen to 9000 tons.' Wazir raced uphill, amidst the brattling sound of chainsaws cutting down trees.

'Three and a half million Afghans, ten per cent of the population, are addicts. Kabul is full of them.'

'Thanks to America.'

'Thanks to America.' I meant it. Wazir and his like wouldn't have existed had America not supported radicalism against the Soviet Union in the 80s.

Wazir pulled over before the wooden gate of the base.

Chapter Forty-Three

Hanif's absence from the praying room gave me breathing space. I walked past the Taliban reciting the Quran and lay down in the top corner, trying to relax. Had encountered so much violence, hatred and brainwashing in the last two days that I feared they'd turn me into a fanatical Ahmad.

I now learned why youngsters willingly turned into fedayi bombers. In madrasas, mosques, homes, on transport, in markets, *everywhere*, conversations revolved around nothing but occupation and holy duty to struggle against it. America and its allies had occupied Afghanistan to 'steal' Islam from us. If these Taliban I was acquainted with had ten lives individually, they'd sacrifice each and every one of them to save their religion.

Man is the product of its time, I remembered Agha saying, and the Taliban's Afghanistan produced machines like Wazir who were programmed to 'liberate their watan from the infidels'. The brave, sincere and loyal Wazir was the kind who'd sacrifice his life for Islam without even thinking about it. Those qualities must have made it easy for the extremists to turn him into a fanatic.

Afghanistan also witnessed a time that produced machines like Frishta, programmed to free Afghanistan from radicalism and replace it with liberalism.

Nobody asked what ordinary Afghans wanted. We cherished our traditional values but Frishta's foreign liberal ideals corrupted them. Likewise, the Islam our ustads and parents taught us wasn't about the outside appearance, but cleansing oneself from the inside from the feelings of prejudice, anger, revenge, envy, jealousy. Khudai saw our inside if no one else did. Islam was a religion of love, peace and patience; not revenge. All human beings were Adam's children, our parents and ustads had taught us, so we should not classify people as kafirs and Muslims or Pashtun and Tajik. But that interpretation didn't suit the Taliban's masters.

Wazir and Frishta's extreme ideologies were tied around us like chains and strangled our values. Sucked our blood like leeches. Demolished our infrastructure like a bulldozer. I lost my home, watan, and nearly all family members in the power struggle between those foreign ways of life, and I didn't know how much more I'd suffer, how much more my people would pay, and what would be next for my watan.

The sad reality was, though, that our own Afghan politicians opened the gates for those alien invaders to enter our watan. Except for a few, all our politicians after Daoud Khan had been shopkeepers, selling what foreign intelligence agencies needed in return for sim and zar. Ironically, they all invoked national interests or Islam for selling their people and watan. Hence, I loathed politics. Loathed discussing politics. Loathed Wazir and wasn't sure about Frishta anymore.

Both possessed unlimited powers and had changed into monsters. One threw me out of the mansion, and the other wanted to cut my throat. I shared nothing in common with either of them. I didn't want to change the world or tell others how to live their lives; global conflicts would have been solved, or wouldn't have been created in the first place, had we stopped imposing 'our way of life' on each other. All I wanted was a modest house, a job, a wife and kids, but their power struggle wouldn't allow me to have them.

A Talib coughed and carried on reading the Quran.

There was another thing that bothered me: why did Wazir ask Shujah's contact number when he dropped me in front of the base? Like my future, it, too, was unknown, a future of which I prayed Mour was a part. I prayed her heart didn't give up. I missed her. I didn't remember spending a day without my mother. *Khudai, give me one more chance to make it up to her.*

I thought of England, how the people of my adopted *watan* were busy watching *Match of the Day* or listening to the terrorist-related news thousands of miles away from them. Mour and I would've been sitting in the lounge sipping tea if we'd been in Durham. We had a lot in life: we just didn't appreciate it. Waited for a better tomorrow; hardly enjoyed today. Never realised today was that better tomorrow. A today in which I hadn't disrespected Mour, told lies or took part in killing human beings. What had become of me? Lips that abstained from uttering an *uff*, expression of annoyance, to Mour called her a poisonous snake; hands that were meant to heal human beings bled them; integrity that had been worked on and built for decades shattered by one dishonest statement after another. A lie was a lie. No matter what, I should've stayed honest to myself and – a wave of pain, not so much physical but suffocating, struck me. The pleasant Quran recitation faded, the green carpet and the arched windows turned blurry and then blackened.

***

A FUZZY MAN with a long beard and round glasses grinned. 'How are you, brother?' he said.

'Soaked in water,' I said.

Wazir's murderous face appeared on my left side. 'You were well. What happened?'

'No idea.'

'Might be the heat,' the man with glasses said. He offered a mug of water. I downed it. Overheard Hanif saying the dua for the Maghrib Prayer.

Wazir told the 'doctor' to go. The man with the round glasses bade me goodbye.

'How's our Ahmad brother doing?' Hanif said, the congregation standing behind him.

'He'll inshallah be better once he hears the news,' Wazir said, throwing me a smile, his bandolier poking forward.

'Let him rest. We can tell him later,' Hanif said.

'The news is his prescription.'

'What news?'

'Time to go,' Wazir said.

'Where?' I resisted showing a pressing pain in my chest, yearning to know about my 'prescription'.

'Let's get some fresh air,' Wazir said.

My head spun around as I rose to my feet. Fought against staggering.

Chapter Forty-Four

Wazir's 'fresh air' turned out to be a tiny, half-lit room high up in the opposite corner of the muddy castle. Maroon Afghan kilims lay on the floor, and an oil lamp burned besides Hanif and two men with chest-long beards, large turbans, and, like Wazir and Hanif, smelling of strong rose scent – the same men from the stoning affair. We greeted. Nobody introduced me to what Wazir called the 'brothers', or they to me.

'I've been right about him all along,' Wazir said to the brothers, sitting next to Hanif, his back to the windows.

Help, Khudai. I sat opposite Wazir, feeling pain in my chest and body.

'He's always been a committed Muslim,' Wazir added.

'Thank you, Meshar Mullah.' I leaned against the built-in cupboard full of files and papers in the hope of reducing the pain.

'We're all in awe of your courage. Allah will bestow upon you Janat once you accomplish your dream, inshallah,' Wazir said.

'Inshallah.'

'It's on tomorrow.'

'What?'

'Inshallah, your mission.'

'What mission?'

'Fedayi.'

My heart fell, lips sealed.

'To remove a mountain of problems from out of our way.'

'I'm here to treat the injured brothers. I can't take lives. I'm a doctor.'

'Ending this life is necessary if you want to save your watan and religion.'

'You're perfect for the mission, Ahmad brother,' Hanif chipped in, leaning forward, the circles under his eyes darkening in the burning orange oil lamp.

'We want to do it before the word of your captivity gets around,' Wazir said.

'Wazir, how can you make such a big decision without consulting me?'

'Fedayi is the highest rank of the jihad,' Wazir said over the clanking sound of the castle gates opening and vehicles driving in. 'We'll put you up in a safe house in Kabul by early tomorrow morning.'

'*Tomorrow morning*?' The words 'tomorrow morning' sank in.

'The scorpion leaves for a conference in America tomorrow afternoon,' Hanif said.

'Get somebody else. You're in desperate need of a doctor in this village. I'll be of enormous help here.'

'Hundreds of fedayis are willing to cut the head of this deathstalker scorpion, Ahmad brother, but unfortunately they won't reach–'

'I have a mother to provide for. I can't do it.'

'Sadly, not anymore. She's passed away,' Wazir said.

'When?'

'On the way to the hospital.'

'How do you know?'

'I spoke to your aka. She was buried this morning.'

Was it possible Mour would never be around? Someone who'd lived 36 years by you, cared for you, loved you, suddenly disappeared from your life forever? Vanished before marrying her son to a 'decent' jelai and feeding her grandchildren on her lap? Died without visiting

Mecca, without the son to read the Quran over her body, pray her Janazah Prayer, and put her in the grave? Was it possible a son accused a mother of a lie she'd never told, making tears come down her cheeks? A mother who'd paid the ultimate price to save her son. Was it possible to lose not just a mother but a father and, worse, a spiritual coach? Who'd advise me that hard work helped you excel in life? Support me to take the A1 exams twice and the A2 exams thrice to satisfy the entry requirements for a medical degree? Remind me, that if you wanted respect in the community, to be guided by truth?

'...Your mission opens Janat's doors for all of your close relatives. You'll inshallah meet her in Janat,' Hanif said and handed me a white embroidered handkerchief like the Taliban flag leaning in the corner.

I wiped my eyes. 'She defended the Taliban all her life. The Taliban gave her death in return. An undignified one.' My voice broke.

'Allah will reward her for the good deed,' Hanif said.

Wazir nodded, uttering an Inshallah. Young Wazir reverted Mour. She, in turn, loved Wazir like 'a son'. His cold approach to her public flogging last night and to her death now displayed that Wazir had no trace of emotion left within him.

'Tomorrow morning you'll be taken to the school the scorpion plans to visit on the way to the airport. As she approaches–'

'*She?*' I cut Wazir short, my heart falling.

'Frishta.'

Another thunder hit me. '*Why* Frishta? She's a good Muslim.' I wiped my eyes.

'She isn't.'

'Listen for now,' Hanif chipped in, placing his finger on his lips. The only fresh lips and face I saw in this mountainous area.

Part of me begged to say, 'Fuck off, bastard Hanif,' but I swallowed the urge. Then a thought sprang to mind: the mission is a Khudai-given opportunity. It can make it easier to escape or give myself up once I'm in Kabul. After all, nobody else could press the button on the suicide belt apart from me. Fedayi bombers frequently gave themselves up to the police. Did I not hear it in the police pick-up on the way to the District Nine Police Headquarters, the day Nazia was still alive?

Wazir was talking. '...She'll pull over when she spots you. Press the button as you feel her touch.'

'Hug her tight before pressing the button – she has seven lives, like a cat,' Hanif said.

The window lightened. One of the men, the brothers, reached the window, pulled the white, embroidered curtains, raised his hand, drew the curtains, sat back in his place on the mattress, and nodded.

'We arranged numerous suicide missions. She survived them all. Make sure you accomplish the mission this time, Ahmad brother,' Hanif went on.

'What if she suspects the plot and doesn't pull over? She must know I'm imprisoned with the Taliban.'

'She knows nothing. I phoned your aka not to tell anyone about your captivity because it'd only make it difficult to release you.'

For that reason alone, Shujah might have told everyone, I thought, but said nothing.

Today once more I felt like a headless goat between my once best friends, a feeling I'd vowed to avoid. Young Frishta was right; no prison was worse than not standing up for yourself but following orders like a sheep.

Wazir said they'd discussed other possibilities, such as meeting her in the office or her mansion, but I wouldn't get past her bodyguards. 'Five identical jeeps escort her. We don't know which one carries her,' Wazir said.

'And the jeeps are bulletproof,' Hanif said, wiping his forehead with his hand. I passed him his handkerchief.

Wazir said the only way they knew which vehicle she was travelling in was to have her pull over. This way, her bodyguards wouldn't search me because she'd let me in herself. 'Hug her and explode. Briskly and confidently,' Wazir added.

'Ashraf, her bodyguard, drove like mad to avoid suicide bombers. I doubt she'll pull over,' I said, wanting to gain as much information about the plot as I could; the more information, the easier I'd form the escape plan and, importantly, save Frishta's life.

'She will spot you,' Wazir said.

'How?'

'Ahmad, you're the only person she won't miss,' he said, giving me a look as if he knew something, the same one he'd confronted me with last night.

'How so?' I genuinely wanted to know. Frishta no longer loved me. What convinced Wazir to think Frishta still cared?

'Ahmad, you know.'

'I honestly don't.'

'Because she's in mina with you.'

'She has a husband and three children.'

'Who'd marry the prostitute? She has no husband or kids. She waits for you.'

'I saw her daughters with my own eyes.'

'They're the daughters of a woman who lives with her. Frishta owns numerous homes where she pretends to look after those whores. In reality, she turns them into non-believers like herself,' Wazir said, beads of sweat coming down his forehead.

'First, I don't think she's got any feelings for me. Second, why would she lie to me about having a husband? Third, Wazir, we know what a committed Muslim she was in school.' Like twins in black turbans and white perahan tunbans and dark grey waistcoats, the two men looked fixedly at me.

'She isn't a Muslim anymore. With the full donation of her American and British backers, she's busy running homes, training workshops and holding conferences to "speak out" for women's "political and social rights". These Western-created rights intend to wipe out our way of life. She refuses to accept women must travel with a male escort or avoid mixing with men in public offices. Her elimination has become a necessity for the mujahideen.'

'Nothing you have said turns her into a non-believer,' I said. Mour's death, the news about Frishta and the imminence of the mission alleviated my anxiety. I spoke almost without fear. I risked their trust, but also knew I was too valuable for them to kill me. 'I hope you understand. Our lives belong to Khudai. Ending them without a valid justification angers Khudai,' I added.

'You won't, inshallah. Trust us, Ahmad brother.'

'I haven't got the answer for why she'd lie to me about her marital status. Plus, I saw her with my own eyes praying the Isha Prayer.'

Wazir looked at the two men. One of them blinked, followed by the other's gentle nod. Wazir pulled out a magazine from under the cupboard behind me and passed it over. 'Read. It'll answer all your questions.'

The cover dedicated itself to Frishta's photo in a black headscarf with the headline and the subheadline: *THE LONE LEOPARD: The Extraordinary Journey of an Afghan Woman—From a Middle-Class Girl to a Beggar, to a Human Rights Champion, to a Member of Parliament and Now a Presidential Hopeful.*

Hanif pulled forward the oil lamp. Under the orange light I began to read the content without hesitation. Frishta had told the story of how growing up in four corners of Afghanistan was eye-opening, how caring her parents were, how she enjoyed her schooling, and how a single rocket took everything away from her: family, home, health and the chance to attend her parents' and brother's funerals. From the rocket part onwards, Frishta wrote...

Chapter Forty-Five

...More children with missing bodyparts poured into the already overcrowded hospital, compelling it to discharge me to free up beds. I had nowhere to go and no one to ask for help. A doctor introduced me to Rahim, who managed an NGO in Khair Khana.

Rahim offered me three meals, a place to live and fatherly love in return for managing the NGO's account.

One morning, a week into my stay, Rahim didn't return from the satellite shop in the Foroshgah Shopping Centre, where he regularly journeyed to make a distant call to the headquarters in America. My heart plodded against my chest. Injuries ached. Stomach hurt. I hadn't eaten anything since Rahim had left. He was meant to come with some bread and tea, but he seemed to have forgotten about his newly adopted daughter. Like the rest of the NGO staff, he, too, might've 'escaped' Kabul.

The second night, a night I'd never forget, the door banged open and two people in white overalls carried a wooden container. A rocket explosion had burned half of Rahim's face; his armless body lay in the wooden coffin. I confirmed his identity, and the men in the overalls said the hospital had informed his next of kin. They'd come from Pakistan – until then, the coffin was to stay in the house. They departed to deliver other coffins. The honourable Rahim, a father figure and my only hope, was no more.

My heartbeats increased as it grew darker. What if Rahim rose from the coffin and strangled me? I wanted to go to another room but couldn't because a large stone hung from my fractured leg. My body trembled with hot flashes and chills. I wept and wept. I hoped a thief entered the broken door - though thieves were so busy in those days that they didn't want to do overtime.

The night turned into day, but no next of kin showed up. I cried. Screamed. Slapped my face. Pulled my hair. Hauled the leg with the weight on. It hurt. If only the rocket had cut that leg, too. If only it sent me on the same journey as my parents and brother. I'd had enough of the unbearable burning pain and smell of rotten meat. Whenever they turned up, I hoped Rahim's relatives found two bodies, one in a coffin and the other without.

A shake opened my eyes to a man and a woman with blue eyes. I screamed. The woman gently pressed my hands and offered me a glass of water. Another man, who cupped his nose with the hand, told me to drink or I'd faint again. The man said the Americans, who looked terrified, wanted to know what had happened to Rahim and how I'd ended up in the building.

I broke into tears. My feeble body shivered.

The woman squeezed my hands again and said to calm down, telling me they, Naomi and her husband John, oversaw the NGO that assisted Afghan women like me.

I told them my story in broken English. We all wept together. The Afghan man, the interpreter, swore to kill the hospital staff for leaving a 16-year-old jelai alone with a dead body.

The couple apologised, reassuring me that they'd help me with my future plans.

'I have none. My journey ends here.'

'Your journey has just begun. You have thousands of Afghan sisters who need you more than ever, young woman,' Naomi said and John nodded. 'I've come from America to help your sisters; you cannot do it here,' Naomi went on.

'I miss my parents and want to join them.' I felt mentally dead and physically alive, only just.

'Who says you don't have parents? We're your parents. I'm your mother.' She hugged me and apologised once more for what had happened to me. 'Janet, our daughter, is seven years old. She'd be over the moon to have an older sister. You are our next daughter.' She pointed to John. 'We'll love you both equally. Won't we, John?'

John's eyes welled up. 'Of course, we will.' He hugged Naomi, telling her how proud he was of her.

'We'll take you to America,' Naomi said.

For the first time after my parents' death, someone cared. After weeks of rejection, someone loved me, really loved me. Reminded me of my relevance. Then and now, I think of Naomi as a loving mother – a blessing in my life.

She employed me in the NGO and helped me improve my English. Brought me plenty of books, not to mention tons of gifts, every time she returned from America.

During the four-year mujahideen government (1992—96) work took me to almost all provinces in Afghanistan, to every single war zone, and I feared no one because I was unafraid of death. I worked to serve my Afghan sisters during the daytime. Learned about Rosa Parks, Emmeline Pankhurst and Martin Luther King Jr at night. These great human beings enlightened me more on human rights, liberty and America's role in women's emancipation. I loved your watan even more.

My watan, however, entered another dark chapter of its history: in 1996, Pakistan occupied Afghanistan through its proxies, the Taliban. They confiscated the NGO and left me in the open. Like Afghanistan, I was back to square one. My foreign colleagues offered to take me abroad. I swore I'd never leave my watan. Instead, joined the hundreds of displaced families in the bombed-out Russian Embassy building; the families whose villages in Shomali the Taliban had burned for having 'supported' the Northern Alliance.

We had access to nothing. No means by which I could contact my American mother. A few NGOs still operated underground, which delivered support to Afghan women. Day in and day out, I listened to my sisters and translated their problems to the NGO workers. I found a purpose in life again after the initial disappointment.

One day an American NGO worker, Jenny, took me to Wazir Akbar Khan District for an 'urgent matter'. On the other side of the satellite, a worried Naomi called my name and asked me to shift to Pakistan until she completed the papers. 'Afghanistan's my America. I was born and will die here,' I told her. I reminded her that she herself urged me to serve my sisters, who needed me more than ever.

Naomi said someone wanted to speak to me. A soft voice called me 'sister' and pleaded that I join her. It was Janet. She said she'd been saving up her pocket money for my tickets. I thanked her and said, hopefully, one day we'd meet.

Naomi suggested another option: I worked from Pakistan, where our NGO's branch still operated. That way I'd be able to serve my Afghan sisters and be safe. She knew why I didn't move to Pakistan. I respected the Pakistani people but was disappointed in its Army's destructive Afghan policy. Naomi offered to transfer money. I needed none. Afghanistan craved books in Dari and Pashto on human rights.

Before the books' arrival, I received something else, however. I detested the burka, a foreign tradition that had caged us for centuries. One day the Taliban arrested me for not being accompanied by a male mahram and wearing the cage 'incorrectly'. I told them the mujahideen murdered all my mahrams and I couldn't buy a husband on the bazzar-e-lilami markets. They lashed me for 'speaking back'. I snapped, shouting that the mujahideen killed us with guns and they with cotton. I hurled the cage at them and screamed I wouldn't be imprisoned with the burka. The worst happened: they threw me in jail.

I turned out to be the only literate among the inmates. The Taliban agreed that I should teach, but only Islamic subjects to prepare the prisoners for the religious test they had to take as part of their release. The teaching of female inmates occupied my days. Jelais had ended up in the cells for what I called the 'Taliban reasons': being in 'mina', venturing out without a male relative, revealing their ankles. One jelai had eloped because her parents pressurised her to marry a Talib who already had a wife. Another woman had run away owing to her husband constantly beating her up for being 'ugly'. Another brave soul had questioned the Taliban ban on women's education and work. The majority of married women, however, had committed crimes, mostly thefts, to feed their starving kids. I voiced their difficulties to the prison governor, who called me *Gwady*, the cripple. 'Gwady, what problem have you brought today?' he'd say every time I showed up.

Prison no longer bothered me when I became a means to help my sisters. The governor nevertheless was pleased to see the back of Gwady after a few months.

The books had arrived. I resumed underground teaching to women and jelais in the abandoned Russian Embassy. I also doubled up as an interpreter, nurse, guide and even a midwife. Midwifed them to deliver babies in the embassy's secluded corner with a piece of black cloth as my only 'equipment'. One woman died for reasons beyond my expertise. I cried all that night.

Our watan was desolate. Everyone forgot about us, even God. Renting videocassettes was like selling drugs. Satellite dishes and TV sets found themselves hung on electricity poles. Female models on imported products had their eyes gouged out. Flying pigeons and playing marbles turned Kabulis into criminals. Boys' long hairstyles became their enemy. The sky of Kabul no longer witnessed its fluttering birds. Public transport was either designated 'male only' or 'female only', or segregated by a curtain. God forbade you celebrated birthdays or played music at your wedding. If you accidentally found yourself in Kabul, you'd think you'd moved back in time to the Middle Ages: the city of black and white burkas and plenty of moving loudspeakers reminding you of the prayer times.

One evening the Taliban raided the dilapidated embassy and caught me teaching. Worse, they found the human rights books. Back to eating bean soup from the Titanic pot and sleeping in the foetal position. The Taliban governor beat me up this time, but the inmates were overjoyed to see me again; though later they apologised for their jubilation. To my pleasant surprise, the governor allowed me to teach classes on one condition: if I uttered a word about human rights, they'd also 'cut my other leg off'.

Sometimes I selfishly thought everyone brought their problems and concerns to me; I had no one to share my worries with. They considered me a strong Gwady, who had no heart, no feelings, no love, no emotions, no past or future. Not once did I get a visit or a gift on a Tuesday, which downcast me sometimes – actually always. Life dragged on without a future.

But then I'd remind myself that God had saved me for one purpose: to serve my sisters, the only thing I lived for. Fighting their cause and trying to protect them from their brothers and sisters' cruelty gave me then and now an enormous sense of purpose. I'd console myself that I possessed a large family; women in prison and outside trusted me as their sister, their 'rock'. They cared and still do. People often ask me why, at 37, I still haven't married and established a family. My response is: I *am* married and *have* a family. I'm married to my dear watan. My brave Afghan sisters and brothers form my family. When you have such a romantic partner and a large family, you don't need to marry in the literal sense. And you're also not a lone leopard!

The Taliban took away my artificial leg and warned me never to step on the Russian Embassy's soil or be seen with foreigners. 'We're watching over you, Gwady,' the governor said as I stepped out of his office for the last time.

What was I to do after 16 months of imprisonment? No place to go to, no one to turn to, no money to spend; at 4 o'clock in the freezing morning, it was me, my burka and a stick. I sat near the prison and chose the only option available to the miserable women of Afghanistan. That day I made 1800 Afghanis, worth tenpence of a dollar; enough for two pieces of bread. That night, and many nights after, I slept at Shah-Do-Shamshira Mosque. Wished one day Khudai gave me the same power as the Saint, the 'King of Two Swards', once possessed, so I rid my watan of the Taliban once and for all. The Taliban beat me up when they caught me begging in the first months, but eventually gave up. Maybe they viewed begging better than teaching human rights.

New books from America took me back to teaching. Jenny always ensured she passed my heartful thank-you to Naomi, John and Janet. I refused to talk to them despite Jenny's insistence. I didn't want my adopted family to worry more about me. They were already doing a great deal for my countrywomen and me. Every time Jenny smuggled me the books, she was petrified. Thankfully, the Taliban never caught us.

Naomi, John, Janet and, of course, Jenny: a big thank-you for what you have done for the women of my watan.

Mornings I begged and late afternoons visited the displaced who resided in girl schools to teach their girls and women. Sometimes the classes lingered and the families let me put up with them. Other times, especially when the refugee camp was located nearby, I travelled back to the mosque.

I carried on as a daytime beggar and night-time tutor until we found out one day that the terrorists extended their poisonous bite to America.

Next we knew the Taliban was on the run.

I went to Jenny's to fetch the next collection of books when Naomi opened the door. She embraced me with tearful eyes, telling me how much she'd missed me. A teenage girl hugged me with welled-up eyes. My adopted sister had just turned 18. John put his hand on my head and stroked me the way my father used to do. I was very grateful to have this family of angels.

Naomi and John introduced me to some Americans in power. They were pleased with my work and persuaded me to elect myself for parliament. The rest you can work out for yourself.

Oh, besides serving as an MP, I registered in evening classes at a university in Kabul and completed my degree in Law, specialising in human rights. Unlike many other politicians in Afghanistan, by the way, I attended all my classes and passed all my exams, so my degree isn't fake. One more thing: I invested every penny I own in my watan. Unlike what you hear, I've worked hard for my business, and after my death *all* my money will go to the charities I run.

Life has taught me a lesson: never stop your ambitions. Accept no one's threats. Don't care if they want to kill you. With each step you'll discover you can take one step further. You'll find you have the guts for things you haven't imagined before, not in your wildest dreams. Now is the time I take the next step: I stand as a presidential candidate, and, if successful, would strive for an Afghanistan with a solid democratic foundation that offers *equal* rights to all citizens regardless of their sex, ethnicity or tribe.

Thank you, Secretary of State Hillary Clinton, one of my inspirations, for your continued support. You, as Americans, too, please support my dear watan and its women. Make sure the US completes its job before it withdraws, or else the blood the Afghan and the American soldiers have spilt would be wasted. The accomplishments we have achieved together would be reversed. Afghanistan has to stand on its feet, or neighbouring countries would increase their jockeying for influence and plunge my watan into another vicious civil war and several occupations. This will, in turn, have repercussions for you and our allies in Europe.

Chapter Forty-Six

'Certain now she'll pull over?' Wazir said, having patiently waited like the rest of the colleagues in the orange-lit room.

'What makes you think so? Nothing in this article backs up your belief.'

'She isn't married, to start with. Second, her book choices. Third, her connection to the CIA.'

'There was no mention of the CIA.'

'You think the parents really are "angels"? Anyway, she asked for you every time she visited me in the Supreme Court. I repeatedly told her I didn't know. I suggested she speak to your tenants. "They didn't know", she said.'

I suspected Shujah kept everything from Mour and me because Frishta could shun his plans. My name had changed from Ahmad Azizi to Ahmad Azizullah. In Afghanistan we wrote our fathers' names in official documents instead of surnames, which Mour and I gave to the Home Office caseworker when we applied for asylum in 1997. Later on, our solicitor advised us not to have it corrected, in case the Home Office suspected we'd been lying. To make matters worse, I was never part of any social media. So no way could Frishta find Mour or me in England.

'Perhaps she asked for me because she had no other close relatives left.'

'That's not what she told me, Ahmad.'

'What did she tell you?' The azan for the Isha Prayer filled the castle and everyone said in unison, 'Allah the most exalted.' We stayed silent until the azan ended, hearing the Taliban's walking to the prayer room.

'One day, she walked into my office. Still hadn't found you. I knew she was there mainly to learn about you. Getting Brigadier's apartment back from a Taliban commander was a pretence.

'I questioned *why* she kept asking for you. She said she trusted me like a brother and revealed, without a trace of shame, she was in mina with you and wanted to marry you.

'I told her Ahmad wasn't the type to think about mina. She said you, too, loved her and had asked her in a letter to wait for your return. She couldn't show me the letter; it was in her diary, which somehow you had. I asked her how her diary was with you? "Long story," she said. I was all ears. She refused to tell.

'I then asked her whether something happened between you two. She suddenly lost it and said she'd never call me a brother, and slammed the door. I was glad to see the back of a 'sister' who disobeyed Sharia law and was in and out of prison. She was a disgrace to her religion then, and an enemy to it now. A female informant who once worked for her told us Frishta "waits" for "an honourable gentleman". So still in mina and still waits.'

I knew Wazir was telling the truth, otherwise he wouldn't have known about the love letter or the diary had Frishta not told him. I remembered reading in the diary how young Frishta trusted Wazir and, unsurprisingly, confided in him.

Astonishingly, Frishta had read my letter. Every day over the past few years she longed to meet me. Thought about her Ahmad and perhaps regretted why she didn't reveal her mina. Two decades later she found her Ahmad, but he broke the news that he was marrying someone else, and Khudai knew what Mour and Nazigul had told her when she visited them after dropping Nazia off. I'd made her wait for 21 years and then told her... Damn it.

At times Frishta could prove the most arrogant person I'd ever met. She'd never disclose her feelings after Mour and I mentioned our wife-hunting mission, especially after I accused her of being a traitor. She must've felt hurt and unsurprisingly lost her temper, exactly what she did years back in Bimaro. She then defended Shafih, even though she had no relationship with him; the day before yesterday, she pretended she had a husband and three daughters.

I was the only person Frishta would share her worries with, like she once told me about her mother. She'd waited to tell her Ahmad how she'd lost her beloved parents, her brother, her health. How the cruel world had turned her into a person who was assumed to have experienced no emotions. She needed her Ahmad to remind her of her womanness. To love her. Hug her. Kiss the hands she begged with. Tenderly stroke the body that got lashed. Listen to the worries that everyone presumed to be non-existent. Praise the accomplishments. Share her happy moments. That was why she came into my dreams. She didn't need my prayers. She wanted me in the flesh. But I'd ruined everything.

If Khudai helped me make it, I'd apologise for the misery she'd been through. Let her know how much I missed her. Tell her I loved her – loved her more than anyone and anything in the world. Releasing myself from the Taliban's captivity hundreds of miles away from Frishta became even more of an important mission, and I begged Khudai to assist me.

'Are you with us, Ahmad brother?' Hanif said over chattering and touches of laughter of worshippers stepping out of the prayer room.

'Totally.'

'No respectable Afghan would marry her, so in a way, she's had no choice,' Wazir said.

'She doesn't need a husband. She has many American lovers,' Hanif added, pointing to the magazine on the mattress.

Wazir nodded, drying his sweaty face with his sleeve.

'Have you personally seen her sleeping with them, Hanif brother?' I found myself snapping.

'It's the first condition of working for the kafirs,' Hanif said.
Wazir nodded.

How could Wazir bring himself to doubt Frishta's chastity? She
didn't need a husband and kids because she already possessed a great
family.

Hanif closed his eyes and nodded at Wazir.

'You remember Mullah Rahmat?' Wazir said.

I nodded with a sinking heart.

'He and his sons kidnapped her during the mujahideen era.'

'Na.' *May Khudai keep you away from the venom of the cobra, the jaw of
the tiger and the revenge of the Pashtun*, was what Mullah Rahmat had said?

'A decade later Mullah Rahmat and his sons' naked bodies were
hanged in Chaman-e-Hozori.'

'Na.'

'Rashid's body was found in a similar position months later –
likewise stripped of his perahan tunban,' Wazir added.

'Rashid?'

'Apparently, Rashid fired the rocket which killed Frishta's
parents.'

No power can hold the bloodsucker for long. I'll be back for you, whore, I
remembered Rashid warning Frishta. Both tragedies befell Frishta
because of me and Wazir. Yet we were planning her assassination.

'Every Kabuli suspects Frishta for the hangings because it's
public knowledge what Mullah Rahmat did to her. But no one dares
to touch her.'

'When did this happen?'

'During the American occupation.'

She took revenge, but in a brutal way, using Mullah Rahmat and
Rashid's 'language' to speak to them. Unfortunately, in Afghanistan
powerful people used rape as a weapon to take vengeance. *Frishta's not
the sort to marry*, I remembered Nazigul saying. The complete sentence
would've included: Frishta was no longer pure. She'd lost her *wyaar*,

pride. I feared Mour might've mentioned this to Frishta somehow during their meeting.

'The American hireling imports books from America to corrupt women. She's evil, Ahmad. Only you could rid Afghanistan and Islam of this evil,' Wazir came to the point, sitting on his knees and towering over like a giant in black perahan turban, bandolier draped over his shoulder.

'Islam needs you, Ahmad brother. Don't let it down,' Hanif said.

'She isn't as patriotic as she sounds. She's a mafia don. Her security firms together with her opium trade are worth half a billion US dollars,' Wazir said.

'Half a billion US dollars,' I found myself repeating. Frishta's supposed capital disturbed me, as she had apparently fallen to pieces like the sand, but shouldn't have surprised me. According to Nadir's thesis, American policymakers were astonished to learn that some Afghan politicians made a billion US dollars a year. Where did the billions of dollars of US assistance and the drugs money go if not into the pockets of high-profile politicians and Taliban? Again she used her opponents' method to gain social and political empowerment for her sisters. Without the money, she wouldn't have possessed the power to solve her sisters' problems or release me from prison; she'd have been a fox among the wolves. Unfortunately, in Afghanistan, you hardly found heroes or heroines. Unlike most of her counterparts, though, she at least served her 'sisters' and would eventually donate all her money to her people.

If I carried the mission, I'd let both my watan and my religion down, not to mention a friendship which I'd broken once and which Wazir attempted to convince me to kill this time. Nobody, apart from Khudai, knew about Frishta's faith. They accused her of being a kafir, even though Frishta referred to the being of Khudai on several occasions. She prayed before me and her room was filled with Islamic duas. Like the young Frishta, the old Frishta sounded a committed Muslim.

'Ahmad brother,' Hanif said, pointing to Wazir, who was talking. Damn it, pay attention, I thought.

'...publicly scoffs Pashtunwali as a set of backward rules favouring only men. Turns wives against husbands, daughters against fathers, sisters against brothers. Beats husbands before wives, and fathers before daughters. She's created chaos, all on the pretext of "protection". Frishta is a cancer that needs to be cut out, or else she'll spread to every corner of Afghanistan,' Wazir said.

Frishta's marital status and her enduring mina for me filled me with hope. But before my life again became complete, I needed to untangle myself from the trap. Thanks, Khudai, a suicide mission was voluntary.

'I've pinned a great deal of hope on you to murder this whore. I know you won't let me down,' Wazir said.

'You want to tell our brother the rest of the plan, Mullah Ghazi.' The few first words one of the big brothers spoke. They had closely observed me ever since I walked into this room – registered my every emotion, every reaction and, worryingly, every inattention. Perhaps also enjoyed two childhood friends debating over whether to murder the third one.

'We'll take you to a safe location in Kabul tonight. Prepare your video there. Shave the following morning and put on Kabuli clothes. Mujahideen brothers will shift you to the location an hour before. Sit in the vehicle until the brothers ask you to walk to the main gate,' Wazir said.

Great, this plan really made it easier for my escape. I must agree to it without leaving a shadow of a doubt.

'Turn a blind eye to whatever is going on around you. I stress *whatever*,' Wazir said.

'Not just you, Ahmad brother, but several others will martyr themselves. Take extra care,' Hanif said.

'Let Khudai accept my sacrifice,' I said, sounding more passionate than I'd intended.

Wazir's face brightened. He rose to his feet, stepped over the oil lamp and hugged me, his pistol poking against my throat as he congratulated me on the special place in Janat. I held to Wazir's rose-smelling arms as the room spun around.

Hanif and the twins stood up and stepped closer to me. Hanif talked of the enormity of the mission and how it'd weaken the foundation of Afghanistan's occupiers.

A medical graduate from an English university blowing himself up would indeed raise questions, I wondered. I let go of Wazir and held onto the cupboard.

Wazir hugged me again and told me how proud he was of me for the third time, adding that Afghanistan would lose a true son, but it was worth it. He promised to see me in Janat.

I'd watched a lot of movies and knew a thing or two about the art of acting. I could tell Wazir wasn't performing, and I didn't know about Hanif, but the two big brothers' excitement wasn't genuine. Such fake acting wouldn't certainly get them into a drama school. I reckoned deep down they were troubled. I could fool Wazir, as they had fooled him, but perhaps not Hanif, and certainly not the big brothers. I feared they knew I was up to something. I suspected they were Pakistani intelligence officers, the masterminds behind Frishta's planned assassination. Unfortunately for them and fortunately for me, they had no choice but to trust me.

They told Wazir to let me have some rest before we set off for Kabul.

Wazir hugged and congratulated them as I stepped out of the room. Wazir sold his childhood friend, someone closer to him than a brother, to the big brothers and, by extension, to foreign intelligence agencies to earn credits. He betrayed another friend, too. The ungrateful Wazir forgot that the young Frishta stood for him against the algebra ustad. Saved him from Rashid. Rescued him from imminent death from the KHAD agent. He then owed his life to her, and his mother, Aday, called her a 'daughter'.

I didn't want to die, especially after learning Frishta's lips were still left unkissed. She still was *mine*. I'd marry her even if the entire world, let alone Afghanistan, stood against me. Hundred per cent support Frishta's wrestle with the wolves, but, inshallah, without having to become a wolf, if Khudai gave me another life. Frishta must also reverse the course of her direction to reach extreme liberalism, a journey no one had or would ever reach in my watan.

It was time I took a final step to inner peace. I'd open a clinic in Afghanistan and spend my remaining life in the service of my beleaguered people. After reading Nadir's thesis, hearing the professor and witnessing the recent events, I felt I had been harsh on my watan. Afghanistan hadn't taken everything away from me. If anything, we Afghans had robbed everything from our watan, all for sim and zar. Perhaps I'd played my part, too, by having abandoned my watan, my flesh and blood; something which at times disturbed me in England, and more and more since I'd returned. It now clicked that I had a lot in common with my watan: we both were turned into headless goats.

I stumbled down the narrow stairs, holding onto the wall. Hanif's statement, *Not just you, Ahmad brother, but several others will martyr themselves*, caught up with me. Were those several others also fedayis? Hands touched my shoulders as I sat before a narrow stream going through the castle. Wazir smiled.

'Who's going to teach me how to detonate the belt?' I asked Wazir.

'Don't worry. Other brothers will take care of it,' Hanif said, and Wazir nodded.

'I have to press the button?'

'You do. You'll be taught in Kabul,' one of the brothers said, standing behind Wazir and Hanif.

'All will be taken care of, don't worry,' Wazir said, adding he'd be back soon, pointing to a doorless entrance under the prayer room. Wazir followed the brothers and Hanif into the entrance of what seemed to be a cave complex.

I did ablutions at the stream, removed my waistcoat, spread it on the grass under the tree with the water flowing and insects buzzing and trilling, and in a sitting position performed nafl-prayers. Looked up at the starry sky and prayed from the bottom of my heart: *please, Khudai, accept what I say to You, please get me out of this trap and save me for my Frishta. Please, Khudai, save both of us. If Your decision is that I die tomorrow, however, I willingly accept it, but please, please don't turn me into a means to kill Frishta. Help her live long. Her life means a lot to her watan...* The same suffocating pain shot around my chest. My body was covered in sweat. The trees turned around, the trilling sound faded, and the surroundings blackened out.

Chapter Forty-Seven

A bleary man smiled and held a mobile close to my right ear.

'How are you, man?' Wazir's voice on the loudspeaker.

'Disoriented.'

'Congratulations on your martyrdom in advance,' Wazir said over Hanif's voice in the background, telling Wazir to let me know that the medication for my heart condition had caused my drowsiness.

'I've never had a heart problem,' I said.

'You'll soon be a hero throughout the Muslim world,' Wazir said.

Hanif said an inshallah in the background.

'Wazir, where am–'

He bade me goodbye and hung up.

The room with white and blue colours wasn't the mosque in the muddy castle.

'Where am I, brother?'

'Kabul,' the shaven man said, inserting the mobile in his pocket. He stood up and stepped away, revealing the room floor bursting with Kalashnikovs, RPG-7 launchers and warheads, machine guns, yellow and white objects like thermos flasks, and shaven men sitting alongside the walls.

'So many weapons?'

'You need to rest, brother.'

'What's going on?'

'Rest, brother.'

'When was I transferred?'

He smiled.

'I can't rest until you tell me.'

His smile broadened, exposing a set of decayed teeth. He offered a plastic cup. I refused. My hands and head were pushed against the mattresses, and a bitter drink pushed into my mouth. The hands released themselves as my head spun around faster. My memory closed down.

***

WHERE WAS I? Footing it to the university? Or to the shops? Where were the shopping bags? Or did I saunter by the riverside, my favourite place at Durham? Why did I stagger, though?

Little jelais in black uniforms and white headscarves – some alone, others in a group, holding each other's hands, cheering, giggling and talking. A jelai shouted 'Nahida' and both entered the school gate. Was I before a jelais' school?

Men in police uniforms pushed against my shoulders and sat me down under fat trees. Vehicles drove in both directions. 'Stay away. Everything is fine,' said one of the policemen as curious passers-by gathered, mostly young jelais.

'We're awaiting the ambulance,' said another.

Red liquid flowed down my head. Had I injured myself?

'Move. To your school. Quick,' a blue-uniformed policeman said, kicking a jelai. The crowd dispersed.

The policeman sitting next to me answered his mobile. 'Just drove past the Supreme Court,' he said to the other policemen.

Who drove past the Supreme Court? A vague memory came to me. Was I here to do something... bothersome? What was it? Why was I disturbed? The policeman who spoke on the phone offered me a cup. I hit it and it dropped to the ground. Why had the police arrested me?

Someone shouted 'Fresh bolanis'.

'Get ready, the ambulance is driving through the market,' the policeman said and put his phone in the pocket.

They pulled my shoulders and raised me on the feet. 'Head for the entrance,' someone said from behind and hands pushed against my back.

'Tffff.' Saliva landed on my face. 'The hypocrite has no shame,' a familiar voice said. The green-uniformed men pushed the spitter away.

Several identical white Mitsubishi jeeps pulled over: men with guns got out and scattered left, right and centre, shouting in authoritative voices like the American Special Forces in movies to clear off. They pushed away the policemen by me before a small figure limped over.

'Ahmad, what's happened?' an alarming voice asked. What's happening? I forced my memory to remember.

Dozens of armed people surrounded the figure and me like bees around their queen. Soft hands touched my shoulders and shook them. 'Ahmad?'

I knew the thin woman.

'Wakil saheb, it isn't safe,' a gigantic man, towering over us, said to the thin woman. 'Shoot anyone who comes near,' he roared at his armed men.

'We need to take him to the hospital, Ashraf,' she said. The name rang a bell.

'We will. You leave.'

Why isn't she safe? Is something bad going to happen? What is it? I forced my memory again. Ashraf. Frishta. Mission. 'Fedayi. Stay away from me, Frishta,' I let out, trying to jump away from her, but the gigantic body crushed both Frishta and me against the ground behind the trees.

The sounds of *deth-deth-deth*, *tak-tak-tak* and *thud-thud-thud* of hitting and deflecting against trees and concretes filled the air. Exchanges of Kalashnikovs persisted. So did Ashraf's shouts, telling

Frishta and me to 'shrink' and to the PPD to keep an eye on the block of flats behind us, to which we were exposed.

Tak-tak-tak, Ashraf fired, his large body over Frishta and me.

A thud sound and Ashraf's body shrank and let loose. Another thwack sound and his body shrank again. Warm liquid entered my left ear. *There is no god but Allah, Muhammad is the messenger of Allah*: Ashraf read the Shahada. His body became heavier like a brick wall.

More fire exchanges and bullet deflections.

A pause.

An ear-splitting *duvvv...*

Blackout.

Chapter Forty-Eight

'Time to go,' I said to Frishta.

'Woh.'

'You'll be live on most TV channels,' Nahima said, holding a notebook in her hand.

'You'll inshallah shine,' I said.

She held my hands and uttered a thank-you.

'Mum and Dad can't wait to watch your speech live.'

'But it's past midnight in America,' Frishta said.

'They've stayed up all night,' Janet said.

Frishta hugged her and plucked a kiss on her head. 'Turn it up, Nahima.'

... like political biographer John Campbell said about Margaret Thatcher, it is equally true about Frishta Afghan: she's the most admired, most hated, most idolised and most vilified public figure of Afghanistan's current political scene. To some she is the protector of women's rights. To others she is a narrow ideologue whose hard-faced views stood against traditional Afghan values. She survived several assassination attempts, including one three months ago where she and her husband, a Western-educated medical doctor, sustained serious injuries. She's passed the first hurdle: the Independent Election Commission qualified her alongside seven others. Whether she will pass the second, the most difficult one, remains to be seen. She is, though, one of the frontrunners...

Frishta switched off the report from the *BBC News*.

'They define you before you know it,' Janet said.

'The gates to the city can be shut, but people's mouths cannot be,' Frishta said, looking at me with a smile, while outside her supporters clapped, cheered and shouted to fight for equality, justice and education for all.

She put her hands on her chest as she set out for the bulletproof glass shield. The cheers and clapping were amplified over Gul Zaman's patriotic song before it died down...

***

IN THE NAME OF GOD. Salaam alaikum. I am so grateful to God that we are all standing here in the Ghazi Stadium, a venue where our men and women were publicly persecuted once during the Dark Ages. Thanks to God and *you*, we've reached a milestone – the first time in our watan's history a woman is running for President.

Today doesn't just belong to us, but to brave men and women who struggled over the centuries to make our resounding victory possible.

Likewise, today's triumph wouldn't have been possible without the support of volunteers, tribal heads, religious leaders, civil societies, activists and all those who have contributed to our campaign, especially our patriotic security forces. And to you, I feel indebted for sharing your stories with me and allowing me to experience your lives physically – you are my *inspiration*, my heroes and heroines, and it is for you that I live. And Ahmad jan, my best friend, my husband and my rock, your wife is and will always remain grateful to you for your patience, understanding and wise advice. I am truly blessed to have you in my life.

As an MP and presidential candidate, I've talked to many of you and learned a great deal about your legitimate concerns. Most of you asked me *one* question: why has America's promised peace, security and prosperity been substituted with war, insecurity and depravity?

By now you all know me. I'll be honest with you. I hate lies and exaggerations. There are several reasons for America's inability to achieve her goals in Afghanistan. Pakistan kept poisonous snakes in its backyard and used them to bite us and our international allies; Saddam Hussein's ghost haunted America's capability in Afghanistan; America aimed at defeating terrorism in Afghanistan and the world, but refused to commit enough ground troops – instead relied on warlords and criminals; NATO allies brought with them hay and straw to build Afghanistan, not bricks and mortar; in the pursuit of a democratic Afghanistan we perhaps sidestepped our own traditional values; Afghan politicians fell in love with the dollar and flushed their watan's national security interests down the toilet; and our Afghanistan's inborn complexities have been turned into major sources of conflict.

While in the coming days and months I'll be talking plenty about this government's failures, including why one district after another keeps falling to the Taliban, today I'd like to talk to you about what contribution *you* could make so we could jointly defeat the evil forces threatening our watan and beyond. I'd like to urge you not to confuse foreign policy mistakes with intention. Our international allies have spent trillions of dollars in Afghanistan. Thousands of their soldiers have lost their lives. They assisted us in achieving unprecedented accomplishments in politics, the economy, human rights, education, telecommunication, health care, free media... The list goes on. I understand our grand desires of peace and security have not yet been accomplished. But please don't become blinded to the achievements we have made so far. Do not fall prey to conspiracy theories propagated systematically by our bullying neighbours. They intend to confuse us, so we can't distinguish friends from foes. To set us one against the other. To divide us.

I believe we'll have a strong Afghanistan when we are together. Lift each other up, not tear each other down. Throw conflict away and embrace cooperation. Give *everyone* a voice in our political system and kick division. Cherish empowerment and fight against resentment.

We're stronger when we fight corruption. Stronger when we support our heroes, the men and women in our security forces.

Stronger when we sustain and build on our institutions, civil society, free media, human rights groups. Stronger when we work with our international allies. But our partners mustn't use Afghanistan as an election bid. Our allies must honour the sacrifices Afghans have made. The streets of Europe and America are safe because of the sacrifices our security forces make every day. Our partners must understand the roots of the problems do not lie in the Afghan villages but over the borders, which has the ideological, financial, motivational, political and military centres of terrorism that enabled the infiltration of insurgents into Afghanistan. So stop killing innocent Afghans and instead find a strategy to deal with those sanctuaries; a strategy that addresses our neighbours' buzkashi game in which they've turned Afghanistan into a headless carcass. But please don't sell Afghanistan to neighbours in return for safety in America and Europe. Think of the lives, toil and money you have spent in Afghanistan. Support me with my reforms to deal with the corrupt elements in the Afghan government.

We'll talk to our brothers, the Taliban. But we can only achieve a stable peace settlement when we respect each other, listen to each other and act with a sense of common purpose.

While I'm willing to talk, I am also ready to fight. My father, the biggest influence in my life, taught me never to back down from a bully. As a Commander in Chief, I'll personally join our heroes in the first line of the battlefield. I won't be hiding in the Arg Palace.

My father also taught me that life was about serving your countrymen and women, and I am grateful to God for having enabled me all these years to do so. I feel that padar jan somehow watches over his daughter, who has become the first female running for President, and he questions the pessimists: Who says that great things don't happen? Barriers can't come down? Justice and equality can't be won?

Thank you, padar jan. I promise we won't give up and won't back down. With the help of God and my people, we'll continue to cross barriers and break limits.

My brothers, sisters, fathers and mothers – whether you're a Pashtun, Tajik, Hazara, Uzbek or any other ethnic group – we are all in this together and I pray you'll join us. Whether you do or not, I, as your president, will make sure you never feel you're left on your own. We are only strong when we don't allow that feeling.

We have a hard task ahead of us. I can't do it without your help. So please, join our campaign. In all 34 provinces. Every phone call you make, every door you knock on, will move us forward.

Today is the beginning; we have a long way to go. If we stand together, we'll achieve a peaceful and secure Afghanistan. Let's go and take the message to every single Afghan.

Long live Afghanistan.

SELECTED GLOSSARY OF FOREIGN WORDS

Afarin Bravo

Agha Father

Aka Uncle

Akanai Uncle's wife

Alef A letter in the Afghan alphabet

Alhamdulillah Thank God

Allahu Akbar God is great

Ameen Amen

Amir Chief/Commander

Ashura A Muslim holy day that occurs on the 10th of Muharram, the first month of the Islamic calendar

Attan A type of traditional dance in a circle

Azan The call to prayer

Bacha-bazi The term means 'boy play' and is a 'custom that involves young boys being forced to dress as women and to dance seductively for an audience of elder men'

Bacha Boy

Barrati Includes cookies, fried fish, jalebi, along with gold, clothing and sweets, which are received by the fiancé's household from the fiancée's family during the 'Barat month' (the month of Sha'ban, the eighth month of the Islamic calendar)

Bazzar-e-lilami A second-hand market

Bolanis Flatbread stuffed with potatoes or leeks

Buzkashi A national game/sport meaning 'goat-pulling'

Chapan A traditional coat usually worn by men

Chup Shush, shut up

Coupons Vouchers that entitled Afghans to a discount off Soviet products in cooperatives

Dar al-Islam The domain of Muslims

Dar al-Kufr The domain of disbelief

Dhol The double-headed drum

Doogh Diluted yoghurt

Dua Prayer/act of supplication, asking help or assistance from God

Dua-e-Qunoot A special prayer or supplication mentioned in the Hadith

Eid Three days of celebration of the holy month

Eidi Includes cookies, fried fish, jalebi, along with gold, clothing and sweets, which are received by the fiancé's household from the fiancée's family during Eid

Ezat Honour/respect/esteem/dignity

Fateha The prayer ceremony (after the funeral)

Fedayi Suicide bomber

Gwady Cripple

Haji A Muslim who has been to Mecca as a pilgrim

Halek Young man

Haram Forbidden by Islam

Harami Bastard

Hashish A type of illegal drug (cannabis) known as *chars* in Afghanistan

Hazaras One of several minority groups in Afghanistan

Inshallah God willing

Jahili The time of 'darkness', the period before the Prophet Mohammad,
    peace be upon him, lived and no one practised Islam

Jan Dear

Janat Heaven

Janazah Prayer for the dead

Jeem A letter in the Afghan alphabet

Jelai Young woman

Jiggy, jiggy A foreign slang word for sexual intercourse outside of a valid
    marriage

Jihad A holy war waged by Muslims against infidels

Kafir A person who is not Muslim/the unbelievers

KHAD The Communist Government's State Intelligence, Afghanistan's equivalent to the Soviet KGB, known by the acronym KHAD

Khairat The voluntary giving of help, typically in the form of money, to those in need

Khalqi A member of the Khalq faction of the Communist People's Democratic Party of Afghanistan

Khastegari Marriage proposal

Khatm The reading of the Quran

Khuda jan Allah, God

Khudai Allah, God

Kulchas Cookies

Lunda Boyfriend

Lundabazi Boyfriend-girlfriend relationships

Madar Mother

Mahram A close male relative with whom marriage is generally not permissible

Manana Thank you

Mantu Meat-filled dumplings

Mashallah Praise God/God's protection of you

Melmastia Hospitality

Mina Love

Mour Mother

GLOSSARY

Mudir School principal

Mujahideen Freedom fighters who challenged the Soviet troops in Afghanistan. After the Soviet Union's withdrawal, they fought each other over power

Mullah Imam

Na No

Naamus Pride/honour/reputation/ esteem/dignity/renown

Naan Flatbread

Nanawatai Seeking refuge

Naswar Tobacco

Nikah Swearing ceremony of a wedding

Non-mahram Women who aren't related to men in blood and with whom marriage is generally permissible

Nowruz New Year

Nowruzi Includes cookies, fried fish, jalebi, along with gold, clothing and sweets, which are received by the fiancé's household from the fiancée's family during Nowruzes

Obro Pride/self-esteem/dignity/honour

Padar Father

Pakol A round-topped hat worn by men

Parchami A member of the Parcham faction of the Communist People's Democratic Party of Afghanistan

Parde awal A style of music

Pari Angel

Pashtunwali The code of honour or the way of the Pashtuns. Pashtunwali's main principles include independence, bravery, loyalty, justice, revenge, righteousness, pride, honour, chastity, hospitality, love, forgiveness, faith [Islam] and respect of elders

Perahan tunban Traditional dress resembling shalwar kameez

Qah-qah Loud laughter

Qaraqul A type of hat made from the Qaraqul breed of sheep

Qataghani A style of music

Qurbani Sacrifice/sacrificial/the feast of the sacrifice

Rubab A lute-like musical instrument from Afghanistan

Rukhsati The end of the school day

Saheb Courtesy title equivalent to 'sir'

Salaam Hello

Salaam alaikum Peace be upon you

Saracha A large living room used mainly by men

Shahid A Muslim martyr

Shia The second dominant division of Islam

Shirini-khori A bigger engagement

Shiryakh Traditional ice cream

Shorawi Derogatory word for 'Russian'

Shornakhud Salty chickpeas

Sim and zar Money and gold

Simyan Homemade snack

Sitara Star

Sunni One of the two dominant divisions of Islam

Sura A chapter or section of the Quran

Tambur A musical instrument

Tarawih The prayers during the month of Ramadan

Tawba-tawba Repenting to God

Toop danda A traditional play/game resembling cricket

Tror Aunt

Tunban Shalwar

Ustad Teacher

Wadah Wedding ceremony

Wah-wah Exclamation of delight, bravo

Wakil Member of Parliament

Walwar Bride price

Watan Homeland

Woh Yes

Yakhni A meat stew

Zina Sexual intercourse between a man and woman outside of a valid marriage

Zoya Son/child (sometimes even 'daughter')

SELECTED BIBLIOGRAPHY

'Afghanistan: The Making of a Narco State', *Rolling Stone*, 4 December 2014.

'Afghanistan: 43 percent rise in estimated opium harvest', *Al Jazeera*, 23 October 2016.

Akkoç, Raziye, 'Mapped: How many migrants entered the EU and applied for asylum in 2015', *The Telegraph*, 4 March 2016.

Andishmand, M.E., *USA in Afghanistan* (Kabul: Bangah Intesharat Maiwand, 2007).

Ansari, Basher Ahmad, *Afghanistan in the Flames of Oils and Gas* (Kabul: Bangah Intesharat Maiwand, 2005).

Apple, R.W., 'A Military Quagmire Remembered: Afghanistan as Vietnam', *New York Times*, 31 October 2001.

Azami, Dawood, 'World powers jostle in Afghanistan's new 'Great Game', *BBC*, 12 January 2017.

Baker, Kim, 'Letter From Kabul: Solving Afghanistan's Problems', *Foreign Affairs*, 30 November 2009, http://www.foreignaffairs.com/features/letters-from/letter-from-kabul-solving-afghanistans-problems.

Baker, Peter, 'How Obama Came to Plan for 'Surge' in Afghanistan', *New York Times*, 5 December 2009.

Bearden, Milton, 'Afghanistan, Graveyard of Empires', *Foreign Affairs*, November/December 2001, http://www.foreignaffairs.com/articles/57411/milton-bearden/afghanistan-graveyard-of-empires.

Begg, Moazzam, and Victoria Brittain, *Enemy Combatant: My Imprisonment at Guantanamo, Bagram, and Kandahar* (New York: The New Press, 2011) https://search.ebscohost.com/login.aspx?direct=true&scope=site&db=nlebk&db=nlabk&AN=51661 8.

Bergen, Peter, 'Confronting al-Qaeda: Understanding the Threat in Afghanistan and Beyond', *Senate Committee on Foreign Relations*, 7 October 2009, http://www.foreign.senate.gov/imo/media/doc/BergenTestimony091007p.pdf.

————, 'Al-Qaeda, the Taliban, and Other Extremist Groups in Afghanistan and Pakistan', *Senate Committee on Foreign Relations*, 24 May 2011, http://www.foreign.senate.gov/hearings/al-qaeda-the-taliban-and-other-extremist-groups-in-afghanistan-and-pakistan.

Biddle, Stephen, 'Assessing the Case for War in Afghanistan', *Senate Committee on Foreign Relations*, 16 September 2009, http://www.cfr.org/content/publications/attachments/Stephen.Biddle.SFRC9.16.09.pdf.

Biden, Joseph R., 'Afghanistan. Pakistan. Forgotten', *New York Times*, 2 March 2008.

Bird, Tim and Alex Marshall, *Afghanistan: How the West Lost Its Way* (New Haven: Yale University Press, 2011).

Blackwill, Robert D., 'Plan B in Afghanistan', *Foreign Affairs*, January/February 2011, http://www.foreignaffairs.com/articles/67026/robert-d-blackwill/plan-b-in-afghanistan.

Blank, Jonah, 'Q&A With Jonah Blank on Afghanistan', *Foreign Affairs*, 7 September 2011, http://www.foreignaffairs.com/discussions/interviews/qa-with-jonah-blank-on-afghanistan.

Boone, Jon, 'WikiLeaks cables portray Hamid Karzai as corrupt and erratic', *The Guardian*, 2 December 2010.

Boot, Max, 'The Road to Negotiation in Afghanistan', *Council on Foreign Relations*, 18 October 2010, http://www.cfr.org/afghanistan/road-negotiations-afghanistan/p23171.

Brzezinski, Zbigniew, 'From Hope to Audacity', *Foreign Affairs*, January/February 2010, http://www.foreignaffairs.com/articles/65720/zbigniew-brzezinski/from-hope-to-audacity.

Bush, George W., 'Address to the Nation on the Terrorist Attacks', 11 September 2001, http://www.presidency.ucsb.edu/ws/?pid=58057.

———, 'Remarks to New York Rescue Workers', 14 September 2001, http://georgewbush-whitehouse.archives.gov/infocus/bushrecord/documents/Selected_Speeches_George_W_Bush.pdf.

———, 'Address to the Joint Session of the 107th Congress', 20 September 2001, http://georgewbush-whitehouse.archives.gov/infocus/bushrecord/documents/Selected_Speeches_George_W_Bush.pdf.

———, 'Address to the Nation on Operations in Afghanistan', 7 October 2001, http://georgewbush-whitehouse.archives.gov/infocus/bushrecord/documents/Selected_Speeches_George_W_Bush.pdf.

———, *Decision Points* (New York: Crown Publishers, 2010).

Cactus with Fawzia Koofi EP 09, 28 February 2019, *1TV*, https://www.youtube.com/watch?v=FzG0x3UO5_M.

Cactus with Anarkali Honaryar on June 13, *1TV*, June 2019, https://www.youtube.com/watch?v=XX5wB8HhNfY.

Cactus Season 03 - Ep 04 [with Shukria Barakzai], *1TV*, 9 April 2020, https://www.youtube.com/watch?v=O8CVu-roD6A.

Cactus [with Farzana Kochai] *1TV*, 28 January 2021, https://www.youtube.com/watch?v=zyLduqYpRSg.

Cactus with Shogofa Noorzai, *1TV*, 25 March 2021, https://www.youtube.com/watch?v=QQ2cXRiRXMk.

Cactus [with Naheed Farid], *1TV*, 13 May 2021, https://www.youtube.com/watch?v=LZrpl8sVf1c.

Carter, Shan and Amanda Cox, 'One 9/11 Tally: 3.3 Trillion', *New York Times*, 8 September 2011.

Chandrasekaran, Rajiv, *Little America: The War within the War for Afghanistan* (New York: Alfred A. Knopf, 2012).

BIBLIOGRAPHY

Cheney, Richard B. and Liz Cheney, *In My Time: A Personal and Political Memoir* (New York: Threshold Editions, 2011).

Christia, Fotini, 'Letter from Kabul', *Foreign Affairs*, 26 June 2011, http://www.foreignaffairs.com/features/letters-from/letter-from-kabul.

Christia, Fotini and Michael Semple, 'Flipping the Taliban', *Foreign Affairs*, July/August 2009, http://www.foreignaffairs.com/articles/65151/fotini-christia-and-michael-semple/flipping-the-taliban.

Clark, Kate and Thomas Ruttig, '"People That Hates US": What can Afghans expect from President Trump?', *Afghanistan Analysts Network*, 11 November 2016.

Clinton, Hillary Rodham, 'Clinton's Plan for Afghanistan', *Council on Foreign Relations*, 6 March 2008.

———, 'Afghanistan: Assessing the Road Ahead', *Senate Committee on Foreign Relations*, 3 December 2009, http://www.foreign.senate.gov/hearings/afghanistan-assessing-the-road-ahead.

———, 'Secretary Hillary Rodham Clinton Testimony [on Afghanistan] to the Senate Foreign Relations Committee Washington, D.C.', *Senate Committee on Foreign Relations*, 23 June 2011, http://www.foreign.senate.gov/imo/media/doc/062211%20Secretary%20Clinton%20Testimony%20for%20SFRC%20Af-Pak%20Hearing.pdf.

———, *Hard Choices* (New York: Simon & Schuster, 2014).

———, 'Read Hillary Clinton's Historic Victory Speech as Presumptive Democratic Nominee', *Time*, 8 June 2016, https://time.com/4361099/hillary-clinton-nominee-speech-transcript/.

Cowper-Coles, Sherard, *Cables from Kabul: The Inside Story of the West's Afghanistan Campaign* (London: HarperPress, 2011).

Craddock, John, 'Countering the Threat of Failure in Afghanistan', *Senate Committee on Foreign Relations*, 17 September 2009, http://www.foreign.senate.gov/hearings/countering-the-threat-of-failure-in-afghanistan.

Craig, Tim and Michael E. Miller, 'Four-way Talks on Afghanistan Start, with Much to Overcome', *Washington Post*, 11 January 2016.

Crocker, Ryan C., 'Countering the Threat of Failure in Afghanistan', *Senate Committee on Foreign Relations*, 17 September 2009, http://www.foreign.senate.gov/hearings/countering-the-threat-of-failure-in-afghanistan.

———, 'Perspectives on Reconciliation Options in Afghanistan', *Senate Committee on Foreign Relations*, 27 July 2010, http://www.foreign.senate.gov/hearings/perspectives-on-reconciliation-options-in-afghanistan.

Cunningham, James B., 'Testimony of James B. Cunningham [on Afghanistan]', *Senate Committee on Foreign Relations*, 31 July 2012, https://www.foreign.senate.gov/imo/media/doc/Cunningham_Testimony.pdf.

Curry, Dayna, Heather Mercer, and Stacy Mattingly, *Prisoners of hope: the story of our captivity and freedom in Afghanistan* (New York: The Doubleday Religious Publishing Group, 2009), https://search.ebscohost.com/login.aspx?direct=true&scope=site&db=nlebk&db=nlabk&AN=721569.

DeYoung, Karen, 'Obama to leave 9,800 U.S. troops in Afghanistan', *Washington Post*, 27 March 2014.

Dobbins, James, 'Ending Afghanistan's Civil War', *Senate Committee on Foreign Relations*, 8 March 2007, http://www.foreign.senate.gov/imo/media/doc/DobbinsTestimony070308.pdf.

———, 'Your COIN Is NO Good Here', *Foreign Affairs*, 26 October 2010, http://www.foreignaffairs.com/articles/66949/james-dobbins/your-coin-is-no-good-here.

Dobriansky, Paula J., 'Democracy Promotion', *Foreign Affairs*, May/June 2003, http://www.foreignaffairs.com/articles/58981/paula-j-dobriansky-and-thomas-carothers/democracy-promotion.

Dodge, Toby and Nicholas Redman, *Afghanistan: To 2015 and Beyond* (London: International Institute for Strategic Studies, 2011).

Dorani, Sharifullah, *From Intervention to Exit: American Foreign Policymaking towards Afghanistan* (Doctoral thesis, Durham University, 2015), http://etheses.dur.ac.uk/11159/1/From_Intervention_to_Exit___American_Foreign_Policymaking_towards_Afghanistan_by_SD.pdf?DDD35+.

———, *America in Afghanistan: Foreign Policy and Decision Making from Bush to Obama to Trump* (London: I.B. Tauris, Bloomsbury Publishing Plc, 24 January 2019).

———, 'America's Afghanistan War: The Poor Relationship between The US and Karzai', *Political Reflection Magazine*, January 2022, https://politicalreflectionmagazine.com/wp-content/uploads/2022/01/PR_Issue30_A2.pdf.

———, 'The Doha Agreement for Bringing Peace to Afghanistan', *Political Reflection Magazine*, 19 April 2022, https://politicalreflectionmagazine.com/2022/04/19/the-doha-agreement-for-bringing-peace-to-afghanistan/.

Doucet, Lyse, 'The Karzai years: From hope to recrimination', *BBC*, 12 July 2014, http://www.bbc.co.uk/news/world-asia-28257108.

Dowd, Maureen, 'Liberties; Can Bush Bushkazi?', *New York Times*, 28 October 2011.

Editorial, 'The Quagmire Issue; U.S. Should Prepare for a Long Struggle', *The Dallas Morning News*, 26 October 2011.

———, 'Inconvenient Truths in Afghanistan', *New York Times*, 29 January 2015.

———, 'Afghanistan's next chapter', *New York Times*, 28 March 2015.

———, 'Nurturing Afghan Peace Talks', *New York Times*, 10 July 2015.

———, 'Is the Pentagon Telling the Truth About Afghanistan?', *New York Times*, 13 October 2015.

Eikenberry, Karl W., 'Statement Of Ambassador Karl Eikenberry [on Afghanistan]', *Senate Committee on Foreign Relations*, 9 December 2009, http://www.foreign.senate.gov/imo/media/doc/EikenberryTestimony091209a1.pdf.

Fair, C. Christine, 'Al-Qaeda, the Taliban, and Other Extremist Groups in Afghanistan and Pakistan', *Senate Committee on Foreign Relations*, 24 May 2011, http://www.foreign.senate.gov/imo/media/doc/Fair_Testimony.pdf.

BIBLIOGRAPHY

Farhang, Sadeeq, *Afghanistan in the Last Five Centuries* (1988).

Farrall, Leah, 'How al Qaeda Works', *Foreign Affairs*, March/April 2011, https://www.foreignaffairs.com/articles/south-asia/2011-02-20/how-al-qaeda-works.

Feith, Douglas J., *War and Decision: Inside the Pentagon at the Dawn of the War on Terrorism* (New York: Harper, 2008).

Freedman, Lawrence D., 'Paying the Human Costs of War: American Public Opinion and Casualties in Military Conflicts', *Foreign Affairs*, September/December 2009, http://www.foreignaffairs.com/articles/65308/christopher-gelpi-peter-d-feaver-and-jason-reifler/paying-the-human-costs-of-war-american-public-opinion-and-casu.

'From Words to Action', *TOLOnews*, 21 May 2018, http://govmeter.tolonews.com/.

Gall, Carlotta, *The Wrong Enemy: America in Afghanistan, 2001-2014* (Houghton Mifflin, 2014).

Galula, David and John A. Nagl, *Counterinsurgency Warfare: Theory and Practice* (Westport, CT: Praeger Security International, 2006).

Gannon, Kathy, 'Afghanistan Unbound', *Foreign Affairs*, May/June 2004, http://www.foreignaffairs.com/articles/59891/kathy-gannon/afghanistan-unbound.

Gates, Robert Michael, *Duty: Memoirs of a Secretary at War* (Alfred A. Knopf, 2014).

Gavrilis, George, 'Why Regional Solutions Won't Help Afghanistan', *Foreign Affairs*, 18 October 2011, http://www.foreignaffairs.com/articles/136598/george-gavrilis/why-regional-solutions-wont-help-afghanistan.

Ghani, Ashraf, 'Manifesto of Change and Continuity', March 2014, http://www.journalofdemocracy.org/sites/default/files/Ashraf%20Ghani%20Manifesto.pdf.

————, 'Inaugural Speech by Dr. Ashraf Ghani Ahmadzai as the President of Afghanistan', 29 September 2014, http://www.hpc.org.af/english/index.php/news/speeches/206-inaugural-speech-by-dr-ashraf-ghani-ahmadzai-as-the-president-of-afghanistan.

'Generation Kill: A Conversation with Stanley McChrystal', *Foreign Affairs*, March/April 2013, http://www.foreignaffairs.com/discussions/interviews/generation-kill.

Ghobar, Ghulam Mohammad, *Afghanistan in the Course of History* (Virginia, 1999).

Gibbon, Kate Fitz, 'Pashtunwali: Pashtun Traditional Tribal Law in Afghanistan', *Cultural Property News*, 28 August 2021.

Ginsburg, Tom, 'An Economic Interpretation of the Pashtunwali', *University of Chicago Legal Forum*: Vol. 2011: Iss. 1, Article 6, https://chicagounbound.uchicago.edu/cgi/viewcontent.cgi?article=1476&context=uclf.

Gordon, Philip H., 'Can the War on Terror Be Won?', *Foreign Affairs*, November/December 2007, http://www.foreignaffairs.com/articles/63009/philip-h-gordon/can-the-war-on-terror-be-won.

Graham-Harrison, Emma, 'Afghan forces suffering too many casualties, says top Nato commander', *The Guardian*, 2 September 2013.

417

Graham-Harrison, Emma and Rob Evans, 'Afghan civilian death toll 'much higher' than the official estimated', *The Guardian*, 8 May 2016.

'Group of Experts and Former US Officials on Afghanistan, 'Forging an Enduring Partnership with Afghanistan'', *The National Interests*, 14 September 2016.

Haass, Richard N., 'Afghanistan: What is an Acceptable End-State, and How Do We Get There?', *Senate Committee on Foreign Relations*, 3 May 2011, http://www.foreign.senate.gov/hearings/afghanistan-what-is-an-acceptable-end-state-and-how-do-we-get-there.

Habibi, Abdul Hai, *History of The Pashto Literature* (1 January 1915).

———, *The History of Afghanistan after Islam* (2001).

———, *The History of Afghanistan in 19th Century* (1 January 2010).

Hirsh, Michael, 'The Clinton Legacy', *Foreign Affairs*, May/June 2013, http://www.foreignaffairs.com/articles/139110/michael-hirsh/the-clinton-legacy.

Holbrooke, Richard C., 'Civilian Strategy for Afghanistan: A Status Report in Advance of the London Conference', *Senate Committee on Foreign Relations*, 21 January 2010, http://www.foreign.senate.gov/imo/media/doc/HolbrookeTestimony100121p.pdf.

Hosseini, Khaled, *The Kite runner* (London: Bloomsbury, 2003).

———, 'Countering the Threat of Failure in Afghanistan', *Senate Committee on Foreign Relations*, 17 September 2009, http://www.foreign.senate.gov/hearings/countering-the-threat-of-failure-in-afghanistan.

Husain, Ed, *Why I joined radical Islam in Britain, what I saw inside and why I left* (London: Penguin Books Ltd, 2007).

Jones, Seth G., *In the Graveyard of Empires: America's War in Afghanistan* (New York: W. W. Norton & Co, 2009).

Joscelyn, Thomas and Bill Roggio, 'Are We Losing Afghanistan Again?', *New York Times*, 21 October 2015.

Joya, Malalai and Derrick O'Keefe, *A Woman Among Warlords: The Extraordinary Story of an Afghan Who Dared to Raise Her Voice* (New York: Scribner, 2009).

Kagan, Frederick, 'We're Not the Soviets in Afghanistan; and 2009 isn't 1979', *The Weekly Standard*, 21 August 2009, https://www.weeklystandard.com/were-not-the-soviets-in-afghanistan/article/240775.

Karzai, Hamid, 'Transcript of President Karzai interview with ABC News, Good Morning Program', 13 October 2009, http://president.gov.af/en/documents?page=2.

———, 'Full Transcript of the Interview by President Hamid Karzai with The Washington Post', *Washington Post*, 14 November 2010, http://www.washingtonpost.com/wp-dyn/content/article/2010/11/14/AR2010111400002.html.

———, 'President Karzai: Afghanistan not Political Lab for New Experiments by Foreigners', 21 January 2012, http://president.gov.af/en/news/6409.

BIBLIOGRAPHY

————, 'Statement by His Excellency Hamid Karzai, President of the Islamic Republic of Afghanistan at the 67th Session of the United Nations General Assembly', 25 September 2012, http://president.gov.af/en/news/13135; also at, http://afghanistan-un.org/2012/09/president-hamid-karzai-speaks-at-the-united-nations-general-assembly/.

'Karzai Slams Govt, Threatens To Oust U.S From Afghanistan', *TOLOnews*, 15 April 2017, https://www.youtube.com/watch?v=p-aCnsIy4Cw.

Kazem, Said Abdullah, *Afghan Women Under the Pressure of Tradition and Modernisation* (California, 2005).

Kerry, John F., 'Kerry Opening Statement At Hearing Titled "Al Qaeda, The Taliban, And Other Extremist Groups In Afghanistan and Pakistan"', *Senate Committee on Foreign Relations*, 24 May 2011, http://www.foreign.senate.gov/press/chair/release/kerry-opening-statement-at-hearing-titled-al-qaeda-the-taliban-and-other-extremist-groups-in-afghanistan-and-pakistan.

————, 'Chairman Kerry Opening Statement At Hearing With Secretary Clinton On Afghanistan And Pakistan', *Senate Committee on Foreign Relations*, 23 June 2011, http://www.foreign.senate.gov/press/chair/release/chairman-kerry-opening-statement-at-hearing-with-secretary-clinton-on-afghanistan-and-pakistan.

Khalilzad, Zalmay, 'The Three Futures for Afghanistan', *Foreign Affairs*, 16 December 2011, https://www.foreignaffairs.com/articles/asia/2011-12-16/three-futures-afghanistan.

Khattak, Khushal Khan, *Divan of Khushal Khan Khattak* (The Academy of Sciences, Kabul, 2018).

Kilcullen, David, 'Perspectives on Reconciliation Options in Afghanistan', *Senate Committee on Foreign Relations*, 27 July 2010, http://www.foreign.senate.gov/hearings/perspectives-on-reconciliation-options-in-afghanistan.

Kleveman, Lutz, *The New Great Game: Blood and Oil in Central Asia* (New York: Atlantic Monthly Press, 2003).

Kramer, Andrew E., 'More Afghan Civilians Being Deliberately Targeted, U.N. Says', *New York Times*, 15 February 2018.

Kurth Cronin, Audrey, 'Why Drones Fail', *Foreign Affairs*, July/August 2013, http://www.foreignaffairs.com/articles/139454/audrey-kurth-cronin/why-drones-fail.

Lemmon, Gayle Tzemach, 'What Leaving Afghanistan Will Cost', *Foreign Affairs*, 9 May 2012, http://www.foreignaffairs.com/articles/137621/gayle-tzemach-lemmon/what-leaving-afghanistan-will-cost.

Letters, 'Is Afghanistan a Narco-State?', *New York Times*, 27 July 2008.

Lockhart, Clare, 'Countering the Threat of Failure in Afghanistan', *Senate Committee on Foreign Relations*, 17 September 2009, http://www.foreign.senate.gov/hearings/countering-the-threat-of-failure-in-afghanistan.

Loyn, David, *Butcher & Bolt* (London: Hutchinson, 2008).

Lugar, Richard G., 'Senator Richard G. Lugar Opening Statement for Hearing on Afghanistan', *Senate Committee on Foreign Relations*, 31 January 2008, http://www.foreign.senate.gov/imo/media/doc/LugarStatement080131a.pdf.

Maley, William, *Rescuing Afghanistan* (London: Hurst and Company, 2006).

McChrystal, Stanley, 'Commander's Initial Assessment' 30 August 2009, http://media.washingtonpost.com/wp-srv/politics/documents/Assessment_Redacted_092109.pdf?sid=ST2009092003140.

'90 Minutes First Program EPS 1', *Ariana Television Network*, 29 October 2013, http://youtu.be/MKIrZJjbQcs.

'90 Minutes Second Program EPS 01, 02, 03, 04, 05, 06, 07', *Ariana Television Network*, 16 November 2013, https://m.youtube.com/watch?v=BqW6XRjKr2U.

'90 Minutes Third Program EPS 01, 02, 03, 04, 05, 06, 07', [on election and democracy], *Ariana Television Network*, 9 December 2013, https://www.youtube.com/watch?v=Rnc7y1_S3T4.

'90 Minutes 4th Program EPS 01' [on economy], *Ariana Television Network*, 21 December 2013, http://youtu.be/3-pGbXp3tck.

'90 Minutes 4th Program EPS 02' [on economy], *Ariana Television Network*, 21 December 2013, http://youtu.be/G28xc-qFn3U.

'90min 5th Program' [on Peace], *Ariana Television Network*, 20 January 2014, https://www.youtube.com/watch?v=4QKsLH2v_c8.

'90min' [on defence], *Ariana Television Network*, 19 January 2014, https://www.youtube.com/watch?v=vKGS7rqLKh0.

'90 Min Show#7' [on corruption], *Ariana Television Network*, 2 February 2014, https://www.youtube.com/watch?v=TYay11NSlsI.

Mohammad Najibullah, 'The Historic Speech Of Dr Najeeb', https://www.youtube.com/watch?v=uT0OVH7CPrM.

————, 'These Words of Dr Najibullah are Truly Worth Listening to', https://www.youtube.com/watch?v=qIbnHYyIvo0.

————, '"Dr. Najibullah - Speech on Shahnawaz Tanai, Coup d'état"', https://www.youtube.com/watch?v=O8oeQ0_l09U.

————, 'Dr. Najibullah's Shamali Speech', https://www.youtube.com/watch?v=-RiyBXMlfwQ&list=PLFEC07C7D08B2CAA4&index=1.

Mueller, John, 'How Dangerous Are the Taliban?', *Foreign Affairs*, 15 April 2009, http://www.foreignaffairs.com/articles/64932/john-mueller/how-dangerous-are-the-taliban.

Mullen, Michael G., 'Afghanistan: Assessing the Road Ahead', *Senate Committee on Foreign Relations*, 3 December 2009, http://www.foreign.senate.gov/hearings/afghanistan-assessing-the-road-ahead.

BIBLIOGRAPHY

Neumann, Ronald E., 'Afghanistan: What is an Acceptable End-State, and How Do We Get There?', *Senate Committee on Foreign Relations*, 3 May 2011, http://www.foreign.senate.gov/hearings/afghanistan-what-is-an-acceptable-end-state-and-how-do-we-get-there.

Nicholson, John, 'The Situation in Afghanistan', *The Senate Armed Services Committee*, 9 February 2017, https://www.armed-services.senate.gov/imo/media/doc/Nicholson_02-09-17.pdf.

Nojumi, Neamatollah, *The Rise of the Taliban in Afghanistan: Mass Mobilization, Civil War, and the Future of the Region* (New York: Palgrave, 2002).

Nordland, Rod, 'War Deaths Top 13,000 in Afghan Security Forces', *New York Times*, 3 March 2014.

Obama, Barack, 'Obama's Remarks on Iraq and Afghanistan', *New York Times*, 15 July 2008.

———, 'Official Announcement of Candidacy for US President', 10 February 2007, http://www.americanrhetoric.com/speeches/barackobamacandidacyforpresident.htm.

———, 'Remarks by the President on a New Strategy for Afghanistan and Pakistan', 27 March 2009, https://obamawhitehouse.archives.gov/the-press-office/remarks-president-a-new-strategy-afghanistan-and-pakistan.

———, 'A New Beginning" Speech at Cairo University', 4 June 2009, http://www.americanrhetoric.com/speeches/barackobama/barackobamacairouniversity.htm.

———, 'Remarks by the President in Address to the Nation on the Way Forward in Afghanistan and Pakistan', 1 December 2009, https://obamawhitehouse.archives.gov/the-press-office/remarks-president-address-nation-way-forward-afghanistan-and-pakistan.

———, 'Remarks by the President on the Way Forward in Afghanistan', 22 June 2011, http://www.whitehouse.gov/the-press-office/2011/06/22/remarks-president-way-forward-afghanistan.

———, 'Statement by the President on Afghanistan', 6 July 2016, https://www.whitehouse.gov/the-press-office/2016/07/06/statement-president-afghanistan.

O'Hanlon, Michael E., 'Staying Power: The U.S. Mission in Afghanistan Beyond 2011', *Brookings Institution*, September/October 2010, http://www.brookings.edu/research/articles/2010/08/25-afghanistan-ohanlon.

———, 'State and Stateswoman: How Hillary Clinton Reshaped U.S. Foreign Policy — But Not the World', *Brookings Institution*, 29 January 2013, http://www.brookings.edu/research/opinions/2013/01/29-hillary-clinton-state-ohanlon.

'Open Jirga 1- Security – BBC Media Action', *BBC and RTA*, 9 January 2013, http://youtu.be/2KMBmnrYROM.

'2. Open Jirga – Economy – BBC Media Action', *BBC and RTA*, 9 June 2013, http://youtu.be/ZAGzNi5Wy7I.

'5. Open Jirga – Afghan President on Governance – BBC Media Action', *BBC and RTA*, 29 May 2013, https://www.bing.com/videos/search?q=5.+Open+Jirga+-+Afghan+President+on+Governance+-

421

+BBC+Media+Action%e2%80%99&view=detail&mid=191169FFA7AEE4F88FBF191169FFA7AEE
4F88FBF&FORM=VIRE.

'Open Jirga 8 on Corruption – Dr. Ashraf Ghani', *BBC and RTA*, 16 July 2013,
http://youtu.be/f7FmIMz8K-Y.

'9. Open Jirga 9 – Security Transition – BBC Media Action', *BBC and RTA*, 10 July 2103,
http://youtu.be/x4MbLZ3xY7o.

'12. Open Jirga – Mines – BBC Media Action', *BBC and RTA*, 16 July 2014,
http://youtu.be/xEBCzAydaFg.

'14. Open Jirga – Election – BBC Media Action', *BBC and RTA*, 10 December 2013,
http://youtu.be/wjWgm0dgbeQ.

'Open Jirga – Role of Elders – BBC Media Action', *BBC and RTA*, 23 December 2013,
https://www.youtube.com/watch?v=rX86bG8PybI.

'18. Open Jirga with Afghan Presidential Candidates – BBC Media Action', *BBC and RTA*, 10 February
2014, http://youtu.be/XxJXEZ8aLoM.

'22. Open Jirga – Effectiveness of Development – BBC Media Action', *BBC and RTA*,
http://youtu.be/djypJwjwYjo.

'26. Open Jirga: Afghanistan and its Neighbours – BBC Media Action', *BBC and RTA*, 11 August 2014,
http://youtu.be/vmBnHjM3Vfo.

'Open Jirga 27 Election Crisis and its Effect on Economy', *BBC and RTA*, 3 September 2014,
http://youtu.be/deBcIxTD1L4.

'Open Jirga 31 New Government's Challenges', *BBC and RTA*, 27 October 2014,
http://youtu.be/27bgm63hoFM.

'Open Jirga 33 Independent Afghan Economy', *BBC and RTA*, 1 December 2014,
http://youtu.be/OqYV-ZG_vmw.

'Open Jirga 36 Narcotics', *BBC and RTA*, 12 January 2015, http://youtu.be/bDtSUgs1Z_Y.

'Open Jirga 37 Independent Defence', *BBC and RTA*, 2 February 2015, http://youtu.be/laDwRJrMiXM.

'Open Jirga 38 Afghan Peace New Prospects', *BBC and RTA*, 16 February 2015,
http://youtu.be/EA6eQGG1E0s.

'Open Jirga 41 Role of Mullahs in Society', *BBC and RTA*, 13 April 2015,
http://youtu.be/SMczxFDKC9o.

'Open Jirga 42 Future of National Unity Government', *BBC and RTA*, 4 May 2015,
http://youtu.be/2cps1ktLatU.

'Open Jirga NUG and Security Challenges. Episode 47', *BBC and RTA*, 13 July 2015,
http://youtu.be/aPGyBEKOefI.

'Open Jirga (Episode 52) National Unity Government Anniversary', *BBC and RTA*, 28 September 2015,
http://youtu.be/A0XbuIubCpM.

BIBLIOGRAPHY

'Open Jirga 55 Militias and its Impact on Security', *BBC and RTA*, 9 November 2015, http://youtu.be/ZhbK_i4cSc8.

'Open Jirga 62 Peace Talks – BBC Media Action', *BBC and RTA*, 8 February 2016, http://youtu.be/6dZ0NbCIgcU.

'Open Letter on Donald Trump from GOP National Security Leaders', *War on the Rock*, 2 March 2016.

'Pashtunwali', *Wikipedia*, https://en.wikipedia.org/wiki/Pashtunwali#:~:text=Pashtunwali%20(Pashto%3A%20%D9%BE%DA%9A%D8%AA%D9%88%D9%86%D9%88%D9%84%D9%8A)%20is,Pashtuns%20in%20the%20Pashtunistan%20regions.

'People's Voice' [Herat], *TOLOnews*, 29 April 2013, http://youtu.be/LpgVdIoDYs0.

'People's Voice: People's Voice: Paktia', *TOLOnews*, 10 June 2013, http://youtu.be/Igj0eWg79Ow.

'People's Voice' [Kunar], *TOLOnews*, 9 July 2013, http://youtu.be/8fjZLPbsrBM.

'People's Voice' [Bamyan], *TOLOnews*, 22 July 2013, http://youtu.be/bJrfXmYWKwU.

'People's Voice' [Khost], *TOLOnews*, 2 September 2013, http://youtu.be/6qSV2viCFSs.

'People's Voice' [Kapisa], *TOLOnews*, 25 November 2013, https://www.youtube.com/watch?v=sTuIE_zlAc4.

'People's Voice: Kabul Residents Share their Challenges', *TOLOnews*, 23 December 2013, http://youtu.be/rYn5gUFGBpg.

'People's Voice: Balkh Episode', *TOLOnews*, 8 September 2015, http://youtu.be/yyzuYWeDnw0.

'People's Voice: Nuristan's Issues Under Discussion', *TOLOnews*, 14 September 2015, http://youtu.be/mjK6DowZ_S4.

'People's Voice: Farah's Issues Under Discussion', *TOLOnews*, 22 September 2015, http://youtu.be/9TkcKEuHXNg.

'People's Voice: Badakhshan Residents Speak Out About Their Concerns', *TOLOnews*, 6 October 2015, http://youtu.be/muo8xVV_MTk.

'People's Voice: Ghazni Residents Speak out about Their Concerns', *TOLOnews*, 12 October 2015, http://youtu.be/BSVAe9R14Gk.

'People's Voice: Zabul Residents Speak Out About Their Problems', *TOLOnews*, 28 October 2015, http://youtu.be/GT-2xQMj934.

'People's Voice: Samangan Residents Speak Out About Their Problems', *TOLOnews*, 3 November 2015, https://www.bing.com/videos/search?q=People%e2%80%99s+Voice%3a+Samangan+Residents+Speak+Out+About+Their+Problems%e2%80%99&view=detail&mid=8995892D006D1751F74A8995892D006D1751F74A&FORM=VIRE.

'People's Voice: Panjshir Residents Share the Challenges They Are Facing', *TOLOnews*, 10 November 2015, http://youtu.be/zZJJSK2P4I4.

'People's Voice: Faryab Residents Share their Challenges', *TOLOnews*, 16 November 2015, http://youtu.be/6p2jCgffpKA.

'People's Voice: Jawzjan Residents Share their Challenges', *TOLOnews*, 24 November 2015, http://youtu.be/jaHrcIgMhJk.

'People's Voice: Baghlan Residents Share their Challenges', *TOLOnews*, 1 December 2015, http://youtu.be/bai-R945dog.

'People's Voice: Sar-e Pol Residents Share their Challenges', *TOLOnews*, 7 December 2015, http://youtu.be/oMBor-0xQMM.

'People's Voice: Parwan Residents Share their Challenges', *TOLOnews*, 14 December 2015, http://youtu.be/6HHWBhOG8JE.

'People's Voice: Paktika Residents Share their Challenges', *TOLOnews*, 22 December 2015, http://youtu.be/0qTwQwx60wQ.

'People's Voice: Wardak Residents Share their Challenges', *TOLOnews*, 28 December 2015, https://www.bing.com/videos/search?q=%e2%80%98People%e2%80%99s+Voice%3a+Wardak+Residents+Share+their+Challenges%e2%80%99&view=detail&mid=812741A62C073C0E18D1812741A62C073C0E18D1&FORM=VIRE.

'People's Voice: Takhar Residents Share their Challenges', *TOLOnews*, 6 January 2016, http://youtu.be/1athc9TdfwE.

'People's Voice: Badghis Residents Share their Challenges', *TOLOnews*, 18 January 2016, http://youtu.be/uplVeMK7W-s.

'People's Voice: Kandahar Residents Share their Challenges', *TOLOnews*, 28 January 2016, http://youtu.be/jRmC4Y18Lnw.

'People's Voice: Logar Residents Share their Challenges', *TOLOnews*, 9 February 2016, http://youtu.be/v4iRVO9yzaE.

'People's Voice: Laghman Residents Share their Challenges', *TOLOnews*, 15 February 2016, http://youtu.be/XgUZBJt4inI.

'People's Voice: Kunduz Residents Share their Challenges', *TOLOnews*, 22 February 2016, http://youtu.be/TidDvzkpcsg.

'People's Voice: Helmand Residents Share their Challenges', *TOLOnews*, 1 March 2016, http://youtu.be/mUSOe1JEgXA.

'People's Voice: Uruzgan Residents Share their Challenges', *TOLOnews*, 21 March 2016, http://youtu.be/NnNkRrqbRCg.

'People's Voice: Nimroz Residents Share their Challenges', *TOLOnews*, 29 March 2016, http://youtu.be/voO3bP82QFw.

Petraeus, David and Michael O'Hanlon, 'It's time to unleash America's airpower in Afghanistan', *Washington Post*, 15 January 2016.

BIBLIOGRAPHY

Pillar, Paul R., 'Al-Qaeda, the Taliban, and Other Extremist Groups in Afghanistan and Pakistan', *Senate Committee on Foreign Relations*, 24 May 2011, http://www.foreign.senate.gov/imo/media/doc/Pillar%20Testimony.pdf.

'Post-ABC poll: Terrorist Attacks', *Washington Post*, 13 September 2001.

Powell, Colin L. and Joseph E. Persico, *My American Journey* (New York: Random House, 1995).

Rashid, Ahmed, *Descent into Chaos: The World's Most Unstable Region and the Threat to Global Security* (London: Penguin, 2009).

Revkin, Mara and Ahmad Mhidi, 'Why ISIS is Rooting for Trump', *Foreign Affairs*, 24 August 2016.

Rahman Baba, *Divan of Rahman Baba* (unknown publisher and year).

Rice, Condoleezza, *No Higher Honour: A Memoir of My Years in Washington* (London: Simon & Schuster, 2011).

Risen, James, 'Reports Link Karzai's Brother to Afghanistan Heroin Trade', *New York Times*, 4 October 2008.

Rohde, David and David E. Sanger, 'Losing the Advantage: How a 'Good War' in Afghanistan Went Bad', *New York Times*, 12 August 2007.

Rosenberg, Matthew, 'With Bags of Cash, C.I.A. Seeks Influence in Afghanistan', *New York Times*, 28 April 2013.

Rowell, Andy, '"Route to riches: Afghanistan" in energy policy', *The Guardian*, 24 October 2001.

Rowlatt, Justin, 'What will Trump do about Afghanistan?', *BBC*, 25 January 2017.

Rubin, Barnett R., 'Still Ours to Lose: Afghanistan on the Brink', *Senate Committee on Foreign Relations*, 21 September 2006, http://www.foreign.senate.gov/imo/media/doc/RubinTestimony060921.pdf.

Rubin, Barnett R. and Ahmed Rashid, 'From Great Game to Grand Bargain', *Foreign Affairs*, November/December 2008, http://www.foreignaffairs.com/articles/64604/barnett-r-rubin-and-ahmed-rashid/from-great-game-to-grand-bargain.

Rumsfeld, Donald, *Known and Unknown: A Memoir* (New York: Sentinel, 2011).

Rustayi, Aubdelmanan, *The Wars of the Super Powers and the Oil Projects in Afghanistan* (2006).

Ryan, Missy, 'We have to end it: Trump takes over Islamic State fight, vowing to finish it', *The Washington Post*, 19 January 2017.

Ryan, Missy and Karen DeYoung, 'Obama alters Afghanistan exit plan once more, will leave 8,400 troops', *Washington Post*, 6 July 2016.

Sageman, Marc, 'Confronting al-Qaeda: Understanding the Threat in Afghanistan and Beyond', *Senate Committee on Foreign Relations*, 7 October 2009, http://www.foreign.senate.gov/imo/media/doc/SagemanTestimony091007p1.pdf. 12/11/2015 Safar سفر [Travel to Khost], *Shamshad TV*, https://youtu.be/5XdUDrj97KE.

19/11/2015 Safar سفر [Travel to Khost], *Shamshad TV*, https://youtu.be/_y9_gEEIZto.

26/11/2015 Safar سفر [Travel to Khost], *Shamshad TV*, https://youtu.be/_pknx44_WXY.

10/12/2015 Safar سفر [Travel to Paktika], *Shamshad TV*, https://youtu.be/QWkiVoxjEvs.

17/12/2015 Safar سفر [Travel to Paktika], *Shamshad TV*, https://youtu.be/W7xebAGVZcM.

24/12/2015 Safar سفر [Travel to Paktika], *Shamshad TV*, https://youtu.be/zE8uHTC-BgQ.

21/01/2016 Safar سفر [Travel to Paktia], *Shamshad TV*, https://youtu.be/TXoNfEJSqqU.

28/01/2016 Safar سفر [Travel to Paktia], *Shamshad TV*, https://youtu.be/KCBM4mYzaNY.

04/02/2016 Safar سفر [Travel to Paktia], *Shamshad TV*, https://youtu.be/dmwfarmpHB0.

24/02/2016 Safar سفر [Travel to Ghazni], *Shamshad TV*, https://youtu.be/mDstfqOMhEg.

05/05/2016 Safar سفر [Travel to Kandahar], *Shamshad TV*, https://youtu.be/hDj1WTzk6Ro.

Saikal, Amin, *Zone of Crisis: Afghanistan, Pakistan, Iran and Iraq* (London: I.B. Tauris & Co, 2014).

Saikal, Amin, Kirill Nourzhanov, *The Spectre of Afghanistan: Security in Central Asia* (London: I.B. Tauris, Bloomsbury Publishing Plc, 28 January 2021).

Salbi, Zainab, 'Perspectives on Reconciliation Options in Afghanistan', *Senate Committee on Foreign Relations*, 27 July 2010, http://www.foreign.senate.gov/hearings/perspectives-on-reconciliation-options-in-afghanistan.

Sanger, David E., Eric Schmitt and Thom Shanker, 'Steeper Pullout Is Raised as Option for Afghanistan', *New York Times*, 5 June 2011.

Scott, Peter Dale, *American War Machine: Deep Politics, the CIA Global Drug Connection, and the Road to Afghanistan* (Lanham, MD: Rowman & Littlefield, 2010).

'Secret Pakistan', *BBC*, 2011, https://www.bing.com/videos/search?q=secret+pakistan+bbc&qpvt=secret+pakistan+bbc&FORM=VDRE.

Seelye, Katharine Q., 'Clinton Talks About Stepping Up Effort in Afghanistan', *New York Times*, 29 February 2008.

Simon, Steven, 'Can the Right War Be Won? Defining American Interests in Afghanistan', *Council on Foreign Relations*, July/August 2009, http://www.cfr.org/afghanistan/can-right-war-won/p19765.

Sieff, Kevin, '5 harsh truths about the U.S. withdrawal from Afghanistan', *Washington Post*, 29 May 2014.

Slaughter, Anne-Marie, 'Afghanistan: What is an Acceptable End-State, and How Do We Get There?', *Senate Committee on Foreign Relations*, 3 May 2011, http://www.foreign.senate.gov/hearings/afghanistan-what-is-an-acceptable-end-state-and-how-do-we-get-there.

Snow, Shawn, 'President Trump and the War in Afghanistan: What You Need to Know?', *The Diplomat*, 21 November 2016.

BIBLIOGRAPHY

'Special Interview: Former NDS Chief Rahmatullah Nabil Criticises Govt's Security Policies', *TOLOnews*, 19 May 2017, https://youtu.be/le8FabjJsnw.

Syed, Baqir Sajjad, 'US asks Pakistan to fight all terrorist groups', *Dawn*, 18 April 2017.

Tanin, Zahir, *Afghanistan in the Twentieth Century; 1900-1996* (M. Abrahim Shareehi, 2005).

Tanner, Stephen, *Afghanistan: A Military History from Alexander the Great to the War against the Taliban* (Philadelphia: Da Capo, 2009).

Tenet, George and Bill Harlow, *At the Center of the Storm: My Years at the CIA* (New York: HarperCollins, 2007).

'The Afghan War Review', *New York Times*, 16 December 2010.

'The First Presidential Debate: Hillary Clinton And Donald Trump (Full Debate) | NBC News', *NBC News*, 26 September 2016, https://www.youtube.com/watch?v=855Am6ovK7s.

'The Second Presidential Debate: Hillary Clinton And Donald Trump (Full Debate) NBC News', *NBC News*, 9 October 2016, https://www.youtube.com/watch?v=FRlI2SQ0Ueg.

'The Third Presidential Debate: Hillary Clinton And Donald Trump (Full Debate) NBC News', *NBC News*, 19 October 2016, https://www.youtube.com/watch?v=smkyorC5qwc.

'The Good War, Still to Be Won', *New York Times*, 20 August 2007.

Thier, J. Alexander, 'Afghanistan: Right Sizing the Developmental Footprint', *Senate Committee on Foreign Relations*, 8 September 2011, http://www.foreign.senate.gov/hearings/afghanistan-right-sizing-the-development-footprint?

'Time to leave Afghanistan, Taliban tell Donald Trump', *Aljazeera*, 25 January 2017.

Tomsen, Peter, 'Statement on Afghanistan: In Pursuit of Security and Democracy', *Senate Committee on Foreign Relations*, 16 October 2003.

'Topic A: Is the War in Afghanistan Worth Fighting?' *Washington Post*, 31 August 2009.

Trump, Donald, 'President Donald Trump Talks With Soldiers Stationed In Afghanistan At The Armed Services Ball', *MOXNews.com*, 20 January 2017, https://www.youtube.com/watch?v=NoXcY7SsL1Y.

Tyson, Ann Scott and Josh White, 'Gates hits NATO Allies' Role in Afghanistan', *Washington Post*, 7 February 2008.

UNCTAD, 'The Least Developed Countries Report 2017', 22 November 2017, http://unctad.org/en/PublicationsLibrary/ldcr2017_en.pdf.

UN News Centre, 'Afghan Casualties hit high 11,000 in 2105 – UN Report', 14 February 2016, http://www.un.org/apps/news/story.asp?NewsID=53229#.V8IJCPR4WJI.

'Unknown Fate from Nimruz', *TOLOnews*, 14 July 2015, https://www.youtube.com/watch?v=hIxPI77PwkY.

Ware, John, 'Afghanistan: War Without an End', *BBC*, 2011, http://www.youtube.com/watch?v=byCH5p_en1A.

Whitlock, Craig, 'US presses allies for more Afghan troops', *Washington Post*, 11 February 2008.

Will, George. F. 'Time to Get Out of Afghanistan', *Washington Post*, 1 September 2009.

Woodward, Bob, *Bush At War* (New York: Simon & Schuster, 2002).

———, *Obama's Wars* (New York: Simon & Schuster, 2010).

Yankelovich, Daniel, 'Poll Positions; What Americans Really Think About U.S. Foreign Policy', *Foreign Affairs*, September/October 2005, http://www.viewpointlearning.com/wp-content/uploads/2011/04/poll_positions_0905.pdf.

Yousaf, Mohammad and Mark Adkin, *The Battle for Afghanistan: the Soviets Versus the Mujahideen During the 1980s* (Barnsley: Pen & Sword Military, 2007).

Zakaria, Fareed, 'The key to solving the puzzle of Afghanistan is Pakistan', *The Washington Post*, 8 October 2015.

ACKNOWLEDGEMENTS

I am eternally grateful to Allah, without Whose grace this novel would not have been completed.

I owe many individuals a great debt of gratitude for graciously supporting me in the research and writing of this book.

First, I should express my sincerest gratefulness to my editor, Matt Rance, at ProofProfessor. I am also especially thankful to my colleagues Helena Maddock, Brian Cunningham, Peter, Cathy Wood, Patricia Porter, David Dwyer and Professor Rahman Dag for their suggestions and encouraging comments. Special gratitude and personal thanks are due to Judy Lindsay for her assistance throughout the writing of this book. Personal thanks are also due to Patricia for the cover design.

My research required many Afghan sources that were not available in the UK. I want to express my thanks and gratitude to my late father-in-law, General Mohammad Akbar Ahmadzai, my uncle, *Qazi* Khaliluraham Momand, and my cousins, Fazil and Faisal Momand, in Kabul for going the extra mile to search and get what I was looking for. To my father-in-law and uncle I will always feel indebted. My deepest gratitude goes to my other uncle, *Qazi* Abdulrahman Momand, for his valuable insight into how Kabulis lived in the 1980s. I also feel indebted to my Afghan interviewees in Afghanistan, the UK, Russia, and elsewhere in the West. Thank you for sharing your views with me and allowing me to experience your lives – you are my inspiration, and it is for you that I wrote this book. Your views are the voice of the contemporary Afghan, and, as I promised you, I stayed committed to voicing them uncensored.

Last but not least, my most profound appreciation goes to my family, my sisters and brothers, and especially my parents, *Qazi* Haji Asadullah and Bibi Haji Dorani, for their continuous prayers, love, encouragement and unwavering moral and financial support, which have made it possible for me to accomplish one of my main goals. The comments of my beloved youngest brother and sister proved helpful to the early drafts of the novel. I am and will always remain grateful to my wife, M Dorani, for her thoughtfulness, patience, endurance and understanding. I could not have completed the twelve-year journey of this book without her unwavering support. Her knowledge of and research into Afghan traditions are this novel's backbone. I am truly blessed and eternally grateful to Allah for having her and my three beautiful children in my life.

AUTHOR'S NOTE

The idea for writing this book was conceived in 1992 when the 'pro-Communist' Najibullah regime collapsed and the mujahideen took over Kabul. Turning Shia against Sunni and vice versa, setting Afghanistan's main ethnic groups of Pashtun, Tajik, Hazara and Uzbek against each other, and accusing each other of uniting with the remnants of pro-Communist members and thus not being Islamic enough, the 15 or so mujahideen groups fought each other in the streets of Kabul, killing tens of thousands of innocent Kabulis, displacing hundreds of thousands, and turning half of Kabul into mudbrick rubble with bombs, rockets and cannon fire.

Taking refuge in the basements of our blocks while the gunfire, shelling and fighting continued, I decided (if I made it alive) to write about what we ordinary Afghans went through. Unlike thousands of Kabulis, I was fortunate enough to live, and 18 years later, in 2010, I started writing about the experience: after 12 years of writing (and extensive research), *The Lone Leopard* is the result. Ahmad, the protagonist, therefore, gives a *first-hand* account of what *I* (and most Afghans) have experienced over the past four decades in Afghanistan (and in exile).

ABOUT THE AUTHOR

SHARIFULLAH DORANI was born and raised in Kabul, Afghanistan, and claimed asylum in the UK in 1999. He has undergraduate and master's degrees in Law from The University of Northampton and UCL, respectively. He completed his PhD on the US War in Afghanistan at Durham University and authored the acclaimed *America in Afghanistan*. Sharifullah frequently returns to Afghanistan to carry out research. He is currently South Asia and the Middle Eastern Editor at The Centre for Strategic Research and Analysis (CESRAN International) and has written nearly two dozen articles on Afghanistan (and the broader region), international relations and law. He lives with his family in Bedford, England.

Printed in Great Britain
by Amazon

85437069R00253